MARIA ROSESTONE

THE
PAWNS
OF
ISOLDA

Other books by Maria Rosestone

Herlot of Alonia (Book 1)

The Pawns of Isolda

(Book 2)

Maria Rosestone

Three Towers Press

Milwaukee, Wisconsin

Published by
Three Towers Press
An imprint of HenschelHAUS Publishing, Inc.
www.henschelHAUSbooks.com

ISBN: 978159598-952-9
E-ISBN: 978159598-953-6
LCCN: 2023938380

Cover art by Mariela Victoria
Proofreading and editing by Elizabeth Jo and Allusion Publishing
(http://www.allusionpublishing.com)

Printed in the United States of America

FOR ZUNIA

A heroine's story of alchemy, love, and battle continues in *The Pawns of Isolda,* Book 2 of the *Herlot of Alonia* Medieval Fantasy Series.

Herlot and Movo escaped execution in *Herlot of Alonia*, yet their journey has only begun as they search for a way to flee the city's walls in *The Pawns of Isolda*. Plunged into an unfamiliar kingdom of Iptans, bandits, and stray children, Herlot struggles to understand whom she can trust while she unearths the magic that has birthed in her heart. As her feelings for Movo grow stronger, a darkness looms–King Felix and an ancient sorcerer await to crush her spirit. However, another darkness has risen, one that threatens the very nature of her golden heart.

Chapter 1
Fabian

Devotio. I believe. I made it. I'm coming back.

Herlot repeated the phrase over and over in her mind. Through every challenge she and Movo had endured since the sun rose, through every forsaken moment that threatened to take their freedom away, through every quickening of her heartbeat at the unlikelihood that Movo and she would be given another opportunity to escape if King Felix captured them again, the phrase pushed her sweat-drenched, fatigued body forward.

Herlot tip-toed to the corner of the empty room of what looked like an abandoned candle shop in the Kingdom of Isolda's capital city, Damalathum. She tried her best to avoid the broken pieces of pottery scattered on the ground. She gritted her teeth to restrain the cry rising up in her throat each time she failed, and blood oozed from the soles of her feet. The freedom to express one's pain was a luxury granted only to those whose lives didn't depend on escaping Felix's inner-city guards.

She squatted in the corner against a stained wall, away from anyone's view from the window, and proceeded to pluck the shards out of the raw skin of her feet. "Movo, how much longer can we keep doing this? This is the *twentieth* place we are hiding in today," she whispered.

Movo held his finger to his lips as he peeked out the doorway. He glanced at her. "We just have to stay—"

"Alert and on the run. I know. I heard you each time you said it. But what happens when we run out of places to run to?"

An almost wild look possessed his eyes as he marched at her. "Don't you think I know that? All I need is time to think long enough before they show up again, which I was in the middle of trying to do, but you keep distracting me with your questions."

"Well, maybe if you thought out loud I could help you—"

"You don't know the city—"

"Shh," she hissed. *Devotio. I believe. I made it. I'm coming back.*

Marching footsteps from outside invaded their temporary sanctuary. If that's what one could even call it. Herlot knew what a real sanctuary was. It had a waterfall and a cave, porridge, milk, and wool blankets. Sounds of clanking iron during the day from people learning the sword. Familiar voices singing and talking in the evenings. The faces of her new family—Enri, Mahtreeh, Asm, Seum, Benyamin, Lucinda, and the rest of the Eraskans. Devotio. This sanctuary was what would keep her moving through any obstacles that stood in her path. As impossible as it seemed, she would find a way back to her family. She would fulfill her promise to Devotio and learn to blend the chestnut tree leaf back onto a tree.

The marching subsided and Movo peered out again. "There are ten lined up along the street. Perhaps there's a backway." He walked up to a door that was boarded shut and began tugging on one of the boards.

"Just wait there and rest," Movo said when Herlot rose to help. "Hope that magic is on our side again and that there's another way out."

The board broke in half as Movo pried it off. He dropped the two pieces on the floor.

"You really believe in magic now?"

"Mhmm." He winked and got to work on the second board.

Magic. It was also on the forefront of Herlot's mind. Movo had asked to hear her story about magic after the sun had magically disappeared and engulfed Damalathum in darkness, providing them with the opportunity to slip away amidst the chaos and lack of light right before they were about to hang on the noose. Movo had always been intent in calling anything to do with magic naïve, foolish, and in his father's case, insane. Yet now he believed and had asked to hear her story.

Oh, how much she wanted to share this part of her life with Movo—Devotio and the unicorns, Emrys and the chestnut tree leaf, and golden heart magic. It wasn't until the rope was tied around her neck, the taste of death on her tongue, that she finally believed it all herself. The stark contrast of death and life made everything that felt real in her life be bathed in sunlight inside a place deep in her chest, a place so real that no evidence could ever do it justice. Yet she hadn't been the one to cause the sun to disappear. Would that stir doubt in Movo?

"Movo, it wasn't me who made the sun disappear, you know that, right?" she asked, hesitantly.

"Yes. It was an eclipse. I've heard of them before. It happens when the moon travels in front of the sun." He spoke between breaths as he pulled on the board. "But that it happened right as we were about to hang, I'm certain that is evidence of magic interweaving itself in coincidence." He chucked the now freed board to the side and began work on the third.

Herlot couldn't wait around anymore doing nothing. She grabbed on to the third board with her one hand, even though Movo protested.

"So you believe in magic because of a coincidence?"

The last board freed instantly when they yanked on it together.

"No. It's much more than that."

"What, then? I don't understand," she said.

"I will tell you later. How about now we focus on ensuring our future is not one of storytelling in a dungeon, alright?"

Herlot nodded toward the door. "Right, cheers to a dungeon-less future. Lead the way."

Movo opened the door.

Herlot's eyes widened as she stared at the scene in front of her. Her brother, Ambro, stood facing her. His eyes were lifeless and his skin was paler than bones. Behind him, five bodies lay covered with blankets. Her father's head was still exposed. His cheek was covered in dried blood.

Ambro grabbed her shoulders. "Herlot, are you well?"

But it wasn't Ambro's voice that spoke. It was Movo's. She blinked and Movo's face appeared in front of her. She grasped his forearm as the room spun around her.

"The boards brought about memories, did they not?"

She squeezed her eyes shut and nodded. "Yes. I saw my family as if I were one of the soldiers entering our home in Alonia." She dug her nails into his skin as the image of her father's face wouldn't go away.

"I'm so sorry, Herlot. I should have known. Listen, I'm going to turn us around, alright?"

She felt his hand on her waist and then her rigid legs struggling to follow his guidance.

"Can you try opening your eyes?" Movo asked.

Herlot opened her eyes. Nothing in the room could stay still.

"Focus on the window. Tell me everything you see about it."

Herlot found the window. She cleared her throat. "There're bricks around it."

"Good, what else?"

"It has a wooden frame. And there's more frames, smaller ones in square shapes, inside it. Some of the glass is cracked." The room stilled and it was easier to breathe.

"Keep looking at the window. I will be right back. We are not going to go through there, but I am going to see if I can find something for us to drink or eat."

Herlot sighed in relief as Movo disappeared. She would rather take on ten soldiers than face that doorway again.

The longer Herlot stared at the window, the more she could feel the blood returning to her legs and she felt confident enough to walk up to the window to examine it more. She ran her fingers over the crack that parted her brittle reflection in two. She had felt so strong and confident in her magic just moments ago. It had taken being on the brink of death and its stark contrast to all that was real and alive to shatter any doubt of Devotio's identity and the golden magic in her heart. She had felt it so clearly. It was in a hidden chamber of her heart. But would this be enough to actually perform the magical task of blending the chestnut tree leaf back onto a tree? Of course, believing that the magic existed was an important step, yet she doubted that the ancient golden-hearted humans had been so...*fractured* like she. How could she have been so overcome by belief at noon and frightened of a doorway by sunset?

She slid her finger up to a pane that was smooth as fresh ice, a pane higher up from the one that showed her reflection. There was still hope that someone else could do it, or at least, someone who might have the potential to teach her: the Emperor of Ipta. As soon as she was back home in Eraska, she would take Seum up on his offer to visit Ipta. This strange man whom Seum had said rarely appeared in public, and who possessed a golden elixir that protected people from crowpox, could definitely be wielding golden heart magic.

She still refused to turn around and look at the doorway when she heard Movo return.

"Here, for you. I couldn't find anything better," he said as he placed a hardened piece of bread in her hand, and then stood at the edge of the doorway. "Come stand by my side. Once a larger group of people come by, we can slip between them and into that alley. Wait for my signal."

Herlot made her way next to Movo's shoulder and nibbled on the bread. After a while Herlot lost track of time. She realized that her hand had slipped into Movo's and she was tracing the creases in his palm with her finger.

More voices filled the street outside. It sounded like several families with children. Herlot could pick out conversations about market goods, school lessons, and poetry recitations. Movo squeezed Herlot's hand.

As soon as the group was outside the door, Herlot followed Movo's lead as he wove them gracefully through the group. A brisk of sunlight danced across her face as the sun set below a large building with towers. At least it would be dark soon. It'd be easier to remain undetected on the streets. Darkness was turning out to be their biggest ally. As soon as they made it into the alley, Movo pulled her behind a wagon cart and looked around its side. "Clear. Come on."

Herlot slammed into Movo's broad back as he halted abruptly. In a flash, he had her up against a wall, shielding her body with his own. Herlot peeked over his shoulder to see what the threat was.

At the end of the alley a soldier had stepped into view. Everything about his dress was crafted for a fight—light reflected off the bits of chainmail exposed beneath his surcoat, high leather boots protected against strikes at the legs, and of course, the sword, which hung relaxed at his side. He seemed at rest, leaning his weight on one leg as he unrolled a piece of parchment. Movo's heartbeat pulsed against Herlot's cheek through the muscles in his back as she watched the soldier run his finger over what was most likely a map. He was probably looking for places they could be hiding. If only he knew, all it would take was a slight turn of his head.

Please walk away, Herlot thought over and over. However, he didn't budge, and as if their situation couldn't get any worse, two more soldiers met up on the opposite end of the alley. Trapped.

Herlot gripped the skirt of her dress in a bunch from the tension. Her mother had woven the dress. That and her leggings were all that there was in her small collection of things to remember her mother by. All their keepsakes, along with her mother's body, had been burned. Torn, stained, dirty. She was in awe that her clothes had survived her journey since Alonia was set on fire. Any moment these men would spot them, and then all that would be left of her would be her clothes in a day's time. If she were to die in Eraska, at least her keepsakes would be cared for by her friends. Here in Damalathum, no one would give them another thought. *Devotio, I'm sorry.*

Suddenly, the sturdy wall Movo had her pressed against transformed into air. She didn't know what was worse—her bottom meeting the stone floor, or Movo's weight on top of her. Both had done a fair job at knocking the air out of her lungs. A memory stirred; as if the impact had jolted and released it from its hiding place in her body. She was back in her home in Alonia the day she had cut her hair and fallen out of a tree. Her father and Ambro were chuckling while her mother's beautiful, stern expression was illuminated by candlelight. She'd give anything to hear her father laugh again.

She swallowed the memory and brought her attention to their surroundings as Movo rolled off her. Movo had had them pressed against a door rather than a wall. Her fight instincts jolted awake as she realized someone must have opened it. Then, a stranger's face obscured her view, hovering above her—a young boy wearing a flat, feathered hat—whose mercy they were most definitely under.

He raised his upper lip high as he smiled, clearly proud of the two front teeth he was missing. He had neck-length, greasy red hair, and a tear in his blouse that exposed his arms, which were just as freckled as his face. He poked her shoulder where she was missing an arm. "Does that hurt?" he asked. He seemed awfully cheerful about the question.

"Not anymore," she said.

"What about when it happened?"

"Yes."

He frowned and this time patted her shoulder. "Close the door and follow me," the boy said. Mercy was served, at least for now.

The boy disappeared through the archway that led into a room deeper within the building.

Herlot took a firm grip of Movo's hand as he helped her to her feet, but the moment he let go of her she found herself swaying backwards. Movo's strong hands were at her waist within a flap of a bird's wings, and her center returned over her feet.

"Again?" he asked, his eyebrows furrowed together in concern.

"No... no..." She yawned before she could speak anymore.

"Exhaustion?"

"Yes. I don't think we need to worry about the awful memories coming back to haunt me right now. If there is a point where memories fall asleep, I think we are getting awfully close."

She wondered if her eyes were as bloodshot as his. Her body was strong, of that she had Seum to thank for, but even the strongest of bodies, even Movo's, needed rest to perform at their full potential. Movo and she needed a safe place to close their eyes if they wanted to avoid making the sloppy mistakes that came with lack of sleep.

She closed her eyes for a moment, lured by the idea of just standing there with Movo supporting her. Just a few moments and she'd be refreshed.

Devotio. I believe. I made it. I'm coming back. Her eyes flew open, and she looked Movo straight into his. She ignored the tired, pink hue around his cold, blue irises, and instead focused on the intensity and depth of his pupils that reflected the same unstoppable determination that she felt deep in her gut.

"Wouldn't it be nice if Enri waltzed in here with her mint leaves?" she said.

His face softened and the right corner of his lips gently extended into a smile. "Stay close to me," Movo whispered. "These children will do anything for a coin. He could be leading us into a trap." He glared behind him at the open door. "Lucky for us, we have no other choice."

Movo closed the door and then they entered the other room. The boy stood in the center with his arms crossed while he tapped his foot. Herlot noticed that his shoes were unusually polished compared to the rest of his clothes.

Herlot looked around the room. She didn't have to be a city dweller to know this place was special. There were dresses, pants, hats, shoes, vests, wigs, and gloves of all sizes and colors slung over chairs, hanging in wardrobes, piled on top of tables. Her eyebrows pulled together as she noticed some of the dresses resembled animals, such as a white one with black spots. Was that a tail attached to one of them?

"What is this place?" she wondered aloud.

"Why it's Madame Lacelot's costumery, of course! It's where our kind get costumes for market performances," the boy said.

"Our kind?"

The boy rolled his eyes. "The dirt class. The filthy. The lower folk..." He raised an eyebrow at Herlot and Movo. "Fugitives on the run..."

"Ah. Movo, wouldn't you feel much better if we were dressed as a chicken and donkey if they caught us again?" Herlot said.

At that, Herlot and the boy started laughing. Movo glared at them. "I'm glad you can find humor in our situation."

It took Herlot three tries of covering her mouth to stifle her laughter into a giggle. The exhaustion was not helping, as it only added to the growing light, numb sensation caused in her body by the laughter.

"Let's move on to matters of business, shall we?" the boy said. "Madame is at the market watching a performance of *Hansel and Gretel*. She's a nice woman and lets me borrow hats whenever I want, but if she catches the likes of you two, there is no doubt she will yell for the guards. Now, lucky for the both of you, I know another way out of here."

A strange exchange began between the boy and Movo, who stood facing him, his legs in a wide stance and his hands on his hips. Herlot looked between the two of them, utterly confused—the boy was much shorter than Movo but had an air of confidence that lifted him up to Movo's eye level. The boy tapped his toe and rubbed his fingers together in the air. Then he exposed his palm to Movo, a cheeky smile on his face.

Movo shook his head. "I can't believe this," he said as he reached into his pocket.

"Hurry up, ex-communicated Prince Movo. Every tick of the clock is worth a coin," the boy said.

Movo held the coin between two fingers at his side. Neither one of them took a step toward the other. Herlot couldn't believe how seriously Movo was reacting to the encounter. But then again, he was everything but predictable since they had made their escape.

One moment he was cursing, his hands balled into fists. Another he was silent like the moments before a storm, focused on counting their coins and planning their next move, and ignored her if she said anything. Then out of nowhere, he would glance at her with the widest smile she had ever seen on him.

"Movo, just give him the coin already," Herlot said.

"No, he has to come and get it himself," Movo said.

She couldn't believe she was witnessing Movo acting so childish. *Naïve. Little. Girl.* Those were the words he had once called her aside from the many other remarks about her "childish" magical stories.

She marched at Movo. "Give him the coin before we fall asleep standing and he takes *all* the coins."

Movo sighed and flicked his fingers, sending the coin spinning toward the boy, who snatched it eagerly from the air.

"Impressive catch," Herlot said.

The boy winked at her, then inspected the coin. He bit down on it.

"I hope you realize that you don't have enough teeth for that test to work," Movo said.

The boy ignored Movo and puffed on the coin before smearing his fingers across the surface. "Pleasure doing business, follow me, you can escape through the roof!" The boy pointed at a hatch in the ceiling. "There's a ladder right over there."

Movo tucked the ladder from the corner under his armpit and then unfolded it right below the hatch.

"Once you're on the roof, there will be another ladder that leads down to the street," the boy said. "But I'll go out first and check for any danger."

Herlot barely heard the boy's steps as he swiftly made his way up, lifted the board, and crawled out onto the roof. This boy was gifted with skills when it came to slipping away. She wondered how many times he had had to put them to use.

A draft rippled through the room, chilling the sweat on the back of Herlot's neck. She rolled her head in a circle to add to the pleasure. If it weren't for the cracking sounds, the motion could have lulled her to sleep.

Movo yawned as he raised his arm and rested it against one of the ladder's steps. He glided the fingers of his other hand over his beard. He began to mutter to himself. "Baker's Street...right...no. No. Maybe somewhere above the cobbler's alley... No, the garrison has someone stationed with a water bowl right below. Damn it."

The thought of having to run through more new places was tedious. In this city, Herlot had lost all sense of direction. If only they could stay in one place where she could watch where the sun rose and set for a few days, perhaps then she'd experience some form of orientation. Surely the forest outside, even though it'd be one she'd never been to before, would be easier to navigate.

"Are you sure we can't make it over the city's walls? They can't be stationed everywhere," Herlot suggested.

"Not tonight. That's what Felix will be expecting."

"We could fight our way out." It'd be worth it just to have the luxury of leaning against a tree for the night instead of one of the city's cold walls.

"Not in this state. We're too exhausted and you need your feet bandaged." He nodded toward the path they had taken from the doorway where several bloody footprints led up to the place where Herlot was standing.

Before she could argue that it was nothing, the burning sensation in her feet seemed to grow stronger. She'd have to make do with imagining cooling them in a stream.

There were few things Herlot loved more than walking barefoot through the forest. The bottoms of her feet were used to all types of textures, from the tickling softness of the grass to the sharpness of twigs and jagged rocks. This city, though, Damalathum, was a completely different environment and it had already challenged her in more ways than she could count. The overwhelming heights of the buildings, the infinite amount of sounds that made her eardrums pound, and the numerous unfamiliar objects that lay on the streets and floors.

The boy reappeared and took a few steps down the ladder before taking a seat. "We have to wait. They're all over this sector right now."

"Thank you," Herlot said. "What is your name?"

"Fabian." The boy extended his left hand.

"Nice to meet you, Fabian. I'm—"

"Herlot. I know who you are. You're all Thomas, Randall, and I talk about."

"Your brothers?" Movo asked.

"Somewhat. I don't have any *real* brothers. And I only sometimes have *real* parents. My father works at the mines most of the time and I only see Mother on special days. I spend most of the time with the boys. We've been playing

Ruelder, and most of the time I play one of the Eraskans, but once I got lucky and got to play Herlot, uh, I mean you. It was great, I pretended to jump off the horse and everything, and the boys tied one of my arms to my side to make it more real."

Herlot smiled. She didn't know how to feel about the fact that a group of boys across the sea from her home were pretending to be her. How often had Ambro and she pretended to be someone across the sea when they had been Fabian's age? But there was something that Fabian had said that disturbed her. "Fabian, how come you only see your mother on special occasions? Is she ill?" Next to her, Movo took a sharp breath.

"She is very well. Besides that, she is a very good mother too. She does all those things good mothers do that boys don't like, when I do see her. I have to wash my knees and comb my hair. She is always proud of my shoes, but all the boys and I, we always have clean shoes because it is good for getting coins. If people see how good we clean our own shoes, then they'll want us to clean theirs too."

Suddenly, Fabian's facial features transformed. His face sagged and he seemed to have aged decades in his eyes. "She doesn't want me marked. As long as they think she doesn't have a child, I'll be safe. They caught me twice, but each time I managed to get away thanks to the boys' help. It's better this way. Even if I ever get caught, they won't be able to trace me back to her." He hooked one of his fingers into the hole on his sleeve and pulled the fabric aside. All Herlot could see was his freckled skin.

"There's nothing there," she said.

"Exactly."

Herlot frowned. "I don't understand." She placed her hand on Movo's shoulder and gently pushed him aside so she could step up on the ladder and be more at Fabian's level. "Fabian, what do you mean by being marked?"

"King Felix makes every child who is five years old spend a month in the dungeons." Fabian's voice fell into a whisper. "No light. No food. Only dirty rainwater every few days. Soldiers given orders to harass them any way they please."

A loud clang rang across the room. Herlot turned her head just in time to see a metal bucket, that Movo must have kicked, go crashing into the wall before he paced out of the room. It was evident that Felix's mad desire for magic – to help him take over the world – was not the only thing making Movo furious. However, he had never told her about this before.

She heard Fabian swallow and turned to face him again. She needed to hear the rest. "Tell me more," she said.

"Then, at the end of the month, if they're still alive, they have a symbol and the shape of a chess pawn cut into their arm. The symbol is created specifically for each child, for them to keep records. It makes it impossible to fake the scars, or we would have done that ages ago."

Herlot gripped the ladder so tight a sliver wedged underneath her skin. She wished it was Felix's neck she had a hold of. How could an evil like him exist? Was he even human? She thought he had given her every reason to hate him and seek revenge, but she was learning there were more reasons.

It wasn't until the day of Ambro's wedding that she had learned about how horrifying the world was. She had had eighteen years of peace before Felix spread the crowpox in Alonia. From that point, her life would forever hold the images of her parents' unrecognizable faces during their last moments.

But at least she had had eighteen years of untainted memories to keep her strong, to be a shining light in the darkness that threatened to engulf her since. But to be five years old and exposed to such horror? She knew what the men under Felix's control were like. Torture was a game to them, and she wouldn't put it past them to use that same type of viciousness toward children, just as she had witnessed them laughing at a child who had fought to not fall into the sea while they shook the plank between their two ships.

Herlot stroked her neck, as if trying to calm her blood that was thirsting with desire—to learn to blend and save Devotio's family, to protect her people, and for revenge. She focused her gaze on her forearm. When her mind rested on the revenge part, as if it wanted to burst through her skin. Felix would pay for the harm he had caused, and when she imagined that moment, it tasted just as sweet as her other desires being fulfilled. What if she could also stop these children from suffering? No more dungeons, no more scars. All accomplishable with the death of one person.

"Fabian, what is a chess piece?" she asked.

"It's used to play a game called chess. You play it on a checkered board. There are two armies, each with knights, towers, horses, and pawns, and the goal is to protect the king. All the children get the pawn on their arms. Only one person has ever had a different scar made—"

"Fabian, go check and see if the guards have left," Movo said, walking back into the room.

"Aye, aye, Captain." Fabian saluted Movo before climbing up on the roof.

"Wait," Movo said, his voice softer, as Herlot made her way down the ladder. She froze as his hand settled on her ankle, his warm fingers wrapping around the top of her foot. She looked down and over her shoulder to see him inspecting cuts on the bottom of her foot. He glanced up at her for the slightest of moments before returning his focus to her foot. "I have a plan..."

He traced his finger over the "S" on her big toe. Seum had tattooed it in golden black ink. Every warrior Seum had ever trained had the same tattoo. It was a symbol for the Iptans: Each time a warrior stepped on to a new place, the soil would know that an Iptan warrior walked the land.

"Before I was born, you know that my father agreed to a deal proposed by the Iptans. They wanted to build headquarters in Damalathum, and in exchange they provided everyone in the city with the elixir that protected them from the crowpox. If we make it to the headquarters, with your tattoo, they may let you in."

Herlot wedged her foot out of Movo's grip and twisted to face him. "What about you?"

"They only allow their own in. It's the best place to hide. It's the last place Felix will look because he doesn't know you could be considered an Iptan."

"But he knows there are two Iptans helping us in Eraska."

"Even if he did think of looking there, he's not allowed in. The Iptan headquarters are Felix's biggest weakness in this city. He is afraid of them. If Ipta wanted to, they'd have this place sacked within days. Nobody. *Nobody* has ever won a battle with Ipta, let alone survived an attack. You have seen how Seum and Asm fight..."

Herlot nodded.

"Now imagine an entire army like that, with siege weapons that none of us have ever deciphered how to build, like catapults that turned cities like Damalathum into rubble overnight."

"Overnight?"

Movo nodded.

Herlot still could not grasp her mind around the amount of buildings in the city. How could it be possible to destroy such a place? And what was the sense in destroying a place one wanted to siege? She was certain that even the Iptans would need more than a night to rebuild a new city from the rubble.

She rubbed her temple. Yes, she had new friends from other lands, but trying to understand their way of life made her head pound. And then, of course, there was Felix himself. "...and Felix really believes some sorcerer could help him conquer Ipta's Empire? That is pure insanity."

Movo raised an eyebrow.

"Oh," Herlot mumbled. "I understand even more now." This was why Movo had lied to her and her people before. He hadn't told them the truth of Felix's intentions, and instead had said that his father was on the search for people unsusceptible to crowpox. He had the intention to study them and find a way to make Ipta's elixir himself. It had been a failed attempt at making his father seem human and obscure Movo's shame for participating in the mission.

"I'm not going to Ipta's headquarters," Herlot said.

"Don't be—"

"I'm not going unless you at least try to get in too. If they accept me, I'll tell them you're with me."

"They're gone," Fabian whispered from above.

Herlot held her stance on the ladder. She wouldn't budge until Movo agreed.

Movo sighed and nodded. "Fine. We can try, now go. And stay low once you're up there."

Herlot climbed to the top of the ladder and then ran her palm over the roof's material. It was hard as stone. Astounding. It could probably rain a pond-full and no water would seep through.

"Why have you stopped?" Movo asked from below.

"What's the roof made of?" she asked.

"Oyster shells, probably," Movo said.

"Astounding." Herlot slid onto her belly and pulled her body forward to the edge of the roof using her elbows.

"Here, try these on." Movo handed her a pair of shoes that must have belonged to a costume, as he positioned himself next to her side.

She rolled onto her back and winced as she slipped them on.

"Thanks," she said as she rolled back onto her belly.

"Look straight ahead, do you see the bridge?"

Herlot shook her head.

"It looks different from all the others," Movo said. "Halfway up it disappears into that large square building. Right into its second story."

Herlot followed Movo's line of sight. *Bridge, bridge, bridge. Where is this bridge? Second story? Square building? Oh, skies, I can't find the strange thing.* Looking out at the city was like seeing a forest without a single tree she could recognize.

If she were in Eraska, it would have been a completely different story. Birch? Found. Elder? Right there next to the cluster of aspens. Willow? Definitely the easiest one. Nothing else could ever be mistaken for a willow. If anyone asked, she could do the same for all types of bushes, wildflowers, and mushrooms as well.

Everything in the city looked the same and completely different... *Herlot, concentrate. You're not about to die just because you can't find a silly old bridge. Now think. What does a bridge look like?* She searched the area for something that arched. And there it was, in a completely unnecessary place since there was no stream below. It was far bigger than she had imagined, a flight of steps on the right leading up to a long walkway that seemed to float above the street until it disappeared into the building. "I see it, Movo, I see it," she said.

"Good. Now watch where I point. This is the path we are going to take. There are guards heading in that direction from the west, they could cross our path if we're too slow. If something happens to me, you run to the bridge as fast as you can, up the stairs, don't worry about being seen—if the Iptans accept you, my father won't be able to do anything about it. Once you're at the end of the walkway, follow the stairs leading down into the building. That's where the Iptans will approach you. Understood?"

Could she leave him behind if something were to happen? Would she risk getting captured again and lose her chance to go back home to help Devotio? Could she run to the safety of Ipta's headquarters while Movo had his hands tied and was dragged back to his father's wrath? The thought was revolting.

"Herlot. Do you understand?" Movo articulated.

Herlot already couldn't remember the path Movo had pointed out. "Show me once more," she said.

This time, she cleared all her worries from her mind and gave all of her attention to Movo's directions. "Understood," she said.

"Boy, oh boy, I wish I could go with you. My friends would never believe me if I told them I raced with the ex-Prince and Herlot," Fabian whispered, having troubles controlling his voice.

"Trust me, this is one race you never want to run," Herlot said. "Thank you, Fabian, for all your help."

"My pleasure, Herlot of Alonia," he said.

"Ready?" Movo asked, rising onto his hands and knees.

Herlot's eyes widened as if waking up from a long night of sleep as she followed Movo down the ladder. Her heartbeat picked up and she felt her familiar friend—freedom—join the strength in her blood, dissipating any of her exhaustion. She could almost hear Seum. *What are you going to run with?* "Freedom," she whispered midway down the ladder, winking at Fabian looking down at them. Not a worry about slipping and falling crossed her mind. It was like her hand and feet instinctively knew where to go, her grip on the ladder strong and confident.

She heard Movo's boots hit the ground ever so subtly, and she jumped, landing just as quietly. Her feet screamed at the impact.

She and Movo didn't exchange any word or look, their intentions perfectly intertwined in harmony as they began to sprint down the street. Herlot's entire being attuned to Movo's body, matching his pace and stride, each one faster than the one before. Her injured feet burned but she harnessed the pain, mixed it with her freedom, and used it for more speed. Her arm pumped at her side, splitting through the air.

They turned onto a busy street where they wove through crowds of people. Smoke mixed with aromas of meat and fresh bread floated out of the windows engulfing parts of the street in a haze. So many different textures of fabrics that she had never felt before brushed against her arm as she ran. So many different faces that blurred as Herlot ran by them. Herlot would need more than a lifetime if she ever wanted to get to know all of them.

A large man wearing an apron froze in his tracks right in Herlot's path. He raised his arms out in front of him, bracing for a collision, and swaggered side to side as if trying to decide in which direction to lunge in order to avoid her. Herlot ran right at him, and the second before she would have made impact with his body, she threw her weight back, sliding between his legs on her knees. She shouted out as the skin on her knees ripped against the ground. *No wonder most soldiers are covered head to toe in armor,* she thought. Either way, it was more of her blood marking Felix's city. She liked the thought of that.

She didn't miss a beat in her run, in her attempt to come upright.

"Anyone following us?" Movo shouted.

Those who run with freedom never have to look behind them, Seum would have said. "Doesn't matter!" she shouted.

"Ha! Is that your magic talking?" Movo exclaimed before gripping the edge of a tomato cart and swinging his legs over it. Herlot followed suit. He didn't turn around to check if she had made the jump with success. She liked that. He trusted her to hold her own, completely opposite of how he had treated her in the past.

"No. Just Seum," she said as she caught up to him. "Movo?"

"Yes?" They both twisted their shoulders in the same direction as they squeezed between a group of women, their chests brushing against one another for the briefest of moments.

"Right now, running feels holy basil good compared to hiding," she said between breaths. It was true, even with the exhaustion and pain. She almost wished it wouldn't end after the continuous stretches of being crammed into small spaces since being captured at the fortress—the ship, the dungeon, the hiding places. Part of her wanted to raise her arms, throw her head back, and howl like she used to while riding Devotio.

"Cheers to that. Almost there," he said.

The archway towered over the buildings up ahead, and they were almost at the last street crossing. This was where

Movo had said a group of guards could intersect them if they didn't run fast enough. Was Movo going to stop and check first? He wasn't slowing down at all the closer they got. Their shadows stretched out long on the ground before them. Just when the head of Movo's shadow crossed into the intersection, he took hold of Herlot's hand. He was going to force them to stop. They were so close to the Iptan archway. They couldn't stop now. How much she didn't want to stop. What if the guards were there?

But then Movo did something she hadn't expected. He swung their arms back, and then swung them forward and up high, the momentum naturally raising Herlot into a jump. Movo shouted, "Whooo hoo!!!!" Herlot's voice naturally joined his without her knowing it. It was everything her body wanted to do after having been forced to stay quiet for so long.

When their feet hit the ground, they didn't look left, right, or behind. They didn't pay attention to the confused looks on the faces of those around them. Herlot's gaze was focused on the archway, just several strides away. They would make it, she knew it.

Once at the archway, they sprinted up the stairs and then jogged the walkway before slowing to a walk.

The closer they were to the entrance, the more nervousness pierced through Herlot's muscles, urging her to slow her stride.

Up ahead, the opposite end of the archway descended into the unknowns of the strange building they were about to enter. What would await them there? And most importantly, would the Iptans allow them to stay?

From the moment Movo had rescued Herlot from the fire in the Alonian forest, it seemed like they had lived a lifetime together, and then another one just within the last week. He had risked everything for the Eraskans. Even more, he had lost everything he had risked. His title to king. Treasure. His home. His life was just as much at risk as her own, Felix hadn't hesitated trying to execute his only son. Only someone purely evil could attempt to kill their own flesh and blood with such ease. The world, even though Herlot had only seen a small fragment of it, would be safer and better off without Felix.

What would happen if the Iptans didn't grant Movo sanctuary? Could she risk her own safety, and opportunity to return to Eraska, in exchange for staying with Movo? The thought alone of being separated from him felt like a tree having its bark torn off. But she had to return to Devotio, to her family, and to the golden leaf with the hidden world of unicorns, before their lives wilted along with the leaf.

Movo's stride was still confident, but his head hung the slightest bit lower than usual, as did his eyelids. A look of defeat. The same look she had seen on his expression at Lorfin when the beasts were charging at the village—just before they would have torn him into shreds had Herlot and Devotio not rescued him.

Herlot looked up at the first stars that had appeared in the sky. She remembered Devotio's last words to her: "*No matter what happens, the stars can see you, always, even when you cannot see them during the day. You're never alone.*" And she had the answer to her question: After everything Movo had given her people, this was not just her journey. It was his too. They were in it together, even if it was just the stars on their side in this city, and she had to believe that the stars would help them find another way. Just before they took their first step down, she focused on the brightest star. *If they refuse Movo, we will find another way.* But first, she would give a-year's-worth-of-wheat-thrashing effort to convince these Iptans otherwise.

She squeezed Movo's hand, waiting for him to look at her. He met her eyes and her breath caught. Her first reaction whenever she looked into his eyes for a longer amount of time was one of fright. They were cold and fierce, eyes that warned his onlooker that Movo was free to harm, kill, or do whatever he pleased without any remorse. In those moments, she remembered that he was, in fact, his father's son.

But when she dared to look longer there was more. It wasn't particularly anything about the physical attributes, it was how his eyes made her feel. That made her catch her breath again, but in a very different way. She couldn't put it into words, but it was so strong that she would stick to her decision no matter what evidence or information was presented to her. She wouldn't leave him.

"Ready?" he asked, his voice hoarse.

She winked at him, straightened her back, then took the first step down.

Good evening, Iptans. May you be well aware that one of your own walks on your land, she thought. With each step, she made sure to press her toe with Seum's tattoo firmly into the ground.

Chapter 2
Stars

Across the sea in the land of Eraska, where swishing trees and gurgling streams took the place of creaking wagon wheels and clanking blacksmith hammers in cities far, far away, there were the villages of Eraska: Alonia—once full of its people fishing and telling stories, Lorfin—where the sunflowers hung heavy and birds wondered where their favorite competitors for seeds had disappeared to, Temes—where skeletons of foreigners lay next to a tumbled wall, and Ruelder—where blood stained the soils of the fields, where the sheep now grazed, and Noray and Bundene—where mature crops wondered what was keeping the hands that were supposed to harvest them. And in this land, in the cave behind Eraska's waterfall, a family of hundreds hid.

Obscured from anyone's view and hushed by the powerful hum of the waterfall, they ate, slept, danced, sang, and most of all, they trained. Train for strength, train for speed, train to protect their lives from the vicious intentions of King Felix's soldiers. Train for the opportunity to return to their homes.

"Anyone who feels strong enough, quicken your stride with me to the liverwort patch," Enri of Lorfin said. She was leading her troop of patients through the cave tunnels. Fresh air was a critical requirement for healing any ailment under the sun. But it was a treatment Enri could not provide to her patients, since they were barely allowed outside unless they were part of a patrol or taking the horses and livestock to graze.

This always had to be done under Asm's supervision. Especially now, since a man named Ivar from the village of Temes had ridden a horse back to his village, to check on their livestock. He had returned in the morning with news of having confronted not a single soldier; however, according to Asm, this may have been a perfect opportunity for Felix's men. They may have left him alive in order to follow him.

"Come on, Enri. When can we stop this nonsense about quickening our paces? The soldiers are gone. Our fields are calling to us!" said Wilson, the expert gardener from Bundene.

Enri glared at him. Aside from possibly leading their enemy right to their hiding place, Ivar had caused even more trouble. He had planted the idea in everyone's heads that it could be safe to go home.

"Ivar... I could throttle you," she said as others whined in agreement with Wilson.

"Enough!" she shouted. "There will be no more talk of going back to our villages until Asm checks the fortress, which, thanks to Ivar, won't be for a while, since Asm now needs to be here with us in case soldiers show up in our cave, over our sleeping heads one night."

The whining stopped, but several people glared back at Enri. Good. They could glare all they wanted. No one was going anywhere for now.

She flicked her long, strawberry-blonde hair over her shoulder, along with her worries about Herlot, Mahtreeh, Movo, and Lucinda. A futile attempt. At least she knew Mahtreeh and Lucinda were together even though no one knew what would await them once they reached the mountains—if they found the allies, would they be friendly? Mahtreeh had almost forgotten to pack his sweater. Their father probably wouldn't believe his eyes if he saw his son climbing a mountain, let alone without his sweater.

As for Herlot and Movo, their fate was hidden in a dense fog. They were in Felix's territory, due for execution. For all Enri knew, they could be dead already and her worries a waste of spirit. The only point of power she had was the present moment, and that meant keeping her spirit bright for her patients, even though they were making that extremely difficult to do today, thanks to Ivar's news.

Sounds of forced breaths and feet clapping against the cave floor echoed back and forth along the tunnel's walls. "Never mind. Everyone up against the wall," she ordered. She squinted to better see the patch of fungus that grew near the liverworts on the wall. She had seen something like it before but couldn't remember where.

Behind her, the injured patients, an array of bandages on their heads, arms, torsos, and legs, shuffled to the side, making room for Asm's troop of Eraskans.

"Have you swallowed a hummingbird, lad? Watch where you put your crutch, last thing I need is to trip and break my other leg!" Cadby, a middle-aged father from Noray, billowed. At the Eraskans' attack on Ruelder, a horse had stepped on his leg. Luckily, the bone had not been completely crushed and was mending with the help of a splint.

"Fool. It is your own crutch you almost tripped over. I've seen fawns with better coordination than you," his brother, Rabbie, said. Rabbie should have been the last person to criticize another's coordination. He had broken his right toe and sprained his left ankle tripping over his own feet while chasing the soldiers away. However, he had been so thrilled by their victory that he hadn't felt the pain until after he rolled down a hill in celebration.

Cadby and Rabbie would both be top fighters once they healed. Cadby had already managed to get his hands on an arm guard, one that Asm had begun teaching the Eraskans how to use. The other night when Enri had ordered him to go to sleep, he resisted until she agreed to practice with him. "Just ten strikes and I'll go to sleep," he had said. So, instead of drinking a sleep mixture, Cadby had balanced on one leg, blocking Enri's sword with his forearm.

Rabbie may not have had the coordination, but he had the motivation. He was reliving their victory all the time. "Hey, Carl! Remember when you knocked your head against the stout one? I bet he didn't expect an old man like you to have the forehead of a boar!" he had shouted early in the morning. Rabbie was one of the first awake and Carl, usually the hardest to wake up and last to finish breakfast, had even offered to help disperse the porridge bowls thanks to Rabbie's motivational efforts.

Remembering every fight detail, Rabbie knew each person's story by heart, and he would sit in the training chamber reminding each one of their previous successes whenever they were struggling. Yes. She had to get these men in top form so that they could begin training as soon as possible. They could use all the motivational spirit possible, especially with Herlot gone and everyone yearning for their homes.

Asm was the first to appear around the corner. Giant was the best word for him. He reminded Enri of the darkest cloud in an oncoming thunderstorm. Physically he was huge, dressed in Iptan gear with a black leather vest that exposed his muscular arms (easily wider than some people's legs), leather pants, and thigh-high boots. However, his person expanded well beyond his body. He was a leader, able to set the tone for any occasion. In battle, Asm was the dark cloud that warned its onlookers there were many more just like him to come.

"Good evening, Enri! Kind of you to make room for us!" Asm said as he pounded by.

"Good evening, Asm!" Then she made eye contact with a heavily bearded, curly brown-haired man who followed a few persons behind Asm. "Good evening, Ambro," she said.

"Good evening," he replied.

xxxAnother couple of words. Perhaps tomorrow it will be a phrase. When needed, Herlot's brother was one of the first to help and he hadn't missed a training, even though Enri insisted he wait until his body became stronger. But he rarely spoke. Who could blame him, though?

Ambro had survived the crowpox attack on Alonia. After that, he was taken, willingly, to the fortress in hopes of reuniting with his fiancée, Manni. Asm, Movo, and Mahtreeh had found him in one of the cells, when rescuing Seum. After learning of how Manni had betrayed their people, telling Felix's soldiers to postpone their invasion to her wedding day, he still refused to believe his love was a traitor.

The rest of Asm's group ran by Enri, and a breeze infused with the aroma of sweat swept over her face.

Cadby held his hands on either side of his mouth. "Hey, Arlette! Afraid to get sunburned?" he yelled to Enri's fellow Lorfiner, who never took off her straw hat. This was followed by a series of sarcastic remarks about how bright the sun was today.

Arlette halted and put a hand on her hip. "Laugh all you want, but you all already have smiles on your face from a little bit of pretending." Then she lowered the rim of her hat and continued to run.

Rabbie stretched out his forearms. "Woman speaks truth, I can feel the sunburn already," he said. "Oh, I'll never complain about working in the field again once we're all back in our homes and get to see the sun every day."

Enri was just about to comment on how seeing the sun every day required one to be alive when she caught sight of Seum and Benyamin at the back of her line. They were huddled toward one another, both leaning their bodies onto their crutches. She would have given a whole nut collection to find out what it was they kept talking about. It wasn't every day that an old villager and an Iptan warrior had so much information to exchange with one another.

"Good morning, son!" Asm called Seum's way.

Seum lifted his palm toward his father, his focus still intent on Benyamin. Yes. There was no doubt that they were up to something. But what? Many people thought that Benyamin was somewhat insane or too old to be of a clear mind. Enri leaned more toward the age theory, although she found him a dear and often thought he might have more wisdom than most people noticed.

And then there was Seum. She had never met anyone like him. Hot. Cold. Intense. Vicious. Deadly. Unpredictable. Last night he had sobbed in front of everyone when he spoke to Hans's family about his death. Now she could add vulnerable to her list of Seum's attributes, which did not fit with any of the others. If Benyamin and Seum were up to something *together*, she was certain she didn't have the wits to even imagine what it could be.

"Carry on," she said to her group as she peered down the tunnel. Seum and Benyamin were turning around, heading in the opposite direction from the group. *You think you're being sly. Well, I see you.*

She put her hand on top of Rabbie's shoulder. "Rabbie, could you lead the group through two more turns and then make your way back? There's something I need to check on."

"At your service, Enri."

"Thank you."

Then, with her finger pressed against her lips to stop anyone from speaking to her, she made her way after Seum and Benyamin. She rolled her eyes at the series of complaints several people mumbled under their breath about being stuck in the cave.

"Couldn't we do these exercises on Ruelder's meadows?"

"No Ruelder meadows. I miss home. After all of this, we could just take on any of those soldiers who came by our village, if there are any even still here."

"I'm so sick of this cave. The bats must get more fresh air than we do."

Enri bit her tongue because it was obvious that her comments were useless. Did some of her fellow villagers really think they could go back to their homes and deal with any of Felix's scouts that might come along? Yes, they had successfully battled at Ruelder, but how much had their element of surprise given them the advantage? Especially now that Felix's soldiers knew that the Eraskans could fight, the villagers had lost their biggest element of surprise. It was critical now more than ever for the Eraskans not to lose their strength in numbers.

She wanted to go home, too, but complaining about hiding in the cave wasn't bringing her any closer to life in a peaceful home. Training and learning how to defend themselves for centuries to come was the only way. Besides, of course, not getting killed because of silly mistakes like falling into the soldiers' traps.

She didn't blame her brother. But, had he and Seum never been caught, she and the others would never have had to perform their rescue mission. Herlot and Movo would still be here. How could so many seem to forget this so easily? One mistake was all it took, and there was nothing more certain than the fact that not a single Eraskan had enough training to know what mistakes could be made, how to avoid them, and how to stay alive in case tragedy struck. If and only if they ensured the soldiers were gone, then they could return home. And first, they would need to come up with plans that included guarding the fortress and continuing their training.

She noticed the light fade as she moved farther away from the torch carriers in her group. Up ahead she could see faint glimmers of gold coming from Seum's tattoos, before the light completely left and she was hugged by darkness from all sides. Her shoulder bumped against a protrusion from the cave wall. This was going to be really difficult and she'd have to do better than tip-toe quietly, for them not to hear her.

"Ten steps until the turn," Seum said to Benyamin.

His skills never ceased to amaze her. Could he really have memorized the paths of the cave so well?

"That's about thirty for you, Enri!" he shouted.

Caught. Enri let out a sigh of frustration. "How do you *do* that?"

Seum laughed.

Enri rushed toward them, glad to join company in the darkness.

"I want to know everything. What have you been talking about? Where are you going? What are you planning? And anything else you might avoid telling me just because I didn't ask the right question," she said.

"Your dress is on backwards," Seum said.

"What? No, it's not."

"It is. We have bets on how long it will take you to notice. Quite impressive that you made it the entire day, never met a woman who cared so little about her appearance," Seum said.

Heat rushed into Enri's cheeks.

"I imagine your face turning the color of your hair right now," Seum said, his voice closer to her ear than before.

She almost threatened to bruise him until his skin matched the black of his hair. He probably would have laughed, but she stopped herself because the sight of him when he was rescued from the fortress still churned her stomach. It was a miracle he was alive. And she was glad he was finally sounding like himself again, because after the rescue mission she had been afraid that the torture he had suffered had scarred his mind forever.

"Before you tell me what you're really up to, because I highly doubt you're sneaking away to talk about my dress, what were the bets?"

"Fine things, Enri," Benyamin said. "Eggs!"

"Great. I'll make sure the winners share their winnings with me. Now, my friends," she put one hand on each of their shoulders, "the truth. Please."

"The truth! The truth!" Seum billowed. "You know what? You will get your truth like the biggest stew you have ever seen in your life, and you will swallow every last drop of it and then see if you ever want to hear the truth again. We have been waiting the entire day for the sun to set so the stars can tell Benyamin if our plan to save Herlot and Movo from execution worked. Every moment you hold us back is another moment we don't know. Now, can you mind your poking until we are outside, so we can get our answer? Then you can get a better explanation!"

Enri's breath caught, as if she was pausing time to allow the rest of her to comprehend what she had just heard. Benyamin and Seum knew something about Herlot and Movo. And from her past experiences, explanations that had to wait until the privacy of the outdoors, with only trees as witnesses, were explanations about magic. "Benyamin, you've been using some form of magic, haven't you?"

Benyamin nodded. "You could call it that." He winked.

"Then what are we waiting for? Outside, now, hurry."

"You sure are quick to believe," Seum said, a tone of surprise in his voice.

"You have no idea," Enri said.

Seum really did have no idea how much she'd believe. She had met a unicorn as a young girl, after all, the same unicorn she was now possibly responsible for helping, if Herlot didn't come back. This help would involve finding a golden magic in someone's heart, in order to blend an ancient world, which was hidden inside a leaf, onto a tree branch. Seum had the best battle skills, yet she was certain she was a "belief in magic" warrior.

They entered the cave's main chamber where the waterfall rushed down in front of the entrance. Only a few patients, too sick to walk, were deeply asleep against the walls.

The trio stepped out onto the path that led down the ledge. Benyamin took occasional glances at the night sky. "Your brother and Lucinda are safe," Benyamin said.

Enri squealed with relief. "Thank the skies."

Once they made it to ground level, a beautifully white-colored figure emerged from the bushes. Devotio. Even without his alicorn, recognition of his wild, magical freedom never ceased to rush through Enri's body at the sight of him.

Enri combed her fingers through Devotio's mane as he took a stand next to her. Since they had lost Herlot, he came and left as he pleased, sometimes spending a night in the woods, other times next to her in the cave. She liked how there was an unspoken acceptance about his freedom, as if everyone knew that the rules, about who and when one could wander away from the cave, did not apply to him. She also liked his peace. If there was anyone dependent on Herlot, it was him, and he seemed to be confident that she'd return. On the other hand, Enri needed more knowledge of Herlot's fate in Damalathum. She turned to Benyamin. "The stars tell you, did I hear that right?"

"Yes. We just have to wait for some of these clouds to pass," Benyamin said.

Seum pointed his finger at the stars as he stared at Enri. "You're not even going to question that?"

"Nope."

"You're not even going to ask him to explain how he does it or how it's even possible?"

"I do admit, I'm curious. But not yet. Besides, sometimes I feel that requiring an explanation for magic defeats the purpose, wouldn't you agree?"

"Huh. Yes, actually," Seum said.

Enri sat on a rock and rested her chin on her palm as she watched Benyamin look up at the sky. The way his eyes jumped around, and the way his pupils dilated, reminded her of her father searching their ceiling for herbs back home. Whatever Benyamin was doing looked like something that took years to master, and for some reason she was certain no one in the world knew how to do it better than him. This wasn't just learning to use a weapon. Benyamin was doing something much bigger, and it sure felt as vast and unknown as the night sky.

"He's like a firefly or something," Seum mumbled. The area around Benyamin seemed extra bright in starlight, as if the stars were focused just as intently on Benyamin as Benyamin was on them.

Benyamin moved his hands above him, focusing his pointer finger on certain areas. He seemed to stroke something with the outside of his finger, like Enri did with sunflower leaves. He chuckled.

"What's so funny?" Seum asked.

Benyamin cleared his throat while continuing the gestures with his hands. "Not all stars like to watch the same stories. Most have a preference. Tonight, ah, tonight is different. Very rare, very rare..." His words drifted off.

"Very rare... and?" Seum said.

"Ah, yes. Most of them were focused on our Herlot and Movo today. Funny how these magnificent lights can act like children sometimes. Right now, they're almost fighting to be the first to share their version of the story. It's a bit difficult to make sense of it."

Enri's palm went to rest against her heart. Experiencing a new form of magic felt like a layer of joy was added to her heart. "This is astounding."

Benyamin looked at her with a large sparkle in his eye. "What is even more astounding, my dear Enri, is that our friends are alive and well."

A sob escaped through Enri's lips. She grabbed onto Devotio's mane and pressed her forehead into Devotio's neck as tears streamed down her face. "Yes... yes... yes..."

Then came the laughter. It sounded hysterical but she didn't care. Her body wanted to express her joy in all sorts of ways it seemed. It only grew when Seum jumped one-legged into the air.

Once Enri calmed down, she wanted to know more. "Benyamin, how? How did they do it?"

"Seum," Benyamin said. "Do we want our friend to join? I'm sure he has been waiting to find out just as much as we have."

"Yes. Yes. Of course," Seum said. That was when Enri noticed Hans's psaltery wrapped around his back. Seum fumbled the instrument and almost let it drop before he sat on a rock and began strumming the strings.

"I don't understand," Enri said. "What friend?"

"Me!" A voice shouted right by her ear. She went flying into the air as she let out a shout.

"Hans!" she exclaimed. "Hans?"

The boy who looked like he had been sculpted out of fog pointed his thumb at his chest. "How did I do for my first scare as a ghost?"

"A ghost…" Enri squeezed her eyes shut and then opened them again. "Before I understand I just need to hug you." She wrapped her arms around Hans, feeling only air that was a bit cooler than usual. She could have let her arms slide completely through him but held them right at the border of his form. Over his shoulder she even could see that he still wore his ribbon to tie his long hair back, just like she used flowers to tie hers back. "It is so good to see you, my friend. This is an evening truly blessed with gifts of the most magical sorts."

"It is, Enri, it is, not just for you, but me too," Hans said. "There are so many who wander and speak to their loved ones. I'm one of the lucky ones that can be heard and seen, all thanks to Seum."

"Seum?" Enri turned to Seum who continued to strum the psaltery.

Hans wrapped his ghost arm around Seum's shoulder. "Seum played my psaltery with so much love that it created a path for me between your world and the spirit world."

"I wouldn't call it love…" Seum mumbled.

A path from the spirit to the physical. Just what Emrys had been able to do, blending the unicorns between spirit form and physical form using the leaf. She looked at Devotio and raised an eyebrow. Did Seum, Benyamin, and Hans know about Herlot's mission too?

Devotio understood her inquiry just by her expression. "They don't know about the unicorns and the leaf, Devotio said. Enri felt the familiar swirl of air around her ear that meant Devotio was speaking to her. Any moment she would hear his voice.

"And this is different, ghosts are physically dead. Hans is in spirit form whether you see him or not. We need someone with golden heart magic to make the switch between spirit and physically alive."

Enri lowered her eyelids in understanding. Then she glanced at Benyamin and back at Devotio. "Does he know about you?" she mouthed ever so slightly.

"Yes."

Enri let out a gust of air. If Benyamin could communicate with stars, he could know everything, right? She was grateful that she trusted him. She had to learn more about his talent, but she assumed he had definitely seen Devotio in his unicorn form when they were children, and that meant he could be trusted. After all, he could have exposed Devotio back then.

"That's right," Benyamin said. Enri was brought back to the matter at hand. "Our Hans loved his psaltery so much that it became part of him. Or he became part of it. Or perhaps a little bit of both. Anyway, what is most important is the path, very much like the one connecting Temes to Lorfin, but in this circumstance it's a path between worlds."

Countless flashes of Enri's father danced through her mind—him hanging herbs from the ceiling, him crushing plants in the mortar, thousands of artifacts left in their home that had no doubt been infused by infinite amounts of her father's love. "Do you think it could be possible—"

She was interrupted by a gentle breeze on her shoulder where Hans now rested his hand. "No, Enri. I already checked. I haven't been able to find your father wandering. He must have moved on."

"Oh." Her shoulders slumped.

Hans bent over so she couldn't avoid his eyes. "It's a good thing. It doesn't mean he's gone or isn't with you. I'm pretty sure of where he is. I—I don't know what it's like there or how to get there..." Hans's figure seemed to shake, certain parts of him becoming clearer and then disappearing. Enri had the sudden urge to back away from him. Just when she was about to, the strange shaking stopped. "Your father, Oliver, he's not stuck. It's a good thing, Enri."

She smiled. "It sounds like he's in a nice place." She twiddled her thumbs. "Do you think he's happy?"

"I think that place has a happiness so happy we probably don't even have a word for it."

That made her smile even more. If there was a place like that, her father deserved to be there. And her mother had to be there too.

"Parents. We wish we could have them forever, don't we?" Benyamin asked.

Enri nodded in agreement. "Oh, parents!" she exclaimed as her thoughts about parents slipped to another mother and father, these ones alive and going through the one thing more painful than losing one's parents—losing one's child. "Hans, before we do anything else, we must take you to your parents."

"I don't think that's a good idea," Hans said.

"I agree," Benyamin said.

"What? Why?" Enri said. "Hans, don't you know how much they miss you? Do you have any idea what it would mean to them to see you? To speak with you?"

"I'm dead, Enri. Nothing will change that. Eventually, sometime soon hopefully, I will have to move on."

Enri sighed. She was almost wild to snatch at any sign of happiness or light around her—something so drastic that it would make up for everything that had happened. The thought of Hans's parents seeing him again had sent her into a frenzy before thinking things through. "You're right, it would only hurt them," she said.

Hans nodded.

"It will hurt us, too, when the time comes," Seum said.

A blanket of silence seemed to hush any words they may have had to speak. Only the psaltery's song penetrated the air. Each time Seum strummed a particularly harmonious collection of notes, Hans became more vivid. But not as vivid as he had been in real life.

"How long do you have?" Enri asked. She hoped it was an appropriate question to ask.

"That's for me to decide. A while, as long as Seum keeps playing my psaltery, I'll be here." All of a sudden, Hans's expression changed. He became dangerously pale, his eyes extra hollow, and his ghost body shook harder than it had before. "I'm not leaving until I know my family is safe from Felix." Goosebumps spread throughout Enri's body as a cold gust of air emanated from Hans.

Seum gripped the hilt of a dagger hanging around his belt. "I won't stop until they are," he said, the side of his lip curling to expose his teeth that shone in the moonlight.

They both had a fire for revenge burning through their souls. Enri understood it too well. None of them had seen her in Dartharus's chamber and she was glad. Something had taken her over as she poisoned him—a viciousness she hadn't known she possessed. She had known that she would poison Dartharus, but she never would have guessed at how much she enjoyed it, like watching the first sunflowers bloom in the fields of Lorfin, a feeling of new life. But in that situation, it had been about knowing that she had rid the world of someone who was bound to destroy another's. Benyamin remained silent, still gazing up at the night sky, and she now really wondered how his talent worked. Had the stars seen her kill Dartharus? And if so, did that mean Benyamin had seen it, too, and how she hadn't stopped with remorse, not for even the beat of a heart?

Seum cleared his throat. "Benyamin... tell us what happened to Movo and Herlot." His fist was tight at his side.

Benyamin tugged at a shard of wood disrupting the smooth surface of his crutch. He peeled it until he had a thin, long piece in his hand and let it drop to the grass. "You're eager to find out if what you did last night had any significance?"

Seum nodded.

"Even more so, you're afraid it didn't."

Seum looked down, as if he were ashamed to be afraid.

"Before I tell the story, Seum, what do you think happened?"

Seum crossed his arms. "All I know is that one moment I was sitting in a room, the next I was climbing onto a winged white horse and flying through the clouds, after which I met Queen Magdalene. Then you mumbled something about moving up the execution to noon that day. I hope it had some influence or else it seems like a warship amount of strangeness for no good apparent reason."

Benyamin chuckled. "Now what do you feel happened?"

"What do you mean, what do I feel—"

"Be quiet for one moment and put your hand over your chest."

Seum slapped his palm against his chest and then let it fall to his side.

Enri found the gesture rather rude, a sign of rebellion, but Benyamin didn't become upset. He tucked his crutch well into his armpit and then pressed his own palm against his chest, smiling, never breaking eye contact with Seum.

Seum's hand shook as he brought his palm up again. The moment he placed it over his chest, this time with gentleness, his body seemed to relax as if lying down on soft, long grasses. "Good, close your eyes. Now try again. What do you feel?"

Seum giggled. *Giggled.* Seum. Giggled. Like a child. His voice was still low, but not as low as always, one pitch higher. Hans giggled as well. "Wow! Did you all hear that? Seum sounded like a boy."

Seum dropped his arm and turned his head away from everyone, but not fast enough. Enri could detect the hint of a blush on his cheek in the starlight. The wind picked up, brushing aside the few strands that had escaped his braid, keeping his flushed cheek exposed. "They're fine," he said.

"Nice to know that you don't need evidence, even as precise as the stories from the stars to know the truth, isn't it?"

Seum tucked his hand into a pocket in his leather pants, as if afraid that it might rise to his chest again.

"I still would like to hear the story. Will you, Benyamin?" Enri said.

"Of course," Benyamin said. He gazed up at the stars again and pointed his finger at one. "Last night, we traveled into the world of dreams and found Movo's mother, Queen Magdalene. I asked her to move the time of Herlot and Movo's execution up a day and to the time of noon. Queen Magdalene remembered the dream and trusted it. That was the part I was worried about, the trust.

So many things are right in front of us and so clear, yet we waste so much time finding more and more proof. Someone like Queen Magdalene would probably have wanted to have several more dreams just like this one before she could trust the message, but in our situation, she didn't have that option.

At noon, the crowds of Damalathum gathered in the city's execution center and waited for Movo and Herlot. The timing worked. This I was worried about too. Had they been too early, our Herlot and Movo would have hung. But noon came, the moon covered the sun, for just enough time. All was dark for them to escape the building. Had we not been cooped up in our lovely cave, we would have witnessed a bit of the same darkness, it's rather fascinating, may I say. Night in the middle of day! The most relied upon routine, our times of day and night, disturbed."

"But, Benyamin, how did you know that would happen?" Enri asked.

"That old gadget he always carries around. It predicts all sorts of strange things about the sky," Seum said. "What's even stranger is how he got the head to even understand the thing."

Benyamin looked smug after Seum's comment. He shoved his hands into his tunic pockets and shrugged, like a little child proud of perfectly planting a row of sunflowers for the first time.

"And now? Where are they now?" Enri asked.

"They were hiding most of the day, and just as the sun set, they entered Iptan headquarters."

"Iptan headquarters!" Seum looked up at the sky as if he had Benyamin's talent. "Benyamin, tell me, what is going on right now. Were they let in?"

CHAPTER 3
BUTTER SWANS

Queen Magdalene had arrived back at the palace as something out of a puppet show—a mixture of disheveled ex-queen and a drunk. She hadn't had a sip, but she sure smelled like one.

She did her best to arrange her legs. They had fallen asleep to avoid yet another drop of wine dripping from the shelf above her. As hopeless as her situation was, she was enjoying the various shapes she had morphed her body into over the last hours. Some of them would have been deemed most inappropriate for a queen. And she could not care less. The only things she cared about now was not accidentally squishing the spider that had been keeping her company, finding her son, and getting out of Damalathum. Based on her location—hiding where the wine barrels were kept in the palace buttery— she was making no progress toward the last two.

"I wonder what you're hiding from," she whispered to her spider companion. "Or maybe you're not hiding from anything, you're just taking a break while your web catches your dinner." Surprisingly she still had an appetite after everything that had happened, but she didn't dare leave her hiding spot. She stuck her finger out to catch a drop of wine. "Cheers," she said and let it fall on her tongue.

Cheers to the Queen who, out of all the places in this city, ran like a damsel in distress back to her palace to hide. Well, at least I did not run back to my chambers, or even better, Felix's chambers. "Good afternoon, My King," I would have said, and probably bowed at that too. "I am guilty of the sorcery you accuse me of."

She was guilty of it, but she felt not a single drop of regret. Each time her eyes opened after a blink, she was certain she'd find herself back in her bed on that night before she had the dream, the dream that changed everything. Today's events simply stripped down to a moment of wishful thinking.

In the dream, an elderly man had visited her and told her to move her son's execution to the present day at noon. The next morning, she had convinced Felix to do so. It had been a choice out of desperation, but by some magic it had fulfilled her biggest wish. It had saved Movo from execution.

Right at noon, the entire city fell into darkness. At that moment, she had known her son would find his way out. She also knew that Felix would kill her for it. Dried blood was still crusted on her forearm from where Felix had dug his nails into her skin to stop her from leaving, but her neck bore no sign of his fingers. She had managed to escape in the darkness.

Suddenly the hinges of the door leading into the kitchen squeaked. Aromas of wood burning and cabbage soup filled the buttery. Magdalene hugged her knees tight into her chest and peeked through a gap between the barrels. A frightening shadow of some creature resembling a dragon moved across the wall before Chef Ademar came into view. He was carrying a butter sculpture of a swan.

"The world may be falling apart, but you have nothing to worry about except for a hot day or the heat from a fireplace, neither of which can harm you here," Ademar said to the swan.

Ademar's kind words to his sculpture were just what Magdalene needed to hear. Surely a man who held such compassion for butter could find it in his heart to have the same compassion for her. Ademar had also never uttered a word about her trips to the kitchen for food to take to the children in the dungeons. Chef Ademar was smart. He knew when he needed to act his part of a worthy disciple of King Felix, but found ways to manipulate his deepest desires while hiding behind his façade.

His smartest act had happened during those awful days when Movo was still in the dungeons. She had helped Ademar trick Felix in a matter so sly and graceful—the same technique she had used to convince Felix to move the execution: making him believe the proposition was to his benefit. Chef Ademar had requested a meeting with the King in his throne room. Magdalene would never forget walking into the throne room and being surrounded by sculpture upon sculpture of swans made of every possible food mixture in the kingdom, decorated with everything from gems to laces. She hadn't even had to fake her side of the deal. Each one of her expressions of awe had been genuine. Since then, not a single real swan had ever been the centerpiece of a banquet again.

She prayed that she could be his next swan.

She stood from her hiding place, her knees cracking as she straightened just as he was walking by her.

"Chef Ademar," she said, and then cursed herself for not taking into mind Ademar's unfortunate tendency toward lack of balance. First came Ademar's shout—"Gahhh!" Then his ankles collided into one another and he swayed forward. And the finale: Ademar face down on the stone floor, his face hidden in what was once the backside of the swan sculpture.

"Oh, no, Chef Ademar." Magdalene lifted the front of her dress and stepped to the top of a barrel, then jumped down, landing on both feet. She ran around his body and knelt near his head.

Ademar pushed onto his hands and knees. "Here, let me help you," Magdalene said. She took the edge of his apron and began wiping the butter from his eyes and nose. His mustache, which was normally perfectly shaped to turn upward at the tips, now drooped, weighted down by, what else, butter.

"Queen Magdalene? Is it really you? How did—ah...ah..." Magdalene bunched his apron in her hand and then squeezed it around his nose as she had done for Movo so many times when he had been a little boy. "Ah-choo!" Butter streamed out of Ademar's nose.

"My apologies, I did not mean to frighten you," Magdalene said.

"Chef Ademar, are you looking for a helping hand?" a woman's voice rang from the doorway. Magdalene scrambled toward a dark corner of the room.

"Absolutely not. Return to your pot immediately before the sugar water over boils!" Ademar shouted.

He then stood, readjusted his hat, and placed both of his hands on his hips.

Maria held her breath as she analyzed his posture. He had not given her up to the other cook, but that did not mean he wasn't about to. He wanted to think about it first, and he was making his decision right now, she was certain of it.

Ademar turned to face Magdalene and sighed. He pitied her. She didn't blame him. Everything about her situation was pitiful.

"My Queen, frightening me is the least of our worries. Felix has just as many looking for you as he does for Prince Movo and the girl."

He wasn't going to rat her out. Magdalene placed her hand over her heart in gratitude for someone she could consider a friend in her world.

"At least they won't look for you here, right under their noses," Ademar said.

A snicker escaped her. Yes, she had made a stupid choice, but there were benefits to it, mainly no one would think she was stupid enough to hide in the palace. It still didn't change the fact that Felix's presence infiltrated every nook and cranny of the palace. He was a ghost waiting and watching in every corner of each room. Some part of his awful person probably knew exactly where she was.

"Chef Ademar, where is Felix?"

"King Felix is in his throne room speaking with the General of the Bowmen and the General of the Cavalry and the Headmaster of Armor."

"What in the world would he need to speak with them for?"

"I do not know, my Queen. The doors have been shut."

These officials were only called in times of a siege, attack, or war. Times when precise and accurate calculations had to be made about everything from the horse fodder that would be required to feed the cavalry's horses going to, during, and then from the battles, to the cost of bows and arrows to equip each archer, and the pounds and pounds of iron and other metals for chainmail, helmets, and shields to protect the soldiers.

Was this her delusional husband's way of dealing with the escape of his son and rebellions of the peasant villages across the sea?— To spill blood in order to gain yet another castle? And which castle? They had run out of space on their continent, unless he had broken his last straw and decided to move into his brother's, King Robin's, kingdom. A nervous giggle escaped her. Ademar raised his eyebrows in question. "Perhaps he perceives me a threat that requires an entire war council to hunt me down. Quite the witch I am. Magdalene. The witch who made the sun disappear. Perhaps he thinks I am the magic he has sought for all these years."

Ademar twiddled his thumbs and laughed nervously. Could he think there was truth in her words? "Chef Ademar! You wouldn't believe such a silly thing, would you?" Was that why he hadn't called on anyone? Because he was afraid of her?

Ademar seemed to fall into a deep moment of reflection as he began molding the smashed butter into forms. "Not afraid, no. But, hopeful. In a dark, dark world where dark, dark things happen, this morning I received news of a Queen who has secretly shown acts of kindness over all the years I have known her, who ordered her husband King to execute her one and only son earlier than expected. The news broke another piece of me. Had the darkness grown too much that it finally overcame the goodness within her, I wondered? Or perhaps could she no longer bear the tragedy that was about to happen, so she found a way for it to happen sooner? Is that what our world has come to?"

Ademar's sculpture somewhat resembled the form of a large duck. He took out a spoon from his apron and began using the edge to carve short lines into the butter form. "But then, at noon, our city was covered in darkness and our prince escaped. No mother lost her son today. Call it what it may be, perhaps it is witchery, but even if it is, it is very, very good witchery."

Magdalene stroked her finger along the butter to smooth out the surface of the neck. "The one thing I have always loved about swans is the graceful curvature of their necks. Now I am also jealous of their wings. Ademar, how will I get out of the palace? How do I manage to leave the city without anyone noticing me?"

Ademar made small dashes with the edge of a knife into the body of the swan, which created the most realistic illusion of feathers. "This is the least of your problem. Before we make any rash decisions, we must have a plan for you after."

Magdalene's face dropped.

"Aha. I knew it. The first mistake someone on the run makes is only thinking of the escape, when really, it's remaining escaped that's a problem. And in your case, my dear Magdalene, it's going to be a very big problem because not only are you very beautiful, your beautiful face is one that everyone knows."

Magdalene's hopes felt like rugs being beaten, the dust flying out and making it hard to breathe through the realization that all the dancing, posture, speech, reading, and writing lessons she took as a girl were completely worthless to her now in this situation.

Ademar was twirling his butter-slicked mustache. "And you're going to have to go far. And when you make it far, then you will go farther."

"I'm glad you're saying *when* instead of *if*. Where will I go?"

Ademar twirled his mustache. "In a few days a ship should be arriving carrying peasant survivors of the crowpox. I have been ordered to prepare crates of apples, wheat, and ale to be delivered along with them to Elfolk. We will hide you in one of the crates.

"These peasants have never seen you before. From what I know the place is relatively safe. Nobody knows what this mystery magician, who asked Felix to perform this atrocious act, wants to do with the survivors. Nobody has even seen the man.

"It could all be Felix's hallucination, which could be my fault. Years ago, I took on the habit of adding extra pinches of nutmeg into all of his drinks, to make him more relaxed. An old trick my father taught me, but he always warned that too much could cause a jelly mind."

"But to the point, this village could be your first far away, before the farther. The first far is the most important. Then you must be smart. You must be patient. Make new connections. Use them. Do not make enemies."

"How do you know all of this, Ademar?"

"Damalathum was my father's 'farther.' He was chef in an eastern kingdom, a kingdom not important enough to name, it would probably not even make it into the history book of most powerful kings and kingdoms. However, my father spilled a hot pot of tea on the Queen just at a time when the medics had a lack of surplus in ointments. My father was smart, though. He always had a plan, just in case."

"And you, have you always had a plan?"

"No. I would take my fate on the noose. The only place up from here would be King Robin's kingdom or Ipta. Robin is much worse than Felix and I am the amateurs of amateurs, when next to an Iptan Chef. Yes, I could give up my position, grow and pick tomatoes instead of cooking them into a soup. But as ashamed as I am to admit it, I have this … marriage you could call it … my position and status. I fear the emptiness that would await me, even more than I am afraid of the noose."

"Not even the master of a swan sanctuary would appeal to you?"

Ademar opened his mouth to speak but stopped. He rested an elbow on his knee and his body seemed to droop with relaxation. He was imagining it, she could tell. "If I managed to become Head Chef to the Emperor of Ipta, and if I survived long enough to retire my craft, that would be how I would spend the rest of my days. Thank you, this will be a thought I return to often in the future."

"You're welcome."

"There is one major hole in the plan that we must mend, so that you are not the orange among the apples, as one may say. The peasants will not recognize you, the soldiers will not look closely at peasants, but something could happen. A mishap blamed on you, some woman accusing you of stealing. The situations are endless and in one of these, a soldier would get a look at you. Magdalene, we must find you a disguise, and I'm afraid that simply cutting your hair would not be enough. But how? How? How?"

"Do not worry about the disguise. I can manage that. Cora will help me. You must contact her as soon as you can—"

"Can we trust her?"

"Yes. Of that I have no doubt. All those years of trips to the dungeons and not once did she whisper a word. Each one of my ladies-in-waiting I could trust my life to. But she will be watched for several days, I am sure. They will question her about my whereabouts and follow her to see if she may be trying to visit me."

"Ha! If only they knew that the chef of all people is the only one who knows of the Queen's whereabouts. No one knows of our relationship. It is good we kept it secret.

Until the ship comes, although it will be rather uncomfortable, we will hide you under my bed during the night. No one will question the extra trays of food because," he rubbed his belly, "well, I always bring extra trays of food to bed with me. Sometimes I wake up from a good dream and crave meats and pudding."

Magdalene gripped her chest at the memory of going to the kitchens late at night when young Movo would have a nightmare. They would sit in the dining hall and share a big bowl of pudding, taking turns using one spoon and talking about all the nice things Movo planned on dreaming about for the rest of the night. "I pray my son has found his way out. I shall never see him again."

"He knows he is being chased, and knowing our Movo, this is his game now. There is no doubt he will find a way. And after such an escape, it would be an outrage if the magic that orchestrated the disappearance of the sun also made events unfold leading to the prince's second capture. Once upon a time there was a prince to be executed, but then night fell in the middle of the day and he escaped. But then he got caught and was executed anyway. Awful. Would never take a seat for such a puppet show at the market. Would you?"

"Oh, I do hope you're right."

"I am! But now, you must find a hint of cheer in your thoughts and future. When your escape succeeds, what will you do? Think about it. Something that gives you a reason to keep moving forward."

"Hmm." Magdalene tapped her finger against her lips. "I will sit in a meadow with five large loaves of fresh bread, butter them to the most un-lady-like extremity, take bites twice the size of that I can chew, and then wipe my mouth clean with the sleeve of my dress."

"And when that day comes, may my lamb shanks burn— and they have always been nothing less than perfection—so I may know my friend Magdalene is well, and myself and Cora will drink mead in celebration."

"Then I hope your lamb shanks burn to cinders very soon. My dream of buttery loaves of bread is tangible, but I also hope my future holds at least one more moment with my son. If I knew I would see him again, I could reach the end of the world and make it a beginning."

Ademar nodded. "We could all use a new beginning. Your spirit gives me hope. But now, I must return to my kitchen, you must hide until I know the corridors are clear before you hide in my room, and..."

Ademar reached into a basket on a shelf and chucked a loaf of bread into Maria's lap. "Someone has to eat all this butter." He pointed at the swan sculpture.

Magdalene swirled the tip of the loaf around the creamy mess. "Cheers to buttery dreams coming true."

Her teeth sank past the crispy outside right into the doughy middle and she had her first taste of freedom.

CHAPTER 1
PENGUINS

The change in temperature hit Herlot like a crashing wave as she and Movo descended down the marble stairs of the Iptan headquarters. It was like stepping from one season into another, from the coldest winter into a heat she had never experienced before. Droplets formed on her skin and warm moisture tickled its way into her lungs as she breathed. The heat engulfed her tired leg muscles that had been cramping underneath her leggings, which were damp from cold sweat.

"Relax, you're safe here," the heat seemed to whisper to her legs. It was a compelling invitation, but she didn't accept. It wasn't too long ago when a group of men told her family and village to hide in their homes where they'd be safe. Nothing could have been further from the truth. If there was one thing she had learned, it was that trust had to be earned by actions exhibited, while belief was a feeling inside when evidence was nonexistent. Regarding the Iptan headquarters and its people, she didn't have either yet. She would not let her guard down.

Movo faltered. "What's wrong?" she whispered.

Movo brushed the air with his hand, then rubbed his thumb and forefinger together. "How could they possibly be doing this? They found a way to create Ipta's climate within their headquarters."

"That's impossible," Herlot said.

He leaned into her as they continued down the stairs. "That's something I thought I'd never hear you say. Unicorns and magical swords, no problem. But a tropical climate in the middle of a northern city? Even you have a limit to what you can believe."

"I guess I do, yet it's real and all around us."

"That it is."

Voices speaking a foreign language and unfamiliar bird songs filled the atmosphere, but it was difficult to see where they were coming from because luscious greens invaded every space of the courtyard. They climbed up the walls and hung off the archways. Herlot was surprised that the greens hadn't consumed the headquarters and the city beyond, so powerful was their presence. Giant leaves of mysterious trees touched at the tips and overlapped a path that opened into the small space surrounding the staircase. "None of these plants should be able to grow here," Movo said.

Herlot hadn't forgotten that the Emperor of Ipta might be able to perform golden heart magic. Perhaps she could learn something here that would help her blend the leaf. Herlot held back a wince as a pebble that must have fallen into her shoe while running, dug into her raw skin.

"Have a seat," the stairs seemed to say, luring her to sit and dig the pebble out. She brushed this invitation off. No way would she be caught small and vulnerable to any stranger they were about to meet. She wedged her foot out of the shoe and then grabbed hold of Movo's shoulder, lifted her foot, and dug the pebble out with her dirty fingers.

She gasped at the sight of her foot and then looked behind her at the stairs. Her blood had soaked through the shoes during their run and there were bloody footprints on the stairs.

"You'll need that cleaned as soon as possible. Last thing you need is to lose a foot or two," Movo said.

"Ha." Herlot pointed behind her. "Last thing we need is me leaving tracks that may stir the curiosity of our pursuers. What do we do?"

"Pray for rain."

Movo pointed at the path, where three figures dressed in purple, red, and blue could be seen approaching through the leaves. "Here they come."

Three men emerged from among the leaves, their hands folded in front of them as they leisurely approached Herlot and Movo. Luscious colors shone from the rich fabrics that draped their bodies, and gold jewelry rested against their skin. Herlot was keen on observing their smiles, trying to judge whether they were kind or sly. They stopped in unison. Everything about their posture was relaxed, and Herlot was jealous at how easily their weight seemed to balance equally over their feet while she had to play the tedious strategy of switching from one foot to the other for relief from the burning pain. If only she could feel the sweet sensation of relief in both.

The man in the middle raised his arms. Slowly. As if the entire world had only afternoons of bird watching and hair braiding to look forward to.

He stepped closer and stopped an arm's length away from them, his presence towering over Herlot like the plants in this unfamiliar place. She was glad she hadn't sat on the stairs. He seemed taller than he was, even though they were at eye level.

"Welcome to our humble abode, my... guests? Enemies? Tell me, what could you be?" the man said, pressing his palms together in front of his chest. He was bald and had a long beard that sharpened to a tip right at his chest, and his lips were spread wide in a smile. He swayed back the slightest bit as he took a breath. Compared to the refreshing aromas drifting from his body, Movo and she were the exact opposite. Last time she had bathed was right before Hans, Seum, and Devotio fell into the trap. Her story from that moment was painted on her by the sweat, dirt, blood, and tears that had dried on her skin and clothing.

The man's words weren't threatening, per se, and the more Herlot studied him, she interpreted the gleam in his eyes as kind.

"Strangers with friendly intentions," she offered her hand for a shake. "Strangers seeking asylum. I am Herlot, and this is Movo."

The one with the beard covered her palm with both of his hands. "My name is Samin and I see I do not have to worry about you concealing false intentions as you do not have another hand to hide behind your back, for attack when the moment is fit." He then shook Movo's hand. "Believe me, many have tried. May I ask about your troubles, and even more, why you believe safety will be granted to you here?"

Herlot was taken aback. Were they oblivious to Damalathum's current events? Did they not know about Felix's troubles in Eraska? On the other hand, maybe they did and were testing her. She would speak the truth.

"King Felix invaded my land, Eraska. Movo is his son, the prince, as I am sure you may already suspect. He has helped my people. We fought bravely but were caught rescuing our friends and brought back to Damalathum—" She was distracted because the man to the right of Samin began waving his arm.

She waved back at him nervously, hoping it was the polite thing to do.

Suddenly, a boy dressed in colorful trousers with a platter of assorted colorful fruit showed up. The man eagerly began picking at a strange yellow-looking fruit.

Alright, he was just hungry. Now where was I before this man just couldn't wait to call for his fruit? Ah, yes. The execution. "Today, when the sun left and darkness covered the city, we escaped execution and have hid in every nook of the city we could find."

Samin's eyes softened as if he was more than satisfied with her explanation. "As much as I wish to help you, part of Ipta's agreement with King Felix was to not interfere with Damalathum's affairs—"

"They are your affairs—" Herlot began but the fruit man started waving again, and already Herlot saw another boy appear from one of the arched and drapery-covered openings. She grabbed hold of the boy's forearm when he got close. She was sick of being interrupted like this, the man could wait to eat his fruit or what appeared to be the nuts on this new platter. "As I was saying, they are your affairs."

Herlot sat on the bottom step of the staircase and crossed her ankle over her knee so that her tattoo was on display for the three Iptans. "According to this tattoo I am an Iptan warrior. It was given to me by an Iptan, Seum, who fights against Felix in my land, and was tortured to the brink of his life by Felix's men. You see? It is your affair, for I am one of you, and one of yours, and his father, Asm, fights with me."

The three Iptans eyed Herlot's toe with suspicion. She knew it was impossible to mistake it for anyone else's. "It is Iptan, I guarantee you. The S is Seum's signature, and it's made with Iptan ink that can't be mistaken for any else in the world." That's what Seum had told her when he did it. It was black ink with hints of gold in it, the same ink as the many tattoos covering his body. She raised an eyebrow at them because they were still not saying anything. "You doubt me? Give me an opportunity and I will show you I have the same skills as any of your warriors."

Samin looked up to the sky where the earliest of stars were gleaming, and then back down at her. If only Herlot could know what was going through his mind.

Samin cleared his throat. "The S, you say..."

"Yes. S. For Seum."

"Do you happen to know the second?"

"E. If you don't believe me, there must be a way you can check. Send a letter to Ipta asking for information on the trainer Seum. S-e-u-m. Seum."

Samin chuckled.

What could possibly be so funny?

"You are familiar with letters and words," he said.

"Yes. I can read and write."

Samin seemed to do a thorough investigation of her with his eyes. "Let me see if I understand you correctly. You come from a poor land yet know how to read and write. Your land was attacked but somehow you have managed to protect it up to this point, and you have received help from Iptans. Did they say why they were in your land in the first place?"

"Traveling. Exploring. They found the mountain that borders the south of my land a challenge and chose to climb it. Then they traveled through Eraskan land until they stumbled upon us fighting Felix's men. Then, fortunately for us, they joined the fight and have been with us ever since."

"And Seum chose to train you as an Iptan warrior. Did he train anyone else?" Samin asked.

"No. I mean, yes. He trained many others, all of my people who are physically capable of fighting." Tiny prickles of anxiety danced around Herlot's belly as she lost sight of Samin's intentions in their conversation. She hadn't expected him to pry this much and didn't know what answers he was seeking. She was an Iptan warrior. The tattoo was proof. That should have been the end of it.

"So Seum turned an entire land of villagers into Iptan warriors?" The man to Samin's left asked, who had remained silent and expressionless up to this point.

"N—no. Not Iptan warriors. But he taught them to fight."

"So you, just and only you, out of all the people in your land, were the only one whom Seum trained to be a warrior through our Iptan methods? You're the only one with a tattoo?"

He couldn't have stated it clearer than that, that was for sure. "Yes."

"Is there a particular reason why you were *singled* out in such a manner?" Samin asked.

She almost winced at her discomfort. "Seum thought I had he ability to lead."

"Why?" The question prickled her right where she hid one of her secrets, her sword. Emrys had given it to her in the leaf's hidden dream world. It was a magical defensive weapon, able to protect her from any strikes aimed at her. But it came with one condition, to never attack someone with it. The Eraskans had been more than happy to believe that it was a special sword given to her by her father, with a magical legend behind it. This wouldn't work on Samin, though, and she could never reveal secrets that would lead to the exposure of the presence of unicorns. Not to anyone that she and Devotio did not trust. She looked to Movo for help, who nodded at her in encouragement, but there was a slight strain of warning in his gaze.

"I was particularly good at defending my people," she said.

"Why?"

She huffed, blowing her hair out of her face. This man reminded her of Ambro and she, when they were children. How they had annoyed Agatha by constantly asking her "why?" as she explained to them which ingredients she was adding to her stew.

Herlot covered her stomach with her hand as the memory churned in her belly, smothering her in pain until she was certain she'd begin heaving. And she did. Her body was fighting to rid her of the unbearable memory of her last connection to Agatha. When Simon, Agatha's husband, had managed to escape through the roof only to be killed with a dagger by one of Felix's soldiers.

Herlot straightened enough to look Samin straight in his eyes. She wouldn't tell him about the sword, but she would tell him something that was just as true. "I was good at defending them because I knew the fate that would await them if I didn't." She almost hissed as she spoke. "Now I need a place to stay hidden long enough to find a way to get back home."

The man to Samin's left whispered something into his ear and Samin nodded. "You will be granted asylum," Samin said.

Herlot's heart fluttered with relief. If only she understood what had made him decide to say yes. "And Movo?" she asked.

She grasped Movo's hand. She had the worst feeling in her. He was ready to leave the moment Samin had agreed to her staying. She wished he would say something in defense of himself, but there was an empty look in his eyes now, as if he had given up already. It bothered her. Didn't he know how important he was to her? She clenched her jaw and pierced him with her gaze. *Say something.* But there it was. That empty look. Whatever Movo was trying to do right now felt like betrayal.

Samin took a breath that he held for a moment too long, as if he was about to bear bad news. Herlot was now sure that Movo's matter would be much more difficult.

"Ipta has committed to not interfere in Damalathum's affairs. I fear we are overstepping our agreement already by offering you sanctuary. However, your friend is Felix's son—"

"Then we're both leaving." Herlot made to turn around before Samin shouted. "Wait!"

What was this? Was that panic in his voice? Did he *want* her to stay? Whatever his reason, she realized she had some power in regard to this decision, perhaps.

"Perhaps we can find a place for him outside of the headquarters. We have friends and—"

Before Samin could finish, she took a step toward him, her hand now outstretched behind her to still hold on to Movo's.

"Samin," she said. "My good friend Seum taught me to fight with freedom, not fear. I understand this is a very important concept in your world. For the past few months, and it's been a few very long months, you would not believe how many times I have heard about your freedoms. *I am Seum, the magnificent Iptan, I am free to do this, I am free to do that, I will never run out of gold, I have power here, I have power there, so free I am and Ipta has a lot of gold—*"

She was shaken from her tangent by Movo clearing his throat. All three Iptans stared at her wide-eyed, and she hoped that her mocking had not caused her to overstep her place. "My apologies," she said. "Now I find myself not only in the company of two Iptans, but in the actual headquarters of these powerful, free people I have heard so much about, and after everything I have witnessed these last few months, nothing shocks me as much as to learn that these powerful, free people aren't free enough to help a man who has made extremely difficult choices without the freedoms you claim to have."

Samin seemed to finally give Movo his full attention. "Prince Movo. I have heard of many of your successes. Two sieges in your first year, eight years of fighting in the front lines when you could have been waiting comfortably in back with your fellow generals. Taking command of a ship after your captain died, and I believe it is you who redesigned the sword hilts of your father's army. The grip is of most comfort, if I may say."

"Thank you," Movo nodded.

"If I may ask, what were you planning on doing, after you turned your back on your own people, after saving these peasants of Eraska from your father's wrath?"

A shudder rippled through Movo's shoulders and Herlot detected the hint of a chuckle. What could possibly be funny?

Movo ran his thumb over the stubble around his jawline and looked back at the staircase leading out into the city. "Not returning to Damalathum, to begin with."

At this, the other three men laughed. "And then?" Samin asked.

"I figured I'd climb the Eraskan mountains and then travel into the southern lands. Have you by any chance read *Sir Maurice's Expeditions and Explorations*?"

Samin eyed the hungry man at his side. "Samin, it is a collection of drawings and observations of a Thessilian biologist from his time in Halia. It is often studied in geography lectures at Damalathum's university."

Samin nodded. "Ah, so you planned on making drawings of the lands you visited."

"Oh, no, I intended to see the animals for myself—the penguins—that Sir Maurice described."

Herlot smiled fondly at Movo. Whatever it was he was doing, his charisma was putting the Iptans more and more at ease.

"Oh, I believe it has been ages since I felt some real humor," Samin said. "Exchanging one's status as future king to see a penguin. I may have to send for a shipment and have them brought to us, then you will tell me if they are worth what you have given up."

Movo laughed along for the moment and then his features turned serious. "Samin, I have only gained since my time in Eraska. Like Herlot said, we need a safe place to hide for long enough to plan our escape. I wish to remain at her side and help her for as long as possible. I would be grateful if you opened your Iptan home to me as well."

"Yes. Yes. I just hope you do not leave before the penguins arrive." Samin rubbed his hands together. "Now, my guests, my good friend Taran will escort you to the baths after which you will be taken to your room. I only have one to spare at the time, but your comfort is guaranteed.

"A month ago, we received silk fabrics made from the most exquisite silkworms in the world. They are so smooth that once your heads lay upon your pillows, you will slide and slip right into your dreams." He frowned. "Or perhaps nightmares based on the looks of you. Ah, and yes, supper will be prepared for you while you bathe. An Iptan specialty."

"Thank you, Samin," Movo said. "May I request a bucket of water first to wash away the tracks we left behind on your bridge?"

"Our guests do not clean. Besides..." Samin's attention turned to a man Herlot had not noticed before, who was leaning over the balcony of the second floor. The man nodded and walked off. "Good thing it looks like rain."

Herlot glanced up at the sky which was nothing but clear. "Samin, if we do not wash the bloody footprints away, Felix's soldiers might be suspicious if they see a trail leading up to your headquarters."

Samin wrapped his arms around their shoulders and steered them toward the path where Taran was awaiting. "Ah, my new friends, you have nothing to worry about. No one investigates our headquarters unless we wish. And besides, the rain will wash it away."

Before Herlot could protest, a giant raindrop splattered on the tip of her nose, soon followed by several others which landed on the top of her crown. The rainwater was warm like she had never felt before. She glanced up at the sky again and gasped at the beauty of it. Most of the sky above Damalathum was covered in a blanket of dark clouds, except for a small section around the horizon where the sunset's colors still thrived. If ever there was a moment to teach a child all the colors of the world, now, looking at this sky would be it.

She glanced at Movo, who was frowning up at the sky. Then, Movo and the color palette above blurred and she could not make out any distinct shapes. Rain was pouring down like a waterfall from the sky and her bare feet were already in a puddle.

"This way, my refugees! This way!" Samin skipped down one of the paths. Before she knew it, they were rushing down the path, slapping against all sorts of plants as the rain hammered onto the giant leaves surrounding them.

Chapter 5
Hanibyn Seeds

Herlot poured herself a fifth glass of water from a gilded pitcher in the bathing chamber. She stared with awe at the crystal-embedded ceiling as she gulped. She took one last sip and allowed the water to rest on her tongue, as if assuring her mouth that it was safe to stop the call for thirst.

She stared at the massive hole in the ground, the size of a small pond, full and bubbling with fresh water. She inhaled the flowery scents as the steam filled the room. It was everything her dirty, tired, and sore body needed, but her heart wished for the cold stream in Alonia, or even better, the fire-warmed bucket of water her mother would pour over her head during the winters.

She jumped and spat out the water as the door behind her opened a crack.

"May I come in?" a female voice asked.

Herlot let out a sigh of relief in knowing that it wasn't Felix's men. She wiped her mouth. This was not her place, and she wasn't the one to make decisions on who could go where. Nevertheless, she appreciated the politeness.

"Yes, of course," she said and faced the door.

In entered a woman carrying a stack of orange and yellow fabrics much like she wore. Her hair was braided into what looked like several hundred little braids, each one a different shade of red. Her nose was decorated with a gold ring of amber gemstones. And then there was her posture. Herlot figured this woman as someone who had never had to hunch over to pick up firewood. The woman was almost a head shorter than Herlot, but because of the way she held herself, no other word but tall came to mind. This seemed to be a quality all Iptans seemed to carry.

"Herlot, is it? I am Aleena, Samin's wife. It is a pleasure to meet you." Herlot shook Aleena's hand. Their hands were about the same size and the pressure of their grip matched perfectly. Herlot had never realized before the intricacies of a handshake because never before had she not had to adjust anything—lessen her grip for a frail hand or match the speed of the shake, so as not to have her body jerked around. Their eyes met and Herlot couldn't help smiling knowing that Aleena was just as surprised to find a handshake that matched her own.

"There are moments that foretell a strong friendship in the future. I believe this may be one of them," Aleena said. A gentle smile grew on her lips.

Herlot looked down at her dirty feet. Aleena's were perfectly clean and had jeweled threading woven around two of her toes and it criss-crossed at her ankles. Based on looks, Herlot was the exact opposite of Aleena, yet this woman was the first person in this city who had a friendliness that reminded her of Enri. This she had not expected.

"It's good to hear kind words, especially ones that entail friendship," Herlot said. "If only I had the time. As soon as we are rested, Movo and I must return to Eraska."

"Of course, but the future is infinite. Now that we have met each other, I'd love to help you get oriented. I'm sure you don't know the first thing about an Iptan bath."

Herlot shrugged. "I was going to sit in there." She pointed at the giant bath.

"Ha! Sit? I mean, you could do that, if you really wanted to... My is it dark in here!"

Aleena's colorful dress floated behind her as she disappeared behind a stone column.

A faint light glowed from behind the column followed by sounds that resembled someone blowing on firewood.

"Do you need help?" Herlot asked. "If it's a fire you are attempting to start, I have done so many times."

"No, no. Ah, there we go. Are you ready to see something beautiful, Herlot? Look up!"

Infinite light sparkled across the ceiling, dispersing from one corner of the room to the other. A gasp of pure awe escaped Herlot, one of those gasps that belongs to children who have not yet experienced the horrors of the world. A sound she thought she'd never make again. "It's like the stars in the sky! My goodness, Aleena, how did you do that?"

Aleena was now back at Herlot's side. "Oh, it's just a little copper and gold trick," she said.

Gold. Magic. The Emperor. She was looking at direct evidence that supported her theory about the emperor using golden heart magic. She could use her time among the Iptans to ensure her speculations. As much as she wanted to jump at this opportunity to ask Aleena, Herlot promised herself that it wouldn't be until she was absolutely certain and in front of the Emperor himself. After she had enough time to judge his character. Then she would reveal about seeking assistance, about blending the leaf back onto a tree.

"How does the trick work?" she asked innocently. "It's quite magical."

Aleena chuckled. "It is, isn't it? It's something some of our very skilled people back home came up with. I wouldn't know the details. You have an interest in magic?"

It appears as though I'm not Iptan enough to be trusted with secrets. Very well. Aleena's gaze seemed to pierce through her. Herlot chuckled just as Aleena had. "Of course, my village loved to tell stories of magic. I always wondered if there were any real occurrences of it in our world. If I may ask, how is it that it's so warm here compared to the rest of the city? I have never experienced anything like it."

Aleena tilted her head and smiled. "Your friend, Seum, even though he gave you an Iptan tattoo, didn't share much with you about our culture, did he?"

Herlot swallowed. Had she pushed too far? She had been trying to learn more about Ipta from Aleena, yet somehow she felt like it was Aleena who was learning more about something Aleena desired to understand.

Herlot shook her head. "No. Our priorities at the time were mainly focused on protecting ourselves."

Aleena nodded slowly. "I see... Well, we all have our little secrets, don't we? Empires have them too."

Herlot exhaled as Aleena approached a stone bench, grateful that the conversation had come to an end. Yet Herlot couldn't shake the feeling that Aleena's statement about secrets had Herlot in mind. Either way, she had learned one thing. Her tattoo and status still weren't enough to help her gain access to Ipta's secrets, but there definitely were secrets being protected.

"I'll set your new clothes on this bench and will take the ones you have before I leave," Aleena said as she set the clothes down.

Herlot stuck her thumb inside the top of her leggings, careful not to irritate the holes as she rolled them down and stepped out. She squatted and ran a finger down a row of threading. There were shadows that seemed more predominant between the rows of wool thread. Blood encrusted into the deeper spaces, her own and those of men she didn't even know. She slung the leggings over her forearm and walked over by Aleena.

Herlot placed her leggings down on a bench. "These leggings tell a story. They are important. I'm assuming you were planning on disposing of my clothes?" Herlot said.

"Yes. I thought you might want to after everything that has happened."

Herlot grabbed hold of the back of her dress, and with even more care than she had given her leggings, lifted it up over her head, afraid that it would rip in half from the weight of sweat, dirt, and blood dragging it down. She allowed the dress to hang over her forearm. "My dress means everything to me. My mother made it. It used to be longer, but I had to cut the bottom portion off. Movo said that the blood stains would cause the people of the village we were about to enter to get sick. I buried that part of the dress in the woods outside of Lorfin Village. That piece of wool had a better burial than my own mother."

"It was your mother's blood that had stained the dress?" Aleena hadn't shied away from the uncomfortable fact that Herlot had meant to avoid.

"Yes."

Aleena closed her eyes and nodded. "Only one who witnesses a crowpox death knows the amount of blood the illness spills." It was as if she were giving Herlot's mother a silent moment of respect in speaking the blunt truth of what Herlot's mother had suffered.

Herlot pointed at the space of the missing right sleeve of the dress. "The sleeve of my dress might still be lying somewhere on the field of Ruelder unless an animal chewed it up trying to get to my arm for its dinner. I think I remember seeing a few pigs at Ruelder. Pigs love bones, you'd be surprised. I was naïve back then. Untrained. Slow. I did the stupidest thing a warrior could imagine, lifted my arm up in hopes of it shielding me from a swinging sword."

Herlot set her dress down on top of the leggings, taking time to fold it with as much care as if it were the newest of all dresses. "I'm grateful for the clothes you have offered me, Aleena, and I will wear them while I am here in the Iptan Headquarters. But—"

"You don't need to explain. Your clothes are like a book. They tell a story that I hope you will share more of with me in the future. I will wash them personally myself."

Herlot pressed her lips together and nodded. "Thank you for understanding."

"You're welcome." She smiled and turned to leave, but then turned back to face Herlot again. "You would fit among Iptan women. They are not afraid to stand in their bare skin. I hear queens in the kingdoms of these lands bathe in gowns. Enjoy your bath and I suggest floating on your back. The experience is...mesmerizing."

Before long, Herlot found herself alone again after the door to the bathing chamber swung shut behind Aleena.

She looked around again. The air had grown more dense, a perfect setting for a game of King Fog. Elvin would have loved it.

Herlot looked down at the dirty sweat droplets dripping down her belly. The steam seemed to be extra concentrated around her body. Herlot knew what this was. Not only had she seen branches conform to Devotio's movements in the forest, she had also looked through the eyes of an owl and visited a hidden world inside a chestnut tree's leaf. There was no fire to heat the room or from what she could see, hot coals to heat the water. This was the work of magic.

Herlot walked down the steps that led into the water until she was submerged up to her neck. How strange it was to see so much water without a hint of wildlife. As deep as she could see there were no signs of rocks, water grasses, or fish. She looked around at the columns, at the places where trees would have been by the stream in Alonia. On the columns were sculpted forms that resembled humans. She wondered why no one had thought of sculpting any creatures. It would have brought the water more to life.

Before her mind was given the chance to think of all the different animals she would have sculpted onto the stone trunks, her thoughts slowed like the evening tide of the sea outside Alonia. Everything about the setting, from the sleep-inducing aromas to the star-mimicking lights shining above, was inviting her to relax. A small part of Herlot fought not to take the bait.

She let out a sigh of relief. The near boiling water bit at her wounds and aching body. It was as if the water was melting away the memories ingrained in the dirt in her wounds.

The water danced around her neckline. Her shoulders, torso, hips, and legs became light. She took a breath and allowed her head to sink under.

Peace. The water engulfing her ears muffled the multiple strands of thought lines running through her mind. She blew bubbles. Underwater there was no sense in trying to speak or form words, and she let go of any worry, of communicating her disheveled thoughts to herself. It was an impossible luxury of peace she wasn't allowed to have and wouldn't have for a long time in her journey ahead. Planning their escape would come with a new territory of worries, but she could enjoy this just for tonight.

Her lungs hinted at air and she gave her body the permission to rise back up to the surface.

She blinked the water from her eyes and smoothed her short hair back. She treaded water, slowly spinning in a circle, enjoying the pressure against her feet and the flow between her toes.

"Hmm," she said. She was alone. She couldn't remember the last time she had been completely alone in a space and she was surprisingly not lonely. It felt good and she didn't know whether to feel guilty about that or not. For all she knew, none of her problems existed in this chamber and everywhere was an invitation for pleasure. No planning. No strategizing. No running for her life. No running for her loved ones' lives. Just her and a human-made pond and stars.

Herlot swam back and forth a few times and then decided to take Aleena up on her suggestion to float on her back and look at the ceiling.

"Now this is something special," she announced to the blissfully empty room. The large amount of bubbles floating to the surface kept the water moving and she felt as if she were out on the boat with her father again, the gentle waves rocking her as she looked up at the stars. It was a delicious feeling of sinking yet being held by compact nothingness. Water was the best mattress.

The lights on the ceiling pulsed in a slow rhythm, like her relaxed heart. She couldn't look away. It was as if she were in a game of "whoever looks away first loses." Some far away part of her panicked at what was happening and was yelling at her to regain control of her body. But the lure of the lights grew stronger and Herlot was barely aware that she couldn't even blink anymore.

Within the lights above her, she made out a pattern that resembled a willow tree. Her arm raised hypnotically and she traced her pointer finger along the shape. Then the stars began to glide along the ceiling. They were gathering into several bunches.

Her chest felt as if it were hanging above a fire. There it was again—the strange warmth in some unknown chamber of her heart. Something that had always been there but impossible to notice on command.

The lights came to a standstill and then began to shake. In what resembled a string, they slid down toward Herlot. Before long they had created the shapes of willow tree leaves and were hovering just above her. She reached her arm out again and a strand of stars twined down it. Another two did the same to her legs, a fourth around her back, and a fifth arranged itself like a cushion below her head. She felt light as a feather and could no longer feel the water.

An unknown music began to play—instruments, voices, and a language she had never heard before.

A gentle breeze danced around her body as she was swayed from side to side. She tried to speak but could not feel her mouth or throat.

One of the star-leaves appeared in front of her eyes and then stroked a strand of wet hair from her forehead. Then it brushed along her eyes, closing them shut, and Herlot's sense of hearing was magnified, absorbing each of the unfamiliar, yet familiar, words of the song.

Her heart fluttered, the words igniting a sense of playful flying within it, as if a butterfly were dancing inside her chest. It was as if her heart had a mind of its own, translating the magic of the song.

Forever Am, forever have been, forever will be.
I and this gold. Before and beyond and foremost within.

Then, all her memories that had been distorted, disheveled, hidden, forgotten, covered, blurred, and misunderstood fluttered around her heart, each one attracted to another and reaching out its hand, forming a smooth bond like the imaginary lines connecting the stars into shapes. Before she could barely recall her past moments of golden heart magic, yet now the memories were sharp and clear. She could finally see how her past moments of golden heart magic interconnected, and the man named Brom seemed to be at the center of everything. Brom—the name of the man who forgot to greet the sun, who Rudi had named in her father's legend, and who asked Emrys to hide the unicorns so long ago.

She remembered searching for the chestnut tree with Ambro the day after her father had told them the legend. Her feet had been drawn to a footprint. *Brom's footprint.* She remembered how it felt when her bare skin made contact with it. A warmth had flown from her heart to her legs and out her feet, entwining with Brom's story at the time he had made the footprint. It had felt like moving back in time.

And then there was the misfortune of coincidence at Ruelder. A spark of the heart and another one of Brom's footprints had led to the events of her losing her arm. As her friends battled on the field of Ruelder, she had been wrapped into Brom's perspective of the world at the time of him making the footprint. His urgency had been her own in regard to the beautiful unicorn that had stood before Brom. Nothing had been more important than to bring the beautiful unicorn to the safety of Emrys's hidden world. Brom's frustration had become her frustration, too, because the unicorn was not willing to wait for Brom's guidance. To the unicorn, Brom had been a potential danger, a gold-less being wishing to kill it for its golden alicorn. It didn't understand that Brom only wanted to take it to the safety of the hidden world. Herlot had agreed fully with Brom's decision to chase it. Too bad this story had unfolded ancient times ago, while in the real world, in Herlot's time, there was a deathly battle occurring on the field that the unicorn ran away too.

Did she regret that day? She didn't know. She was certain that she never wanted to feel the pain again. She hadn't felt the sharp metal of the soldier's sword slice into her arm, it had been that quick. She remembered still trying to stand up after it had happened. But then when her senses caught up to what had happened, it had been excruciating. She was terrified that this body that she was in could one day have her experiencing the pleasure of a cool stream, yet also have the potential to turn even breathing into a nightmare, so powerful could the pain be.

Then there was the moment in the cave with Seum. Once again, her gold had begun to flow from her heart, coincidentally at the same spot where Brom had once stepped, again. How often did a coincidence have to occur to not be considered a coincidence anymore? Was some hidden part of her purposefully seeking out Brom's footsteps? Or were Brom's footsteps somehow calling out to her?

When she blended in the cave, Brom's mind had been disheveled. He had been dying, very possibly. His conscious thoughts were like a fading ring around the moon. He had painted his palm and pressed it into the wall. There was something special about his palm, and she remembered his urgency to communicate something. He was praying for his knowledge to be shared with someone. If only Seum had not stirred her out of that moment, she might know what this vital information was. Furthermore, that palm print did not exist there anymore. Someone had carved it out of the cave wall and taken it somewhere. Who and why?

"Herlot? Are you in there?"

Like distant sea waves, Herlot heard voices, but she couldn't stir herself awake, nor did she want to. The longer she stayed here, the more information and understanding she might gain about how to control the gold in her heart and make sense of past events.

She could maybe really do it, blend the leaf all by herself. She couldn't stop imagining what that moment would be like when she blended the leaf onto a branch. It would be a moment of blissful joy—to look Devotio in his rainbow-tinted eyes and know that she had not failed him, that she had given him magic the same way he had lit her days with magic when she had been a little girl.

Had it not been for the fire, the leaf would still be attached to the same chestnut tree where it should be. An entire world that held the memories of beautiful ancient times, a last remaining trace of what this world could be, wouldn't be threatened. If she didn't find a way to blend the leaf back onto another tree, the unicorns and Emrys would be forever gone. Their trace and how the world had once been would forever be forgotten.

All because of Felix.

She was beginning to feel her body again, the rage caused her muscles to twitch, and angry tears burned her eyes. If she could rid the world of this one awful person, so many future awful events could be avoided. It was unfair, unjust, and had to be fixed, how one person could cause so much harm with such ease compared to how many people and how much good it took to create good things such as a home in her Alonia. One week to build a home, a few breaths to burn it down. She promised herself that she'd do everything in her power to ensure Felix never hurt anyone again. *And...and I hope he suffers.*

Suddenly, a sharp pain in her chest caused her eyes to fly open. She fought to scream at the scene above her. There were no more Iptan stars. The starry willow tree leaves were now large, round tendrils that were tightening their grip around her. Everything went black.

Herlot could not believe such darkness could exist. Even if the sun, stars, and moon were taken from the sky, it could not be so dark. It was a color that rose the most uncomfortable, undefinable fear from the pit of her soul and prickled sharply at the inside of her skin as if it wanted to pierce itself out. She didn't know if the darkness engulfing her or the fear fighting to pierce itself out of her skin hurt more. She was screaming but no sound came out of her.

The darkness was heavy. Strong. Powerful. It massacred the future. Any flower would never obtain bloom within its presence. It would be born and grow into a withered, wilted, and rotted expression of death. Here not only death was death, life was death too.

Somebody help me. I beg someone to help me. Please someone help me.

Herlot had never cried harder or screamed louder in her life, but no tears streamed down her face and no shout could escape her lips. Instead, her screams and tears intertwined into a thorny vine inside her head before plunging down into her chest, only to make her pain twice as intense. It was an endless cycle that she couldn't stop. More screams, more tears, and then more pain.

A distant pounding, a sound of the physical world, sounded from far, far away before she was swallowed back in. The only comforting thought was that one day when infinity ended, this pain might end. But before that day, the pain would grow and grow until she shattered, and then it would torture her by sewing her together with a sword, leaving her a scarred and damaged version of what she had once been. And then the cycle would repeat, the edge of infinity never in sight.

"Herlot!"

Movo's voice blended with the piercing pain. Somewhere, some part of Herlot remembered a memory of what it was like to breathe.

"She's not breathing. Take the shot. In the foot first," another voice said.

Something pinched Herlot's ankle. A beautiful, physical, normal pain and the memories of breathing grew more vivid.

"Once more before she suffocates. In the back!"

"Are you certain?"

"Yes! You did not get trained to aim for nothing. Now take the shot!"

This time the beautiful pain pinched her back and burrowed into her insides. Her eyes flew open. Her lungs expanded. Tears streamed. And she screamed, loving every vibration of her sound escaping, the now again starry ceiling above her grew more distant. The impact with the water smacked the entire surface of the back of her legs, waist, ribcage and shoulders as the throbbing pain grew in her ankle and inside her belly, and she thanked the skies for these pains. As much as it hurt, it was right, understandable, and how pain was supposed to be.

She was sinking into the water and saw Movo's beautiful face blurred by the surface before he dove in, fully clothed. His strong arms cradled her naked body, and water was rushing past her as they rose together toward the surface.

All was so well when they broke the surface. Herlot couldn't help smiling as she coughed and breathed normal air in the normal world, feeling her normal pain. She had her arms wrapped around Movo's neck and her forehead pressed against his jaw.

Aleena, Samin, and a woman Herlot had not met were standing at the edge of the pool, talking as they passed a strange weapon between themselves. From what Herlot could make out, they were admiring its craftsmanship.

"She's bleeding!" Movo shouted at the trio as he swam them toward the staircase. Herlot noticed the streaks of red liquid blending with the water.

Aleena glanced their way. "Don't worry, new friend. Our medic will be here and Herlot will be a shiny, gold goblet before we know it."

Movo's angry grunt reverberated in his throat.

"Movo. I'm fine. Very fine, please don't be upset or worried," she whispered and smiled against his neck.

"Trust me, you are very far from fine and I'm very far from being not worried. You sound like a drunkard off the streets from whatever they did to you in here. We are leaving tonight."

He marched up the stairs and nearly knocked Samin, Aleena, and the woman over as he pushed past them and headed toward the door.

"Movo, my new friend, wait. She needs to be taken care of," Aleena said.

"Yes, Movo, stop—" Herlot said.

"Do not call me a friend. She was not even here an entire evening and she nearly suffocated to death before you shot her with that weapon of yours. We will take our chances outside of your damned headquarters," Movo said, not stopping his stride.

Just then the door opened, and a young man dressed in a robe and a long sleeping hat entered. He was holding the door open with his side as he shuffled in, both of his hands occupied carrying a long, black wooden box.

"Be reasonable. No one in this city can mend those wounds as well, and as quick, and as easily as our medic. What if you can't find a healer or get caught? Herlot's wounds will be infected by sunrise if you leave," Aleena said.

Movo stopped in his tracks.

"And she's butt naked if you have not noticed. That is sure to bring you unwanted attention, especially because the bandit's neighborhood is just around the corner," the woman with the weapon said.

"I have noticed," Movo said under his breath.

"They're right. Please, let them help me. After everything we have been through, I don't know if we need a naked adventure through a bandit's neighborhood," Herlot said.

Movo turned back toward the pool. "Fine."

The medic swished past them, a cheerful bounce in his step that caused the long strip of his hat to bounce. Normal pain and bouncy hats. There was sanctuary in this city after all.

A man carrying furs, most likely his assistant, entered the room and was soon on his knees unrolling the blankets.

"No worries, sir," the medic said to Movo. "Hanibyn seed wounds are the simplest thing under the emperor's sky to heal, and everyone always has a joyous time watching the treatment. I find it more fascinating than gardening on any day, if you ask me." His style of speaking was completely opposite from his form of walk, his words smoothly strung together like the stems of a flower crown. "Just lay the lady down, on her belly, if possible, on the furs."

Movo cleared his throat. "Samin," he said.

Samin turned so that his back was to them.

Herlot caught a glimpse of the assistant pouring water out of a clay pot over the medic's hands as Movo lowered her down. He did it so gently that the wound on her back was not bothered by the first contact with the hairs of the furs. "Can you roll over on your own?" he asked.

"Yes," she said.

Immediately Movo straightened and turned so he was facing away from her. "Hanibyn seeds? What are they? Is that what you shot into her?" he asked.

Herlot balanced on her hand and knees for a moment to gain trust in the strength of her muscles before lying down on her belly. The assistant had already draped a silky-smooth blanket over her, and she was enjoying the feel of furs between her fingers. They reminded her of running her hands through long blades of grass in Alonia.

"Hanibyn seeds," Aleena said. "They are the hardest, toughest seeds in the world and bloom the most gentlest of flowers. One strong gust of wind is all it takes to cause a petal to fall, hence why they grow best in personal gardens with someone who has all the time in the world to take care of them, and only in pots so they can be taken to shelter if the winds grow strong."

The medic wiped something cold and wet across Herlot's back. "Absolutely never can they be left out in the mid-day sun, only in the early morning hours and just before evening," he added.

"Right," Aleena said. "The seeds, however, will pierce through anything, just like an arrow. Unlike the arrow, though, they are not poisonous and are easily extracted. Yes, they are great ammunition for battles, but are also very helpful in, for lack of better words, waking someone from their stupor. Many a bad idea was prevented from coming to fruition thanks to these little seeds. And then there are the few occasions of the trance. I've seen it happen a few times. Once when I was a girl my father had fallen so deep into a trance of dance during a festival, and only a shot of the Hanibyn seed woke him from it."

"Who took the shot?" the woman with the weapon asked.

"My mother."

Samin chuckled.

"I don't know what is amusing about injuring someone stuck in a trance," Movo said.

Herlot giggled as the medic poured something into her wound that caused her skin to tingle. The tickling continued down into her belly where the throbbing pain had been. She ignored the sound of displease Movo made.

"Is that what happened to Herlot? She was in a trance?" Movo asked.

Samin let out a sigh, trilling his lips as he did, like Agatha used to do to entertain newborn babies. "That's what it looked like, but I think only Herlot can tell us the answer to that."

Herlot mimicked Samin's sigh. How could she put what had happened into words? "I was floating on my back, as Aleena had suggested, looking at the fake stars. I must have fallen asleep, and I dreamed that I floated up toward the ceiling." She stopped there, not wanting to share the part about her memories of when the gold in her heart had sparked. "I started having a nightmare and it was awful. I couldn't get out of it until you shot me. Thank you."

"Do you always float when you sleep?" Aleena asked.

Silly question. Herlot furrowed her eyebrows. "No. That's impossible."

A moment of silence followed and Herlot was certain they were all wanting to say something, but thinking of the right way to say it.

"Sometimes the best thing to do is to just start talking instead of thinking about how to say what you don't know how to explain. It figures itself out on its own," Herlot said.

Aleena was the one to take Herlot's cue. "People *do* and *can* float. You are living proof of it. You were just an arm's reach from the ceiling," Aleena said.

"Oh." She hadn't expected that. Yet it was true, how could she have fallen into the water otherwise?

"And your skin had turned blue because you weren't breathing," Movo said. The way he said it was as if he were testing her, trying to get a rise out of her, like a father making sure his child understood the seriousness of having broken a bone falling out of a tree that he was not allowed to climb.

"Oh," was all Herlot could manage. Well, was this not a festival of calf births? Herlot's life was intent on presenting her with more and more questions with no answers and she didn't know if it was worth it to worry about this instance. More than anything she wanted it to be stored away with no need to decipher, explain, or understand. The floating was nothing compared to the darkness. She didn't know if it was a trance, but if that's what it was, she never wanted to fall into one again. Also, at least it hadn't been real. Her relief at the idea was hindered, though. *If it wasn't real, then my mind conjured the awful experience.* If it ever happened again, how could she stay sane knowing her mind's ability to torture her? Real things one could run away from. She'd never run away from this unless she lost her mind. She shuddered.

Herlot felt the tip of a metal object on her back. "Take a deep breath. You may feel some discomforting pressure but that is all," the medic said.

Just like he had said, the pressure was there but it was nothing to cry over. Herlot wished she could see what he was doing.

"I am ready for the water," the medic said.

Herlot caught a glimpse of the assistant taking a tube-like glass structure filled with gold-tinted water out of the box.

"Movo, you may wish to see this. It is quite fascinating," Samin said.

"What is so fascinating? I'd like to see," Herlot said.

The medic patted her on the shoulder. "You'll see when we work on your ankle."

He poured the liquid over the sore spot on her back and then she felt something wiggling.

"Holy basil," Movo said.

Herlot smiled at his use of the Eraskan term and how naturally it had come out of him. Suddenly, all the pressure in her back released. She turned her head to the side and saw the medic dangling a green sprout attached to a black pellet-sized seed at the end. "That was in me?" she asked.

"Mhmm. Now let's turn you over so you can see the process for yourself."

The medic held the fabric covering her, giving her enough room to turn over. As soon as she was on her back, he covered her chest, torso, and hips.

Herlot rested on her elbow so she could watch the medic work. "Can I see that?" she nodded toward the sprout now in the assistant's hands.

"Of course."

Herlot wiggled and struggled trying to find a position she could easily hold herself up in so she could use her arm to take the sprout. Seum always made her do countless exercises so that her belly area was strong. However, each time she moved to lift her arm she thought she would collapse backwards. Her belly was clearly speaking to her and saying that no matter how much training it had received in the past, it was now going to sleep, and soon her other muscles were to follow.

Movo seemed to have heard and understood her belly as well. He took a seat behind her. "Lean back," he said.

She let her head fall back against his chest. "Thank you." Her arm was now free to examine the sprout.

The fabric covering her body slipped a little as she reached for the plant. Movo tucked it in firmly just below her armpit.

Herlot rolled the seed between her fingers, sending the sprout growing out of it into a twirling dance. The seed was in fact the hardest thing she had ever touched, and it left imprints in her fingertips.

This time she saw the metal tool the medic was using. He placed it a bit into her wound, and as he pulled the top two pieces open, the two pieces in her spread as well. He flicked the end of his sleeping hat over his shoulder before taking hold of the glass with the liquid gold. "That's a lovely hat," she said.

"I cannot sleep without it," he said.

"And he sleeps most of the day and night," Aleena said.

"Really? Why?" Herlot asked.

The medic pouted his lips as if thinking about how to answer the question. "Well, it just feels so incredibly nice. I trained and studied, then trained and studied again, since I was a boy. Now, unless someone needs my help, and especially because this kingdom has no scenery of interest to me, I prefer to relax and dream of Ipta."

"You never have troubles falling asleep? Eventually you must not be tired at all." Herlot said.

"Never. As long as I think the right thoughts I can do it whenever I please."

This man was incredibly interesting to Herlot. "What kind of thoughts?"

"All sorts of thoughts. Memories of falling asleep to begin with. Hammock designs. Pillow materials. Ocean waves. Thunder. Rain. Harp music."

Herlot smiled. "I like thinking about ocean waves, thunder, and rain too. I have never heard harp music."

"It's somewhat like the psaltery," Movo said. He tapped the assistant, sitting back on his heels. "The water?"

"Samin, we must call for the harp player if she is not due to entertain Felix's court. I can't remember the last time I heard one either," Aleena said.

"She was just here last week," Samin said.

"I would love to hear this instrument. I hope she is able to come before we leave," Herlot said. "What does it look like?"

"Before we all fall asleep, would it not be best to clean and treat Herlot's wound as soon as possible?" Movo said.

"Right," they all answered in unison.

Herlot watched the assistant hold the edge of the strange tube right at the entrance of her wound. Several drops fell in and then she felt the tickle sensations again. Then, right before her eyes, faster than she had ever seen a plant grow, the sprout appeared.

"Holy basil," she said.

The medic pinched the top of the sprout between two fingers and plucked it out, seed intact.

"A beauty," he said. "Aleena, would you like to plant it in your garden?"

Aleena widened her eyes and reached out her palm. "Any chance it will bloom silver?"

"Yes, with certainty. As far as I know, we only received barrels marked silver Hanibyn seeds," said the woman with the weapon.

Herlot found the Iptans more and more amusing and she felt more and more at ease around them. She liked how humorful they were about an event that would have been horrifying to most. "Can I keep this seed?" she asked.

"Consider it yours. To remember your stay with us," Samin said.

"Thank you."

Herlot yawned.

"I know exactly how you feel," the medic said. "Let me just care for the bottoms of your feet and we can all retire to the dream world."

Movo fidgeted behind her. He brought his arm across her belly and brought them both to a more upright position. "That won't be necessary. If you provide me with vinegar and cloth, I can do it," he said.

The medic nodded. "That we can do. I'll have my assistant bring the supplies to your quarters."

Movo rose to his feet, the whole time keeping a supportive arm behind Herlot's back. "Get dressed and I'll wait for you outside," he said. Before Herlot could respond, he was already at the door.

As much as Herlot was at ease with the Iptans, there was no doubt that Movo felt the exact opposite. It was clear that he wanted to get out of the bathing chamber as fast as possible. Did he have something important to tell her? She smiled at her new friends who had managed to shoot her and heal her all in the same evening, and she remembered how it was naïveness that had allowed Felix's soldiers to invade Alonia with such ease.

Herlot cleared her throat, thanked the Iptans for their help, and asked for privacy to get dressed. After putting on her Iptan dress, she hurried to the one person she knew was safe and who knew much more about the new world she found herself in—Movo.

CHAPTER 9

STARS DO NOT LIE

Enri sat on the edge of a rock, her face in her palms, crying.

"Oh, are you certain Benyamin?"

"Stars do not lie," Benyamin said. "The Iptans agreed to offer them sanctuary for the time being."

"Had I not given her that tattoo..." Seum said.

"But you did give her the tattoo and the Iptans took them in and now they're fine," Hans said.

"Could you stand still?" Seum snapped. While they had waited for Benyamin to learn the story from the stars, Hans had started floating around them. Enri found it fascinating to watch him drag his pointed toes without having to put his feet one in front of the other to walk.

"No," Hans said. "My, never thought there'd be things I'd enjoy about being a ghost." He concentrated his float in a circle around Seum, and Seum attempted to swat him away like a fly.

Enri smiled and shook some of the tears off her palms. Life had become twisted with the darkest and the lightest of things. Herlot and Movo were stuck across the sea, but they had escaped execution. Hans had been tormented to death, but he was with them and still finding joys in life, or afterlife. Things didn't feel so bad, they felt somewhat well.

"My, I wish we could tell everyone," Enri said. She loosened the collar of her dress allowing fresh air to run through. Emotions could make one terribly hot. "Can you imagine their faces? And to know that it was all thanks to you, Benyamin." She took his old, dry, wrinkled hands into hers. "Thank you. Thank you for saving our... family."

His smile sent an array of creases across his face. "It was my pleasure. But Hans and Seum are to thank too."

Seum grunted. "I just rode an imaginary horse with wings. You're the one who knows how to read some mysterious metal object and coordinate events to match an eclipse."

"Your love and play of the psaltery brought us Hans back, and Hans led us into the dream world."

"Yes, and–!" Hans lifted slightly off the ground. "Oh basils, that feels weird. I wanted to say that Queen Magdalene was wonderful too. She believed her dream."

Enri nodded. She was fascinated by Movo's mother. She had believed her dream and taken such a risk. Had her dream been wrong, she would have killed her only son a day early.

Yes, Enri believed in magic, but she was aware that understanding what was magic and what was not could be difficult. One could make plans and decisions based on something that was not even real. She reckoned it was a unique gift, some sort of intelligence that some people could have that helped them distinguish.

Maybe Enri had it. After all, everything Benyamin, Hans, and Seum had said could be wrong. Maybe Herlot and Movo were dead. Maybe they had never spoken to the queen and just thought that they did. She couldn't explain it but there was a confidence, something that made the events seem more real than if they had actually been there to witness them physically.

Her eyes widened at a realization. "Benyamin, can you see if any of Felix's men are still in Eraska?"

Benyamin glanced at the stars. "They all left with the ship that sailed, which Herlot and Movo were on."

Seum threw both of his arms in the air. The psaltery went flying and Hans disappeared. Enri slid and rolled just in time to catch the psaltery before it hit the ground.

"All this time, Benyamin!" Seum yelled. "All this time you could see where these men were, and you didn't think to tell anyone?" He pulled on both of his braids and stared at the night sky. "Oh, great emperors, please help me!"

Enri and Benyamin exchanged looks. "Seum, do you really think anyone would have believed him?" Enri said.

He raised his palm toward her. "You don't seem to have a problem with believing in magic. No one had troubles believing in Herlot's sword story. Skies, based on the way they train I'm sure half of them still believe in faeries that will magically do the work for them."

Enri ignored the last part. Seum did have a point, though. "Benyamin, surely there were so many things you could have seen. The traps, their location... why didn't you help?"

It was the first time Enri saw Benyamin looking ashamed. "I wanted to, but I had my reasons."

"What could have been more important than keeping us alive?" Seum asked.

"Life was always my intention, I assure you. Our operation with Queen Magdalene was out of pure desperation, and I will soon know if the damage was done. That is all I will say for now."

"That is all I will say for now," Seum mocked and made his voice a bit raspy like Benyamin's. He shook his head. "Unbelievable."

Enri let her shoulders drop in defeat; however, she did notice that Benyamin's gaze was particularly intent on Seum when he spoke about the damage. Speaking of damage, she thought of Manni, of the reason they had been exposed during their rescue of Hans, Seum, and Ambro at the fortress.

"Did Manni leave with them?" she asked. "It would be nice to tell Ambro she didn't think twice about staying for him."

Benyamin tapped his lips with his pointer finger. "Manni... hm. I don't believe I know who you speak of."

"Surely you've seen her in Alonia for many years. Manni, Ambro's fiancée. She called the soldiers on me when I was in Dartharus's chamber."

Benyamin searched the stars. "Ah, yes, I do see someone like that. Yes, I do think she left on the ship..."

"Where is she now?"

"I can't seem to find her. I will have to take some time to look longer. Not many of the stars seem to watch her, or perhaps I just haven't found the ones that do."

"Don't bother. Waste of time that woman is," Seum said.

"You're right," Enri said. "Speaking of a worse matter at hand, what are we going to tell the others? Every other person in there is yearning to go home, and everyone needs fresh air. I don't know how they'll react to hearing that the soldiers are completely gone."

Seum scratched his beard. "Hmm...Benyamin, what is Felix doing?" Seum asked.

Benyamin stared at the night sky in silence. Then he frowned. "How strange..."

"Elaborate, please?" Seum said, sounding annoyed.

"I've never seen it happen quite like this before. One would be surprised at how many places starlight can reach, but there are some places in this world that are more difficult to read. Often it comes back as a reflection...the stars just see themselves, such as with our mountains. I have never been able to test the theory, but perhaps there is a frozen lake hidden somewhere in the range, which makes it so difficult to see.

But this...there seem to be several stories of Felix. A distortion of some sort. But why? One moment I see him entering his palace, and in the other he has still not left the execution arena, not spoken a word unless it is asking if Herlot, Movo, or Magdalene have been found..."

Benyamin seemed distraught. Enri was concerned that visiting the dreamworld, combined with his body still healing from his injury, may have been too much. It would make sense, especially with him also not being able to see Manni. "Benyamin, perhaps you need to rest," she said. "I'm sure the stories will be clearer tomorrow."

"Yes... yes... perhaps," he mumbled.

Seum rubbed the side of his neck. "We will all go to the fortress and continue training there. That way we are prepared if they come back."

"Do you really think he would send soldiers back again?" Enri asked.

"Yes. Men like him are vengeful and spiteful. He'll send a ship here with men looking for Herlot and Movo, eventually, especially if he doesn't catch them in the city," Seum said.

Enri bit at a nail. "I know I can convince the Lorfiners to come to the fortress. I don't know about the others...I'm afraid they will want to go home if they hear the soldiers are gone. If Herlot made the order, it'd be a different story."

"Then we won't tell them yet. We will say we are going to siege the fortress back for ourselves. Meanwhile, we will keep emphasizing the need to create a long-term plan to protect Eraska's coast and continue training."

Enri chewed on her cheek. She didn't want to lie to her family, but this was the one way to ensure everyone stayed together *and* got the fresh air they all desperately needed. "Fine, it's a plan."

"To sleep under the stars again..." Benyamin mumbled. "And to no longer smell the rotten leaves."

"Rotten leaves..." Enri thought out loud. There was something important about rotten leaves. She squeezed her eyes shut trying to focus.

"Ennnn-riiii!" A masculine voice shouted. Enri made out a figure, Rabbie, standing at the top of the cliff near the opening to the caves. "Emergency!"

Oh, no. Someone was probably hurt.

"Quickly now, child. Someone needs your help," Benyamin said.

Holding the front of her dress so as not to trip, she raced up the path.

"What is it, Rabbie?" she asked as droplets from the waterfall covered her left side.

"I—I don't know. They were fine one moment, stretching with Asm, and the next thing we knew they fell over."

Oh no. More than one. She hurried inside.

Asm had everyone waiting in the tunnel section, his face clearly one of distress. The two patients sat close to one another as far away as possible from the rest, back to back, using one another to stay upright. One of them was a Temesian girl named Clement and the other was Keswick, a father from Noray. Both of their families could be seen trying to look over and under Asm's arms that were outstretched, blocking anyone from coming closer to the patients.

"Why don't you both lie down so we can see what is happening?" Enri said as she walked toward them.

"We wanted to, but the dizziness worsened when we tried," Arlette said.

"I see. Then let's keep you both the way you are for now."

"What if it's crowpox?" someone in the crowd asked.

Enri's knees wobbled and the room spun a little as she knelt next to them. This could be their worst nightmare if it was crowpox.

"You know, dear Enri, it was the strangest thing. One moment I felt fine, except for how much I was sweating while running. Then like a rain-drenched stalk, I couldn't keep myself upright anymore," Keswick said.

"That must have been terribly uncomfortable," Enri said. She held her palm up against Keswick's forehead. Very hot. Not good.

"Holy basil, that awful smell is infesting our main chamber now too," Cadby said.

Enri's stomach churned as she inhaled.

Oh! Rotten leaves, yes. It makes sense! She closed her eyes and remembered joining her father on a visit to Arlette's home when she was young. Arlette had been barely able to speak through her cough and was dizzy whenever she stood. *Oliver, the smell. The colors of the trees have only begun to change, yet it reeks of a pile of rotten leaves in here.* Arlette and her family had stayed with them for the next few days as her father had ordered another home for them to be built. She remembered him showing her one of the stones that was covered in a dark green slimy substance.

It's on the cave walls! Enri remembered seeing the same strange substance near the patch of liverworts during their run through the tunnels.

"It's not cro—" The room spun again, and Enri had to put both of her hands on the ground to stop from toppling over. Sweat from her forehead sprinkled onto Keswick's tunic.

"Enri?" Asm's bear tone rang from the tunnel.

"It is most definitely the crowpox," Tanya of Bundene announced loudly to the crowd. "We need to leave before we all get sick!"

Shouts of agreement responded to Tanya.

No, Enri thought. She wanted to shout at everyone to stop, but another wave of dizziness washed through her and her arm muscles simply didn't have the strength to hold her up.

The room became blurry from the spinning. She felt awful for landing on top of poor Keswick.

"We have another! Asm! Help us, Martina is sick too!" someone shouted, returning to the main cave room from the tunnel.

"Everyone out before we all get sick!" someone shouted.

"It's not crowpox," Enri managed to say, but no one heard. Everyone was busy finding their families and urging them to rush out of the cave. All Enri could do was watch helplessly through her blurred vision. She had lost Herlot's army.

***

Seum hobbled toward the path leading up to the cave.

"Stop," Benyamin said.

Seum hobbled another step forward. He dug his crutch into the ground, leaned his weight onto it, and prepared for his next step. He saw Benyamin's move out of the corner of his eye. Even on a crutch it was an easy attack to react to, yet it was the first time someone had truly caught him by surprise, just because it was Benyamin. And he was so slow doing it. Benyamin swung his own crutch way out to the side and then right at Seum's foot. *Is he really about to try and knock me over?* Seum thought. He didn't react just to see if this was truly happening. Oh, it was. The crutch hit him perfectly in the ankle and he lost his balance, not enough to fall over, though.

What for the blessing of the emperor!? He is doing it again? And he was. Benyamin, as if frustrated that his first swing had not done its job, recoiled the crutch and swung at his ankle again. Seum's weight charged toward his toes, then beyond his toes, and then Seum the almighty flopped face first on the ground.

"Are you insane, old man? I'm injured!"

"I told you to stop," Benyamin said.

Seum struggled with repositioning his crutch and leaning his weight on it to get back to his feet. "Well, what if I did not want to? From what I remember, your people don't like being forced to do something they don't want to do."

"Seum of Ipta, you cannot avoid our conversation forever."

"What do you want to talk about, you malicious moth trotter?"

Based on what Seum had learned of Benyamin's ability to see the stories of the stars, he had a very good idea about what Benyamin wanted to talk about. What Benyamin shouldn't have even known could be talked about.

"I'd like you to stop making decisions based on the projections of the black star that your Iptan brothers and sisters attempt to read," Benyamin said.

"You don't know anything," Seum said.

An amused expression crossed Benyamin's. He glanced up to the stars. "Oh, really? Seems to me that I know a lot more than anyone thought."

"Well, you don't seem to know a thing about the black star or else you would be more concerned."

"Oh? And what do you think it tells you? What have your sky watchers seen? Some awful threat, I presume, that you must fight to stop?"

"It tells the future. It has always been right before."

Benyamin nodded slowly. "Of course, of course. Always right. Always right."

Seum straightened, as if he were standing strong behind those words.

"And tell me, Seum," Benyamin said. "What is it that the black star has shown your sky watchers this time?"

Seum sighed and slouched, as if the burden of the vision was too much to handle. "You know already from spying on our conversations, don't you? Yet you want me to say it, to trick me into thinking there's something to be ashamed about. Well, I am fully confident in my brothers and sisters. The black star predicts a war in the skies. There."

"Ahh... a war that will make the once undefeated Ipta vulnerable once and for all? And tell me, who is this awful enemy the black star has shown you?"

Was Benyamin mocking him? Seum's tone turned aggressive. "Not just Ipta. All of the world. Our sky watchers have seen enormous winged black creatures. One of them is at least twice the size of the largest human I know."

"And how does Ipta plan to solve this?"

Seum faltered for a moment, as if saying his response out loud would make it laughable. He even shook his head a bit before he spoke. "We are searching for a way to fight them in the skies. I once thought it impossible."

"Until you stumbled upon a girl with a magic sword. You decided to stick around, because it was the best thing you had found before that point of your journey. And then you found the paintings of the white winged unicorns."

"What do you want me to say? That you are so old and wise and right? Well, you are. But don't ridicule me for attempting to protect my own people, rat bones, not just my own people, yours as well and every other damn being that walks on a piece of land." Seum pointed at his chest. "I am not the enemy." He pointed at the sky. "Those beasts awaiting to invade our world are the enemy. Not me."

A sadness glistened in Benyamin's eyes. "And tell me, Seum. Herlot, what is it that you plan to do with her?"

"We will take her to Ipta."

"You really think she can solve the problem?"

"She is the closest thing I have found so far. The paintings of the unicorns in a cave on the same land where a peasant girl runs around with a magical sword. There is something there. And one of our watchers once saw a woman of her resemblance and a slightly different creature than the beasts. That creature has a striking resemblance to the unicorns painted on the caves and the one that took us into your dream world. Anyone would be a fool to not look into it further."

"Oh!" Benyamin swayed. "Seum, I find myself awfully dizzy. Could you help me—"

Seum pulled Benyamin to the side just as he was about to topple over.

"Only a fool would never pause to think that just maybe the black star was making you create what it wants," Benyamin said.

Seum felt as if he had been slapped in the face with ignorance. He had much to say to Benyamin. But the moment he opened his mouth to put the insane man in his place, he stopped, realizing he had been slapped with wisdom. His jaw dropped at the possible reality of what the black star watchers of his empire may have caused.

He barely heard the crowd of villagers pushing their way out of the cave. He barely heard his words as he protested. Benyamin's family was pushing him along, saying they were going back to Bundene as Benyamin fought to be left alone.

Once Seum had awoken from his shock, he couldn't see Benyamin anymore. The forest below was filled with Eraskans heading out in all directions. But instead of wondering what was happening and how to stop this mistake from happening, he could only think about the black star. If the black star operated as Benyamin said, was Ipta about to cause the biggest disaster their world had yet to witness? No, it couldn't be. Benyamin might have a gift, but that didn't rule out the possibility that he was not mentally well. It was better that Benyamin's family took Benyamin back to Bundene before he could interfere with Seum and his father's plans upon Herlot's return to Eraska.

CHAPTER 7

HONEY AND PICKLED CUCUMBER

Mahtreeh slid off of his horse and dragged his feet toward the well of Bundene village. "I can't believe we finally made it," he said.

"Don't celebrate too soon. We still have a mountain to climb," Lucinda said.

"Now there's something you don't hear every day." Mahtreeh tugged on the well's rope, wetting his lips in anticipation of the fresh water. Usually he wasn't the one to pull the bucket out of the well because just looking inside the endless hole made his knees weak to the point where he was afraid they might give way and he would fall in. He definitely had made progress in being less afraid of things. He glanced up at the mountain range that rose toward the sky at the horizon. *Don't call yourself fearless yet,* he thought. *You still have a mountain to climb.*

Lucinda didn't seem to be worried at all. While he was still working on getting his water bucket, she had already started the fire at Bundene's hearth. Everything came easy to this girl, just like everything came hard to Mahtreeh. They were complete opposites, and the entire ride to Bundene they had not had too much to talk about, but he didn't mind. She didn't complain about his bird songs. He didn't inquire about her reason for being so silent. At a deep level they understood each other and felt like family, even though the only thing that they had in common was that they were both from Eraska and had suffered loss.

Mahtreeh appreciated Lucinda for not pushing him or making snarky comments in areas where he lacked. Every time he needed a quick break under the shade, or when he could not steer his horse correctly through a turn, or even when he threw up his breakfast, she didn't act bothered. He knew it was because he reminded her of Hans. Both he and Hans had been the worst at training. Both he and Hans had a talent for music. Mahtreeh and his whistling, Hans and his psaltery. They could have made beautiful music together.

The two horses gathered around him, one on each side, as he hauled the bucket. He really wanted to dunk his entire head in and drink, but all it took was a nudge of the nose under his elbow from one of the horses. He put it down on the ground and let them have the first drink. "There you go," he said as he patted the horse along his neck.

When they were finished, he lowered the bucket back down. *Are you seeing this, Father? Two water retrievals in one day. You wouldn't recognize me, I bet. I hope you're proud.*

As soon as he had the bucket again, he scooped a bunch of water into his palm and drank. Then he scooped again and splashed his face. He was about to dunk his head when Lucinda arrived at his side. She hooked him elbow to elbow. "Come on, let's go see what smoked meats may be left over. Or would we rather graze like the horses?"

Mahtreeh's eyes widened. What kind of a woman was this? He knew she was intense. After all, she did come from a village haunted by beasts in the night. But to eat grass?

She chuckled. "You don't think I'm serious, do you?"

"I—uh. If you are, I definitely appreciate a woman with the digestion of a dragon."

Mahtreeh closed his eyes and looked up, as if he could see right into his head. His stupid head that made him say stupid things. *Father, if you're listening, now might probably be a good time to leave. Go check on Enri.*

"Oh really? How do you know so much about dragons?"

"I don't. But remember Herlot's story about them? If they can blow fire out of their nostrils, they can probably eat anything too. I wouldn't want to be a fish in that stomach."

At that, Mahtreeh's stomach grumbled.

Lucinda kept her elbow locked with his as she led them toward the storage shack. "I wouldn't either. I do wonder what they eat. Fish probably wouldn't be enough. You suppose they could take down one of the Temes beasts?"

Mahtreeh tapped his finger against his chin and then realized it had water dribbling from it. He wiped it away quickly with his sleeve. "I suppose so. I mean, they can fly. The beasts can't. All they'd have to do is float above them."

"Must be nice to be a dragon. You can hunt and cook your food at the same time. Never have to worry about starting a fire. I bet all the animals would be jealous because the dragons would be the only ones who could eat cooked meat. If I were an Alonian, I'd tell a nice dragon story. You know, one for the kids so they would sleep good at night? It would be called the dragon feast and there'd be a family of dragons that'd invite all the forest animals for a feast. And the other animals would bring things. Let's see... the family of rabbits could bring vegetables they had found in a garden. All it'd take was a sneeze from one of the dragons and they'd be crisp and delicious to perfection."

Mahtreeh laughed at that. "I see it's not only the Alonians who have a vivid imagination. I must be honest, Lucinda. You don't seem like someone who can come up with children's stories."

"You're right. Hans would be the one good at that with all those songs he'd play for them. If we ever get to go back home, someone will have to help the children sleep at night. Maybe telling stories will be the way."

"And that way, a little bit of Alonia will live on too," Mahtreeh said. He wondered if that would be considered a happy end, what with Ambro now being the lone survivor. Mahtreeh couldn't imagine his once childhood friend ever regaining his spirit. A lump formed in his throat as he thought about Herlot. He squeezed his fist and promised himself to make his grieving wait.

They were at the door to the shack now. "What do you say, Mahtreeh? Do you think we'll be lucky and find smoked salmon?" She nudged the door open. Mahtreeh squealed as a family of spiders paraded from a web in the corner, some falling right on top of Lucinda's head. He jumped several feet away and watched in amazement as Lucinda calmly picked them out of her hair and set them down on the ground. "These ones don't bite, come on, while we still have daylight to see."

Mahtreeh swallowed and followed her inside. The familiar scent of salt tickled at Mahtreeh's nostrils, and right away memories of salting meats came to his mind. Instinctively he rubbed at his palms, remembering how dry and cracked they would be after a day's worth of pressing salt into the strips of pork. Once his hands had hurt so bad that he had had to sleep with them in jars filled with milk.

"Something pickled...something honeyed...maybe some dried apples..." Lucinda was saying to herself as she searched through a barrel.

Mahtreeh checked one of the barrels. "Well, Lucinda, we are rich in mead tonight."

"And pears. Lots and lots of pears. Open your mouth," Lucinda said.

Mahtreeh dropped his jaw and didn't have the time to wonder why. Lucinda flicked a dried pear and it landed perfectly on his tongue. "Great aim," he said.

"Thanks. That's what Seum always tells me. He said that he wished he had the tools and materials to make me an axe like Asm's."

Mahtreeh couldn't imagine anyone big or strong enough to handle Asm's axe. Last time he saw it was with Herlot. He had just barely realized her throwing it when it cut into the ropes and dropped the fortress gate. Thanks to her, they had gotten away.

"Huh. Maybe that's my problem. Maybe I'm just not good with a sword," Mahtreeh said while trying to chew the pear without getting it stuck in his teeth.

"That's not bad thinking. Seum talked about a flute-like weapon and when you blow into it, poisonous pellets shoot out at your attacker. With all that whistling that you do, I'm sure your breath would be more than strong enough."

Mahtreeh's mind filled with images of facing one of Felix's men. Of course, the man would think he was weak and an easy target. But then, just as he got close enough, Mahtreeh would blow into his flute and prove him wrong. That man would think twice before coming anywhere near him or his family. Mahtreeh definitely wanted to learn more about this weapon.

"What other weapons did he tell you about?" Mahtreeh asked as he took the lid off of a barrel. This one was filled with the prize they had been looking for. Smoked salmon.

"The bow and arrow, and that we're lucky the soldiers who came here didn't have any. Not only can they be shot from a distance, they're poisonous too. We wouldn't survive without shields, and even if we had them, sometimes they don't do much good."

"If they're such deadly weapons, why didn't they bring any?"

"I asked Seum that too. He said that arrows are expensive to make. Most kings save them for real threats, like battles or if an invader is trying to siege their fortress or castle. Enemies you don't want to fight up close."

Mahtreeh sighed. "Then maybe it's a good thing we were never a threat to begin with."

"I agree. We would not have stood a chance against the bow and arrow. If we got anywhere near their range in Ruelder, they would have taken us down one by one."

A breeze blew and shut the door to the shack, leaving them in complete darkness. "I think that's the weather telling us to stop rambling and eat. We need our strength," Lucinda said.

"Right. You lead the way," Mahtreeh said. He wasn't planning on moving until she had the door open. Too many things in the way that he could trip over. He didn't want to embarrass himself anymore in front of Lucinda, even though he was sure the embarrassment was entirely on his end. It was as if she didn't notice his silly remarks or his cowardly reaction to the spiders.

Once Lucinda had the door open, he picked up the barrel of dried fish and headed toward the light. Lucinda held the door open for him and he set the barrel down next to the fire she had made. He was on his way back to help carry more things, but he stopped when he saw Lucinda, holding a sack, standing right in the doorway, one foot in the shack and the other resting on top. Her head and shoulders sagged, as if she were deep in thought.

"Lucinda?" he said.

She looked up at him. "I was just thinking. Do you think that where Hans is right now is completely dark or completely light?"

Mahtreeh marched toward her and took the sack off of her arms and slung it over his shoulder. "Light. Think of the lightest place you could imagine and double that. That's how light it is."

He was expecting her to question his statement from all sides and ask for answers that he couldn't give, but she didn't. Mahtreeh knew that he didn't know where his comment had come from and that he didn't have proof of it, but it was a place that he imagined his father and mother were, and that was good enough evidence for him. Without it, he feared he would go insane.

"We should eat outside, don't you think?" he said, guiding Lucinda toward the fireplace. "The one thing I am loving about our journey is that we have been in the sun and fresh air for two whole days now."

"Mhmm. I don't miss the cave air at all."

"If you ask me, that is not air in there."

Lucinda bit into a piece of smoked salmon. "If it's not air, then what is it?"

Mahtreeh poured honey onto a piece of pickled cucumber and quickly rushed to lick the bit that was about to drip off the side. The kids from Lorfin always asked him to eat this delicacy in front of them. They wrinkled their noses and laughed at the absurdity of the combination while he chewed. He enjoyed putting himself on display for them, and even more so, enjoyed what he believed to be the perfect concoction of sweet and sour.

"Bat farts," he said. "We have been breathing bat farts."

Lucinda's laughter filled the deserted village. "Bat farts! That is the funniest thing I have heard in ages!"

Mahtreeh chuckled not only at his joke, but because he felt so sly for bringing Lucinda to such laughter.

Lucinda wiped a tear from her eye. "Oh Mahtreeh, I don't know if I'll be able to think of anything else when we return to the caves."

"Good! But now, Lucinda, look at where we are. We have a whole village to ourselves, good food, a beautiful view, and all the fresh air in the world. I say we perform a special cheer to that."

Lucinda's sharp eyes narrowed. "The mead."

Mahtreeh winked. He searched through his sack for a mug and then told Lucinda to keep her seat as he took her mug from her and went to the shack to fill them with something much better than water.

He began singing as he danced his way back, stepping one foot to the side and then sliding the other toward it, all while holding the mugs above his head.

> *"Many forests I have traveled,*
> *Many streams I have swam,*
> *Never in my dreams did I think I would find,*
> *A drink for a dreamer like me."*

"I know this one!" Lucinda stood, grabbed her mug and joined Mahtreeh in the side-to-side swaying. Together they continued to sing.

> *"All I need is the warmth in my ears*
> *And my eyes to see through my fears*
> *Then with my mead and this tune*
> *I'll dance with my lady and my dream will come true."*

Mahtreeh held up his mug to his lips. "Up for a race?"

Lucinda took a wide stance, as if she were preparing to train, and held her mug up the same. "A drink for a dreamer like me!"

That was the cue. Mahtreeh allowed the liquid to pour down his throat. He tipped the mug even higher. He was certain he'd be first. As soon as the last drop of mead rushed down his throat, he stretched the mug out in front of him where it clinked with Lucinda's.

"Tied!" they shouted in unison.

After that, they sat for a long time not speaking much. Lucinda would occasionally hum the mead tune and Mahtreeh would join, whistling.

The day continued to turn into night around them. "The sunset seems so big here." Lucinda stood and turned in a circle. "I always felt bad for the Bundeners for being so far away from trees, and never thought they might be benefiting in other ways. This is it."

Mahtreeh also found the display of colors above them fascinating, spread out in a half sphere above them from one horizon line to the next. A beautiful arc from blue to black.

"You ever think about magic, Lucinda?" Mahtreeh asked.

"No. Maybe if I saw it first-hand, I'd think about it more."

"Did you ever think you might be seeing it all the time and maybe just not noticing it?"

She put her hands on her hips and her eyebrows furrowed together. "No. I have not. That makes me feel somewhat strange. Quite a disorienting thought, to be seeing something I can't, well, see. What about you, Mahtreeh of Lorfin? Do you think about magic?"

"All of the time. And I have seen it too. First-hand, I swear."

A smile spread across Lucinda's face. "Then what is it?"

Mahtreeh thought about telling her about Devotio. As hard and strict as she appeared on the outside, there was something about her, something like a familiar scent, that said that not only could she be trusted with such information, she would also believe it and love it. But Devotio was Herlot's story to tell, and it was his secret not to tell. But he believed in magic very much and knew that it was everywhere.

"It's something so real that you can't explain it, and if you think about it too much you get confused. Like how the colors of the sky changed around us. It was so subtle. From blue to orange to pink to black, it somehow mixed all together and there is not one moment you could say this is exactly where it changed from blue to orange or from pink to black. It's like sunflowers growing. You can't see it happening but it's happening all the time."

Mahtreeh stared at Lucinda. "You're pretty magical, too, Lucinda!" He jumped at how loud he had said it and she did too.

He giggled. "But really you are."

"Why, thank you, that's one of the nicest things anyone has ever said to me. I think."

"Well, good. Nice things are good to say and to be told." He wondered if his comments even made sense. Lucinda covered her mouth and he thought she was trying to hide a laugh, but she just yawned. A really long yawn, and he could almost feel her soul stretching. My it would feel good to yawn, he thought, and before he knew it his jaw was stretching down to the ground, and the familiar ear thunder of a yawn engulfed his sense of hearing.

"It will be good to sleep on hay again," Lucinda said.

"So many homes to choose from, where do we sleep?" Mahtreeh asked.

Lucinda pulled out a candle from her sack and stuck the tip into the fire. "Hmm... let's look inside a bunch of them and see which one feels the most... magical."

Mahtreeh really liked that idea, and especially because it had been Lucinda's idea.

They walked along the paths of Bundene, peeking inside each home they came by. They were all filled with the same things that most of the homes in their villages had. Some chests, hay mattresses, a fireplace. But as repetitive as they seemed, each one was different. A subtle change in smell, perhaps, or an unusual organization such as a mattress right in the center instead of up against the stone walls. It was evident that each home had housed a unique family. Some had a few herbs hanging from the ceiling, but there was not one single home like Mahtreeh's. His had a forest hanging from the ceiling.

They had made it through all the homes except for one. It lay a little bit on the outside, closest to the mountain. As soon as Mahtreeh neared the doorway, he could sense it was different. The air seemed more vibrant. He stretched his hand out and could practically feel the air, a subtle pressure against his palms. How strange. Lucinda was mimicking his movements next to him. "Do you feel that?" he asked.

"Mhmm. Magic, right?"

"I don't know, but it sure is different."

Mahtreeh gently nudged the branch door from where one edge dug into the ground a bit too much, careful not to snap anything. The branches creaked. They needed tightening. He was upset that the villagers had not found a way to fix this door. He was certain whoever had lived in the home could not do it themself because no one would want to fuss with such a door, let alone suffer through a winter with it.

He finally got it unstuck and then slowly guided it open.

"Oh, my," Lucinda said. "I think we found the one."

Well, Mahtreeh had sure found a home that resembled his own. But it wasn't a forest that hung from the ceiling, it was seashells, seashell dolls, to be exact.

Mahtreeh and Lucinda both walked up and examined one and then looked at one another. "Benyamin," they both said. They were all like the ones Benyamin had given Enri for helping him after he had fallen into the hole in the ground when they had first found him. He had said his wife used to make them. The seashells themselves were from Alonia.

"Mahtreeh, I don't think they're just dolls. Here, look. It's like they're acting out scenes. You see this one? This piece here looks like a boat, and the doll must be the captain."

"Huh. You're right." Mahtreeh examined the seashells strung tightly together to form the shape of a ship. All of a sudden, he became very sad. Why had nobody helped fix Benyamin's door? Did anyone even come to visit him here? Did they know about the magic that hung from his ceiling?

He continued to look at the seashell scenes. There was one corner that had many little dolls sitting on horses and holding sticks that had been carved to resemble spears. A war. Next to them was a building that resembled the Eraskan fortress, but much bigger. A castle. Benyamin had an amazing imagination. Or else he had to be able to read and had gotten his hands on a book meant for Alonia in order to create such details. There were some things that resembled creatures and plants most likely, but Mahtreeh didn't recognize them. Had Benyamin traveled the world? Impossible.

Then he stopped by a scene that sent a large wave of heat from his head to his toes, and then goosebumps traveled up his arms like ants. He knew this scene. He had lived this scene. He was in the scene. And he was certain there was no way Benyamin could have been there.

One seashell structure resembled a pine tree, and next to it were five dolls: two girls, two boys, and a unicorn. Herlot, Enri, Ambro, Mahtreeh, and Devotio. This was the night Herlot had introduced them to Devotio, and Devotio had taken them to the tree Mahtreeh's mother had planted.

What did this mean? How could Benyamin have possibly known this happened? No matter how good of an imagination, people couldn't imagine things that had already happened or were currently happening. Or could they? His teeth began chattering at the influx of thoughts and questions about his discovery.

"Are you cold?" Lucinda asked.

"Yes! Very! I'll be right back with our things!"

He skipped outside, wondering why he was skipping and why his nerves always made him do the most unexpected of things. Happy people skipped. Incredibly confused and overwhelmed people did not.

Once he made it to the fire, which was now just a glow of deep red, he shuffled through his sack in search of his sweater. "I wish I was actually cold," he mumbled. But he had to put the sweater on so Lucinda wouldn't question him anymore.

As he fought with sleeves and finding the hole to put his head through, he tried to calm his thoughts and breathing. He told himself that no matter how Benyamin and his wife had come to make the scene, they probably didn't mean anyone any harm. And Benyamin had never said anything. And no matter what, his main mission right now was to find the Eraskan allies in the mountains, show them the ring, and get them back to the cave as soon as possible. And when he got back, Benyamin would answer questions. A lot of them.

Mahtreeh hauled both sacks over his back, noticing a small difference of ease in carrying them. At least all the training had made him a little stronger. He found the horses still grazing on a path and thought about taking them inside one of the huts, but then decided not to. After being cooped up in the caves, they deserved all the fresh air they could get. He was sure that Lucinda and he would be sleeping with the door open for the same reason, even though that meant a few bugs would be joining them in their slumber.

He was almost back at Benjamin's home when he stopped in his tracks. A shadow had disappeared behind a home. He frowned and fought the fear bumps that were crawling around his body. He squeezed his fists tight. *Mahtreeh. It's me. Not scared Mahtreeh. Reasonable Mahtreeh. Your imagination is at a height because of the seashell dolls and you're over exaggerating things that you see. There is no one behind that home. Don't even go check. You would have heard footsteps had there really been someone there.*

He let out a sigh and decided to listen to his voice of reason. However, he quickened his pace when he walked by the house where he had seen the shadow, and as soon as he was back inside Benyamin's home, he shut the door.

"We don't want to let the fresh air in?" Lucinda asked. She was already lying underneath a wool blanket on a mattress in the corner of the home.

"Bugs," Mahtreeh said.

"Oh, alright. Can you blow the candle out?"

"Yes, of course," Mahtreeh said.

He bent over to blow out the candle, but then decided he wanted to see the dolls one more time. He held the candle up to one of the boys, it was either him or Ambro, and noticed the smile that had been carved and painted into the shell. The same smile was on the rest of the children. The entire scene radiated a sense of warmth, gentleness, and kindness. Whoever had made the scene meant Devotio no harm. Whoever had made this scene had noticed the joy Devotio had given to the children. And this was a very good sign. Whoever had made the scene, appreciated and knew the love that came with magic, and that was a person Mahtreeh could trust.

He blew the candle out, at peace about Benyamin, and curled up on the second mattress. He didn't use the blanket because he already was warm enough, especially because of his sweater. He closed his eyes and tried to imagine his body becoming cold. He decided to take his sweater off, even if Lucinda wasn't sleeping yet and she might complain about his fidgeting. Then he tried again. *Think of snow*, he told himself. He thought of submerging his entire body in fresh snow, but it wasn't working. He sighed out of frustration. *Maybe I should open the door to let the breeze in*, he thought. Then he thought of the shadowy figure he had seen, and a cold shiver ran up and down his back. Before he knew it, his body was cooled down and he reached for the wool blanket.

Mahtreeh startled awake as the comforting hug of his blanket disappeared off of his body.

"On your feet, Mahtreeh. With a cheerful grin, please. The sky is clear and there's a mountain waiting for us," Lucinda said.

The first thing he wanted to think about when he woke up was breakfast, Not climbing a mountain. "Not inspiring enough, Lucinda. Sorry, the mountain can wait." It felt nice to whine and complain, which he had never been able to do if Asm, Seum, or Movo woke him for training.

"How about bread and jam?"

Mahtreeh kicked his knees up and rolled up, bouncing up a bit into the air as he straightened. His head hit one of the dolls. He rubbed his head. "How did Benyamin move around in here with all these dolls?" he wondered out loud.

"I suppose it might have something to do with finding ways to make room for things you love."

"No wonder Benyamin has such a hunch."

"Probably. But if you keep your back straight and just bend at your knees when you walk, it's very good exercise." Lucinda showed off her training idea as she made her way to the door. "If we ever make it back to Temes, we will practice this way blindfolded. It will help us if we ever get stuck in the dark with the beasts."

"You really think we'll be able to go home again one day?" Mahtreeh dropped his head low and hunched forward as he shuffled his way after her. This morning he would eat and hunch and not do a single exercise. Well, at least not until they arrived at the mountain. Now that he thought about how soon the occasion of climbing that giant actually was, he was certain that he needed an extra-large breakfast.

"Of course. Why else are we doing all of this?" Lucinda said.

"Don't get me wrong. I want to make sure Felix leaves us alone forever, just as any other Eraskan, but... I don't know. It's kind of nice getting to know the other villagers. I don't think things can go back to how they were before."

Lucinda smiled wide. "No, not like they were before. I'd miss you too much, Mahtreeh of Lorfin. We will see each other many times after this is all over."

Mahtreeh watched after Lucinda as she headed toward the smokehouse. "Well, morning sun, I think that's the best thing I've heard in a long time. Give me a hand if I need it on that mountain today, alright? I think I just might have a future to look forward to."

Lucinda was in an awfully cheerful mood as they ate breakfast. *How could she be so relaxed with what they had ahead of them?* Mahtreeh just stared ahead at the mountain where their supposed allies lived. He could imagine the mountain laughing at him right now. A silly young man trying to climb it while searching for something that was not even there. He'd probably fall and kill himself in the attempt.

"Hey. Have you even heard a word I've said?" Lucinda's voice came rumbling through his thoughts.

"I was just thinking, what if there's a storm?"

Lucinda pointed her finger at the sky. "Does that look like storm weather to you?"

He shook his head. "What about the horses?" he asked.

"I think it would be best to leave them here. We'll leave buckets with the water out for them, and there's more than enough for them to graze on. The walk to the mountain doesn't seem too far, we should be there well before noon."

"What if something happens to us? Who will take care of the horses?"

"Nothing is going to happen to us. We'll be careful and go slow. If something is too dangerous, we'll come back down and know that at least we tried."

That sounded like a perfect plan to Mahtreeh. He just hoped Lucinda and he had the same understanding of dangerous.

They finished breakfast, scouted chests for winter gloves and jackets that they folded tight and then stuffed into their sacks. Then, after petting the horses and letting them know they'd be back soon, they began their venture toward the mountain.

It wasn't long before Mahtreeh struggled in keeping pace with Lucinda. Not that a fast walk was difficult for him, but he preferred to take his time getting to things that he was afraid of. If anything, Lucinda was in a rush to climb that mountain. She was probably even looking forward to it.

"Tell me you're not scared at all of climbing," he said.

"I'm not scared *at all* of climbing," she said.

Was that a skip in her step as she said that? He rolled his eyes. She was looking forward to the climb in a way that little children looked forward to maple syrup.

"I am scared of who we will find if we find them, though."

That took Mahtreeh by surprise. She was scared of the allies? That was just plain silly. Why would she be afraid of a group of people who wanted to protect them?

'They're going to help us. They're the last people we should be afraid of."

"If there's anything this summer taught me, it's that the only thing worth being afraid of is people. King Cloudian had a deal with these people, that's all we know. They have never shown their faces at any of our villages, that's a good sign. But Vincent went looking for them and he never came back."

"Vincent probably climbed the mountains and is off somewhere in the southern lands enjoying his freedom," Mahtreeh said.

"Let's hope so."

"I can't stop thinking about why they hide. What kind of a life can they have in the mountains? What do they do?"

"I don't know, but neither one of us has ever been to a mountain. We have just heard stories. It might be a wonderful place to live, for all we know," Mahtreeh said.

"It could be, but not based on anything Seum and Asm had observed when they climbed it. Just a lot of rock and snow at the top. I don't understand how they survived."

The conversation was making Mahtreeh more and more nervous. Lucinda was right. It was silly of him to be so quick to trust. There he was making the same Eraskan mistake all over again. Had Herlot not showed up at Lorfin when she had, he knew his people would have trusted the soldiers just as the Alonians and Ruelderians had.

But they were both at a slight advantage, he realized, as his attention was brought to the swords hanging on their backs. If these mountain people meant them harm, they wouldn't be prepared for Eraskans who were trained in fighting, let alone with swords. He wasn't a good fighter by any means, but he had killed soldiers and he had survived up until this point. That had to mean something.

Soon the ground became more and more steep to climb, and before he knew it, the village of Bundene could be seen. Mahtreeh was surprised at how well he was taking the climb, even though it was just the beginning and they weren't even near the steepest parts yet.

The familiar shrill of a hawk sounded. Mahtreeh looked up to indeed see a hawk soaring near them. "What in the world are you doing here? You won't find any mice or fish on this mountain, my friend." Following his spoken words, he responded to the hawk in the same shrill. Sometimes he felt like his words were better communicated in bird calls.

"Did you ever think he might be watching out for you?" Lucinda asked.

"Yes. Sometimes I feel like they call me as much as I call them."

"That's what I always thought Hans' songs were doing. His music sought him as much as he wanted the music."

Mahtreeh thought about that. So many sky creatures around him that made him feel like he was truly seen. They communicated with him just as much as he did with his family. He wondered if his mother had had a connection like this with pine trees, based on the poem she wrote.

"Makes the world seem like not such a lonely place if birds and music look for us as much as we look for them," Mahtreeh said.

"Yes, yes, it does. Let's take a break and eat and drink a little." Lucinda sat on a rock and slung her sack off her shoulders, sighing in relief. "It feels good to have that weight off."

Mahtreeh followed suit. As he chewed his nuts, he reached his hand into the bottom of his sack until he found the hard stone he was looking for. He took the ring out and examined it. It had many sharp edges and was a see-through pink and red. It was beautiful. He could see why the allies had chosen to give it to King Cloudian with directions to present it if Eraska ever needed their help. There was probably no other stone like this in the world.

"Pretty, isn't it?" Lucinda said as she leaned over to look at it too.

"Very."

"Not much you can do with it, though, if you think about it. Just like that gold the whole world seems to be in love with."

"I agree, but there's something more to it. Yes, it's pretty and nice to look at. I'm sure that's part of it, to get your attention. But the longer you look, I don't know, there is something else there." Mahtreeh could not find the words to match what he was sensing. He wanted the words. He wanted the understanding. And it was right there, just a bit from his reach. His mind felt very large all of a sudden, as if it wanted to stretch out further.

"Let me try." Lucinda said.

Mahtreeh handed the ring to Lucinda who put it on her finger. She began to stare at it. "You're right," she said. "It's so interesting."

"Yes," Mahtreeh said.

"So... complicated."

"Yes!" Mahtreeh said. "An interesting complicated."

Mahtreeh wiped a drop of sweat off his brow. The sun was straight above them and he figured that they were still low enough to not worry about getting cold. He was about to take a layer of his ensemble off when a flicker on the mountain wall caught his eye.

Lucinda was waving her fingers around, looking at the stone from every angle, and right as she twisted her hand in one direction he saw the flicker again.

"Lucinda, hold your hand like this." He positioned her hand until he saw the flicker, now a stable pink spot on the mountain wall. "Do you see that?" he said, pointing at the spot.

"Yes."

They both approached the spot, Lucinda adjusting her hand so that it would not go away. Once they reached it, Lucinda began her hand dance again, this time very slow, and then another flicker on the mountain caught their eye.

When they made it to the new spot, she repeated the motions and yet another spot appeared. "It's like a path," Mahtreeh said. "Do you think this is how we find them?"

"I don't know, but it's a much better idea than searching the entire mountain aimlessly."

They followed the trail along the wall deep into the afternoon when they came to a crevice in the mountain, large enough to fit two people through. As much as Lucinda moved her hand, no more spots appeared.

"I think we have to go in there," she said.

"I was afraid of that." He took a deep breath. As unsure of himself as he was, he definitely didn't want Lucinda going first and getting hurt by something. "I'll go first."

"Don't be silly, there's enough room for us to walk side by side.

"No, I will go first."

With one hand extended to protect them from the world's greatest doom, Mahtreeh made his way in, telling himself that nothing stood a chance against his palm. It wasn't as bad as he thought, it felt just like being back in the cave. No light, the same cold dampness on the walls. The farther in they went, the less fresh the air became. Mahtreeh reminded himself that if the air became too difficult to breathe, all they would have to do is turn around. Simple and with an easy escape plan. This journey couldn't have been suited more to Mahtreeh's needs.

His palm was beginning to get bored when it smacked right into a wall. "I think we've reached the end," he said.

"Are you certain?" Lucinda came up beside him and they both began searching along the wall in front of them and to their sides for some farther opening.

"Well, we just wasted a day following some spots to only reach a dead end. Maybe if we back-track we'll find something else," Lucinda said.

Mahtreeh doubted that. The entire time he was sure that there had been nothing besides mountain stone on either side of them. "Maybe we should try looking up instead," he suggested.

He reached his hand up high to see if he could reach the top. His fingers brushed against more stone. Something rumbled.

"What was that?" Lucinda cried.

Oh no. Lucinda was panicking.

But before he could panic, another rumble sounded and reverberated around them, and the next thing he knew the ground beneath him disappeared and he was falling. Lucinda right alongside him, shrieking, while his panic was still trying to catch up to him. One of his worst nightmares had come true. He was falling into the dark abyss of a well, not knowing what would break his fall. And the worst part was, someone he truly cared about was falling right along with him.

Wooden Unicorn Figures

"Would you please sit down and let me take care of your feet?" The smell of matches filled the room as Movo lit another candle in their guest room.

Herlot brushed his comment aside and slipped another fruit in her mouth. From one window to the other she paced back and forth, looking at the city lit up by torchlights and at the long wall that closed it in from the rest of the world. She leaned over the windowsill. A cat sat on a barrel below, cleaning its ears. She wished she could reach out and pet it.

"You know, falling out of a window is possible. It's happened many times." Movo said.

There was something about looking down from so high above that kept calling to Herlot. It made it difficult to feel her legs yet, at the same time, some part of her seemed to want to jump. It was thrilling and nerve-wracking all at the same time. She had no idea how she would sleep knowing how high up they were.

She leaned away from the windowsill and took another piece of fruit from a bowl that was sitting on a stand, this one a yellow color. A brisk sweetness danced across her tongue and her mouth watered for more. She put two more pieces in her mouth.

"How come so many people here like to be so high up above the ground?" she asked after she swallowed.

"I don't know if they like it, it's just how cities are built in order to fit more people, makes it easier to get to the places they need to go to."

"Like where?" She turned around and looked at him. He was sitting in a gilded chair painted in shades of dark blues and reds. The table next to him was just as decorated. The room in its entirety was the most colorful place she had ever been in. Movo placed the roll of cloth he had been holding on the table and sighed.

"I don't know. The shoemaker."

"Oh. Yes. I suppose that would be a problem to walk so far to the shoemaker if you needed shoes."

Herlot looked out the window and spotted a small quarter of the city that seemed more lit up than others, and she thought she could hear music coming from there. "What are people doing in the lit-up part?" she asked.

"That is the bandit's quarter. You could say most of the less civilized spend their evenings there."

"Bandits. Hmm." Her attention went to a long, thin tower that looked like it could topple over any moment. There was a light glowing from a window way at the top. "What about the tower? What is in there?"

"That's the old, abandoned tower. Most people try not to walk too close to it because they're afraid it will topple over. It's filled with old, useless things."

"I don't think it's abandoned. Someone is in there."

"Probably a bandit. Some homeless spend their nights in there."

"Homeless. Hmm. There are so many homes here, though. How could someone not have a place to stay?"

"It happens to those who fall into trouble, trouble that they usually can't fix without the help of another, but once they reach that point, it's hard for others to see them."

Herlot's eyes narrowed. "It's not like they become invisible because they don't have a home. They should be easier to see if they're out on the street."

"It's not like that here."

"Of course, it's not. I should have guessed that."

Herlot tapped her fingernails against the windowsill. "How would I know, if I wasn't seeing someone?"

Herlot jumped when Movo started speaking right behind her. She hadn't heard him approach. "I don't think you will ever need to worry about that," he said.

She turned to face him. His cold, blue eyes jarred her but there was something different about them. The longer she looked, the more she noticed a warmth that hadn't been there before.

"How do I know when there is nothing more left to see?"

His lips curled up in a smile. "I wasn't the best philosopher in my studies, but I would assume that as long as you're asking that question, you have not reached the end. Now, will you come sit down with me? Your feet really need to be bandaged." Movo took the bowl of fruit and set it on the table, and then slid another chair right in front of him.

"When did you learn philosophy?" Herlot asked as she sat down across from him. A butterfly danced in her belly when Movo took her foot into his hand. He set it right in his lap. He dipped the cloth in the bowl of vinegar and then pressed it to the bottom of her foot.

"From my tutor, and then I attended several lectures at the University whenever I had time between expeditions."

"What did you learn about?"

"Virtue, justice...my favorite lectures were ones that speculated on what constitutes matter. One idea that I found particularly interesting is the notion that everything is built of many smaller parts, and that there must be a piece of matter that cannot be broken down any further."

Herlot bit her lower lip as she pondered the idea. Her mind filled with images of all sorts of objects…apples, flower petals, spoons, and shells, hearts, being cut in half over and over again. "How small such an undividable piece must be…" she wondered out loud. A smile formed on her lips. "Even if we can't see these smallest parts, as much as life may try to shatter us, we can't break at the most fundamental level. I hope it's true."

"For the time being, it seems we are limited by what our eyes can see. Proof will have to come in a different form."

"We are back to the subject of seeing. I bet philosophy often travels in circles."

"It does. Now we can ponder how one sees past the limitations of the eye if he wishes to see farther."

They both stared at each other. Herlot blushed and brought her attention to the leg that was not in Movo's lap. She couldn't seem to keep it still. It kept wiggling as if it had a mind of its own. Movo pressed his palm against it. "It's exhaustion nerves. We experienced it often during long stretches of battles," he said. "Just take some deep, slow breaths, as soon as I am finished you can finally rest."

Herlot blew air out of her mouth and focused on Movo's work on her feet. The warmth of his hands, the gentle pressure of the cloth, the slight sting of the vinegar. Then the wrapping of the cloth, a perfect pressure that felt like an embrace.

"Why were you in such a rush to get away from the Iptans?" she asked.

Movo glanced up at her. "They like you too much."

Herlot's chair screeched against the floor as she straightened her leg and sat up. "They like me too much? Holy basil,

Movo, there's people in this kingdom intent on killing me, and you were upset that someone actually likes me?"

Movo lifted an eyebrow. "That's not what I meant. It felt like you were falling into a trap. It seemed like they were trying to make you one of them." He calmly continued to work on her foot.

Herlot's back slumped back into the chair. He was right. She had felt at ease with the Iptans. Too at ease. "I made the exact mistake that I promised myself I wouldn't." She was confident in her skills with a weapon if it came to a situation where she needed to protect herself; however, danger didn't always come dressed in chainmail and holding a sword.

A breeze flew through the room from the window and extinguished the candle on the table. Movo leaned back and stretched his arm out to grab a lit candle from a stand, which had a sculpture of a woman with plants growing out of her head for its foundation. He used the flames tip to relight the candle.

"It's not that I don't believe you're intelligent enough to maneuver in this world, but you need more experience to understand how things work, and that requires time," he said as if he had read her mind.

She wiped a stray strand of hair from her forehead. Then with more force than she wanted, she tapped the back of her head against the chair she was sitting in. "And that kills me, Movo, I don't think you realize. I feel like a child learning to walk again when I should be able to run."

"But you're not alone. I'm with you."

"You were willing to leave me alone here."

"That was a matter of desperation."

She closed her eyes. "I just don't want it to happen again," she said.

"What?"

"A mess that could have been prevented if I hadn't been naïve."

Movo put both of his hands behind his head and leaned back into his chair. The sound of his back cracking reverberated through the room. Then he pressed a knuckle to each side of his jaw to crack his neck, as if what he was about to say was something he was ready to fight for.

"Your villagers..." he looked her straight in her eyes, "your parents, Ernest and Ilvy of Alonia, died, but they did not lose. They won long before I arrived to torture them. Yes, they were naïve, but they were good. No matter how big of a mistake you might make in the future, remember that you're good."

Her stomach sank because the way Movo said it made it seem like he didn't believe that he was good. If only he could hear the kindness in his voice when he spoke of her parents. "Their names, you remembered my parents' names."

He smiled. "There's a lot about you I enjoy remembering."

Herlot glanced to the side, suddenly very aware of his eye contact. She cleared her throat. "Alright, so tell me what you're thinking about the Iptans."

Movo took her other foot into his lap. "The moment Seum was mentioned, Samin and his men became intrigued. I could see it in their faces. As nice as they seem, they are not Eraskans, Herlot. They don't heal people like Oliver used to. You should see the medics who work for my father, they race to help him or the closest person to his level for the sake of earning prestige."

Herlot sighed. "What is it that all these people in the world are racing for, to get this prestige?"

"Gold. And to have the most of it. If you don't have any, you serve the people who do, and then you work to get as close to them as possible."

Gold. Of course. Herlot thought about Emrys and De-votio's story, how people had lost their golden hearts and then searched for gold everywhere, including the unicorns' alicorns. "And what happens if you have the most of it?" she asked.

Movo rolled his eyes as if annoyed just thinking about the answer. "Many things. Power, like the Iptan Emperor. Importance. Freedom to have and do anything you want. Some believe it gives them immortality."

"Seum told me that his emperor has a place in forever, and that thanks to him, all the Iptans will also have that after they die."

"Hence why I am so bothered by what happened in the bathing chamber. That medic should not have cared as much as he did, that is unless you had something of importance to them. And the way Samin reacted when you threatened to leave... he clearly wants you to stay. Now I always thought there was more to Seum and Asm's story than they were saying—"

"They helped save our lives. And look at what Seum suffered through for us."

"Exactly my point."

Chills went down Herlot's spine. Could Seum and Asm have been helping them only because they really wanted something from them? "What in the world could they want from us?"

"Or maybe just from you."

Herlot struggled to stand but Movo sat her back down. "I'm almost done."

"But what do you mean just from me?" Flashes of Seum streamed across her mind. His interest in Devotio the first day they had met in Lorfin, his speeches about her being a leader.

"I don't know. But there's a story about magic I'd still like to hear from you. It might connect."

"So...do you think your father may have been right about Ipta having powers of magical origin?"

"The rain...those strange seeds...I don't know. Everything about Ipta and these headquarters has been a mystery to everyone in this city. I think that if we're discreet about it and study them, we might find out more."

Herlot nodded. "Well, it all started—"

"Not now." A pained expression formed on Movo's face. He had his palm facing her as if pushing away any of the words she might continue to speak. "I want to hear your story. Just, not now."

Herlot nodded. "Alright. Not now."

"This is not the place to start having delusions due to exhaustion. We need to rest," he said, but Herlot was not so sure that was the reason he did not want to hear it.

"All done," Movo said.

"Thank you. My feet feel much better."

He smiled and nodded. "No more pacing by the window, though. Go lie down."

"What about you?"

"I have some things to think about first."

"Oh. Alright, then." She looked around the room trying to decide where to sleep. Everything along the walls resembled a mattress nicer than she had ever seen before. She guessed that all she had to do was pick the color she liked the most.

She stood and walked over to one covered in green fabric. It was so silky smooth that she was certain one could slide on it. She wondered if the Iptans ever went sledding on hills made of these fabrics. She crawled in and the coolness of the silk calmed her throbbing, tired muscles. She rested her cheek against one of the yellow pillows. All this comfort was almost too much to take. "Movo?"

"Hm?"

"We need to find a way to get weapons."

"I was thinking the same."

These aren't pillows. These are clouds, she thought. It felt like she could sink into the pillow forever. Before she knew it, the sinking feeling transferred to her eyelids.

* * *

When her eyes opened, she was met by darkness as colorless as her dreams had been. All the candles had been blown out and she wondered where Movo was sleeping. She adjusted her vision toward the window, where a little starlight shown in, and that was where she noticed the outline of his figure. He was wearing only his trousers, the small hint of light reflecting off his bare chest made her catch her breath for a moment. He had one leg bent up on the sill, an arm draped over it, and the other holding a small figure. She assumed it was the wooden unicorn figure he had shown her just before they had to escape from their hiding spot in the city. She was curious about the story behind it.

She didn't want to say anything and let him know she was awake. She just wanted to keep looking at him. It was as if some part of him was exposed that he otherwise would never show. Beautiful was a word that came to mind, but it wasn't the perfect one. She tossed through words in her head. "Magical" seemed to be the right one, but she reached for others. Movo and magic did not blend. Or did they?

"Are you cold?" he asked.

She jumped as if she were a little girl caught stealing another maple treat. "How did you know I was awake?"

"Your breathing."

Herlot rolled her eyes. "Are you ever off guard?"

"I try to be, but it's become instinctual."

Herlot stretched her arm above her head and pointed her toes, after which she stood and walked over to the windowsill, sitting on the edge of it to face Movo. The Iptan dress glided against her bare skin as she adjusted her seat, very different from the scratchy fabric of her Alonian dress. She grabbed hold of his hand and turned it so that she could see the unicorn figure he was holding more precisely.

"My mother's lady-in-waiting, Cora, slipped it into my hand right before we were about to be hung. It was one of the toys I played with before—when I was young."

"Are those burn marks on it?"

"There was an accident. I didn't know my mother had salvaged it."

Herlot smiled. It was nice to know a queen would save a toy such as this even though she could have had another one made for her son. She remembered Movo's mother from the execution. She seemed completely different from Felix. "You have never spoken to me about your mother."

"Once I began training, I rarely saw her. I have good memories of her from when I was a child, though. We both loved these toy figures."

That Herlot had not expected. Eraskans usually saw their parents every day. They usually saw everyone every day. She wondered what it had been like for Movo to have a mother but rarely see her. "Did you miss her?"

He looked up from the toy figure. "What?... Oh, no."

She wanted to ask him to elaborate, but something about his distant look stopped her. Instead, she decided to focus on the toy figure.

"You know, this reminds me a lot of the figures Rudi used to make. He was my father's best friend and was known all over Eraska for his woodwork. Almost every child had a toy

made by Rudi. He made all kinds—animals, people, trees..."
Inside she was smiling. Talking about Rudi out loud felt good.

Movo cleared his throat. "I'd like to hear your story now if that's alright with you."

"It's about time." They both laughed quietly. Herlot felt herself slip into her memories, to the night her family and Rudi's family had had supper together and she had wanted to hear a story about real magical creatures. "It began the night when my father read us a legend, the legend of the unicorns, he called it." She smiled. "My memory of it is still so vivid that I can even still feel the heat from the fire... According to the legend, a long time ago, all humans had a unicorn. They had an alicorn on the center of their foreheads." Herlot touched the spot between Movo's eyebrows. "And they would fly up into the sky together to greet the sun every morning." She waved her arm up and down as if it were a wing. "Then, one day, a boy named Brom skipped the greeting and later returned without his unicorn. After that the people changed. They began hunting the unicorns for their golden alicorns. The unicorns were so sad that their human friends didn't greet the sun with them anymore and had instead turned on them, that their wings disappeared. It was too dangerous of a time for them, so they hid inside a tree, waiting for a safer time to return."

Movo's expression was still relaxed. He wasn't frowning, that was a good sign.

"I met Devotio the evening of my first tree sitting." She had started speaking slowly but now she felt the need to rush. "I got lost following two elks after I unknowingly used magic to blend through the tree. A storm came and when I woke up, he was there. He had an alicorn back then. He warmed me and took me home. Then he met my brother, Enri, and Mahtreeh." There. Done.

A stone formed in Herlot's stomach and she held her hand over her belly.

"What is wrong?" Movo asked.

"I—I just didn't know how hard it would be to talk about it."

"I didn't think so either. I was under the impression that your story of magic made you happy."

"That's just what it is. Movo, my childhood with Devotio, it was—it was so much more than magic. It was freedom, love, *happiness*. Yes, there were magical things that happened, but it was that feeling of me and Devotio together, free, riding through the forest and meadows, not afraid of what might happen, and knowing something wonderful would. And to know that such a life is even possible, I think that's what hurts so much. Especially now that I know more about the world and how ugly it is. All that ugliness, it could be beauty. I just don't understand why things are the way they are."

"I don't either, but maybe there's an answer in the legend. If it's true, everyone had a life like you and Devotio at one point, right? And then something happened. Brom, that's his name, right? Something happened after he didn't greet the sun, something that caused the others to change. How true is this legend?"

Herlot almost laughed at how easily she could answer his question. Finally. "It's real, Movo. Just as real as our heartbeats and battle scars. I know, right here, and that is all the proof I need." She pressed her palm over her heart. "I wasn't always that certain, though…"

"Tell me more," Movo said.

"Well, one day Ambro told me to stop playing games, that we had imagined Devotio. I ran to my father and demanded to know where the legend had come from. He said that he had written it. It was just a silly story that he had once made up, a

THE PAWNS OF ISOLDA

story that he had called real to satisfy my wish to hear a story about a real magical creature. I went back to the woods that day and Devotio still looked and felt real, but I didn't believe in him anymore. I said goodbye."

"What? You said goodbye to him?" Movo sounded like a child upset at a part of a story.

"I did, and it hurt. I had lost my dream come true, a best friend. And I lost my trust in my own sanity. He came back, though. He rescued me from the fire. I would have burned in my own home had he not knocked the wall down. I thought I was hallucinating, but something in his eyes urged me to trust. And then, he took me to his hiding place and entrusted me to save his family."

"So there's more unicorns?"

"Yes. This is where it gets very complicated. Are you ready?"

Movo nodded.

"Just like in the legend, Devotio and his family are hiding in a tree, a chestnut tree to be exact. There is a woman there, Emrys is her name. Movo, this woman, she is one of the ancient people from the legend, that's how long she has lived. There is one thing my father's version left out, and that's that these ancient people had golden hearts that disappeared after Brom came back. But, Emrys still has a golden heart and she can perform magic with it, the same type of magic I have to learn to use if I want to save Devotio's family. In her version of the legend, Brom was the first one of the ancient humans who had lost the gold in his heart. Whatever happened to him, after not greeting the sun, caused him and everyone else to lose their gold."

Movo chuckled and rubbed at the spot between his eyebrows. "I thought this story would be much simpler. I thought it would be about a unicorn. One piece of magic to understand. This is magic on top of magic rolled together in magic. Sailing on a ship of magic."

"Oh, there's more. And by the way, that ship might be sailing on an ocean of magic. Ambro lost Rudi's boat once. Devotio introduced us to a family of whales that found the boat and brought it back to us. And these weren't normal whales. They're even more mysterious than the unicorns. Even back then, before the unicorns went into hiding, the whales rarely showed themselves. They know all the mysteries of the sea. It's like a whole different world with different kinds of magic."

Once again, Herlot checked Movo's expression. Any moment she thought he would tell her to be quiet and any interest he had shown in her story would be gone. She wouldn't even be surprised if he decided she couldn't be helped if she believed in such rubbish, but his eyes were wide. If anything, he looked more interested than ever before.

"Huh. Unicorns have made their way into stories. Not once have I heard of magical whales... Go ahead. I'm understanding more than I thought I would. This is good. Tell me more about Emrys."

"Once I was in Devotio's family's hiding spot, I learned that we weren't exactly inside a tree. We were inside the leaf of the tree. Emrys told me that back in the day, when her people came up with ideas that they did not want to forget, they would touch leaves and the leaves would hold onto those ideas for them. Then, if it was time for the leaf to fall and they still had not done anything with their idea, it was understood that it was not meant to be."

"That's smart. These people valued patience and thinking things over before making a decision..." Movo said.

Herlot nodded. "And what Brom decided to do to save the unicorns would require an eternity of patience for the unicorns and Emrys. After most of the humans lost their gold, Brom found Emrys before she could lose her gold, and asked her to hide the unicorns in a leaf. He made sure that she did not see him though, because all it took was to look at someone without a golden heart to lose one's own. Emrys touched the leaf with the idea of a hidden world for the unicorns to hide in, and then using the magic of her golden heart, blended herself and the remaining unicorns into it."

"But there was a serious problem," Herlot continued. "Although Emrys had found a way to keep the leaf alive and prevent it from wilting, by pouring her gold into the lake of this hidden world, the longer they stayed in the leaf, the more they felt that they were losing connection to the real world. Every twelve moons the sensation of being lost would come back if they didn't leave the tree. Emrys could blend the unicorns out, but it became more and more dangerous for her to leave. Imagine if she left and something happened to her? Or she saw someone without a golden heart? The leaf would wilt along with the unicorns inside it."

"She could have blended the unicorns out first and gone last. Then all they would have to do is find another tree."

Herlot shook her head. "It still didn't eliminate the risk of being seen. There are a hundred unicorns. Especially during those times, Eraska was more populated. Can you imagine what a gold-hungry person would have done if they stumbled upon a hundred unicorns? So Emrys decided to let our world go and forever stay in the leaf world."

They both took a breath at the same time. "Brave," Movo said.

"Very." Herlot took a breath. "Emrys also explained to me about my magical abilities. I used the gold in my heart on several occasions as a young child. I never understood it. Like the time when I blended through the tree trunk. I was too short to climb out without help. I remember wanting to follow the elks, and then suddenly it was as if I had become one with the trunk and then just simply stepped out of it on the other side. Emrys said I was able to blend, just like she and the people of her past could. She said my heart sparks gold, and that in those moments I can do magic with the gold." Herlot steadied her breathing. Talking about this part out loud made her entire mission seem overwhelmingly huge and impossible. She focused on the sound of a dog barking and the fresh breeze to ground back into the present.

"I think I know where this is headed. She needed you to take the leaf so that it would not burn in the fire. And you have to use this magic and find a new tree branch for the leaf."

"Yes. In twelve moons. Now ten. That's how long the unicorns have before they're stuck in the leaf forever. They need the tree to create a link between the real and leaf world. And that is the magic of trees, I guess. Firmly rooted in the ground but reaching toward the sky where the dream worlds are. A bridge between ideas and reality. I always liked that part."

Movo frowned and then let his head drop. "Not only did I destroy your world, I almost destroyed a whole other world too."

She tilted her head to get a better look at him. "Yes, but you changed. You gave up everything. I saw you clearly that night at Temes, Movo, you were willing to get torn to pieces by those beasts to protect the Temesians."

Movo's jaw tightened and his fist squeezed around the unicorn figure. "I have done much tearing apart in the past, Herlot. Don't think your village was the first."

Herlot bit her lip. She knew that. She didn't want to know the details, but she was certain she'd be shocked if she did.

What she knew of battles was nothing compared to the battles Movo must have fought in in the past. As awful as it had been, the battle at Ruelder had been short. Perhaps someone in Movo's world would refer to it as a fight rather than a battle. The ones Movo had been in could have lasted an entire day or more. And she also knew that it wasn't just a battle here and there to defend his city. Once one battle was over, he was preparing and training for the next.

"I know," she said. "And yet, here we are, and I trust you."

"And I believe you."

"If that isn't proof of how things constantly change, I don't know what is," Herlot said. They both laughed.

"So tell me how you're supposed to blend this leaf?"

Herlot crossed her ankles and leaned back. "Simplest thing in the world. Make the gold in my heart flow and use that to attach the leaf to another tree."

Movo raised an eyebrow.

"I was trying to add humor to the problem," Herlot said. "Well, first I need time. As soon as we're back in Eraska, I'm going to find chestnut trees and see what happens. If that doesn't work, my plan *was* to have Seum take me to Ipta. Seum said people barely see the Emperor. I can't help thinking that he might have a golden heart, or at least, from what we have seen, there is a possibility that they are using some form of magic. If only I knew what their true intentions are. I'm not so sure about my option of going to Ipta with Seum anymore. Based on what I have told you, is there any connection you see between Seum and Asm's presence in Eraska and my own story?"

"Possibly. But how would they have known about your golden heart magic, or the unicorns?"

"I don't know," Herlot said. "Perhaps the same way my father somehow knew about the legend in a way that caused him to make up a story that was actually true."

"There has to be an explanation for that. People learn the truth, they can't just make it up." Movo carefully unrolled a bandage for her other foot. "Perhaps it was a story that carried on from these ancient times that you speak of. Each generation changes the history books. In your land, each generation may have lost pieces of the legend. Your father may have overheard it as a child and didn't remember."

Herlot tapped her finger against the table as she thought back to the night her father told the legend. "Perhaps, but it's unlikely. My father's version didn't have a name for Brom. Rudi was the one who came up with it while my father was telling it. Could he really have guessed Brom's name? So that would mean Rudi would have had to have overheard it too... But a story like this not being more well-known in a story-telling village? Movo, that's practically all my people lived for. However, our land did have its occasional wanderers. Maybe that's how they overheard it, or how it spread to other lands like Ipta..."

"More coincidences," Movo mumbled. "Suppose there are more trees like this. Surely Brom and Emrys weren't the only ones who thought of hiding the unicorns. What if Ipta has their own versions of stories about unicorns in their land and they're now searching the world for unicorns?"

Water welled in Herlot's eyes at the thought of this being true. "Devotio is right there in plain sight of Seum and Asm. If he still had his alicorn—" she shook her head.

"Why did he lose it?"

"He wanted to come with me, and the only way to do that was for him to dissipate it in the lake, the same one that Emrys forged my sword from, so he could blend in as a horse.

But he's still different. Seum was particularly curious about him when he saw him for the first time at Lorfin." Could Seum and Asm, who seemed to have fought alongside them with the best of intentions, really be in Eraska for alternate reasons? "Why would Ipta be hunting for unicorns? It can't be for their golden alicorns, they already have so much gold!"

Movo fell silent. She could tell he was thinking hard. "When my father began his search for magic, Dartharus came across rumors that Ipta was preparing for a war in the sky. No one ever took it seriously. People are always imagining stories about what the Iptans do inside their closed city. But if that's true... what if it's not the alicorns they need, it's the wings?"

"But all the unicorns lost their wings," Herlot said, exasperated.

"They might not know that, depending on which version of the legend they heard. And if there are others, perhaps not all of them lost their wings."

Herlot's jaw dropped. Sharing her story with Movo might have been the most important thing she could have done. "I could kick myself for leaving the leaf in the cave room that Seum knows about." She dropped her head into her hand. "What if Enri or Mahtreeh say something? Or worse... what if Devotio decides they're trustworthy and reveals to them that he can speak? Skies, I can't sit here waiting."

"We will make it back. I promise you. Right now we just need to be patient and think things through. Just like the ancients and their ideas," Movo said as he rubbed her shoulder. "We can even find a way for you to start practice blending the leaf. It shouldn't be too hard to find a potted plant to bring back in here."

Herlot exhaled a gust of air that caused her bangs to lift up. "In the past, every time I have used golden heart magic has been by accident. I can't do it by command. It's incredibly frustrating—to know you can do something but you can't control it."

"Is that what happened in the bathing chamber?"

A whimper escaped her as she remembered the trance and the tendrils, pain, and emptiness. She took a breath and focused on the first part, the part where she had been clearly able to recall with clarity her past experiences of blending while being under the influence of her golden magic. "My chest became very warm, that's usually a sign that it's starting, but whatever happened in that chamber made it possible for me to recall my moments of blending in the past, clearer than I ever have before. Usually I can't remember much. When I was under this trance, I realized that I have often blended with footsteps Brom took in the past. It's like I become and see the world from his view."

Movo scratched the side of his jaw. "Can you do this with other footprints?"

"Possibly. I don't know if it was blending per se, but I always loved being barefoot, and could easily find people when I needed to find them as a child. It's only with Brom's footprints that I actually *become* the owner of the footprint."

"That's very strange. Out of all the footprints in the world, why Brom's?"

"If only I could answer this question...I've been lost in my own story my entire life, believe me, our conversation tonight has only raised more questions."

Movo was still rubbing his jaw, deep in thought. "What do you see when you...become him?"

"The first time was when he was going to ask Emrys to hide the unicorns. Then, at Ruelder, I relived a time when he chased after a unicorn." She slowed her words. "It's how I ended up in the field..."

Movo winced at that part. "That worries me," he said. "If it's something you can't control, it could happen at any moment. Something could take over and make you walk out of here into a soldier's arms."

"No. I don't think there's anything to worry about as long as Brom's footprints aren't anywhere around here."

"Herlot, you didn't see yourself in the bathing chamber. This is serious. Until you get this under control...it could kill you. Are there any other signs that it's happening?"

"Barely. Just the warmth. Back in the cave, Seum took me to a room with unicorn paintings on the walls and there was a moment when it happened. I was Brom again and wanted to press my hand to the wall. I think Brom was dying and trying to communicate something. Anyway, when it stopped, Seum had not even noticed and I just kept looking at the pictures like nothing had happened."

"So no strange look in your eyes or anything?"

"I... maybe. I guess nobody has ever looked at my eyes before it starts."

Movo nodded. "If you ever feel that same warmth, you have to tell me right away."

"I will."

Well, there was her story. Movo knew it now. She had expected him to doubt things more, to put up a fight against everything she said. But he had done just the opposite.

Suddenly, she felt the warmth of Movo's hand under her jaw. His finger gently traced a line from her chin to her ear and then combed through her hair. "You didn't tell me what else happened in the chamber." His hand fell back. "I have seen many awful scenes in the past, but the way you were stuck in the air and how you began to turn blue, it—it really terrified me, Herlot. It was as if something was there trying to kill you. Something powerful."

No matter how hard she tried to breathe, she couldn't get her lungs to fill up all the way. She opened her mouth and gasped for the climax of a normal breath but couldn't reach it. Cold waves rolled down her legs, sharp pains poked at the back of her head and sweat poured from her skin. Her lips trembled. "I'm so afraid," she managed.

She didn't know if it was she, who had thrown herself into Movo's arms, or if it was he who had pulled her to him. She gripped at the space between his shoulder blades. "It was a place where all color disappeared. Even the color black," she managed. And then she cried as if that awful experience had some heart, could care about the pain it was causing her and thus leave her alone. But she knew deep down inside that it didn't. Whatever had visited her in that bathing chamber, whatever had happened, this was something without a heart, without a soul. And what if this creature was hidden some-where deep in her mind? What if the trance had woken it, and right now it was finding its way out? How could she run away from something that was inside her? What if it was her?

Then, she was being swayed. Soft strokes through her hair. A loving, quiet voice at her ear. "You're safe right now, Herlot. Whatever that was, I'm here."

And then, just how her body had sunk into the comfort of the Iptan bed and pillows, her mind fell into the safety of Movo's rocking embrace, and she slipped into blackness with all the colors of the world at her side.

* * *

Herlot ran out on the cliff overlooking the sea and stretched her arms up toward her mother. Her mother's hands grasped firmly below her armpits. She lifted Herlot up and the child wrapped her legs around her mother's waist.

"What are you doing here, Mother?" Herlot asked.

"Listening to the bells," her mother said.

"What are bells?"

"They are big pieces of metal that swing back and forth and make beautiful sounds from the tower at the fortress."

Herlot scrunched her nose. "Mama, I don't hear anything."

"*Ding, ding, ding,*" her mother sang.

Herlot smiled. "Now I can hear them."

Ding, ding, ding.

Herlot's eyes fluttered open.

Ding, ding, ding.

At first, she didn't know where she was and where the beautiful dinging sound was coming from. Then she felt the bare chest and breathing below her cheek.

"Movo!" she cried as she pushed herself off of his body. "Wake up before someone sees us!"

Then she saw that he was already awake. "Don't worry," he said. "I've been watching the entire time. No guards."

Had he slept at all? She was about to ask when the door to their room flew open.

"Happy morning, happy morning!" Samin walked in holding both hands up in the air. "Now that my new friends are awake, we can finally begin our first day together. You are both invited to join us for breakfast in the courtyard once the sun has risen a little more. But first, before the best breakfast of your adventurous lives, let us discuss adventurous undertakings, shall we?"

Herlot straightened her dress as she stood. "How did you know we were awake?"

Samin flopped himself on one of the cushions around the wall and fluffed a pillow. "It happens when your special guests, may I not forget to mention the special guests who are being sought after by every guard of the city, decide to sleep on the windowsill in plain sight for every guard who passes by. I would not be a good host if I didn't deter every person from the area." He winked.

Herlot blushed and glanced over at Movo who was now sliding a chair toward the spot where Samin was sitting. "Thank you," he said. Resting one elbow on top of each thigh, he leaned toward Samin. "What would you like to discuss?"

Samin, not the least bothered by Movo's close proximity towering over him, examined his fingernails. "I have made plans for your escape."

"Oh?" Movo said.

Herlot walked over and stood next to Movo.

"Yes. Several weeks from now an Iptan ship will be in the vicinity of Damalathum before it docks at Skara. I will arrange for it to anchor nearby for the night, the same night in which you will make your escape out of the city. I'll have a rowboat hidden for you near the beach, one you can use to row to the ship. Beautiful, isn't it? Simple, elegant, ah, just beautiful."

Herlot restrained her natural urge to cry out in joy. It sounded too good to be true. She almost patted herself on the back for the skepticism that had risen since her conversation with Movo. *A sword protects my body, skepticism protects my mind*, she thought.

"And how do we get out of the city?" Movo asked.

Samin clapped his hands. "This is where the adventure comes in! My sky watchers will request to use a certain part of the wall that night, the exact same spot under which a sewage tunnel opens up into the moat below. First you will enter the sewage tunnels. Unspotted, of course." Samin began motioning his arms in wide circles as if he were swimming. "Then you shall go for a swim in the moat, climb out..." Now he stood up and began jumping from foot to foot. "And run, run, run. Beautiful and adventurous plan, right?"

Well, I sure hope it will be as entertaining for us as it seems to be for you, Herlot wanted to say.

Movo interlaced his fingers and shook his palms as he stared down at them in thought. "And where will the ship take us?"

"Why Eraska, of course!"

Much too good to be true, Herlot thought. And she really didn't like the part where they would have to wait for several weeks. Something did not feel right about the ship. After everything she and Movo talked about last night, Iptans didn't seem like the type of people who would go out of their way to arrange a ship just to take two people to a land that they had no interest in. What was in it for them? She wanted proof that the ship would, in fact, take them back to Eraska. She wanted to ask these questions but wanted to give Movo time to take the initiative. Based on his experience in this world, he would know what questions to ask to make Samin reveal more about the plan. Movo lifted his head. "It is, Samin, as you say, a very beautifully thought-out plan. We can only be grateful to you."

Herlot frowned. Where were the questions? Why was he trusting him so easily? She was at a loss for words, many words that she wanted to voice, but all it took was Movo turning to look at her and smiling happily to stop her protests. "We are going home," he said. She smiled the same smile back, one that for any person observing would look genuine, but communicated a whole conversation between the two of them. He was acting. And so would she. "I can't believe it," she said. "Thank you." She understood now. The best way to learn about the Iptans was to ensure that they didn't know that she and Movo were suspicious.

"It is my pleasure. Of course, if you wish to repay me in any way, I am highly fond of entertainment. Herlot, I would love to see how well Seum trained you. And, Movo, I would love to see how the former Prince of Damalathum, wields his weapons of war. I have a few men who would love to train with you. Would you be willing?"

"More than fair," Herlot said. Weapons. Exactly what they needed. "Do you have a staff or just swords?"

"For you, I have both."

Herlot grinned wide.

"Now I will leave you to yourselves, and please come meet us in the courtyard when the bells ring again."

"For the best breakfast we will ever have," Herlot said.

At this Samin grinned from ear to ear. He shook hands with both of them as he walked out the door. Just before he had closed it all the way, he opened it again. "The best!"

Herlot waited for the door to be closed and then again a little more, to make sure Samin wouldn't return.

"We are not—" she and Movo began at the same time.

"Getting on that ship," Herlot finished. "What are you thinking about the first part of the plan?"

Movo walked around the table in the center of the room with his hands on his hips, as if he was studying a map unfolded on top of it. He was probably imagining the city and the environment around it.

Herlot stared at the stand with the sculpture of the woman, which she could see with more clarity in the morning light, as compared to the dim candlelight of the night before. The woman had tree branches growing from her head with leaves gilded in gold. *Part tree. Part human.* She wondered about how a person would come to the idea of sculpting such a woman. If there's anything that could represent a woman blending with a tree, this piece of art would be it. Was this another hint about golden heart magic?

She examined the woman's face and posture more closely. Her features were soft, graceful. Although she was frozen in place, it looked as if her arms were about to flow into a dancelike motion. She bit her cheek. If this is what she would have to look like when she wielded her golden heart magic... well, if the ancient humans could see her right now, they were probably laughing.

"We will escape through the sewage tunnels like Samin said. The way the city's walls are angled makes it possible for groups to see us at two of the stations, once we're in the field, if we give them a reason to look. If the spot right above the sewage tunnel will be taken by Iptans, as Samin says it will, we can make it. If we catch the attention of anyone else..."

"Archers, right?"

Movo nodded.

Herlot could already feel eyes on her back and the anticipation of the sharp metal piercing the spot between her shoulder blades.

"We'll run fast," she said and walked over to a basin in the other corner of the room. She splashed her face and then examined several items scattered out on a stand. She picked one up only to see her face looking back at her, like her reflection in the stream yet much clearer. "Mirror," she said out loud. She had read about them in stories. It was strange to see herself so clearly, her gray eyes, uneven strands of hair, the creases in her lips, the irritation around her neck from where the rope had been fastened. She scrunched her face together, wanting to laugh at how silly she looked. Then she relaxed her facial muscles and ran her hand over her cheek just how her mother used to do. She smiled. "Beautiful," she thought out loud, and wondered how real the reflection was.

"What was that?" Movo asked.

She held the mirror up to catch him tying his boots. She walked backwards until she reached where he was sitting. She knelt down and played with the mirror until she could see Movo's reflection when he finished tying. Instead of looking into the mirror, he looked at her and raised his eyebrows. "What do you find so fascinating?"

"Look at it," she said.

He looked straight at the mirror and then back at her. "Happy?"

"Longer."

He looked back at it and she studied every part of his face in the reflection. Everything about his face was strong and reminded her of the sharp cuts in the sea cliffs outside Alonia.

She lowered the mirror down into her lap. "Now look at me," she said.

He leaned an elbow on his thigh and turned to look at her, some of his hair falling over his forehead. "You don't like being looked at?" she asked.

"It reminds me of having my portrait painted."

Herlot remembered the portraits of Movo's father that hung in the palace.

"How long does it take to paint one?"

"It depends on the artist. I preferred the ones that could finish by noon."

"Hmm." She smiled, examining his features. "The real image is better."

He chuckled. "Very true. For that reason I never understood why anyone would paint food."

Herlot became aware that she was salivating and the room was filled with delicious aromas. "Do you smell that?" She stood and sniffed, then sniffed again trying to catch the names of the scents. "Oatmeal. Apples. Oh. Mmm. Bread? I don't know that one. Or that one. Well, there's many I don't know. Do you? Oh, I am hungry." She held her hand over her rumbling belly.

"Cardamom and nutmeg," Movo said.

"Come, Movo. Let's taste the best breakfast we will ever have," Herlot said.

Movo raised his hands in the air and wiggled them like Samin had and she laughed. She wrapped her arm through his and pulled him toward the door.

Chapter 9
Cinnamon and Apple Oatmeal

The moment the door opened Herlot almost stumbled backward from the heat. She had almost forgotten about the strange temperature change in the headquarters. Their room had been cool in the night due to the open window. She had never experienced heat like this before, even on the strongest of summer days in Alonia.

They stepped out onto the long balcony and looked down into the courtyard. Iptans could be seen everywhere between the spaces of the large leaves. The aromas were even stronger. Her tongue tingled with anticipation.

Butterflies and bright-colored birds flew among the trees. Luxurious, carved bird feeders and baths hung from the branches. "It's a jungle. Ambro and I read stories about them as kids. I saw pictures of these birds."

"It is. But jungles do not appear in northern lands. They shouldn't."

"How do they do it?"

"That's the question, Herlot, that everyone who is not an Iptan wonders," Movo whispered. "There are many strange things about them that no one has answers for. Anyone who was stupid enough to attack their capital died of thirst. It is surrounded by a desert that takes a year to cross, and supposedly the city itself is surrounded by golden structures. Nobody knows how they survive in such conditions. How they thrive in such an environment. Seeing this, it makes sense, it has to be magic."

Movo scanned the entire premises and ran his hand through the air. "And also seeing this makes me realize it's probably a magic more powerful than anyone may have suspected."

"How so?"

"They're controlling weather, Herlot. You saw those clouds last night. And this right here should be completely impossible. Even with magic, it should not be. It's not natural."

"Are you afraid?"

He straightened his arms against the balcony bar and looked around again. "Yes, I think so. Not of them, the Iptans, but of the magic. It's different from yours."

"I can sense it too. Everything that happened with Devotio always felt good. This is different. It feels *forced*. Whenever Devotio took me for a ride in the woods, we never had to worry about staying on a path because the forest adjusted to his motions. I once asked Devotio how it was possible that the branches moved to make room for him, and he said that he hadn't forced the branch to do anything, he *asked* them. This feels like forcing a branch, if that makes sense."

"It does. But what you say might be the key to under-standing how to use your magic. Whichever branch you pick to attach the leaf to, the branch should have a say about it too."

All Herlot had worried about up to this point was how to make the gold in her heart flow. After that, she had no idea how to actually apply the magic. Enri and Mahtreeh were a huge help in that they believed wholeheartedly in Devotio and her mission. However, now that Movo believed her, he also had helpful insights. And holy basil, did she need them, especially if she would end up without the option of getting help from the Emperor of Ipta.

"I wonder if blending with golden heart magic requires language," she said. "Last night during my trance, magical happening, oh I don't know what to name it... but when I saw the willow tree leaves descend it was as if they were singing a song, but it was in a different language. Maybe if I could learn this language it could help with speaking to the branches... but they were words I can't repeat."

"Words I can't repeat! Words I can't repeat!"

Herlot stared horrified at the colorful bird sitting in the branch that had just repeated her words.

Movo took hold of Herlot's elbow and steered her down the balcony path toward the stairs that led down to the courtyard. "And that will be our sign to head down for breakfast before our entire conversation gets announced to the Iptans," Movo whispered. "As for speaking to a plant, I wouldn't know a book on this planet that might teach you to do that."

Herlot kept staring back at the bird but was in too much of a daze to walk back toward it. "It talked. Movo, that bird talked! It must know about the magic I need to work. We have to go back."

Movo chuckled. "No, Herlot. My apologies, but that bird knows no magic. It's supposed to talk. It's a parrot."

Herlot's shoulders slumped. Of course, it couldn't be that easy. She leaned in toward his side as they walked down the stairs and whispered toward his ears. "All this time you found it completely normal for a bird to talk, so what made it so impossible that my Devotio could?"

"I'll show you *Lucius Havelot's Anatomical Drawings of Beasts* and then you'll understand. A horse's anatomy does not support making human sounds."

"A book?"

"Yes. Maybe they have it in a library here somewhere."

They continued walking a path that led around the edge of the courtyard. All along the building were stands displaying foods that made Herlot salivate. One stand had about ten different kinds of smoked fish. Another had massive platters of herbed butters. Wide tables with assortments of chopped onions, tomatoes, cucumbers, and chard. As Movo and she mingled into the crowd they were greeted by Iptans left and right.

"Hello there. Blessings to the Emperor!"

"Good morning."

"I hope you are enjoying your stay."

Being in a place surrounded by Iptans, it was evident how each of them shared one quality in their form of speech: they all spoke louder than most people. And they loved to laugh. Their mornings began with as much humor as an Alonian ale festival. One woman held her pregnant belly as she bent over near the bread stand, laughing at something her partner said. A man wove past her, apologizing as he bumped into Herlot, and then continued to chuckle at something he was reading on a scroll. A group of children squealed at the funny faces an older man was entertaining them with. "They're so...cheerful."

"Being rulers of the world is good for the mood it seems," Movo mumbled.

"May I offer you both a plate and utensils?" a young girl, with two braids rolled into buns on the sides of her head, asked.

"Why, thank you, yes," Herlot said. "That's very kind of you."

Then she got a look at the plates. She had never seen anything like them before. In the center was a large bowl surrounded by a gentle curved flat space that could easily hold breads, meats, vegetables, and fruits. "What a great idea," she said. "A master carver must have made these."

The girl reached a plate out to Movo, and as she was attempting to separate a spoon and knife from the collection in her hand, the utensils began to fall. "Oh!" she cried out.

With a swift motion Movo caught the spoon and knife just before they would have hit the ground.

The girl tilted her head up at the sky. "Argh. How is a girl to master balance and coordination if she can't master her utensils?"

"No worries, no harm done," he said. "Want to try again?"

"Again and again until it is right," she said.

Herlot leaned down. "With a little less fear and a little more freedom."

The girl gazed at her with intent. There. A remembrance of the Iptan way. Herlot recognized it in the girl's eyes in how the pupils dilated. It felt like a wave of wild freedom rippled out from the girl, just as Herlot often felt around Seum.

"Ready?" Movo asked. He maneuvered the utensils up and down, waiting for the girl's agreement, a nod that said she could handle them being thrown to her.

"Yes."

He chucked the spoon and then the knife. Each one spun a little. The girl caught the spoon right on the stack of plates and then she caught the knife by its handle, facing upward like the rest of the utensils in her hand. "Your utensils," she said, handing them right back over to Movo.

"Thank you," Movo said.

The girl stared with worry at Herlot's shoulder. "Will you need help scooping your oatmeal?"

Herlot looked at the stand surrounded by people scooping the delicious-smelling oatmeal into their bowls. "Oh, I had not thought about that." Back at the caves, Herlot had always set her plate down on the ground and scooped her porridge into it. Here everyone was standing, holding a plate in one hand while using the other to scoop.

"I'll help her," Movo said.

"Good. Because she needs to eat so she has her strength to show us how well she can fight." The girl disappeared into an area that had all sorts of loaves of breads on display in large, woven baskets. Each one was sprinkled with nuts and seeds. Herlot couldn't wait to try the bread too.

Herlot and Movo joined the line to the oatmeal. There were about ten different pots, each one emitting a different aroma, and the oatmeal inside was decorated with flower petals.

"Which one is the cinnamon again?" a girl carrying a pot asked someone behind her as she lowered the pot from where she had been holding it on top of her shoulder, ready to pour.

"Third from the right."

Herlot watched the endless amount of oats lazily crawling their way out from one pot to the other.

"Do you want to try this one? It looks like apples," Movo asked.

Herlot really wanted to try the one she had just seen getting refilled, but hesitated. Actually, she wanted to try a little bit of each. She didn't want to burden Movo, though.

She nodded and extended her plate. "Yes, the apple one sounds good."

"Or do you want the cinnamon one?" he asked.

"No. I said the apple was fine." Part of her wanted to take the oatmeal and go hide back in their room to eat it.

Movo dropped the big scooping spoon back in the pot.

"Is something wrong?" he asked.

Just wonderful. Now they were stopping the line. There were plenty of Iptans behind them waiting.

"Movo," she said through gritted teeth. "Just give me the apple oatmeal."

She could feel his gaze studying her features. Then, he practically ripped the plate from her hand and scooped a bit from the first pot. Then he took another bit from the second. Then the third. The fourth. Fifth. When he returned, she had a plate of the best-smelling disastrous mixture of ten different sorts of oatmeal.

She stood there holding her plate, too speechless to say thank you, as he scooped a large portion of apple oatmeal on his plate. "Let's find a place to sit," he said, and with a hand on her back, guided her out of the crowd.

She paced ahead, eager to be away from her helpless moment in the oatmeal line. The large leaves jutting out at every angle into the path were not as interesting to her as they had been when they first arrived. Having the plate in one hand made it impossible to brush them aside, and each one seemed intent on giving her a small slap on the face as they walked by.

Movo caught up to her and held the next branch in their path to the side. "To think all this time I've been preoccupied learning to work a sword and staff just to find myself in a line, dependent on someone else's help for feeding myself," she said. She stopped in her tracks. "I'm sorry," she said. "I should have thanked you instead of complaining. Thank you."

"You're welcome." Movo didn't say anything else and she was glad that he kept quiet. She didn't want any cheering up, what she really wanted was a way to let her frustration out. She couldn't wait to see the staff and swords Samin had promised.

She almost sighed in relief when they finally came up to a circular space with an empty hammock hanging from one tree to another. She gladly flopped her seat into it, then waited for Movo to join her before resting her plate in her lap.

The hammock swung gently back and forth, loosening the rigid rocks of frustration that had built up inside her. They didn't feel as rigid anymore, a little more like water rocks, if that was possible, still hard but not as rough around the edges. She wished they would go completely away so she could enjoy the best breakfast in the world.

Maybe if they could swing more the tension would dissipate completely, like salt crystals in water.

Poor Movo. He had just taken the first bite of his oatmeal and he looked like he was really enjoying it, already getting more on his spoon. She waited for him to swallow, and right before he began to prepare his next bite, she said, "Can you wait a moment? I was hoping you could help me make saltwater."

"And how do we make saltwater?"

"Look. Like this," she said. She began bending and extending her knees, each pump causing the hammock to go a little higher.

Movo didn't object at all, as if he needed the swing just as much as she did at that moment. As they were swinging, the hot air was not as hot as it breezed back and forth through Herlot's hair. Swinging was exhilarating. Just when she thought the whoosh forward would go on forever, it stopped, and then whooshed in the other direction. One moment there was pressure at the front of her body, the next it was at her back, but no matter which way she swung, she knew she would not fall down. And suppose that she did? Of course, she would get right back on the swing.

Losing her arm had been a nightmare and living without an arm would always be a challenge. It would swing her into frustration one moment and then relief into the next. An inability to scoop cereal while standing. A friend to help move branches aside. Right now, fighting was her hammock that kept her feeling stable. If she ever fell off, she knew she had the freedom of training to fall back to. What she couldn't do is forget the pleasure that was woven into the swing, the exhilaration it caused when paths changed.

Her frustration rocks were now saltwater. "Alright, unless you want to swing more, the mission is complete," she said.

Movo laughed. "I'm glad to hear that."

They both dug into their breakfast. Herlot tried each flavor separately and then mixed two together, then sometimes three. She was completely engrossed in an experience of flavors and pleasure on her tongue, endless combinations possible. Movo left to come back with another plate of several pieces of different types of bread and butter, and the tasting experience only deepened. Some of the butter had hints of garlic in it, and soon she had expanded her combinations to bread topped with butter and oatmeal. Every tastebud on her tongue was fully awake.

Suddenly, a spoon that did not belong to her invaded her feasting plate. Movo was in the same tasting trance as she, for he was attempting to taste the oatmeal with the yellow pieces of fruit.

"If I lived in Ipta, I would eat bananas every day," he said while chewing the stolen spoonful.

Seeing him enjoy something was just as pleasureful as enjoying something herself.

"Oh!" Herlot cried as a leaf from one of the trees fell on top of her bowl. She looked around to make sure no one was watching. She picked it up and held it up to the branch closest to her as she chewed.

"Shouldn't you try that in a more private setting?" Movo hissed.

Herlot rolled her eyes and let the leaf fall. "It wasn't going to happen now. I was just curious to see if I might feel anything at all."

"And?"

"Just as I expected. Nothing. Too bad this isn't something I can learn from a lecture like those you spoke of attending."

Movo chuckled. "You will definitely not find that on any curriculum in the botanical studies."

After a few exchanges of insisting that the other finish the plate, they decided to take turns. They sat cross-legged on the hammock facing one another. They were like two birds calling to one another, each sounding an expression of pleasure as they ate. "Try this one mixed with this one," Herlot said.

"There's still plenty of cakes to try," Movo said.

Herlot's eyes widened. "If I had known I would not have eaten so much! How I wish I had another stomach."

"Me too."

Herlot dropped her spoon. "Really?" A sinking feeling of shame poured over her.

Movo stopped himself from putting the spoon in his mouth and set the spoon down. Herlot could practically see it, a large pot hanging above both of their heads, tilting, and instead of oatmeal it was shame flowing out. Here they were having the time of their life, safe and secluded from the rest of the world, their biggest worry that of if they could still enjoy cake after breakfast.

"No, not really," Movo said. He looked around at the Iptans. "There's something about this place, these people.

Being around them makes it seem like the rest of the world doesn't exist."

"I'm making a new wish. I wish to go back home," Herlot said.

"And I wish to take you there," Movo said. "Let's not forget that while we're here."

Herlot nodded as she took her last bite of bread. "Agreed."

"Ah, there you are, my friends," Samin said entering the circular opening. He was followed by Aleena and the same men who had been with him the other evening.

"Good morning again to you," Herlot said.

"Did you enjoy your breakfast?" Aleena asked.

"Very much, thank you," Movo said.

"Would you like some cake?" Aleena asked.

"No," Herlot and Movo answered at the same time. They patted their stomachs as a sign of their fullness.

"Understandable. There will be plenty more cakes after our supper feast. Now, may I introduce to you my dear friend, Gold."

Herlot half expected to be introduced to a piece of golden jewelry, but a man who had been standing behind Samin stepped forward. Could someone have really named their child Gold? She held back a laugh at the idea and focused on rocking her way out of the hammock in order to shake the man's hand. The moment Movo tried to stand, her weight collapsed in on him and they were both back in the hammock. They both started giggling.

"Oh dear!" Imagining what the scene looked like to their onlookers sent Herlot into more laughter. "Please just give us a moment, we're a little tangled up here."

For the next few moments Movo struggled to push his weight back upright while Herlot tried to find her footing on the ground.

As soon as she was standing, she ran her hand over the front of her dress. "It is nice to meet you, Gold, you have a very creative name," she said. Gold reminded Herlot of Seum, except that he had blonde hair a shade lighter than her own. However, it was long and tied into a braid that ran down his back. As he extended his hand, she noticed the same golden tattoos that covered Seum's body just above his wrist.

"You, as well, Herlot. And I prefer to think otherwise. I wish my parents had given it more thought. And you, Prince Movo, it is nice to meet you as well," he said.

"A pleasure," Movo said.

"I wish to inquire if you are well rested and fed enough to perhaps join me in a light-hearted duel?"

Herlot's blood seemed to awaken and a rush of freedom pulsed through her veins. "Absolutely," she said. "Here?" She noticed that more Iptans had arrived from the paths that led to the circular space.

"Yes." Gold smiled. "Do you have a preference for a weapon?"

How nice it was to have a question she could answer with ease. She knew exactly what she wanted. Her soul craved the iron extension of her hand as compared to the wooden weight of the staff. "Sword."

It was not long before Herlot found herself surrounded by onlookers, Movo was back in the hammock, squished between Samin and Aleena now. He looked miserable and she knew he was waiting for his turn.

She brought her awareness to her body. Her bandaged feet were secured in Iptan sandals. The two slits running down each side of her dress ensured that she would not have to worry about ripping the fabric. And her hand, now comfortably wedged between the pommel and guard of a leather-wrapped sword handle. The blade looked fresh, not even a scratch.

She put a slight bend in her knees, just so her weight could ground more into her feet. Like movable roots, they sank endlessly into the earth below, past her bandages and shoes, then the stone and anything else that was between her and fresh soil. Her head was in the clouds, able to observe everything, especially her new opponent. She was like a tree in this moment, she thought. She was magic.

"Shall we?" she said.

Gold's sword jabbed at her feet in less than the blink of an eye. Like a bee escaping the entrapment of a collapsed hive, she whizzed backward and her body molded into a new position of freedom. She advanced, her sword coming within inches of Gold's arm. Before metal could meet skin, he blocked her attempt with his forearm guard. Again she advanced. Again he blocked. She was closer than a sword distance to him, but just as she swung her leg to knock him off balance, he jumped and was now at her exposed right side. She felt the breeze from his swinging sword above her as she ducked and rolled away.

They laughed at the same time. It was as if relief poured through both of them in their recognition of a partner of equal ability. Herlot lunged fully into the dance, as did Gold, neither holding back for fear of injuring the other.

Soon Herlot was entranced in a space where her body felt no limits. She bent and slid in ways she hadn't been taught, no fear that trying something new could cause her damage. It was an exhilarating song of freedom—the breath, the metal, and the wind. She didn't want the singing to end.

On the outside she was breathing heavily. On the inside her breath was the calmness of crickets in the evening. Had someone been able to hold their ear to her chest, they would have said her heart was pounding heavily. But on the inside her heart was singing a lullaby to her mind.

It was only the short glances she managed to steal at the sky that told her they had been fighting a long time. Time seemed to stop when one was free.

The rhythmic clanks of the swords meeting one another. Gold's body facing one direction, she adjusting her own. His foot forward, her foot back. More rhythm. More steps.

Flashes of metal in the sunlight. An entertained smile of Gold's. And again. He smiled a lot.

How ironic it was that yesterday her execution would have entertained a crowd in Felix's arena, and today her skill was entertaining strangers from another world.

She stole another glance at Gold's expression, but it wasn't his smile that was there. It was Felix's nasty lip curl and vicious eyes that looked back. She blinked twice and was almost thrown off balance. She knew it was Gold in front of her, but Felix's face refused to leave her mind. Oh, she hated it so much. She wanted it to suffer.

Her charges became fiercer, quicker. Gold was having trouble catching up.

More images of Felix.

More rage.

Teeth gritting together. She imagined how hard she would squeeze if she had her hands around Felix's throat. She wondered how it would compare to being hung on a noose.

This feeling was uncontrollable. But it was powerful, and she was certain she liked it more than she didn't. If only it were Felix she was fighting. Everything in her yearned for the feeling of victory. Felix gone, so many safe. It would taste like honey sprinkled with Iptan gold. If she could only get a taste of it now.

Quicker strikes.

Gold's sword slipped from his grip.

Felix's face again.

A perfect angle to slice his throat. How much she yearned for it.

Herlot, that's not Felix! some distant part seemed to be screaming at her.

It was not until someone's clap invaded her trance that this screaming part was able to send a clear message to stop.

"I thought she was ready to complete the deed," an Iptan standing to her side said to another. She realized that there was a man standing next to her who had a firm grasp on her forearm.

Would she have completed the deed? Had she almost tried to fulfill her desire? Would she have killed an innocent man? Her fingers, which were wrapped around the hilt of the sword, trembled as she thought about what she had almost done. She dropped the sword. The man let go of her arm.

The sun was high up above her head, almost noon, and Gold, his body glistening in sweat, flashed her a large smile before toppling onto his back and looking up at the sky. She draped forward and sweat dropped from her forehead onto the path.

"That was wonderful," he said.

Wonderful. If that's what he called it, it was quite a relief. If Gold didn't feel threatened, it really couldn't have been that bad. Her sword had come nowhere near Gold's throat. Thinking about doing something was very different from actually doing it, right? And, aside from the disturbing images at the end, she felt wonderful. She was certain her eyesight had even improved; such was the clarity the fight had created. And she was hungry again. Very.

Gold appeared at her side and patted her on the back. "I know the events leading up to your arrival at our Iptan home in Damalathum caused you much suffering, but I am grateful for your presence here and hope we have more plays like this throughout your stay," he said.

He really had enjoyed himself as much as she had. Of course, the thought that she would have tried to hurt him at the end was completely absurd. She couldn't believe that it had really worried her. Yes, to the onlookers it may have looked different, but it was Gold and she who were in the fight. He didn't feel threatened, and she knew herself better than to worry about hurting someone who was innocent. She decided not to worry and enjoy this wonderful moment. She returned the pat. "Me too," she said.

"Impressive, entertaining, inspiring," Samin said, and several other Iptan voices agreed with him.

"A piece of cake, please," Herlot said, walking over to the group in the hammock. One of the giant leaves kissed her on the face and she didn't mind it one bit.

Aleena laughed. "I doubt a piece will do. You need an entire cake, one with a warmed butter-cinnamon sauce and filled with walnuts. Herlot, that was absolutely astounding! No different from an Iptan warrior."

"Oh, I beg to differ," Samin said. "Those howls you make give it a lovely touch of wildness. Our boys and girls are not trained to do that."

What howls? Herlot wondered.

"Prince Movo!"

Herlot turned to see Gold balancing the tip of his sword on his palm. "Your choice on the weapon. I would prefer, however, a different one from the sword."

"Shield and spear," Movo said as he rose from the hammock.

Shield and spear? Was Movo still tired? He had been awake when she had woken up in the middle of the night, and on top of that, they hadn't fallen asleep together in the most comfortable position. Maybe that was why he had chosen to fight with such a simple weapon that her father had sometimes liked to use for fishing.

"You were nothing less than inspiring," he said to Herlot as he passed her on the way to the center of the courtyard.

Pride filled Herlot to receive a compliment from Movo on her skills. His alone meant more than the entire crowd combined. She sat in the hammock, right where Aleena and Samin had left a space open between them.

"Oh my, you are drenched. I'm so sorry, Herlot. We should have given you separate clothing for the fight." Aleena said.

"Maybe we shall pause the activities so Herlot can have some time in the bathing chamber?" Samin said.

Herlot was well aware that she did not smell appealing. Samin did not know what it was like to spend days on end in a cave close to people who trained all day. The smell of sweat was the result of hard work. Lifesaving work. It was meant to be celebrated, at least for a little bit. She put both arms behind her head and leaned back in the hammock. "Samin, my friend, entertainment does not always smell like fresh flowers," she said.

Aleena guffawed at that, as did a few other Iptans around them. "The girl speaks truth," an Iptan said.

Before she knew it, a plate of cake sat on her lap but Herlot's attention was stolen by the man entering the space who carried the shields and spears. The strangest things could make a person feel as if they had the world taken from under their feet, and the sight of the spears in that moment had that consequence for Herlot.

These weren't the simple wooden spears her father had used to fish. Her arm ached just at the thought of carrying it, let alone balancing it so it could extend at a perpendicular

angle from her body. Her stomach rose to her throat at the
thought of what would have happened had the soldiers had
these weapons in Eraska. Seum, Asm, and Movo had mentioned on several occasions how lucky Eraska had been that
Felix's soldiers had not come equipped with more weapons
and armor, since no one ever thought a land made up of
simple villages would ever stand up to them. She fully understood now.

A sword fighter would need a miracle to get close enough
to do the person carrying the spear any damage. And if they
did, the spear fighter would have been equipped with a shield
that would have made the task that much more difficult. Her
appetite for cake was replaced with a desire to study every
move that was about to play out in front of her.

The fight was much slower than sword fighting. She
noticed right away that each attack relied on how much
weight and force Movo and Gold could put behind a weapon.
Completely different from the quick, fluid motions of the
sword. This was a battle of bone-shattering power. This was
not a fight that could last as long as the one she had had with
Gold. Each attack that Movo or Gold deflected, whether with
their shield or spear, sent a shock through the opponent's
body that Herlot could almost feel. The clang of the impact
reverberated around the courtyard each time. Everything
about it seemed uncomfortable, the opposite of freedom. Once
Movo or Gold committed to a position with the spear, a
surprise move from the other meant a lot of time needed to
adjust.

"What do you think, Herlot?" Samin asked.

Herlot swallowed, watching Gold's powerful blows coming
at Movo from above and below his shield, and then vice versa.
"It's like a snake attack, over and over," she said.

"Good observation," Samin said.

Then something about Movo changed. Herlot doubted anyone else would have noticed it, but she did. The slightest hunch in the shoulders. His shield dropped the width of a twig. Then, Gold made a mistake, exposing his left side to Movo. The fight would be over.

Movo didn't take it.

He didn't take it.

Gold's next moves made Herlot push farther back into the hammock with each powerful strike that landed on Movo's shield. The shield wobbled as if the person underneath didn't have the strength to hold it up. That was not Movo, yet it was. With each strike, Movo's feet struggled for balance more and more, a pathetic shuffle as if he were making an attempt to run on water.

Then Movo was on his back, his arm still holding onto the shield at a defeated angle. Gold's spear was pointed right at his heart.

If this had been a battle, Movo would be dead.

He wouldn't talk again. He wouldn't walk again. He wouldn't breathe again.

She wouldn't see him again. She wouldn't hear him again. She wouldn't touch him or feel his touch again.

She could talk to him, but he wouldn't respond.

His story would be over, right when she felt as if a new story was beginning—their story. She would never learn who the Movo with warm blue specks in his eyes was.

She never wanted to eat cake again.

She heard a few sarcastic comments from the people about the "Prince's" skills.

She watched, still speechless, as Gold extended his hand and helped Movo to his feet. They clapped one another on the shoulders and exchanged a few words. Gold laughed. And Movo laughed, too, like an alive person.

Just hearing his laugh made the cake not seem so bad anymore.

She took a bite, but it did not taste as good as she had imagined. The rocks in her belly were back.

Chapter 10

MARZIPAN

Herlot could not have been more wrong when she had thought that Movo and she had started a new story. She was in their room sitting on the floor in front of a potted plant that Movo had bought from an Iptan. She was holding a fallen leaf, holding it right up to the twig that used to be its home. She had sat like this for hours since their first day in Ipta, with no success. She had tried speaking to it, imagining it reattaching, imagining a gold string between the leaf and the twig, and over and over again she had attempted to stir the warmth in her chest. Nothing. And Movo was clearly not around to offer any suggestions. She was at a loss.

It had been several days since the spear fight, and he had barely spoken to her. They would wake up, eat breakfast, train, eat again, then Movo would train while she went to spend time with the plant, eat again, and take baths. He was always back to their room and asleep before she came back. However, the few times she had managed to catch a glimpse of his eyes, the warm blue specks were still there.

There was one good reason for his behavior, and it was also why she didn't push him to talk. His training sessions were awful. Every single one. She had seen him use every range of weapons possible—sword, staff, mace, dagger, and of course, the spear and shield—and he barely lasted several strikes into the duel. And it was not Gold's talent either that was causing him to fail so bad. There was really something wrong with Movo. He fought like a complete novice. It was like all his years of training were forgotten. It worried her because soon they would have to leave the city, and they both needed to be in top shape to fight anyone who might block their path home. But the way Movo was fighting, he would cause more problems in their escape, and she depended on him to make it possible for them to leave.

Later that evening, she had just left the bathing chambers feeling fresh in a new outfit of Iptan clothing and then stood in a secluded spot holding a leaf that had fallen up to a branch. She had been doing this every night after her bath, in case there was something about the pot that wouldn't make it work. She tried to remember the words she had heard, but it was of no use. She hoped just getting accustomed to holding a fallen leaf to a branch might eventually develop into something. Practice and patience were her only allies.

After she was satisfied with her unsuccessful practice session, she realized that the last thing she wanted to do was go back into the quiet quarters with Movo, practicing more with the potted plant without success while thinking herself into a frenzy while he slept.

That was when she spotted Aleena on one of the paths.

"Good evening, Aleena," she said as she caught up to her.

"Oh, Herlot. Good evening."

"Where are you going?" Herlot asked.

"Nowhere in particular. Just strolling the paths for an evening walk. Would you like to join me?"

"I was actually wondering if you could help me find something."

"Oh?"

"Yes. It's a book, actually. *Lucius Havelot's Anatomical Drawings of Beasts.* Do you know it?"

"Hmm. Anatomical drawings have never been a source of pleasure for me, but we may have it in our collection. Bodies are lovley on the outside, but the inner workings are the nectar of nightmares, at least in my opinion. Come, follow me."

Aleena led her into one of the rooms that was partially exposed to the courtyard, a popular place for desserts and drinks in the evening. Several Iptans sat at a table drinking wine. A few others were deep into a game of cards, their table covered with sweets.

At the back of the room was a staircase leading below ground. Herlot faltered at the steps, remembering the last time she had seen stairs leading into the ground—Felix's dungeons.

"Come, nothing to be afraid of. Not a single rat, I promise."

She wasn't afraid of rats. She actually preferred them to people who locked people underground in cold, dark places.

She reminded herself that this wasn't Felix's palace by far, and that she was considered a guest here. No one had shown the least bit of a sign that they wanted to capture her. Then she thought back to the conversation Movo and she had had, and she thought about how that would be the perfect way to capture someone—wait for them to ask for it. Was she being stupid? Should she go down the stairs? She wished Movo was here to either warn her or encourage her, but he was intent on sleeping and not speaking to her. She had to make the decision herself.

One thing Movo had been certain of was that she could fight her way out of a situation. She didn't know if Aleena could fight, but if she did, she'd be an equal match.

She followed Aleena.

Once they reached ground again, Herlot saw that indeed there was nothing to be afraid of. Curious? Yes. But not afraid.

She found herself in a gigantic room, probably the length and width of the entire headquarters. The columns that seemed to be the only thing holding the ceiling up made her nervous, but everyone else in the room seemed to be at ease.

All over were cases and shelves filled with books and Herlot had to tell herself to wait a moment before taking them in. There were more books here than she ever imagined existed in the world, and ladders scattered throughout to reach the ones on the highest parts of the shelves. She looked at the Iptans sitting with quills and parchment at desks. Some sat together, quietly discussing something while others worked alone. Torch light shone from the walls and candle-light glowed from each desk with an occupant.

There was something about the people here that made her incredibly happy. It was not an entertaining scene such as her training sessions that Samin loved to watch, or a dance, or a person wearing an astoundingly beautiful piece of textile. It was quiet but the air was filled with ideas. Each murmur between the people at the desk seemed to have a world behind it, like the roots, stems, and leaves of a flower that worked so long and hard for their flower to bloom. How much she wanted to sit down at one of those desks and join the conversation.

"Follow me, let's see if we can find this Lucius Havelot book of yours," Aleena said.

Herlot followed Aleena into the forest of bookcases. Herlot snuck a twirl of joy when she thought no one could see her. The possibilities in what these books held were endless. The places her mind could travel were endless. She wanted to touch, smell, and read every single one.

"Ah, here it is," Aleena said. Herlot watched Aleena use her pointer finger to lean the book away from the others. There were so many squished together on the shelf. As soon as Aleena had loosened the book enough, she had to use her entire hand to free it from its neighbors. Herlot smiled. These books loved to be together, like a family.

"There." Aleena handed her the book.

There was not a single scratch or tear on the leather cover. Smooth, gilded words spelled out the title. Even though it was one of so many, the book felt special, just as every book in Alonia was treated. It was like a familiar friend, one whom she could talk to. *I promise to bring you back to your family,* she thought.

"You are awfully quiet tonight," Aleena said.

If only Aleena knew the conversations one could have in their mind. "My apologies. I'm somewhat speechless, I guess. I've always loved books, and there's so many here."

"Samin mentioned that you could read. I'd love to hear more about how that happened. It's not often someone from a peasant background can."

"That's true. Only the people in my village, Alonia, were able to. We were always considered the curious village. That's what happens when you live on the coast. We'd see so many ships dock at our fortress, and sometimes sailors would come wandering by. It's how the love for stories started among my people."

It was strange speaking about her family and friends as if they were only a part of history now. But that was the truth. It was a good history, though, one that was probably not half as adventurous as some of the stories in the books surrounding her, but it was good. "Our King liked to do nice things for us. Not just our village, all of them. He and the kings before him would trade with the sailors for books, and when his stewards made their rounds to my village, they would gift them to us."

"That's surprisingly comforting to hear. I don't know how else to say it, Herlot, but trust me when I say that it is not often you hear nice things that are not entangled with obscured intentions in this world. Maybe one day you can write down the story of your Alonians."

Herlot couldn't help laughing. She could almost hear the other Alonians laughing with her. "Perhaps. Perhaps. I never was much of a storyteller, though. I was actually the only one who was not a storyteller."

"Oh, really? Why is that?"

Herlot heard it in Aleena's voice. Blanketed yet not blanketed enough. Curiosity that teetered on the edge of suspicion. An intent to gather information.

"No particular reason. I just couldn't come up with stories or poems. I had no trouble reading or repeating them, though. My recitation, a rite of passage in my village, well let's just say that there weren't many people clapping afterward." she said. She didn't mention that at the time she had been far more interested in the unicorn in her life.

"Huh. From what I know, villages like yours are like one big family. How did the other Alonians react when you didn't follow village tradition?"

Why all these questions? Herlot was not about to tell Aleena that her village was used to her being different because of her "skill" of finding people, even at a young age. Nobody, even herself at the time, didn't know that she was blending with footsteps. Maybe she was overthinking Aleena's questions. Maybe Aleena was just trying to get to know her better. "Uh, I suppose some were shocked when I didn't recite. My family was not upset. Evenutally I found other ways to be useful in the village. I worked a lot and did some of the things that were harder to do. I even helped my brother build his home. I was strong. I managed to blend in after all..."

"I'm sure that strength helped you after the attack," Aleena said.

"I'm much stronger even now." She spoke the words with a slight tone of warning in them.

Aleena cleared her throat. "Well, you are welcome to take the book back to your room with you."

Herlot looked over at the Iptans sitting at the desks and bit her lip. "Aleena, if I would not be intruding, would it be alright if I sat over there for a bit?"

"Why, of course. I would have offered, it's just that I assumed you'd be in a hurry to return to your lover."

"My *what?*"

Aleena raised her eyebrows. "Oh, Herlot. I am sorry. I thought that Movo and you—"

"Oh, no. No." Yes, she did have strong feelings for Movo, but lover? Absurd. Peasant and a Prince on top of everything that happened? Absolutely not. This was not an Alonian fairy tale.

"You're blushing," Aleena said.

Was it because part of her wished it could be an Alonian fairy tale? She wished someone would slap her wrist for even thinking about it. "Aleena, any thoughts of something like that are a waste of time for me."

"But why? You're a beautiful, young woman."

"A woman destined to die soon." Herlot gazed at the space in front of her lips as if she could study the words that had come out of her mouth. She didn't know she would say them. She didn't even know she was thinking them. But they were true. She knew it the moment those awful black tendrils had a hold of her in the bathing chamber. Even if she and Movo got lucky and actually managed to escape back to Eraska, something awful existed, somewhere, possibly within her. She didn't know where, but it did, and it could kill better than any weapon even the Iptans could invent. She hugged the book closer to her chest.

"Listen, I know you have been through a lot, but you'll make it out of here. And that probably won't be the end of your troubles, but you shouldn't let that stop you from, I don't know, enjoying something even if it only lasts for a short while," Aleena said.

Herlot managed a smile. Aleena didn't understand. She hadn't felt the complete hopelessness that had engulfed her after those tendrils got a hold of her. She didn't feel the complete nothingness, the emptiness.

"Herlot, I'm going to leave you alone now. I-I'm sorry, I feel like I may have asked or said too much. Listen, I think you might really need a friend. I'm here if you want to talk. I understand that all of us here may seem very different, even strange to you. But we're good people. People fear us because of our power, but I have never met an Iptan out to cause anyone harm. When you have everything you need, you don't need to use people for personal gain. You can trust me."

Herlot hadn't thought about it that way. What Aleena said made sense, but Movo's precautions still rang deeply in her mind.

"Thank you, Aleena. I'll keep that in mind."

Herlot followed Aleena to a spare desk with a candle and they said their goodbyes. She sat in the chair taking a moment to just stare at the others deep in study, embracing the fact that she soon would blend in. She would get to be a woman exploring the mysteries of a library in a city far, far away from her home. Would it really be that bad if she allowed herself to experience the tiniest portion of Ambro, Elvin, and their dreams of exploring the world?

"Cheers to you, Elvin. I'll enjoy this for you," she mumbled. Then she looked at the book in front of her and opened the first page. Time stopped and her world was filled with pictures and words of foreign animals. She laughed when she found the penguins that Movo had spoken of. "What a strange -looking creature!" she exclaimed. She covered her mouth and apologized to everyone who had looked up from their studies. She shrugged. "First time seeing penguins." One man winked and held his cup of tea up to her before taking a sip.

When she was finished, she returned the book to a shelf and chose another. *A History of Damalathum*. She stared in awe at the drawings of little stone huts with small paths woven between them, and how the picture changed every few pages until it reflected the city in how it was today. She couldn't believe Damalathum had once been the size of Alonia. Perhaps there was a semblance of her life here. After all, it had formed from something very similar to what had once been her home.

Next she headed to a different shelf. It was filled with books on weapons and battles. She almost cried with joy at the thought that all the information that people like Movo, Asm, and Seum had received through experience was attainable for her, right here at her fingertips, in books. She didn't know where to start. She closed her eyes and reached for one. *Diruptio*, it said. "Huh, never heard of it."

She sat back at the desk. She frowned when she skimmed through the first few pages. There were pictures and symbols she didn't understand. Was it a different language? They didn't look like letters, though; it was symbols and strange names. Lots of the pictures looked like they had smoke and fire in them.

"Fights during the day, studies at night, when does the woman sleep?" a masculine voice said.

Herlot whipped around in her chair. "Gold!"

He chuckled. "Did I frighten you?"

"No, I just forgot where I was for a bit." She stared at the strange golden object he had slung over his shoulder. "What is that?" she asked.

"This? It's a telescope. It makes it easier to see things from far away, like ships and stars."

Herlot's jaw dropped. "That's phenomenal."

"It is. If Felix wasn't so intent on searching for you, I'd love to take you to the city wall so you could see."

Herlot's shoulders slumped at the possibility of getting just a taste of such an adventure but having no way to experience it.

"We could try in the courtyard, but the tree leaves block a lot of the view. It will still be nice, though," he said.

"Oh, could we, please? Now?"

"Yes, but not right now. The sun is beginning to rise."

Herlot hadn't realized how much time had gone by. She wasn't tired at all. She just wanted to keep reading. "Can I ask you a question?" she asked.

Gold nodded.

"What is this book about?"

Gold leaned on one hip and flipped through a few pages. "Explosives. Formulas on how to make them, depending on what kind and how much damage you'd like to cause."

"I don't understand."

"Most people won't. It's a form of war technology only Iptans have. There are probably thousands of people who would kill to get their hands on that book if they knew it existed."

Herlot pushed the book a few inches away from her, as if she had opened something she wasn't allowed to see.

"You want to see?"

Herlot looked up at him with wide eyes. Did she want to learn a war technology more advanced than Felix's? It was a question dropped to her from the skies.

Gold slammed the book shut and tucked it under his armpit. "I take that as a yes. Come, follow me."

Jaw hanging open, Herlot shuffled behind Gold to the back of the library feeling like a child being let into an adult secret. He opened the door of a wooden cabinet. Inside were hundreds of vials filled with powders of different colors.

"These are powdered crystals that have been blessed by our Emperor. Each one will do something different. Some will cause just smoke and make it difficult for the enemy to see, the lapis could take down an entire city, this one here is poisonous. Sleep, hallucinations, weak muscles, vision impairment, hearing impairment..." Gold kept running his finger down the vials listing the gruesome things they could cause. "Ah, this one will be perfect. Just a loud noise to cause distraction No harm done. Let's get it ready," he said.

Herlot shook her head. "Y-you want to use one, r-right now?"

A part of her felt like this was a circumstance that she should ask Movo about; but then again, Movo didn't seem to want to talk to her lately. She would have to learn the ways of this world without him this time.

"It will be safe, don't worry," Gold said. "Certain plants help the process. This one benefits from dried clovers." Herlot watched him pour the crystal powder and clover into separate glass jars and then placed them on an object that had plates hanging from both sides. He opened the book again, ran his finger down a page, and then poured some of the crystal mixture back into its original jar.

"What are you doing?"

"Weighing them. The proportion matters. Too much of both makes the effect more powerful, not enough of one could make it not work at all."

"That's pretty important information." Herlot wished she knew the language written in the book. To think this whole world of knowledge was unavailable to her because she could not understand the words.

"That should be just about right," Gold said as the plates teeter-tottered at a certain point. He then poured the contents of both jars into a tightly woven cloth to which he attached a short rope.

"If only Enri could see this," she murmured.

"A friend?"

"Mhmm... like a sister. She's skilled at using plants to heal people."

"It's always fascinated me that all plants are beautiful, never seen an ugly one, yet some of these beauties heal, while others kill. It's like you and this Enri friend of yours, a healer and a killer."

"I've killed but I'm not a killer. I was protecting myself and my people."

"Yes, you are. I can smell it in your sweat when we fight. Not a killer of many, perhaps, but of one. Every strike you take, you're preparing it for that one person. It's Felix, isn't it?"

Herlot's jaw dropped. So he had felt it when they fought. He knew more than she ever expected. "Yes. But like I said before, it's only to protect my people."

"If you knew he'd leave you alone forever, could you continue living without fantasies of taking his life?"

Herlot wished she could say yes. She shook her head.

"And if he were standing right here, defenseless, would you let me perform the deed?"

Herlot ground her teeth together. "No."

He pointed at her eyes. "There it is. It's about much more than protecting. You want it, the satisfaction of being the one to do it."

Herlot put her hand on her hip and walked in a circle. She couldn't find the words to defend herself. She faced Gold again and shrugged. "Alright. I'm a killer. But just for now. It will end after Felix."

Gold raised an eyebrow. "If you say so."

What was that supposed to mean? She frowned. "I do. Now are you going to show me how to use that thing or no?"

Gold swung his arm toward the stairs. "After you, warrior," he said.

"Grab a candle," he said as they passed the desks.

Once they were outside, Gold led them toward the archway that led out of the Iptan Headquarters. Herlot faltered and looked up at where she and Movo's room was, half expecting him to stand there and tell her to stop. Leaving their hiding spot was the last thing she should have been doing, especially with the sun beginning to rise. But this was her chance to learn more about Ipta's strange magic, something even Movo did not understand. She quickened her pace up the steps.

They both looked down over the bridge. The cobblestones were glossed with rainwater. A gentle breeze rocked some of the shop signs, and all that could be heard was their creaking.

"Good. No one is out on the street yet," Gold said. "Give me the candle and you hold this."

Before she knew it, Herlot had the bundle of powders, power, and magic in her hand. Its weight felt surprisingly light in her palm, yet she was overwhelmed by the heaviness of responsibility that came with it. "Wouldn't it be better if you held it. I mean, I'm not—"

"You have to throw it the moment I light the tip of the rope. No hesitating," he said, as if there was no doubt that she could do it. "It won't harm anyone as long as no one is standing next to it."

She nodded.

"And stop shaking."

She glared. "You'd be surprised to learn what I and some of my friends can do while we're shaking." Like Mahtreeh, when they fought together at Lorfin.

Gold held the candle flame to the tip of the rope. The moment the flame caught, she chucked the thing as far as she could with her shaking hand.

Her ears popped and all she could hear was a ringing. She covered her ears, and then panicked at only being able to cover one. She felt as if she had stood right next to a lightning strike. She needed to find something to hide under. Her body went limp with fear, and all of a sudden she felt as if she was floating. Just wonderful. Gold was carrying her. Apparently, she couldn't do as much as she thought while shaking. This was the second time since she came here that she had to be carried. The stairs blurred beneath her and she barely felt the return of the dense, hot atmosphere in the Iptan Headquarters.

"Put me down," she wanted to say, but her words came out slurred. There was still a ringing in her ears.

"Gold, were you throwing thunder globes on that good ol' Felix's streets again?" Herlot barely heard Samin say through the ringing. "You know that frightens the city dwellers, and I'm going to have one of those messengers with a letter of complaint within the hour."

"I know, I know. I was just trying to entertain our guest," Gold said.

"I don't think she's fond of loud noises," Samin said.

"What the hell was that? What happened to her?"

Herlot rolled her eyes. Wonderful. Movo had arrived. She started wiggling in an attempt to signal that she wanted to be put down. Once she felt the ground beneath her feet, she shoved Movo's helping hands aside and wobbled toward a bench. She sat down and put her head between her knees. Meanwhile, the three men kept bickering back and forth. This was the last thing she wanted to listen to.

"I'm going to go to sleep," she managed to say and didn't care to wait if they had heard her. Then she wobbled her way up the stairs and toward her room. She flopped onto the cushioned bed and covered her head with every pillow she could find. After a while she heard Movo enter the room.

"Herlot? Can I get you anything?"

"Quiet," she said. He didn't speak again, and eventually she fell asleep dreaming of the last time she had been frightened by such a loud sound. She had been a young girl, lost in the forest, and a lightning strike had scared her so much that she fainted. That time she had woken up to warmth, light, beauty, and magic—Devotio. She'd give anything to relive that moment, or anything to live long enough to wake up in peace to see her best friend.

* * *

Herlot groaned when she woke up. The awful ringing was still there. Not as loud, but still painfully annoying. She looked out the window to see that it was dark outside. She turned to her side to see Movo in the corner of the room. She watched him splash his face with water and then lean his weight on both forearms as he looked at himself in the mirror.

"What were you thinking, going out on the archway with Gold?"

"Learning Iptan magic tricks that help them win wars. I may have hearing loss for the rest of my life, but at least I got some information. Your turn. What were you thinking when you decided to barely speak a word to me for a week?"

Movo wiped his face with a cloth and let it drop on the edge of the sink. He walked to the table and picked up what looked like two cloaks hanging over the chairs. "Since you're so eager to risk your life, let's get out of here for the night. Here, put this on."

"Where are we going?"

"Bandits' quarter."

She took the cloak from him. "And...what are we going to do there?"

"You're going to tell me what you learned. I'll tell you what I've been thinking. But first, we're both going to drink."

Herlot smiled wide. She kept her gaze locked on him as she slid the cloak over her body. "Prince Movo, there is nothing I'd enjoy more than pretending to be a bandit with you tonight."

A hint of a smile showed on his face.

"Are the cloaks enough for disguise?" Herlot asked.

"Luck was on my side today while I explored the head-quarters. These people find creative ways to spend their time living here. I managed to purchase two wigs from an Iptan, and from another, a pair of pirate boots for you."

Movo lifted two large clumps of what looked like long, wavy, black hair from another chair, and then a pair of boots from underneath the table. He threw the wig toward Herlot and she caught it.

Herlot adjusted the black wig over her head and then went to the mirror to see what her reflection looked like. "Ah!" She turned around and burst into laughter at the sight of Movo in the wig.

"You look like Seum," Movo said.

"You do too!" Herlot turned around again and began braiding the wig hair. She forgot what it felt like to have long hair.

"He lived. He had to," Herlot said, as she thought of Seum's state when they last saw him.

"I have no doubt. No one is tougher than Seum."

Soon they both lifted their hoods and went out on the archway. Once they were assured that the street was clear of any guards, they made their way down. A rush of pleasure flooded Herlot the moment her booted feet touched the city's street. She was still within walls, but it felt a little more like freedom.

Their surroundings changed as Herlot explained to Movo about the powders blessed by the Emperor and clovers to make the "thunder globe." Groups of people swayed merrily as they neared the bandits' quarters, often with arms around one another's shoulders. Music and aromas of cooked meats drifted out of several spaces. It was a merry atmosphere. Each place that she peeked into, she saw people who did not seem all that different. She had met Iptans and soldiers, but it was just now that she was realizing that these foreign places were not made of only royal figures whom she had read about in books.

As they entered the bandits' quarter, the looks of the people changed a bit and the sounds coming out of the taverns were louder. "Who are these people, exactly?" she asked.

"Bandits, vagabonds, and the occasional pirate here and there."

"And your father allows them to have an entire area of the city to themselves?"

"No. It's a way to keep them all concentrated in one place so that they are easier to control."

Movo stopped in front of an inn. "Ready?"

Herlot couldn't explain how much she craved to be around people who were not somehow entangled in the past tragedies, people who didn't know of or didn't want anything to do with her. "More than ever," she said.

The moment Movo opened the door Herlot was swarmed with an array of the pitches of singing and laughing. So much happening in such a small space, everyone too busy in their engagement of drinks and company to even notice she and Movo had stepped inside. She would have skipped with joy if it weren't for the packed crowd.

She followed Movo toward a space by the wooden bar. Behind it was a tenant who seemed brutish in manner and wiped his nose on his sleeve as he thrust a cup at a group of men sitting on stools. Whatever was in the cup splashed onto the surface but no one seemed to mind. A man carrying two large cups stumbled past them but then turned as another yelled curses at him. He began shouting threats back through a pipe that was hanging in his mouth. He raised his arms to promote a fight but realized the liquid in his cups would spill if he did so. "I'll get those for you," Movo insisted as he took the two cups off the man's hands, as he was already charging at his persecutor.

Herlot and Movo squeezed themselves through the callous crowd until they found an empty space on a bench that they attempted to share. Pressed against Movo's side, Herlot sipped the drink.

She wrinkled her nose and squinted at the man sitting at the table across. "What is that smell?" she asked as she studied the man's long hair that seemed to be held unnaturally in place in an intricate flow.

"Burned butter. His tribe is known to use it in their hair."

Then she tuned in to the hair man's words, not a single one of which she could understand. It was the harshest, most guttural language she had ever heard. "*Ghh...bhrr*" she attempted to mimic.

Movo started laughing and covered his mouth with his elbow as he nudged her in the ribs with his other. "That's the best impression I have ever heard. You might want to stop before they hear and think you're mocking them."

Herlot mimicked the words again to make Movo laugh even harder before she took another sip of her drink. She closed her eyes and pondered the bitter, refreshing taste. She licked her lips and took another sip. This time she recognized a small hint of blueberries in the flavor. Next she took two long gulps. The flavor penetrated her palette. "Delicious," she said.

"Slow down, you don't want it to get to your head," Movo said.

Several snarky remarks were at the tip of Herlot's tongue as she peeked into Movo's cup and saw that it was already half gone. She also wanted to tell him about the times she, Ambro, and Elvin drank the strong ale back home, and how she was perfectly comfortable with it getting to her head; however, a man leaned over the table and into their space. He was tall, thin, and had maybe three teeth, at the most. Behind him were two other men who had much larger frames. "Up for an arm wrestle?" he asked.

Herlot and Movo eyed one another. She opened her eyes wide with eagerness, hoping he'd understand that she really wanted to try. At that, Movo rolled up his sleeve and set his elbow on the table. "Be my guest," he said.

Herlot dropped her hood, and whipped her braid back over her shoulder. Then she pushed her hand through the hole of the cape and winked at one of the men behind the one who was preparing to wrestle with Movo. "Have a seat," she said in as low of a tone as she could foster.

The men who had been sitting on the other side of their table sounded their protests about being pushed off the bench, but then stopped once they realized it was for the occasion of an arm wrestle. He turned and mapped the size of Herlot's arm to his companion's using his thumb and pointer finger. "I might have me a chance!" he exclaimed.

Herlot smiled at her opponent as she squeezed her hand into a fist and then stretched her fingers wide. "Ah, left-handed I see. Not my best side, but you look scrawny. Shouldn't be a problem. Ready?" he asked.

She curled her fingers around his hand. "On three," she said. "One, two…three!"

Herlot watched her opponent's eyes as they twisted and turned in all directions, as if nudging the veins that were protruding along his temples. She knew that she could beat him even now if she wanted to, but wanted to watch him a little while longer. "You always fancy looking a fellow into his eyes during an arm wrestle, lad?" her opponent said.

She glanced over at Movo's battle. He and his opponent took turns gaining advantage, their arms leaning toward one side until just an inch from the table, and then slinging back to the middle to begin the slow descent toward the opposite side. Herlot cheered Movo on as he closed the gap between the last inch and won. Movo raised his eyebrows at Herlot's opponent, reminding her to get back to her own task. "Oh!" she exclaimed, realizing she was several inches away from losing. She took a deep breath and then slammed the man's hand into the other side of the table. He shook his hand with a pouting expression on his face.

"Come on, let's find someone we can beat," he said to his companions.

"If only they knew they had just wrestled with the Prince," Herlot whispered.

"Or a hero," Movo said, eyeing her.

Herlot blushed.

"Out of my way!" the tenant shouted as he made his way toward the bench. He practically threw a roasted carcass of some sort of meat on the table. Before Herlot could react, half the inn attacked the meat. Sounds of a flute and drum began playing from somewhere she couldn't see. All around her, men licked grease off their fingers before grabbing for another piece of meat. Herlot took another sip of her drink as she swayed to the music.

All of a sudden, her arm-wrestling partner returned. "Hey, let's try the other arm, what do ye say?" he asked.

"Next time," Movo said as he pulled Herlot to her feet. Her heart was pounding and she prayed that this man would leave them alone. If anyone noticed that she was missing her arm, their disguises would fail to protect them, and although these people seemed very different from the rest in Damalathum, she doubted anyone would keep a secret of having found the ones that Felix was looking for to execute.

Her heart slowed as they stepped outside, and she took a breath of the fresh, crisp air.

"So, what did you think?" Movo asked.

"Oh, I barely had time to think there was so much happening. I wish we didn't have to leave. I would've loved to listen to the music more."

"Maybe we still can. Come, let's follow this street."

They slipped into the shadows of an alley alongside the inn. Movo climbed onto a barrel and fidgeted with a window until it budged open slightly. Once again, Herlot could hear the mixture of the crowd and the flute and drums. Of course, much fainter, but still enough to imagine what it was like in there.

"Hungry? I managed to sneak this before the inn guests got their hands on it," Movo said as he unfolded a piece of cloth with roasted meat in it.

Herlot eagerly took a piece. It blended perfectly with the bitter taste of the drink still lingering in her mouth. "Mmm."

Herlot took a seat on a barrel and leaned the side of her head against the wall of the inn. She closed her eyes and listened to the life happening inside. "Why can't it all just be like this?" she said. "It could all be so simple, so happy. It's happening within the walls of a city whose ruler hurts so many people. It's also happening outside of the walls. Do you think there's any way the awful parts could just... drop away? All this life would still remain, wouldn't it?"

Movo sat on the barrel across from her. "I once thought that my father's way of ruling a kingdom was the only way. He's a malevolent king, but he's not the only one. I've met many others. His brother, Robin, for example, could be considered even worse. As a child, I didn't really know any-thing else. I just thought it was how the world was supposed to be. There were those who worked all day and sang, danced, and drank at night, there were those who fought, and there were those who ruled. I never questioned it, maybe because I didn't have much of a choice. But now I do think that life would remain if the rest just dropped away. It could just be hard work, and then singing and dancing like you say."

"Do you think it will ever be?"

Movo shook his head. "No. Too much awful has happened. Once that much has happened, it's like everyone decides it has to keep happening. Probably because if it stopped, we'd have to face our own shame for letting it happen in the first place."

"Hmm. So you think that all these kings who do awful things, deep down inside, they may not want to rule?"

"In my father's case, no. He wants power more than his own life. And if there ever came a time when he decided to stop, I don't think he'd be able to keep breathing if he really thought about all the harm he has caused."

"You've been thinking a lot the last few days..." Herlot said.

Movo didn't say anything. She tried again. "You've been thinking a lot the last few days."

Silence.

"Movo, what is wrong with you? And what has happened in your training? You look like you just picked up a weapon for the first time."

"I'm not much different from my father, Herlot."

"You are nothing like your father."

She saw a glimmer of fierceness in his eyes.

"I know you have fought in a lot of battles. I also think that is very different from infecting people with crowpox and locking five-year-old children inside dungeons," she said.

She noticed his jaw tighten at the mention of the dungeons. Slowly, she slid off the barrel. She stopped right in front of him and reached her hand out and into his cape sleeve. She traced her fingers over his forearm until she found what she was looking for—a scar, but not in a usual straight shape that would come from a blade. She followed the curves, curves that could have never naturally happened, signs that someone had deliberately and slowly focused on carving this design on to his body. "A chess piece, right? I can't believe he put his own five-year-old son in the dungeon," she said.

At that, like a lightning strike, Movo had a grip on her arm. "I wasn't a victim in the dungeons," he said. She took a shaky breath as he tugged her an inch closer, as if he had information to tell her that he wouldn't allow her to get away from. When he spoke, his words felt as cold as the void in his eyes.

"I was ten years old when my father ordered me into the dungeons. I was twelve when I left."

Two years? Yes, he was older than the other children, but two years? How could he not see himself as a victim? "Movo, keeping anyone in a dungeon for two years for no reason aside from frightening them is unforgivable. I don't care how old you were, I'm sorry you had to live through that."

"You should ask me how I got out."

"Alright. How did you get out?" she asked, but then regretted it the moment she did when she saw his expression. She felt the same way as she had the first time she had seen his eyes. She wanted to run.

"You really want to know?" he asked, as if he could sense her tension. She felt his grip tighten on her forearm as if he were warning her that if she said yes, everything she thought she knew about him would change. The Prince who had helped her in every way he knew how would not be who she really thought he was. The only person she could trust and depend on in this foreign place could be the danger she was trying to protect herself and family from. The man who made her heart warm could have the soul of her worst enemy, Felix. It was her choice now. She could believe an illusion, or she could face the truth. She could be naïve, or she could be smart. It was her moment to prove that she had learned from her mistakes.

Her heart screamed at the cruelty of the world with every word that came out of her mouth. "What did you do to get out of that dungeon, Prince Movo?"

"I killed a little boy."

A whimper escaped her, but she pushed through and forced herself to keep looking in his eyes. "H-how?"

"I first broke each one of his knees, just like my father told me to. And then I put a dagger in his heart."

He kept a grip on her arm, as if challenging her to see how long she could last being near him. She continued to use all her strength to fight the urge to pull away. She fought so hard, every moment she stayed near him was an attempt to rescue everything she thought Movo had been to her. Then she saw a look of pity come over his eyes and he released her arm. She stumbled back, not realizing how much she had been trying to pull away.

Feeling wobbly, she sat back down on the barrel and stared at the cobblestones, while images of Movo killing a child flashed across her mind. A man and woman walked by, their elbows hooked together, laughing about something. They didn't even notice them sitting there. Maybe they were so far away from happiness that happy people couldn't see them anymore.

Could she have hurt a child when she was twelve years old? No. But what if she had been locked in a dungeon for two years? She hoped not, but she didn't know. After all, before this summer she never thought she'd kill someone. And she had killed many, and would kill more. Even more important, did she even have a right to judge Movo for what he did? Perhaps, if it meant that this information would help her make sure that he'd never get close to anyone she loved again. Her stomach churned at the thought. Even knowing this, the thought of Movo not returning to Eraska with her hurt, as if home wouldn't be complete without him there.

He had changed. Every one of his actions since the fire showed that he did. He had been a child when it happened, and his very own parent ordered him to do it. What would she have done had her father asked her to perform such an unspeakable act?

"Why did Felix make you do it?"

Movo sniffled. Was he crying? His voice was clear and steady, though, when he spoke. "It was meant to be my first lesson in training to become a good soldier and then a good king one day. He wanted me to understand that the king always has to be the last one standing, that is the only way to win, even if it means he has to sacrifice those underneath him. I wasn't allowed to leave the dungeon until I learned. One day I broke. Those two years were a battle between holding on to myself and seeing the light. I broke. I wanted to see the light again."

Herlot didn't know what to say. No sunlight for two years. She couldn't imagine.

"What was it like when you saw sunlight again?" she asked.

"After that day I stopped caring for it even though I got to see it every day."

"Oh." Her heart hurt. For the little boy. For every child in that dungeon. For Movo. She didn't know how it was possible because she didn't think she could hate Felix more than she already did, but it felt like more wood had been added to a fire of revenge inside her.

"Did his plan work?" she asked.

"Brilliantly. I knew exactly what to do to not hesitate in a fight. I knew how to not feel regret and remorse, to not think about right and wrong in a battle."

"You say knew as if that's not the circumstance anymore."

"You're right. I can't do it anymore, and it shows. You've seen me fight the last few days."

"I don't understand. What happened?"

"You."

"Oh." *Oh.* The rate at which her emotions were changing throughout this conversation made her feel as if she were being rocked in a boat during a storm. First the thrill of the inn, then the confusion, hurt, fear, and revenge, and now...she refused to think of the word. It was an impossible endeavor. But what else could it be? She had just learned the ugliest truth she could learn about a person, and beneath all the hurt feelings there was a stable feeling that could be no other than love. Even after learning this about him, she still wanted to be near him, she still cared for him. She also really wanted him to know, but she didn't know how to say it. She wanted him to know that no matter what he did, that would not change how she felt about him. And she also remembered her conversation with Aleena, and her very own reason as to why this would never work. But they did have now.

She noticed that the crowd inside had quieted. There weren't as many people there anymore, and the music was now a mellow tune played by something that sounded much like the psaltery.

"Too bad we did not dance," she said.

Without hesitation, Movo pulled Herlot into an embrace, interlocking his hand with hers and bringing it up between their chests. She rested her head below his chin as he swayed them from side to side and in circles to the music. Even though they weren't inside where the instruments played, the music was even more beautiful as it interwove with the wind, tamed from the tall walls that encircled the city. Herlot's mind, previously distracted by the commotion in the inn, now fell into a place of easy rest as Movo's heart beat a rhythm of peace that caressed and mesmerized her spinning thoughts. "*Ding...ding...ding...*" she whispered along as a bell off in the distance chimed three times.

When the bells chimed four times, they were still interlocked in their embrace even though the music had stopped. Herlot was barely awake. Her eyes were half closed, but open enough to see the glimmer of starlight between her eyelashes. She wasn't asleep, but she was resting deeper than she had in a very long time. Perhaps because being in Movo's arms was better than the best of dreams. Maybe it was even a dream come true. It had now happened for the second time in her life. First meeting Devotio. Now, it was being locked in an embrace with Movo. She had never before spent so much time in someone's arms, and she did not want it to end.

And he wasn't letting go either. At first, she waited for him to be the first one to let go, but that moment didn't come, and it still hadn't. Did he love this embrace as much as she did?

Slowly the starlight started mixing with hues of the beginning of the sunrise. The dream come true was going to end, soon.

Her stomach grumbled. Movo chuckled. He put his hands around her waist and ever so slowly leaned her away from him. "Have you ever had marzipan?"

The moment she looked into his eyes she felt blood rush into her cheeks and she stared down at her boots. It felt like a butterfly was dancing in her stomach. The blue in his eyes had never felt so warm before. He was unbelievably handsome.

"Herlot?"

How was he able to act so natural after what had just happened? She barely knew how to speak a word to him.

"Ah, yes. The marzi...pan?

"Marzipan."

"Right. The marzipan. No. I have not."

"Some of the market vendors might be setting up early. Maybe if we are lucky, one of them sells the marzipan. Would you like to risk your life with me for a delicacy?"

"Which way to the market?" she asked. She sighed, grateful that she was able to speak again.

They started walking in the cold, dewy morning air, and she remembered the couple who had walked by earlier. Hesitantly, she extended her arm and then wove it around Movo's elbow. She could feel his gaze down on her, and then he mimicked the gesture of her elbow. She smiled wide.

"How dangerous do you think it is for us to visit the market?" she asked.

"In this weather, mostly everyone will be wearing a cape. We won't look suspicious."

As they continued to walk, more and more delicious aromas met Herlot's nose. "Mmm," she murmured as they walked by a bakery on the narrow street. How she wished she could go in.

The path they walked soon opened into a large square space. Several groups of people were working on attaching large cloths over their spaces. People walked with carts filled with fruits and vegetables. Movo steered her toward a woman stacking fresh loaves of bread on her table.

Movo slipped her some coins. "The marzipan, please," he said.

Herlot made sure to keep her head down so that her hood covered her face.

"This way," Movo said and continued to walk at a slow pace along the path that wound through the numerous stands. "Give me your hand."

Herlot took a moment to feel the weight of the ball-shaped delicacy in her hand. Out of the corner of her eye, she saw Movo put an entire piece in his mouth.

She took a small bite and looked at him in shock as pleasure danced across her tongue. She had never tasted anything so delicious. He smiled. "What is it made of?" she asked.

"Honey and almonds."

"Psst... pigskins for sale," a voice that Herlot thought she recognized said. She turned to her right and saw Fabian waving them over to his stand.

"Oh, no," Movo said.

"Oh, please, Movo, let's say hello." She nudged him toward Fabian.

"Pigskins for sale," Fabian said again and winked as they reached where he was standing. "Still haven't found a way out?" he asked once they were close enough for no one else to hear.

"Soon, hopefully," Herlot said. "I thought you polished shoes?"

"I do. But I came across these and thought I'd take a chance in selling them."

"What are they used for?"

"Nothing. We don't need them," Movo said.

"I hear they can help you breathe underwater. Just imagine. You're trying to escape out of a city and your only way out is going through the moat, but you have to wait underwater to make sure there is no archer standing over you on the wall."

"We need them," Herlot said. "How much?"

"Two coins, please."

"We will not need pigskins," Movo said, but Fabian had already handed Herlot her goods.

"Pay the boy," she said. She and Fabian giggled as Movo fumbled through their coin purse.

It felt good to see Fabian. Herlot thought she'd never see him again.

Fabian handed her a pigskin, but she dropped it as soon as she had it in her hand. Horns blared through the market and city. Herlot covered her ear and nearly dropped to her rear at the surprise of it.

"I think it'd be best if you both hurried out of here now," Fabian said as she scrambled to her feet.

Herlot only managed to catch a glimpse of Fabian's worried expression before Movo pushed them toward an alley. She bumped into someone. "Apologies," she said and caught a glimpse of the woman she had bumped into who was walking with her partner—the same couple who had walked past them in the night. She and Movo had looked so much like them just moments ago. And now they were on the run again. How could she have expected a peaceful morning at a market to remain peaceful?

Herlot watched as red strips of fabric rolled out from every window she could see. Echoes of undecipherable cheers reached her ears from far away. "Movo, what is happening?" she asked.

"A war announcement. Every time Felix decides to go to war, every person who lives in the city must hang a red flag out of their window and chant the name of the enemy. It symbolizes that the entire kingdom stands behind Felix and is coming for his next victim."

The chanting grew closer to them, and Herlot noticed the people standing next to their windows, mothers and fathers holding their children, many still in their night garments, awaiting to hear the name they were about to join in chanting. The chanting began to transform into more and more ordered syllables as it approached them.

Once the name arrived, it hit her with the impact as if she were standing under a waterfall.

"Eraska! Eraska! Eraska!"

Herlot felt as if someone had poured a boiling pot of rocks inside her. The chanting voices seemed to slow, and the street scenery blurred. "Eraska...Eraska...Eraska..." she repeated the words, barely able to believe that all these people were chanting the name of her home.

"Herlot, now is no time to slow down."

She shook her head to knock herself out of the stupor.

"Stop!" she yelled.

Movo turned and started to speak but she cut him off. "No!" A fire was blazing inside her, so strong was her rage. "Your father is declaring war on my home?"

For a moment she thought he'd dare to push her along toward the Headquarters, but something stopped him. "Yes." He let go of her hand, as if it was too hot to hold.

"What does that entail?"

"Many ships, armored archers, cavalry, siege weapons, fire—"

"He is sending an army to attack what's left of a small group of peasants?"

"Yes. And since your land is useless to him, he'll make sure it's useless to them too. They will burn everything. Now, can we hurry? We'll be of no use if we get caught now." His eyes were pleading. She didn't care.

"And every single one of these people saying the name of my home supports him in doing this?"

"No. They're forced to do it." Movo looked around, probably to see if they were catching anyone's attention. Herlot didn't care about that either right now. If there's anyone she wished she could see right now, it'd be King Felix.

"If every single person under your father's tyranny stopped being afraid of him, would he still hold the power that he has? Every single one of these people is Felix as far as I can tell."

She lifted her cape and unfastened the dagger tied to her leg. She turned on her heel and glared at the first person she saw in a window threatening everything she loved. She raised her arm and aimed at the window. But before she could swing her arm, something made a strong impact with her head, and before she could do anything about it, the street and the chanting disappeared, and she was engulfed once again in darkness; however, this time, the darkness was tinted red.

CHAPTER 11
ELFOLK

As soon as the wagon stopped, she pushed the peasants aside and hopped off. She lifted the front of her dress as she hurried toward the hill. Her boots slid in the mud as she climbed. She threw a harsh comment at a soldier who asked if she needed help. She would never need help from these people.

Once she reached the top, she held her head high as she walked past the skulls and totems outlining the field in a circle. She was the only one allowed closer to the mound, and she loved hearing the curious whispers from the soldiers outside the perimeter.

However, this time, she paused for the first time ever before entering the mound. She had never failed her master before. Her trip to Damalathum had been a failure, two times over. And the wagon of crowpox survivors she had ridden with from Damalathum definitely didn't look like they had someone capable of slipping her master's grip for the gold in their hearts.

She entered the tunnel that led to the living quarters. The door to his private quarters was open, but she did not dare enter without an invitation.

"You have returned," she heard him say from the room.

He emerged in the doorway, his face obscured by his hood. Never before had she seen his face.

"Y-yes."

"And?"

"I-I failed. The girl, Herlot, she escaped the execution. I wasn't able to find her after."

The hooded head tilted to the side.

She swallowed. "I found Manni, too, but after I ran back to the execution arena to look for Herlot…"

"Yes?" His words seemed to wrap around her throat.

"I lost her too."

Silence.

"I'll go back and look again." She turned to leave.

"No. You will go to the village and see if any of them catch your attention. And you will do so every day from now on."

She frowned. "I am certain Herlot is our best chance. She caused the sun to disappear right at the moment of her hanging."

"Stupid girl. It was an eclipse. If you had lived as long as I have, you would know better than to deem it unusual. A rebellious peasant is the last of my concerns at the moment."

"Have you felt any fluctuations in gold from the direction of Damalathum?"

His voice hissed around her ears. "The direction is always obscured due to Ipta's experimentation on the crystals, hence we will be concentrating our attention on the peasants right in front of our noses. Now make yourself useful and study the new ones who have been brought to me."

She bit her lip. She yearned for gold. She had been weeks without it. Did she dare ask?

"May I ask for—"

"You will be satisfied after you perform your duty."

At that he disappeared into his quarters again.

Wearing a dress that would help her fit in with the peasants, she walked from her master's home. It was a stupid idea to wear the dress. Even in filthy cloth, her beauty intimidated them enough to keep silent and be wary of attempting anything out of the ordinary, she was certain.

She kicked one of the skulls that lay in her path as she crossed the field. Like a queen, she made her way down the hill and toward the village, not once glancing at the sunset. She used to watch those every day. Now she had better things.

The guards saw her from far away and already stood at attention. She loved that she had more power than their King Felix.

Her head held high, she walked right through the opening in the fence that had been constructed around the village. It now held many people since all the survivors of the southern lands were being held here. Walking the paths was tedious. She hated accidentally grazing her shoulder against one of the dirty people. And the smell was awful. Aside from the sweat and dirt, their aroma was mixed with traces of the sea. It made her want to vomit. Her master hated the sea.

The sound of the blacksmith hammering sent irritation through her veins, as did the stupid song some of the men were singing from the tavern. She couldn't wait for this awful trip to be over. But she would complete her task. Anything for him.

She missed the taste of gold. Oh, she could barely wait to return and sink into an abyss of golden euphoria.

"What is your name, dear?" an elderly peasant woman, whose entire dress was covered in patches, asked. She was sitting on a chair outside of a chicken coop. She was the one with the annoying cough who always seemed to be watching her.

The question prickled at her, and she did her best to focus on the pebbles on the dirt path. When that did not help, she began to count them, only to pause to enjoy an image of strangling the old woman who had asked for her name. That would make her feel better, but her master would be upset with her. These people were meant to be studied, not killed, although she doubted that any one of them was worth the study. The gold stealer she was looking for would surely be less…common.

Her craving grew stronger, yet she still had to finish her task. She wouldn't report back to her master without that. However, she couldn't take it anymore, and would need to settle for the next best thing: blood. She quickened her pace and exited the town out the opposite side, after which she raced into the woods. She stomped on a family of wildflowers that had managed to escape being run over by a wagon wheel.

From a pouch attached to a belt that was wrapped around her hips, she took out a blade and headed into the woods.

With a firm grasp on the blade, she scavenged through the woods for her victim. The first bird, rabbit, or squirrel that came into her sight would do. She didn't want to waste time hunting for something larger.

She whipped her body in the direction where she had heard the chirp of a squirrel. It was probably communicating to another one about a nut it had found. She chucked her blade, admiring its perfect spin as it traveled through the air, right into the tall ferns growing near a black walnut tree where she had heard the chirp. The sound of metal on flesh announced her victory.

She wrestled the ferns aside and found the squirrel. Without another thought, she dove her teeth right in. To her surprise, she was still used to the taste and texture of the raw meat. This was how she had lived before. Before he made everything right that had been wrong. She had always known there was something special about her, even throughout the worst of times. She had always known he was looking for her.

She had sensed him long before knowing he even existed and could be found, much like Manni, she was sure. She had called to him so many times. She had wandered for so long until she had come close enough for him to recognize her as the one who had been calling him.

"Hoot, hoot."

She groaned. "Not you again." That forsaken owl was up in the tree branches. She had hoped one of the guards might have captured it to make into a wall decoration for that Felix king's palace.

She wiped the squirrel blood from around her mouth. "You don't have anything better to do, do you?"

Maybe a threat would make it go away once and for all. She raised her blade up and looked up into the branches, the owl the first thing she saw when she looked up.

"You see what happened to this squirrel? I didn't even have to see it, that's how good I am. If you keep following me, you'll be next."

The owl readjusted its claws on the branch and continued to stare. Was it mocking her? Was it daring her to follow through with her warning? Its gaze lowered just a little bit. It was as if it could see through her chest, right into her heart. She gritted her teeth, telling herself that the discomfort of exposure was just her imagination. Then the owl returned its stare right into her eyes and hooted. In that same moment, the peasant woman's question pierced through her mind again, but this time in the low tone of the owl's hoot. *What's your name?*

She gritted her teeth against a memory that followed. Her lover from a time long ago appeared in the forest carrying pelts across his shoulders and calling her name. She saw him mouth the words, but could not make out the sound.

She narrowed her eyes at the owl. "I don't know. There. Are you happy?"

She threw the squirrel down on the ground and paced back toward the village.

Wings flapped alongside her, and that awful owl hooted again. This time she was certain it was laughing at her because she couldn't remember her own name. She didn't remember when she had forgotten it. She knew she once had one. One day it had just seemed to slip away. From the time she met her master, there were more important things to focus on, such as euphoria. Who cared about names when feeling so good?

This time, the owl hooted without end, haunting her until she reached the village, as if saying that that was the most ridiculous thing she had thought of yet.

Once most of the families and their guest survivors sat down to dinner, she began making her rounds. Many of the survivors barely ate. A few asked if she wanted food, to which she did not reply. She was here to observe them, not to make conversation.

Once she was finished visiting the last home, she sighed with relief and finally made her way to the mound under the dark sky. She swayed her arms along her sides as she entered the field, blissful about the fact that she was the only one who was allowed to walk in the field, in the vicinity of her master, without being killed.

She stopped in her tracks when she noticed that her master was standing in the opening to the mound. He rarely did that unless something outside was upsetting him.

"Something has happened?" she asked. "Is it the one who steals the gold?"

It would be wonderful if he had finally found the person. It would finally be over once and for all, and they wouldn't have to worry about this person's method being learned by others.

"Perhaps. From the direction of Damalathum."

From what she was informed, there was not another ship due to return with survivors for at least another week. "Then it must be another experiment by the Iptans and their crystals," she said.

"Perhaps."

"Two times in the course of a week. They're usually months apart... Shall I go in and wait for you?" She was hungry.

"Yes. I will feed you and then you will tell me more about Herlot."

She could practically taste the euphoria already.

She was lying still, awaiting her master to come to her. She thought of her past lover and tried to read his lips in her memory when he spoke her name. She made sounds to see if anything felt familiar, but it didn't. Then, finally, she felt her master's presence above her, and within a moment her mouth was filled with a golden mist that traveled down her throat and warmed her entire body. As the euphoria built, any thoughts of her name or the image of her past lover's face faded, as did the sound of the hooting owl.

CHAPTER 12

RED FLAGS

Herlot stirred awake. The side of her head was pounding, and someone was pressing a cold, wet cloth to it. Images of the red flags, sounds of the horns, and those awful voices chanting, they all clouded her mind. She sat straight up almost bumping heads with Movo who sat in a chair next to her. She rubbed her head and thought of the last moment she could remember. Then she glared at Movo. "Did you *punch* me?

"Yes. You were about to kill an innocent person and cause a scene."

"You don't have a right to make choices for me!"

"Yes, I do. Because it seems you need saving from yourself right now."

Rage pulsed in her veins and she lunged at Movo, sending the chair tumbling backwards. Before she raised her fist, with a swift move he had her on her back. More rage. She struggled to kick her legs and flail her arm, but he had her pinned down, just the way Seum had shown her how to do. How could she have fallen for it? She swung her head up to knock her forehead against his, but he gracefully deflected it. "Let go," she said.

As if not worried at all that she might retaliate, he pushed himself off of her.

"You haven't been quick to respond like that in days," she said, as she pressed herself up onto her knees.

"You haven't acted foolish like this since I met you."

His words felt as if he had punched her again. What had she been thinking? Every time she thought of Felix, more rage and hatred grew in her, so intense that she couldn't think straight. Had she really almost thrown a dagger at an innocent person?

Movo shuffled through some papers on the table. "Samin was able to get information about Felix's plans. The fleet sets out for Eraska in four weeks."

"We need to get back now."

"The ship won't be here for another two weeks."

"We need to warn them now!" she yelled. She felt so helpless that she was on the verge of tears.

"Listen, Herlot. We have one option and one option only. We need to stay alive during our escape so that there is someone to warn them. No leaving the Headquarters again. No rash decisions. I need you to understand that if you decide to do something stupid, you're putting everyone's life at risk back home."

She walked over and stood next to his side as she read the notes on the papers. Supply lists. Arrows. Armor.

"Movo, how are we going to make enough armor to protect everyone from the arrows?"

Silence.

"We can't." She gripped at her hair. "We're going to have to fight an entire fleet absolutely defenseless."

"You're right. We can't. And we won't."

Herlot leaned and turned to look Movo in the eyes. "What do you mean? Do you have a plan?"

A glimmer of hope. How grateful she was. She just knew Movo would have thought of something.

"Can you sit down?" Movo asked.

Herlot sat in the chair with her back straight, eager to hear the genius plan.

"There was something else Samin and I discussed. He is offering to give orders that will require the ship that was supposed to take us to Eraska to take all of the Eraskans back to Ipta."

"W-what?"

"Herlot, we don't stand a chance. Escape is the only logical thing to do."

"After everything, *everything*, that that monster did to my people, you expect us to just leave?!"

"I remember that even before Ruelder, escape was an option."

"But that was before we were able to fight! Who are you? Weren't you the one warning me to not trust the Iptans? I thought we weren't even getting on that ship. Now you seem more than happy to take all my people to Ipta?"

Movo grabbed her by the shoulders. "Herlot, listen to me. I don't care how much training your people may have had. Not a single one of them will survive this siege. If my father leaves any survivors, they will be left with a burned land. I wouldn't have agreed to Samin's offer so easily were it not such a risk. Please, trust me."

Herlot's jaw trembled. "Please, Movo. He's already taken so much." Her face was so hot with desperation and rage that she thought it could boil the tears that were streaming down her face. "There has to be something we can do. If Ipta offered to help them escape, maybe they will give us armor?"

Movo dropped his head as if defeated. "I already asked about that. They will not interfere militarily with affairs that are not of Ipta's interest. Gifting weapons is outside of what they are willing to do."

Herlot gripped Movo's shirt into a bunch and let out a helpless cry. "He's right here. Right here in this city. We could—"

"No. No matter what our skills, that would be the stupidest thing to do right now. If we get ourselves killed, Eraska's lost. No one will warn them."

Herlot released her grip and ran her hand over her dress. "It's me he wants. This is all because of me. Had I been executed, he wouldn't want revenge, right? I'll go there right now."

Movo's entire body grew stiff and his fists clenched. "It's too late for that. And how dare you even think of sacrificing yourself after everything we have been through? And if you believe any part of your story about magic, how could you think of doing something like this when you have Devotio depending on you?"

"If I surrender myself, I might be able to get close to him."

"No!" Movo paced the room. "I won't let you. Skies help me, Herlot, if I have to tie you to that chair until it's time to leave, I will. Would you just listen to yourself? You're not thinking for them, for Enri, Mahtreeh, Devotio...*me*."

"How can you expect me to sit here and do nothing when the man who wants to destroy everything that matters to me is just a walk away?! Don't tell me I'm not thinking of them. Everything I do is for them."

"If that's true, you'd realize that what's best for them is having you alive. What you're thinking is the weak thing to do. It's giving up."

Herlot tapped her foot against the ground and fell into deep thought. Could she really ask her people to relocate to Ipta, a place whose people they were still learning about? Could they trust them?

"What if Ipta has alternate motives? What if we're falling into another trap, one we are both too naïve to realize?" she asked.

Movo's shoulders relaxed. "Whatever their motives are, it's not to kill any of us. For now, it's better than what my father has planned."

Herlot took a deep breath. "One step at a time, right?"

Movo nodded.

"If we do this, Movo, and all my people end up in Ipta, you do realize we'll be in the hands of the most powerful and dangerous people of this world if things go downhill, right?"

"Right."

She went to stand and look out the window. Somewhere out there was her worst enemy. She would agree to Movo and Samin's plan for now, but she would certainly not give up trying to find another way. She refused to live in a world where King Felixes could determine the future of one's life. Where he or she lived. *I will come for you, Felix,* she thought. *Sooner or later, I will come for you just as you have come for me. And it will be worse. That I promise you.*

CHAPTER 13

WALNUTS

"We need to go to the fortress," Enri croaked from her tent at the campsite. She wanted to say more, but another coughing spell shook her body. Lisel, a girl she had always admired for her patchwork, appeared at the entrance to her tent and handed her a cup of tea. Enri chugged it all down, hoping it would strengthen her voice so she could speak some sense into the others, at least those who were left and hadn't already returned to their villages. People didn't like listening to toads, apparently.

"I hate missing the sunflower harvest," Arlette said. "Karen, aren't you worried about your chickens? What if the others were right? What if it's really time to put this nightmare behind us and go home?"

Several others around the fire mumbled in agreement. Raspy voices joined, those who like Enri were still recovering from the fungus illness that still lingered from the caves.

Enri chucked a walnut at Asm, who was blowing his nose into a cloth. "Say something," she mouthed.

Asm cleared his throat. His voice sounded as raspy as her own. "The smart thing to do would be for your people to continue training. There should always be someone at the fortress, as the main defense. And you need to establish a plan for communication. It is crucial for times when you need to rally for an emergency. But there is no use in me training any of you if you do not wish to be here."

At that moment Seum hobbled through the trees and entered Enri's tent. "Anything?" Enri asked.

Devotio had been missing for three days now. Seum shook his head as he checked on the psaltery.

Enri touched the necklace with the leaf hanging around her neck. It had taken all of her strength to find it, and Herlot's sword, while she was sick and everyone was preparing to leave the cave.

"We know how to fight now. Even if they did come back, we'd be able to stand our ground," Arthur from Lorfin said. "How many villagers in this world can say that they sent a whole pack of soldiers, from one of the most powerful kingdoms in the world, running with their tails tucked in between their legs?"

Enri watched Asm close his eyes and shake his head.

"That was once, Arthur," Enri said with a feeble attempt at sternness in her voice.

"You speak as if we could go on living like things were before."

As she heard Ambro speak, Enri whipped her head too fast, so much so that it made the pressure in her ears grow.

"Yes. After all, wasn't that the plan?"

Ambro laughed. "Is it? You," he poked Arthur in the chest, "know nothing. You are lucky. None of those men set foot in your village thanks to my sister. My sister who, by some miracle, managed to survive and stay sane after what happened to me and my family. You chased a few soldiers down a hill, that's what you did. You never witnessed what these fiends are truly capable of."

Ambro's voice dropped. The firelight danced across his face and Enri could tell his gaze became unfocused. "The...the memories. They're like poisonous weeds, grasping at anything they can touch in your head. And the whole time they're rotting. It's a kind of rot that will never stop and just go away. These weeds can't disintegrate like real things do with time. They just keep rotting, and they spoil every memory they touch. That's what these people are capable of. They have the ability to infest any happiness that we have ever felt, our memories, stories of our ancestors passed on for centuries, and also any dreams we may have of the future. I once had memories of snowballs and stews. Now the snow is tainted red from blood, and there's maggots in the cooking pot…"

Enri swallowed to fight the bile that was rising in her throat. Based on the silence, she knew Ambro's words had given everyone a glimpse of the torment he lived with every single day.

Ambro looked at the others and straightened his posture. "We need to train. We need to live closer to the fortress. We need to be able to become an army in a moment's notice if we are to survive in this world. Most of all, we need to learn. And we have two Iptans willing to teach us. And you're all just going to throw that away to return to your ignorance…and your death."

Most of the people nodded in agreement, and the others, for the time being, did not argue. It was far from an enthusiastic cheer but Enri felt like she could sleep for the night. So many had left already, and more left each day. Benyamin was gone and Devotio was missing. Her brother still had not returned from the mountains with Lucinda. She had to keep believing that tomorrow would bring better news.

"I still think we should go and try to get Benyamin from his family in Bundene," she said to Seum, who was unwrapping the psaltery from the blanket it was wrapped in.

"No. He needs to be with his family. You saw what star watching did to him. The more he did it, the more obscure what he saw became. Yes, he has a gift, but it's not one we can rely on. I stand strong behind what I told you before. If we care about him, he needs rest and to be with his family."

Enri frowned. She really didn't think Benyamin was that bad off. Especially now that he was in fresh air, the fungus illness would soon subside. She was already feeling much better.

"It's what a responsible healer would do," Seum said.

She cringed. Was he right? Was she so preoccupied with Benyamin's gift that she had lost sight of following in her father's footsteps? Would she risk someone's health just to gain the advantages of their gift?

"Alright... but I'd feel better if eventually we send someone to check on him."

"That we will do."

Seum began strumming and Hans appeared just as Enri was preparing her place for sleep.

"Hans, will you teach Seum to play a lullaby tonight?" she whispered, as her ghost friend appeared.

As the music changed, she spoke to the skies as she closed her eyes, wishing for the safe return of her brother and Devotio. She also asked for Herlot's forgiveness as she overheard more and more families making plans to return back to their villages in the morning. At this rate, she'd be lucky to have ten people to welcome Herlot back to Eraska.

Chapter 11
The Fingerpainters of Orfolk

Herlot tapped her fingers against the table holding the chessboard. She was preparing her next move as she waited for Movo to return with more jam to enjoy with their bread. She was interrupted by the sound of the graceful, soft landing of a leaf that had fallen from the potted plant in their room.

She rose from her seat and sat down cross-legged on the floor in front of the plant. It was still several days before their escape. How much she wanted to return and give Devotio the news that she had learned to work her magic. She held the leaf up to the twig it had fallen from.

Come on, heart, she thought. *Somewhere in there, I know you have the gold to do this.*

She thought back to the moments before their execution and how she had thought about all the people she loved. She thought of their faces, and how powerful the thread that bound them in a relationship felt.

Then she saw Felix's face. The faces of her loved ones disappeared, and she was consumed in Felix's face contorting in agony as blood splurged from a dagger she had driven into his heart.

She stirred out of her fantasy as someone banged on the door of the barber's shop across the street.

She stared down in horror at her hand holding the leaf. Her fingers were wrapped in a fist, the delicate green of the suffocating leaf peeking through the space between her fingers. She unraveled her fingers and let the crumpled leaf drop to the floor. She pressed her palm against her chest and backed away from the scene. "I-I'm so sorry," she whispered.

She had tried to reattach the leaf to life but had only ended up killing it more.

The doorknob turned and Movo entered the room. "Everything alright? You look like you've seen a ghost."

Herlot shook her head. "No, all is well. Just nerves about tomorrow."

She followed him back to the table with their game of chess next to the windowsill, where they could play with the remaining light of the sunset.

Movo looked out the window as a shout reverberated throughout the street. "Oof... sounds like the barber had to pull someone's tooth."

Movo set a small bottle of nerve tonic down next to Herlot's side of the chessboard.

"Another one?" Herlot asked. "I thought you were getting more jam."

"That's for you to decide. Last night, one didn't work, so perhaps two will help you sleep tonight."

"The only thing that might help me sleep is if I was returning to Eraska with a ship full of armor and weapons." Every night, all she could see was Felix burning her defenseless land. Every village, the trees, the plants, numerous places where families had made memories would soon be gone.

"Even if we had that luxury, we'd be outnumbered."

"Skies, what evil exists in this plagued world that one man can destroy so much?" Her hand was shaking again. "If I had the opportunity, I don't think killing him once would be enough," she said through gritted teeth.

Movo covered her hand with his own. "Herlot, I know you're suffering, and I know the rage you feel. But trust me, please, as painful as it will be to lose your land, it is nothing compared to a field full of corpses of your own people. If you were to stay and fight, you'd lose the land *and* your people. Ipta is the safest place away from Felix. Remember that, alright?"

Herlot nodded. She plugged her nose and took the shot of nerve medicine. Across the street, the man at the barber shouted again.

Movo cringed. "Sounds like it's more than one tooth."

"I can relate to his agony." She sighed as she set the empty bottle down. "I'm starting to think that the only reason this stuff ever helped my mother was because the taste is awful enough to make one forget her problems and only focus on the taste of burned rotten apples stuffed with fish guts."

Movo wrinkled his nose and pushed his plate of bread smothered in berry jam to the side. "Did you decide on where to move your pawn while I was gone?"

"No. I think I might want to move the horse, instead." She jumped the figure over her pawns and one spot to the right. She knew right away that it had been a good choice because Movo unknowingly started tapping one of the pawns he had taken from her against the table as he fell into silent concentration.

While she waited, Herlot unrolled a piece of parchment that Movo had returned with. She frowned. "It speaks of the collapse of a mine. Isn't that where Fabian said his father works?"

"Mhmm. But that wasn't my father's mine. It belonged to his brother, King Robin."

"You have met your uncle, right?"

"Often, but it is far from what most people would consider a relationship between an uncle and nephew. From what I remember as a child, any visits with him were rushed in fear of war being declared between the two of them." Movo jumped his horse and Herlot scanned the board to see which one of her pawns had become vulnerable.

"Is he like Felix?"

"Some say he is worse. His methods are more cruel. Unless one is a member of his military or court, they are practically slaves. The people of his kingdom are provided with rations, and the only way for them to gain any coins for themselves is if a member of the military or nobility decides to gift them some. It's a cold kingdom with no homeless but only a few free. People here are free to leave at their will. Nobody is allowed to leave my uncle's kingdom."

Outside they could hear the patient offering his utmost thanks to the barber, while holding the side of his cheek. "If that barber were to live in Robin's kingdom, he could be executed if he did not open his shop when it is expected of him. Unless it's crowpox, they're required to work."

"What if it was?"

"Anyone showing signs of crowpox gets killed on the spot by an archer. No one is allowed near the body for several days. Families are not allowed to give proper burials."

"Is that what it was like here before Ipta gave everyone the elixir that protects against crowpox?"

Movo nodded.

Herlot bit her lip so hard that she tasted blood. She had never thought about how well Felix must have known what a crowpox death looked like. He had probably seen many suffer and die from it. Yet he had been willing to perform the despicable act of infecting her people for the sake of a stupid game of power in this world infested with gold and prestige.

Herlot pushed the chessboard away, and several of the pieces toppled over on one another. "This game is stupid," she said.

"You were winning," Movo said. "A few more turns and you could have checkmated my king."

"It's not a game I want to win. I'm going to head to the library for a while."

She rushed out of the room and slammed the door behind her harder than she wanted to. She didn't want to hear the word "King" for the rest of the night.

As soon as she was in Ipta's library she could breathe easier. Several of the people at the desk, now used to her daily visits, waved and greeted her. She noticed one of them, Thissel, writing in a book with a quill and pen. She looked over his shoulder and noticed that it was a map.

"What is that, Thissel?"

He set the quill aside and cracked his knuckles. "I am revising a map of the boundaries of our empire. Once I am complete, my drawings get sent back to Ipta so more of these books can be made."

Herlot noticed a stack of books at his side. "Are these past ones? May I have a look?"

"Be my guest."

Herlot opened one of the books. Each page was numbered with a date. As she flipped through the pages, she noticed how each map's boundaries changed—sometimes slightly, sometimes significantly; however, the only thing consistent was the Iptan Empire's growth. It never receded. It grew at a steady rate throughout centuries. Would they continue going until all was conquered? If so, they had found the right method to do so. A little at a time, so that it was barely noticeable, and the conquered people had time to adjust. From the book she had read about past battles in Isolda's lands, even if there was a siege, it was difficult to maintain it. People had to be willing to accept their conquerors. It was only successful if the new conqueror instilled enough fear, or offered them more gold than their previous King.

"Fascinating," she mumbled as she reached the end of the book and still had not witnessed a single recession of Ipta's borders.

She said goodbye to Thissel and ventured into the bookshelves, searching for the books she had previously read and looked at. She took out book after book, flipping through them until she found a page that felt just right. One of her favorite things was finding markings of the books' previous readers—dirty fingerprints, dried flowers, blots of ink. It's as if the readers became part of the stories as much as the people who had written the works. Earlier, she had carefully unraveled a thread from her leggings and cut it into small pieces using a knife and now, into each book that she had read from, she inserted one of these pieces. Part of her now lived on in a history of pottery, an encyclopedia of war weapons, a children's book about a friendship between two clouds, and a cooking book consisting of every recipe known to man incorporating a tomato.

She decided to venture off into a part of the library she hadn't visited before, to leave more of her threads. She used the skirt of her dress to wipe away dust off a row of books. The shelf was so dusty one couldn't see their titles. "Hmm... *The Fingerpainters of Orfolk*," she wondered out loud. She grabbed the book and set it on the floor. She knelt over it as she opened to the first page. Soon she learned that it had been written and illustrated by an exiled dye-maker who had stumbled upon cave paintings.

She held her hand against her chest as she looked at the first page. An illustration showed a cave wall covered from top to bottom with hand and fingerprints. There were some footprints there too. *Just like Brom's handprint that someone had carved out in the caves in Eraska... These had to be ancient humans.*

She saw it before she heard anything. Out of the corner of her eye a shadow moved across the bookshelf, heading toward her. She pretended to keep reading, humming out loud. Then, when the shadow seemed to make a wide motion with his arm, she spun around and pinned her attacker against the bookshelf, her forearm pressing hard into his chest.

Gold belted out laughing. "I'll remember not to try that again!"

She narrowed her eyes. "Why would you sneak up on me like that?"

"I was very curious to see if your reflexes are as good in moments of surprise as they are when you expect it. What are you reading tonight?"

She lowered her arm and let him free. "I found this book...these cave paintings are astounding. Why so many handprints?"

"Huh... that is interesting."

"Do you know of anyone who might know more about them? They were found in a place called Orfolk."

"Herlot...I assure you I can introduce you to many who can tell you about much more meaningful art than this... Thissel, himself, could paint a portrait that only mirror reflections can compete with."

Herlot shook her head. "No, I want to know about these."

"Alright. Does not hurt to try." He grabbed the book and marched toward the area with the desks. Herlot rushed after.

Gold raised the book up high above his head. "May the Emperor be blessed on this lovely evening. Does anyone happen to know about the finger paintings of Orfolk?"

"Gold, if you're trying to impress the lady, show her the newest textile shipment, not some old pages in a book," Thissel said.

Gold shrugged. "I guess we won't find much help among this serious bunch."

Herlot noticed Thissel stick his tongue out at Gold, behind his back.

"That's too bad. I was very curious about them."

Gold lifted his finger in the air. "I have an idea. Meet me in the courtyard in an hour."

"Oh, no. No more surprises. I would like to spend my last week here without needing someone to carry me. No more lost feeling in my legs because of another experiment."

Gold pressed his palms together in front of his chest. "Iptan honor that it won't be loud or dangerous. If anything, it will be leisurely."

Herlot examined his features. "Well, you're not lying, at least I think you're not. Alright. I'll meet you, but at the first sign of anything strange, I'll sail away like a pirate sieging a rum ship. Alonian honor."

* * *

"Gold is preparing a surprise for me in the courtyard in an hour. You coming?" Herlot said as she swung the door open to her and Movo's room.

Movo shoved a set of maps that Herlot had not seen before aside and headed to the door.

"You're not going to wear your boots?" she asked, pointing at his bare feet.

"Oh." He glanced down. "I guess I've grown accustomed to it."

"What were you looking at?" she asked as he closed the door behind them.

Movo eyed the parrot sitting on the balcony railing. He rushed Herlot forward a few steps. "I'm studying the currents at this time of the year," he whispered. "In case something happens and we can't get on that ship or we find something out while we're on it, I want us to be prepared."

Currents. Another thing to add to her list. She would have to find a book about them, hopefully still tonight.

"That tonic is really not working, is it?" Movo said.

Herlot twirled on the steps. "Not a bit!" The gold gilding of her dress shimmered in the moonlight. She looked up at the night sky. *Nine moons left until the leaf wilts.*

Herlot and Movo sat on the edge of the fountain as they waited for Gold. There was something about the courtyard in the middle of the night that made the leaves seem more prevalent than during the day. It was as if the quiet allowed Herlot to notice the conversation that the plants were having between themselves, a quiet conversation that otherwise went unnoticed. The air was thick with plant words.

"What do you think this surprise is?" Movo asked.

"I don't know. I found a book with illustrations of cave paintings, much like the ones in Eraska. I suppose it might have something to do with that."

They both turned at the sound of the loudest yawn the world had ever heard.

The medic appeared at the top of the stairs, holding a bucket. Behind him were Gold, Samin, Thissel, and Aleena, all holding similar buckets.

Herlot and Movo met them at the bottom of the stairs.

Gold stood proudly with his hands on his hips. He motioned at the buckets. "We have paint..."

Samin followed with a similar gesture, aiming at the building. "And we have walls."

Aleena waved her hand. "And hands."

The medic yawned again. "And no bed."

Thissel yanked the medic's hat. "Wake up, finally something out of the ordinary happens around here and all you can think of is frolicking in the dreamworld."

The medic slapped Thissel's hand "Don't touch my hat."

Movo and Herlot looked at one another, both clearly confused. "Gold," Herlot said. "You don't mean to tell me we're going to paint these walls?"

"Oh, that's exactly what we are doing," Aleena said. "It will give this place a nice touch. Think of how surprised and delighted everyone will be to look at something different when they wake up for breakfast."

"Samin, why don't you do the honors and be the first?" Thissel said.

Herlot watched eagerly as Samin dipped his hand into one of the buckets and then slapped his hand onto the courtyard wall.

They all stood back and looked at the handprint.

"Well, what are we waiting for?" Aleena said as she waltzed to a bucket.

"Trust me, you won't have to ask me again," Herlot said as she dipped her hand. "Ooh," she sounded as the cold paint engulfed her entire hand. She couldn't wait to see what it would feel like to leave her handprint in such a place.

The paint oozed between her fingers as she pressed her palm into the cold wall. She admired the handprint she had left. She rushed to dip her hand again. Before she knew it, she had made at least ten handprints on the wall. Something about this felt so...good. She looked around at the others who seemed just as focused on their handprint artwork as she, including Movo.

"We need more colors!" the medic said.

"I'll get them," Gold said.

"Make sure to grab a blue and gold," Samin said without looking away from his print.

Herlot pressed her palm to another spot, this time closing her eyes. She searched for words to describe the feeling of how her palm and its many lines were transferring onto the stone. The closest thing she could compare this to was telling a story. Yes, a story, but much easier than the one she had had to come up with for her recitation in Alonia. A true story, her own, exposed and so clear to see by anyone who stumbled upon her handprint. "Here I am, this is me," each of her handprints seemed to say. Every crevice twist and turn seemed to fill in the spaces of a story one could never fully tell another.

She had never thought about it before but if she would ever want to share every moment of herself, her experience, her story, then words wouldn't be sufficient. There was something about these handprints. If only one could read them, it's as if they could learn everything.

She was certain more than ever now that Brom had been trying to communicate something when he made the handprint in the cave. But what? What?

"It's so...honest." Aleena broke the silence.

"Yes, better than any portrait," Samin added.

Thissel was kneeling with his chin resting on his fist as he stared at his handprint. He was so engrossed, Herlot wondered if he knew that he was going to have paint all over his face.

She had spent much time among the Iptans now, and there was so much to question about them still and about their intentions. But right now, she realized that beneath the mysteries, the gold, the talents, the skills, they really were people. Even with the many certainties their statuses gave them in life, there was a part of them that wondered about the meaning of their own, unique handprint — as much as any other person. Right now, the courtyard was filled with individuals being curious, in wonder, and even being confused about him or herself.

She walked over to Movo, who had been leaving his handprints on the wall near a fountain. "What are you thinking?" she asked.

"I'm thinking that I'll never have enough time to know what all these patterns mean. It's like my handprint knows me better than I ever will myself."

"That's a good way of putting it. There's so much there, how much have we missed out on and will never know..."

"Gold! I want to do my feet. Help me," the medic yelled across the courtyard.

Herlot and Movo watched, laughing as Gold lifted the medic beneath the armpits and first dunked his feet into a bucket before swinging him up so that his feet made contact with the wall.

"Now take me for a walk!" the medic ordered.

Samin, Thissel, and Aleena now joined in on the laughter as Gold held the medic sideways as he walked across the wall.

They ended the evening in happy spirits. Herlot was sure everyone felt a thread of kinship of a sort as they said good-night to one another with bashful smiles, as if they had revealed precious secrets about themselves.

When Movo and she returned to their room, Herlot crawled onto Movo's mattress with a book and rested her head on his chest.

She yawned loudly as she opened the book.

"Sounds like you're finally ready to sleep."

"Yes, but I really want to end the night with a story."

"Oh?"

"Yes... you know those places that felt so unknown in the handprints? Well, I could be wrong, but perhaps we can find out more about it through our imagination, and there's nothing like a children's story for a healthy dose of imagination."

And then she started reading from the children's book. It was about a fairy without wings who had to climb to the tip of the tallest blade of grass in order to find her way back home. Herlot read until she didn't know if she was still reading out loud, or if her voice had continued to speak into the first kind dreams she had since learning of Felix's plans for Eraska.

Chapter 17

The Handprint

I t was the evening before their escape. Herlot and Movo were going back to their room after their last Iptan dinner. Aleena had arranged a harp player, and the music was still playing as Herlot closed the door behind them.

Herlot went to the corner and poured water into a bowl. Then she splashed her face and leaned over, letting the water dribble off her face. Tomorrow was only the distance of a night away, the day she had been waiting for would soon be a reality in her present.

"We need to sharpen these," Movo said, referring to their daggers.

She remembered the sounds of weapons being sharpened in the caves. All the effort the Eraskans had put into learning to fight was now for nothing. How could she return home and tell her people that after all the hiding and training, and being pushed beyond their limits, they were going to run?

She took the mirror and gazed at her reflection. No matter how long she looked, she could not see a woman who would run away. She could practically hear Felix laughing as he burned Eraska into ashes. What would her reflection look like then? She'd forever see someone who abandoned the land she loved.

"We're better than him," she said.

"What was that?" Movo said.

"If we had the armor, we would win the war."

Before Movo could respond, she was racing out the door and down the stairs.

I have to try. I have to.

She bumped right into Gold as she was running down the stairs to the library.

"Herlot, what's the rush?"

"I need to see Samin and Aleena right now, do you know where their room is?"

"Why, yes, of course. I'll take you right to them."

She shifted her weight from foot to foot as Gold knocked on a door at the other side of the courtyard.

"Herlot, Gold, what—" Aleena started.

Herlot pushed past her and stumbled into a sculpture as she headed toward the center of the room. She realized it was a sculpture of Samin as she steadied it from tumbling over. Then she caught sight of the ceiling. There must have been thousands of framed golden squares, each with a painting on the inside. There were all sorts of animals—elephants, parrots, snakes, and people she didn't recognize, and large, pyramid-shaped structures. The space smelled of a sweet wood that calmed her racing thoughts. Then she noticed a bubbling sound and turned just as Samin was wrapping a robe around his body next to a private bath.

She cleared her throat and looked into each of their eyes before speaking. "Please, if there is anything you could do to help my people get armor, I am begging you, help us," Herlot said.

Aleena and Gold sat down next to Samin, who was now sitting on a cushioned seat that could sit at least fifteen people.

Aleena and Samin eyed one another, and Gold stared down at his hands folded in his lap.

Herlot fell to her knees. "Please, I am begging you. If not armor, weapons. I know you have weapons capable of wiping Felix's army out. I know you have magic. You can change the weather and manipulate lights in a way that should not be possible. Please, I don't need to know Ipta's secrets, I just need the tools."

Samin sighed. "Herlot, I can't. Our resources are spread too far as it is."

She gritted her teeth. "That's not true. You are currently fighting no wars or battles."

"But we will if we take such a bold stand against Felix," Aleena said.

"Supposedly, from what I've heard, you could sack this city in a day," Herlot said.

"Our orders are not to disturb the peace in Damalathum."

"Why? Because your sky watchers would lose a nice view of the sky?"

Aleena cleared her throat. "Herlot—"

Herlot raised her hand. "Stop. I don't want to hear the excuse. I'm already disappointed enough as it is."

A silence followed. Herlot looked around at the room. There were luxuries here that she could not even name. Everything was gilded in gold, even the window frame and curtains. "What good is having all of this gold and power if you can't help a friend in need when they need it?" she wondered out loud. "And we are friends, aren't we?"

"It's not what you think," Gold said, having spoken for the first time. "There is a larger threat. Upon all of us, not just Ipta, not just Damalathum, and not just Eraska. All of us, all the kingdoms, and all the lands without kingdoms."

Herlot raised an eyebrow. *What was he talking about?* "Go on," she said.

"Gold—" Aleena started.

"No, she deserves to hear this," Gold said. "They're not just watching any old stars in the sky. They're watching the dark star. Most people can't see it, only some are born with the ability. It's a star that tells the future."

"And what future does it see?" she asked.

Gold eyed her suspiciously.

"Just like that, you believe this?" Samin asked.

Herlot almost rolled her eyes. Stars that told the future were nothing compared to what she had experienced. "I do. Gold?"

"Beasts. Giant, winged, dark beasts will descend upon our world. For years we have been preparing to fight them. We'll need every man and weapon we have. Everyone will. But no matter how many weapons we make, the watchers still see the same future. The beasts will defeat all of us. So we make more and more until the future tilts in our favor, hopefully before this vision becomes a reality. That ship you are to board has a crew searching for new materials to make weapons. There are many Iptans searching the world, as we speak, for something that might be able to tip the odds to our advantage."

Herlot's stomach churned. Movo had been right about the war in the skies. She dipped her hand into a water bowl sitting on a marble column. She scooped the water that had rose petals floating in it, and took a sip.

"That's for hand washing," Samin mumbled.

The water could have been for barn animals, she couldn't care less at the moment. The same fear she had felt in the bathing chamber filled her veins. This darkness, these beasts that Gold spoke about, were they of the same nature? "You need to tell them. Everyone. Everyone in this city. Everyone in every kingdom and all those in between," she said.

"They will think it's an Iptan ploy," Samin said.

"Why would Ipta need ploys?" Herlot asked.

"It's a nice way of taking control of land without having to fight for it," Gold said.

"Then tell them and leave. You could go and tell Felix now. It would stop him from attacking Eraska and give us all time to prepare."

Samin chuckled. "Herlot, you have learned so much about the world outside of your kingdom, but you have not yet fully realized something. Most of these people are too busy fighting for gold and power to care about their own life. If I tell King Felix about the beasts, he will only see it as Ipta being occupied with a problem, a sign of weakness. He will use it to his advantage and start another war, one none of us should be wasting time on now."

"Yet you agree with his intent to start a war with my land?" Herlot said.

"Of course not. But like we said before, we are not in a position to lend military help," Samin said.

Herlot nodded. "Very well." If this was true, and that awful feeling in her belly told her that it very well might be, Ipta had to focus their forces on finding a way to protect the world against the beasts. Or would they only protect them-selves? Was she really in a situation where even if she did manage to win a war against Felix, and then blend a leaf onto a tree to save a world of unicorns, there still lurked a more powerful enemy? Would it ever end?

"Asm and Seum..." she said. "Is that what they were doing this whole time? Looking for something that might help fight the beasts?"

"Yes," Aleena said.

Another thing Movo had been right about. She tilted her head back and stared at the ceiling. *Skies, please keep my Devotio safe from Seum and Asm.*

"That leads me to a very important question, Herlot. Does Eraska have something special that would cause Samin and Asm to stay there for so long?"

Unicorns. "Yes, it does. People. Lots of very good people. You don't think that was enough to make them stop and help?"

She would never forgive Seum and Asm for fooling them. Her thoughts jumped to the cave room with the unicorn paintings that Seum had shown her. How much did he know?

The room began to spin. She splashed her face with more rosewater, quickly said goodbye to the Iptans, and ran back to Movo.

* * *

"If Ipta is hoarding their resources, then it must be serious," Movo said. They sat together at the windowsill, watching the sun set into the city's buildings and wall. "Then again, I have yet to see proof of any winged creatures like this, including your unicorn." He smiled gently.

"When I think about these creatures, I see a magic and unicorns, but the exact opposite of what Devotio and his family are. I feel the same thing I felt in the bathing chamber, and it's real, the most terrifying kind of real one could imagine."

Herlot felt Movo's palm on her thigh. "One catastrophe at a time. Tonight we focus on our escape. Then we focus on Eraska. After that, the leaf, and, if by some miracle we're still standing, then we focus on evil, winged creatures. And who knows, perhaps these dark star watchers are not well in the head, and it may turn out we have peace sooner than later after all. What causes my doubt in this story is that they have been preparing for this war for at least two decades now and nothing has unfolded. These headquarters were built for the sky watchers, and that was before my birth."

Herlot sighed. "It makes me worry, though. I was so hopeful that Ipta's Emperor might be able to blend, but now I doubt it. Surely he'd be able to have a better plan against these creatures if he did have these capabilities..."

"It doesn't matter if he can or not. You're going to be the one to do it. I know it."

It was Herlot's turn to smile. "You don't know how much it means to know that you believe in me so much."

The air seemed to thicken between them and Herlot's heart began to race. All of a sudden she felt incredibly shy as she felt Movo's gaze upon her.

She felt his fingers under her chin, lifting it ever so slightly so she couldn't avoid his eyes.

Right then someone knocked on the door.

She closed her eyes as Movo brushed the back of his fingers against her cheek and then proceeded toward the door. Torchlight shone into their dark room and she saw Gold standing at the door.

"I hope I'm not interrupting," he said. "I didn't have a chance to say goodbye. And there's something I would like to give to both of you."

Herlot slid off the windowsill and walked over to them. Gold handed her a satchel. She swung it over her shoulder and opened it to see what was inside. She let out a sigh of relief.

"What is it?" Movo said.

"One of Ipta's best-kept secrets," she said as she stared at the three balls wrapped in fabric.

Gold chuckled. "It may not be the armor and weapons you were hoping for, but I want you to have them in case you run into any trouble tomorrow. Needless to say, these should never find their way into the hands of someone capable of deciphering the ingredients and proportion, so you must promise to stay alive until you use all three. We wouldn't want Felix using them to his advantage."

"Gold, I don't know what to say," Herlot said.

"Don't say anything. Listen. This one—smoke. That one—fire. And this one here, you use as a last resort. It will take down at least a quarter of their perimeter around the city."

Herlot nodded. "Smoke, fire, last resort. Understood."

Gold turned to Movo. "What do you say, Movo? One last round?"

"I'll meet you in the courtyard," Movo said.

Once they both disappeared down the stairs into the courtyard, she found a spot on the balcony where she could watch. She leaned over the railing as the first clank of the swords sounded. She knew Gold had arranged this more for her than for Movo. She needed to be put at ease that Movo was able to hold his own tomorrow. His form and speed had improved since they had arrived, but he still was not the same fighter she had met in Eraska. She cringed as Gold disarmed Movo and his sword went spinning into a nearby tree. Gold put his hand on Movo's shoulder. His lips were moving but she was too far away to hear what he was saying.

She gripped the railing of the balcony the moment they started to fight. Movo's sword whistled through the air with a fluid grace. There was a lightness to his movements, as if he had previously fought while bearing a weight on his shoulders. His strikes weren't explosive with fierce freedom like the Iptan style, but they were quick and fluid. It was beautiful.

A couple and a family of three who had been going for a walk on the paths that wound through the courtyard stopped to watch. Herlot gritted her teeth as Gold attacked with more power. However, Movo struck back almost instantaneously after blocking the attack.

And then it happened for the first time. Movo swiftly took a step forward, his foot wedged behind Gold's, and the next thing that she knew, Gold was on his back, and the tip of Movo's sword was pointed at his neck.

He did it. The family clapped and Movo looked up and met Herlot's gaze. He winked.

Herlot took in the entire premises of the Iptan Headquarters. It would never be a home, and she still had not reached a point of clarity about the Iptans, but she had made friendships here, ones that she would not forget. Soon she and her people would be living among the Iptans, and her time here had at least given her enough evidence that they wouldn't be harmed once they arrived in Ipta.

She was just about to return to her room when she noticed a shadow move on the other side of the courtyard, directly across from her balcony. She waited for her eyes to adjust, and that's when she noticed them. Three people wearing telescopes on their backs, and the man she had only seen once before on their first day, the one Samin had signaled just before it began to rain.

Then, as if they had become aware of her noticing them, they retreated into a room.

Herlot sorted through her memories of their time spent in the Headquarters. She didn't know if she was imagining it, but she could practically see flashes of these four at a corner table near the breakfast line, passing by a bookshelf she was examining, on a balcony hidden mostly by the tree leaves while she trained, or purchasing flowers at a stand at the market. And then, she even pictured them in the crowd at their near execution.

The nerve tonic must be getting to me, she thought. But she remembered the maps of Ipta and how their borders expanded at a slow and even pace. Patience. Could they have been watching her this entire time?

* * *

The moment she slipped her dress over her head and it settled into place, Eraska finally felt tangible. Soon her feet would walk the land. Soon she could touch the bark of its trees, even if for one last time. Soon she would embrace her family. Wearing her dress felt as if she was announcing to the world that she was ready to come home.

She wiggled into her leggings and then got to work at tightening several belts around her legs where she would keep her knives hidden. As she worked, she became aware that there was one thing different about her clothing. It smelled Iptan. She was grateful that the blood stains and sweat had been washed out thoroughly, but these clothes would be somewhat different now. Wool that had once been woven by her mother had traveled across the sea and been handled by people her mother would have never met.

She checked the button on the pouch she had sewn onto the skirt of her dress, the one holding the three globes Gold had given her, to make sure it was secure. Lastly, she folded the Iptan garments she had been given by Aleena and placed them on a chair. She wanted to take them, but they were heavy for clothing, and she couldn't risk taking anything else that might slow her down.

Movo had one leg up on the chair, fastening the last belt around his legs. "Sun is about to rise. Now or never."

Without exchanging another word, they left their room and headed into the courtyard. At the steps leading out of the Headquarters stood an Iptan they hadn't met before. "The street is clear, you are safe to leave," he said.

Swiftly they crossed the bridge and found themselves on Damalathum's street.

"This way," Movo said.

Herlot followed him down the street and into an alley. From what she remembered on the map, there were three more turns they would have to make before reaching the part of the city with the pothole they had to climb into. From there they would follow a complicated route through the sewage tunnels until they reached an opening into the moat. Then, when the sun set, and if things went by plan, a group of Iptans, not archers, would be stationed right above them pretending to look at the sky. From there, all they'd have left to do is jump into the moat, avoid the spikes at the bottom, climb out, cross a vast field into the forest, find a boat hidden behind a bush, and row to the Iptan ship without being spotted. Simple. Herlot wiped a bead of sweat off her brow.

Movo stopped at the end of an alley and glanced both ways onto the street they were about to enter. "No soldiers, as planned."

The Iptans tracked where and when soldiers were stationed; however, there was always the chance that some things didn't go by schedule. So far, the schedule was on their side.

"That's the pothole." Movo pointed down the street. "Ready?"

"Yes."

Herlot's heart started pounding faster the moment they stepped onto the street. So close to safety. In moments they'd be hidden underneath the city with nothing to worry about until sundown. She increased her pace. "Slow down," Movo said. "No need to rush and attract attention."

There weren't that many people out. She kept her focus on her feet, but she could sense the presence of them. A little chatter to her right. Footsteps to her left. Someone singing from an open window. Horse hoofs. Wheels turning over the cobblestones.

"Whoa...whoa!"

Herlot's eyes shot up and her breath caught in her chest as she watched a man standing on a carriage pulling on the reins as he tried to maneuver his horses away from a woman walking in the street. It happened fast, but to Herlot the next motions seemed never ending because she felt Eraska slip farther and farther away from her as the carriage wobbled on just two wheels and then toppled on its side. Right by the pothole.

"No," she cried. Herlot could not stop herself staring at the wheels of the carriage still turning, as if they understood the urgency of moving the carriage away from the pothole. She couldn't believe their plan had failed right at the beginning.

Movo nudged her and kept walking as if nothing had happened while more people appeared on the street, many from the doors of the surrounding buildings, to check on the people in the carriage. Calmly, Movo turned into another alley, this one with such uneven cobblestones that most people would avoid.

"With that many people right around the spot, we'll never climb in unseen," Herlot said. She looked around her nervously, feeling completely exposed, like ducks in the center of a pond surrounded by hunters. They needed somewhere to hide. Light began to fill some of the shadows of the alley. The sun. If they waited any longer they'd have to climb into the pothole in broad daylight. It wasn't going to work. "Can we make it back to the Headquarters?"

"We'd have to circle around..." Movo said. He took out one of his maps. "But if we go back, the plan is over. We'd have to wait until evening to enter the pothole, and by the time we make it to the wall the skywatchers will be replaced by archers. From what Samin told me, their agreement requires schedules to be set at least a week before."

"Another pothole," Herlot said. "We can find another one. Where is another one?"

She grabbed the map from Movo. Her nerves were on fire and her inner voice yelled at her to focus. "Why aren't they marked on here? You know this city, where is another one?" More light made its way on the map.

She looked up at Movo and noticed how the sun shone on his face, the Prince's piercing blue eyes recognizable amid the cover of the cloak.

"Are you lost?"

They both looked up at a woman on the balcony holding a child on her hip. "Darling, why don't you go downstairs and help these people. They seem lost," she called to someone inside.

Movo snatched the map from Herlot. "The tower," he said.

He took hold of her hand, and once again they were on the move. Eraska seemed to be shouting to her from the tunnels underneath the city. The longer the distance grew between them and the pothole, the louder the shouting was.

They took a right at the end of the alley, and the tower Herlot had noticed before came into view. Being close to it now made her understand why people didn't want to go into it. It looked so fragile that a gust of wind could make it topple over.

They climbed the steps and stopped in front of a tall wooden door. Movo pulled on a metal ring near the center and cursed. "It's locked."

Movo pulled out a knife and began to fumble with the lock. Herlot buried her face against his shoulder as if it could hide the fear emanating from her. She was sure people around them could sense it and would know they were up to something suspicious.

"Out of all the places, I didn't expect to find you two here," a childish voice said from behind. "Looking for a key?"

Fabian pushed his way between them. He slapped Movo's hand aside. "Master would be very upset if this lock was broke." The miracle child pushed a key into the lock, turned it, and creaked the door open. "Quickly, unless you have more tricks under your belt to save you from a hanging."

Herlot rushed in, and once the door was closed behind them, she stared at Fabian, absolutely dumbfounded. By Movo's silence, she knew he felt the same.

Fabian grinned up at them, showing off a loose tooth.

Movo ran his hand over his beard and then to the back of his neck. "I'm starting to believe those fortunetellers who always say the ancestors are watching over you. Wish they had an explanation for why ours are consistently sending a little child."

"Because they're smart. Hey, that means they're probably Herlot's," Fabian said.

"You're not supposed to disrespect them," Movo said, appalled.

"I have no respect for anyone who had anything to do with our King," Fabian said, his back straightening. Then his features softened. "The Queen, however... well, alright, apologies Movo's ancestors. I didn't mean what I said."

An urge to touch Movo took over Herlot as she watched his features sink at the mention of his mother. He looked down at his feet. "Is there any news of her?" he asked.

"None! Just like the two of you, they haven't been able to find her. My boys and I haven't seen a sign of her anywhere either. And we usually know when new vagabonds join the city, we know every nook and corner. Have to when you're constantly running from guards who want to put you in a dungeon." Fabian stood on his toes to tap Movo on his shoulder. "She must have gotten out."

"Or Felix is holding her prisoner in the castle," Movo said. He turned and walked to a window and looked out into the street.

Herlot's heart hurt for him. If only they could know what had happened to Queen Magdalene.

"Anybody home?" Fabian called toward the top of the tower.

Herlot finally took a moment to look around. There was a winding spiral staircase that went all the way up to the top of the tower. All around it were platforms with shelves filled with all sorts of books and gadgets. Movo had mentioned before that this was where old and useless junk was stored.

All of a sudden, several heads appeared from one of the platforms. "Fabian, is that you?"

"Come down here, there's two people I'd like you to meet."

"Fabian, is that Herlot of Alonia?" one of the boys shouted.

Herlot waved back at one of them.

"And ex-Prince Movo?"

"Come down and see!" Fabian shouted back.

Herlot watched the group of boys rush down the spiraling staircase and she wondered how they managed not to get dizzy.

"Rotten Felix fingers, you weren't lying when you said you really met them!" One of the boys circled Herlot. He stopped and smiled up at her. "Hello!"

Herlot giggled. "Hello, nice to meet all of you."

Several of them blushed, especially the one who had taken a seat on a stair, letting his legs dangle off the edge.

"Movo, would you like to say hello?" Herlot said. He was still looking out the window, as if deep in thought. He turned his head for a quick moment, said a greeting and went back to looking out the window. Only a few of the boys responded, and they all seemed to huddle closer together, as if afraid.

"He's not going to kill you," Fabian whispered, but not quiet enough for Herlot not to overhear. Now she understood. All these children knew about what Movo had done to get out of the dungeons.

"Listen up, here's the plan," Fabian said. "Thomas, you lead the boys over to Mallory's favorite shoe-shining spot. There's a pothole there that our friends need to get into. Figure out a way to create a distraction to clear any people out of that area of the street."

"How do you know that we need to get into the pothole?" Herlot asked.

"I was paid to keep an eye on you," Fabian said.

"By who?" Movo said, his voice raised. The other boys cringed and Herlot was sure they were about to run away.

"Calm your horses, Prince. A nice Iptan lady. She thought you both might need some help."

"Aleena," Herlot said with a smile.

"That's just great. How did she think the help of a street child would do us any good?" Movo said under his breath.

Herlot watched Fabian's face fall. "The same reason why she trusted me to help you the first time. I'm more skilled than you think I am."

Herlot's jaw dropped, and she and Movo made eye contact.

"Fabian, did I understand correctly that Aleena had you help us before we ever made it to the Iptan Headquarters?" Herlot asked.

Fabian nodded.

"They were watching us from the moment we entered this city. They were practically expecting us," Movo said.

Herlot swallowed. She was wishing more and more that they had another option aside from Ipta's ship to get back home, and then somewhere else to get the Eraskans to safety.

"Why didn't you tell us this before?" Movo asked.

"She asked me not to," Fabian replied.

Herlot shook her head. It was as if Ipta had their eyes everywhere. Was there some way they could have overheard the private conversations between her and Movo?

"Hey, where is Mallory anyway?" Fabian asked.

"He hasn't come back yet... he'll make it back, though!" one of the boys replied with forced cheer.

"Yeah, Mallory wouldn't let those geezer guards catch him," Thomas added. "Now let's clear that street for this lot."

Movo grew pale at the comment. She observed him closely as Fabian ordered his friends outside the tower on their mission. She could not read his expression and wished she had the willingness to ask, but she feared that it was not her place. A presence emanated from him that seemed to warn her not to even try. He stared out the window after the boys as they made their leave. She herself didn't know how to cope with the guilt of having children risk being thrown in one of Felix's dungeons for the sake of helping them.

She decided it best to leave Movo alone. With that she climbed the spiraling staircase, wishing to look at some of the things stored away in the tower.

"Don't go too far. We need to be ready to leave at any moment," Movo said.

"Mhmm." She realized she was gripping the stairwell harder than she meant to. She couldn't protect Eraska from Felix, she certainly couldn't protect the people of his own city from him. How she wished they could take the children with them.

She stepped off on one of the platforms and made her way over to one of the bookshelves. She ran her hand over the sides to swipe the dust off in order to see the titles. "Interesting," she said, as she realized they were in a language she did not understand. She opened one of them and smiled. It looked like a children's story. There were drawings of fairies on some of the pages, and some of the first letters were decorated with butterflies. She wondered why such a beautiful book would be hiding in a tower, far away from anyone who knew the language that it was written in.

If it were up to her, she would get on a ship and take it to the people that knew the language. A sadness sat on her shoulders at the thought. She wasn't in a world where magnificent things like ships would ever be used to take a children's book to someone. Ships in her world were used for wars. Her thought turned to the unicorns. Would there ever be a time safe enough for them to return? That's what it would take after all. A world where ships were used to transport children's books.

She slammed the book shut and put it back on the shelf.

She climbed the staircase another level. This one was filled with drawings and sketches, some so unwanted that they were scattered on the floor with dirty footprints on them. She sat down on the floor cross-legged and picked up a batch of papers. They seemed to be a collection of nature drawings. Forests, plants, fields. A tree was drawn with such skill that it made her feel as if her nose was right up to its bark. She stacked them and put them back on a shelf. Stopping a moment to sneeze from all the dust. She climbed up another level.

More shelves. More gadgets. There was a podium-like object in a corner with a glass cover. Curious, she made her way over to it. She frowned as she got a closer look at the drawing underneath the glass cover and then gasped. "It can't be," she said. She rushed to the railing and leaned over it. "Fabian! Come up here!" she called, and then hurried back. She lifted the glass cover and set it down and picked up the parchment to hold up by a window.

"Unbelievable." Several sketches of a cave. One with unicorns painted on it. It was the exact same paintings that were in the room Seum had taken her to in Eraska. Underneath one of them was a handprint, the exact spot where someone had carved out a piece of the cave wall. On the right side of the parchment was a detailed sketch of the handprint, with lines and writing pointing to particular parts of the palm.

"What is it?" Fabian asked, as he bounced his way over to her side.

"Do you know anything about this? Did you not say the master of this tower lets you stay here? Where is he?"

Fabian stood on his tiptoes to get a closer look. She lowered the parchment so he could see. "Ahh... this. It was several years back when a man visited my master to show a piece of stone that he had brought with him from some place across the sea. I remember them calling on a palm reader to decipher the handprint that was painted on it. They didn't get very far."

"Where is the stone now, Fabian?"

"I think the man took it with him."

"Where is your master?"

"I do not know. He left several days ago and has not been back since."

Herlot ran her hand through her hair and looked closer at the writing.

"Tell me about this palm reader," she said.

"Well, it's quite strange. She's able to look at people's palms and tell them about their life."

Herlot studied the notes. *A life spent fixing a catastrophe without success.*

Herlot had a sudden urge to put her hand over the sketch of the handprint, as if doing so would resemble being able to touch the actual handprint on the stone.

Warmth seemed to emanate from the drawing onto her palm. "What's your name," she whispered, as if she was greeting the person before shaking their palm. She could feel the name inside her chest, and her mind was fighting to find a word to match it. She ran her finger along one of the lines. And then it happened. As clearly as if she were speaking to a person right in front of her, a voice began to speak. *I am old, sick, and wounded, but most of all I need your help. I have awoken a dark creature, dangerous beyond anyone's belief. If you are one who walks this world with a golden heart, I give you the responsibility that I was too weak to accomplish in my time. It took me years, but I believe to have found a way to stop it.*

And then the voice stopped. She opened her eyes and looked down at her finger where it had come across a spot where the ink had smudged.

"What's happened?" She turned around to see Movo climb over the railing.

She held up the parchment for him to see, still unable to speak about what had just happened. He skimmed it and then looked into her eyes, asking for an explanation.

"It's a drawing of the room with the unicorn paintings in the cave. Th-the sketch of the palm print speaks. It's Brom. The same man whose footprints I have been s-stepping in."

She tried to take a deep breath, but it caught in her throat.

Movo stared at her. "What did it—he say?"

"Hey!!! Where are you lot hiding? It's time!" one of the boys shouted from below.

Herlot rolled the parchment and slid it into a pocket in her cape.

"He was speaking of a dark creature," she said as they ran down the steps. "And how he found a way to fight it. Then, it stopped."

"What else?"

"You both are stranger than I thought," Fabian chimed.

"He needed someone with a golden heart to do it," Herlot said. "Fabian, do you have any idea where the man with the stone could have gone? Think, please, if there's anything you can remember."

"I'm sorry, I don't. We would have to ask my master."

"Maybe we should wait," Herlot said when they reached the bottom of the stairs.

"And miss the ship?" Movo asked.

Herlot bit her lip. She couldn't believe she was suggesting it, but the urgency she had felt in the palm print seemed crucially important, just as much as returning to Eraska. She had to find the stone and learn more.

"Herlot, are you absolutely serious?" Movo asked. "Are you certain, absolutely certain your vision was real?"

She pulled at her hair. "I don't know. I don't know." She took a breath and couldn't believe the words that followed and came from her own mouth. "That darkness I felt... I think that's what he is talking about." She hugged herself, as if having to protect herself from what she was speaking about.

He put both of his hands on top of her shoulders. "Are you certain? You know what this would mean... if we miss the ship, I don't know when our next chance will be to escape. And my father is coming for Eraska. Perhaps we could hide on one of his ships…"

The list of matters was unmanageable. Escape Felix. Blend leaves. Fight a dark creature that nobody had ever seen before based off of a handprint. Herlot put her hand over her heart. *What is most important right now?*

"Time to go," she said with certainty. "This will have to wait."

"Good choice," Fabian said.

Within moments they were back to following Fabian through alleys. At the corner of each one, he'd stick his head out, check for soldiers, and then motion to them that the coast was clear.

Finally, they were just steps away from the pothole.

"What's the plan?" Herlot asked as she stared at the busy street. There were people everywhere, unlike in the early morning. There was no possible way someone wouldn't notice them climbing into a pothole.

"Just wait. Maven and Randall should be making their way here any moment now."

Herlot noticed Thomas standing in the alley opposite of them, looking down the street as if waiting for something.

"Please give our thanks to your friends," Herlot said.

At that Fabian turned around to face her. For the first time, his playful look was not present. His eyes were wide and hopeful. "Take me with you."

"Absolutely not," Movo said.

"I could be helpful. I can help fight even. You have seen how useful I can be."

"Fabian, your home though, your parents—" Herlot started.

"I can't see them anyway! It's too dangerous. Every day I spend here is just about hiding so I don't have to go in Felix's dungeons."

"You have the master of the tower, though. You have friends. Eraska is going to be dangerous when we return there, and we don't know what our journey away from there will be like," Herlot said.

"Yes, but at least I wouldn't be trapped in his city. I can't even leave here. They would check my arm the moment I'd try to cross the bridge over the moat."

"Fabian, we have to get across that moat, too, tonight and there's a chance that the archers will see us. I'd rather have you hiding in here for the time being than dead out there," Herlot said. She hated having to let him down.

"Fabian," she said. "Once my people are prepared to fight Felix, I promise you, he will never be a threat to you again."

Fabian's shoulders shuddered, as if he was holding back a sob. "Tell your people to fight for us too. For me and my friends and every child born in this city."

"We promise," Movo said.

Fabian nodded with approval at Movo. Then, Thomas in the alley held two fingers up in the air.

"Here we go," Fabian said.

Herlot watched as a tall figure, also wearing a cape, appeared on the street. He seemed to have troubles balancing, and would stagger to one side for a moment before continuing on a straight course.

"They need to work on that," Fabian said. "I wonder if Maven is on Randall's shoulders or the other way around."

Thomas slipped out onto the street. He whistled as he walked with a skip in his step, heading toward the boys sitting on each other's shoulders. Then, the caped figure tripped and fell over.

"Perfect execution," Fabian said.

Thomas ran over and lifted the hood of the fallen "person."

"Crowpox! Crowpox! Everyone, run!" Thomas shouted.

Herlot couldn't believe the chaos that broke out in the street. People shouted for help and ran in a frenzy in all directions.

Herlot looked up at Movo. "Why are they running away from him if they're protected by the elixir?" She knew that the supposed crowpox victim was actually two healthy young boys, but the other people didn't, and they supposedly could not catch crowpox. Why would they run from a sick person with an illness they were safe from? "Movo, they are terrified from something they're safe from." She didn't know how to wrap her mind around it.

"The elixir doesn't protect against fear and its power to take hold of the mind's reins," Movo said.

Seum had taught Herlot to transform her fear into freedom. But right before her eyes she was seeing the power of the emotion, even when there was no danger in sight.

"Would you run?" she asked.

"No."

"I wouldn't either."

At least she hoped she wouldn't. Was there something she was afraid of that did not even exist?

"Now!" Fabian shouted.

Another one of his friends, whom Herlot had no idea where he had been hiding before, was already holding up the cover to the pothole.

"We wish you safe travels!" the boy said as Herlot readied to climb in.

She swung her legs in first and then slid inside, not knowing when she would find ground. It wasn't as far down as she had imagined, but enough to send a shock through her body as she landed on the slimy ground. In a moment, Movo was at her side.

She looked up and waved to Fabian, a knot forming in her chest as the lid blocked out the sight of his face and the daylight. They were in complete darkness, and all that could be heard was the trickle of water and their breathing.

She listened to Movo scramble for something. She heard the strike of a match, and then his face lit up behind the flame. He held the match to a candle. A faint smile appeared on his face. "We made it," he said.

"We made it," she said. Saying that made her feel as if their chance of surviving the run across the field could be accomplished too.

They sloshed through the tunnels without exchanging a word. Only the occasional squeak of a rat accompanied them, along with the dim glow of the candlelight. The entire time Herlot searched for words to say to Movo. She didn't know if she wanted to ask him a question, or tell him something. For a moment she thought she might just need to think out loud about the parchment they had found, but no, this was specifically something different, something specifically to him about...them?

"What else did you see on that parchment?" Movo asked.

The words echoed around the tunnel.

"I didn't see anything, per se. I held my hand to it, and I could hear Brom speak. He was speaking of a dark creature, and needing a golden-hearted person to fight it. He said he knew how to fight it, and then I couldn't hear anything else."

"We never learned how Brom lost the gold in his heart, and how that made everyone else lose their gold too. What if—" Movo stepped aside to let a rat run by. "What if that's why you always seemed to step onto his footprints? You're the first golden-hearted person since his time. What if his memories, or whatever is imprinted into his footsteps and handprint, knows that and calls out to you?"

"Movo, think long and hard about what you're saying to me..."

"And that *thing* you experienced in the chamber. Herlot..."

"Stop. I am not destined to fight some dark creature that no one has ever heard of. Holy Basil, Movo, listen to yourself. Part of me almost wishes you didn't believe my story. You haven't even questioned once this entire time whether or not this dark creature is even real."

"Alright. I'll stop."

Part of her wanted to take the parchment out of her pocket and leave it in the tunnel to be eaten by a rat.

"My life is not an Alonian fantasy story about monsters," she said.

"It is not."

"Exactly. And there's a limit to magic."

"A definite limit."

"Stop trying to calm me down."

Movo chuckled.

"This isn't funny."

She brushed her bangs out of her face, as if it could help her see more clearly. She couldn't believe the thoughts that were going through her mind. Her entire life she had been fascinated by magic. But if for once she were put into a position where life actually asked her what she wanted, the first thing that came to her mind was the couple whom she had seen at the morning market who were walking with their elbows hooked together. The most wonderful adventure she could think of right now was to wake up to a day busy with feeding chickens and thrashing wheat, and then to end the day sitting by a fire listening to stories, perhaps next to someone she deeply cared for, a very specific someone.

Sounded a lot like Alonia. She scolded herself for thinking these thoughts. How dare she have wishes like this when there were so many more important things at risk?

After a time that felt like eternity, a faint orange light began to join them in the darkness. Up ahead, she saw the opening to the moat and a glimpse of the sunset. Once they reached a few steps before the edge, they stopped. Movo blew out the candle. All that was left was to wait for the sun to set. They had no way to tell if there were archers standing right above them, or if they were gone and replaced by Iptans.

Then Herlot focused in on the field. Just beyond it was a patch of woods, and beyond that the beach. Then the sea, then the Iptan ship that should be waiting for them, and then, far beyond that, Eraska—Devotio, Enri, Mahtreeh...Ambro. Last time she had seen her brother he had reminded her of a malnourished, thinning tree, and she had not been kind to him. She did not regret it, but she didn't know what to expect when they would see each other again. She was different, and he loved a traitor. She wondered what had happened to Manni. Was she in Damalathum as well? If only she knew where. Maybe it was better that way, because if she had known, she would have found a way to sneak out of the Headquarters just to finish what she wished she had been able to do the last night at the fortress of Eraska.

"I still don't understand what exactly it was Manni was trying to do when she told your people to wait for the wedding to invade," Herlot said. "You said that something was wrong with your memory?"

"Yes. Not one of my men was able to think logically. She appeared on our path and told us to wait. None of us stopped to question how she knew what we might be doing. And after that, it was like we all forgot that we had met her."

Herlot rubbed her fingers against one another, as if she were trying to untangle a long string of yarn that had tangled itself into several different knots. So many problems, yet they all felt tied together, as if they were all part of the same string—the unicorns, Felix, Brom, Manni, golden hearts, Ipta's war in the sky, the darkness that had engulfed her, and Brom's dark creature. If only she knew her instinct was right, and if it was right, if only she had the wisdom to know *how* it could be all connected.

Herlot looked at Movo's face and how it was lit up by the setting sun. She still didn't know what she wanted to say to him. She felt so much. Maybe there was another way. She raised her palm and touched the side of his face. She focused on each part of his sharp features, as if memorizing them. She ignored the curious look in his eyes, as if he didn't understand what she was doing. She realized that everything she wanted to say led to one thing—that she wanted to feel closer to him. There were so many things she wanted to learn about him, to really know who he was. He was like peeling an onion, and their time in Damalathum had given her time to learn that there was so much beneath the surface. Why did she feel that any opportunity she would have to learn more was over? That somehow her only chance had been during their time in the Iptan Headquarters, and now that was over?

The last glimmer of light disappeared from his face. She looked out of the tunnel and caught the last glimpse of sunlight before the sunset and night arrived in Damalathum.

Her mind cleared. Her sense of sight sharpened as her eyes adjusted to the darkness to make out the water below and the field.

"Can you hear anyone?" she asked Movo.

"No."

"Then it's now or never."

"Together?"

"Yes," she said.

They didn't count down. At the same time as Movo, she kicked off the ledge. For a moment it felt like she was floating, and then her feet made impact with the moat water. She began to kick the moment she felt it, knowing that if she sank too far down, she'd meet the spikes that were waiting to pierce any person attempting to invade the city. She felt something sharp grace the side of her leg. Close, but still safe.

Her head broke through the surface, and she swam toward the brick wall. Her heart sighed in relief at the sound of swimming right next to her. Movo had made it too.

She gripped at the brick with her fingertips and used every muscle strength in her body to climb. She grounded her footing and then sprang to reach her hand an inch higher. This was the most difficult task to accomplish with one hand. *Quicker. Faster.* Her knees scraped against the wall, but she didn't care. All she thought about was the possibility that someone above was noticing her right now and drawing his arrow. She gripped at the grass blades and pulled. Movo was already out and grabbed the back of her dress to help her climb out.

They didn't pause for a word. Herlot imagined what it was like to ride Devotio and forced her legs to run the same. Faster. Faster.

Bells. Shouts. Something buzzed right by her ear.

"Get down!" Movo shouted.

Herlot threw herself into the grass and began hauling herself forward using her elbow and knees.

Her heart screamed in agony as she heard Movo hiss in pain. She stole a glance and saw an arrow sticking out of the back of his leg, but he was still pushing forward.

She shouted as two arrows pierced the ground right in front of her, as she rolled to the side. More arrows, all around her. It was over. "Ah!" she cried as one grazed the side of her arm. She felt the blood trickle as she prepared for the next arrow. She wanted to close her eyes, as if that could stop what was happening.

And then the sun came back.

She was dead. She had to be. Too much light. She was surprised at how fast the arrow killed her, so fast that she didn't have time to feel pain.

Yet the ground was still underneath her. She looked up and rolled on her back in joy.

"Movo! Look!"

"I see it!" He was laughing as he sat up and broke off the end of the arrow. "I see it!"

All around them, to the left, to the right, above, was a swarm of fireflies only a child's heart could imagine. She lifted her legs and arm in the air and wiggled with joy as she squealed. No archer would be able to spot them. There had to be thousands and thousands of fireflies.

"Come." Movo grasped her hand and pulled her to her feet. He wrapped his arms around her and spun her in a circle. She lifted her arm and wove it through the air, gently touching the fireflies.

When her feet touched the ground, Movo's hands didn't release their grip from around her waist. She wrapped her arm around his neck.

She closed her eyes, engulfed in the warmth of his chest and the firefly glow. She sank into the feeling of his lips as they came together and couldn't help smiling as their kiss continued.

An arrow whizzed by her ear and they broke from their embrace. They were invisible, but that wouldn't stop the archers from shooting. They were probably making their way out onto the field at any moment.

"Is your leg alright?" she asked.

"Good enough," he said.

And once again, as they had done many times, they broke out into a sprint toward the cover of the trees, but this time not fearing for their lives. Herlot kicked off the ground and jumped into the air cheering, and even stopped to spin in a circle.

"Is this magic your doing?" Movo asked, a few paces ahead of her.

"I think it's unicorn magic!" She stopped in her tracks and looked around. "Devotio?" It couldn't be. He couldn't be that close. Yet it felt like he was there, watching somehow. "I'm almost home, Devotio." They had survived the most difficult part of their journey. It would be as easy as eating fresh berries by the handfuls from this point on.

She ran at a leisurely pace onto a path that led into the forest.

"Just a bit more and then we have to look for the boat," Movo said.

A few of the fireflies had followed them into the forest, just enough to make it easy for them to see where they were going.

"Can you explain any of this?" Movo asked as he pointed at the fireflies. Herlot sped up to run alongside him. "Devotio told me a story once about how the fireflies became, it was when Brom's unicorn Ola's heart shattered because she was so sad that he had not come back to her."

"Wonder where he had gone?" Movo said between breaths.

"Wherever he did go, it has to do something with how he lost the gold in his heart," Herlot said. They both jumped over a tree trunk.

"And it's most likely where he would have come into contact with this dark creature he warned about in his handprint."

"You sure can talk a lot while running," Herlot said.

"As can you." Movo slowed his pace. "That's the blueberry bush up there, I think."

Herlot prayed that they would find the boat hidden behind it as Ipta had promised. She could smell the ocean and hear the waves. They were so close to escaping.

As they approached the blueberry bush, Herlot picked a few berries as Movo stepped behind it.

"It's not here," he said.

"Maybe we're at the wrong bush," Herlot said. "Let's have a look around. There has to be more of these around here."

"You take this side, I'll search over there," Movo said.

Herlot walked farther into the woods and stepped over several logs with grace as she searched for another berry bush. Even though the soldiers could be following them, she sighed in relief to be surrounded by trees, ferns, wildflowers, and all the wonderful forest plants that she had missed.

"Just one moment of freedom," she said to herself, as she untied her boots. She hummed with pleasure as she spread her toes and sensed the wet soil beneath her heels. "Alright, boat, where are you?"

She wandered deeper into the woods.

"Find anything?" Movo called from afar.

"Raspberries," she said as she popped more berries into her mouth. She was so relaxed. How could that be after what they had just survived? "Must be the relief of survival," she mumbled to herself.

Even though she had eaten well in the Iptan Headquarters, fresh berries off the bush made her tongue feel as if it was awakening from a long sleep. A comforting warmth spread in her torso. It reminded her of eating a warm Eraskan potato and leek stew.

Then she stopped in her tracks as she realized the heat was concentrated in her chest.

"Movo!"

More heat. A footprint. Her foot adjusted to match its angle. Flashes of past memories. A blue dress. The hollowed-out oak tree. Chasing a unicorn out onto the field. The cave with the unicorn paintings. *My name is Brom. May I share a memory with you?* a voice said.

You couldn't have picked a worst time, Herlot thought. She should be looking for the boat, not blending with Brom's memory. But what had Brom been doing here so far from Eraska? And what if she missed an opportunity to learn about the dark creature? How long would it be before she could come back here? They were heading to Ipta, on the other side of the world. She had called for Movo. He had to be approaching soon and would shake her out of the blending. She could at least see a bit of what Brom had experienced here at this time.

Before her mind could analyze anymore, her heart spoke: yes. And then she opened her eyes, and before she knew it, her legs took off without her influence into a fast run.

Oh, no. No, Brom, stop! Never before had Brom's memory begun with a run. How stupid could she have been to not have thought of this possibility. This was bad.

She paid attention to the second strand of thoughts running through her mind. Yes, she recognized Brom's voice, but he was thinking incredibly fast, and she could not decipher the words. She had to calm down and focus. *Alright, Brom, what are you doing and where are you taking me? And most of all, how do I get you to stop?* The fact that any moment she could run right into a soldier's arms followed her like a lightning bolt ready to strike.

She was able to make out more words in Brom's thoughts, scattered as they were. He was rushing, that she was certain of, and fearful, yes, fearful.

What if she goes into the field before I get there? I was supposed to be there yesterday.

So she knew that he was rushing to meet someone. But what field? And why would that be a problem?

What if she took off her blindfold?

A-ha. So he was meeting a golden-hearted human, just as he had Emrys. Was this another person he had found who could hide unicorns? Now she had to know whom he was going to meet. Any moment she, or he, *or they,* would arrive. After all, how long could he keep running like this?

Brom slowed his pace, but didn't stop, nor did the memory. As much as she wanted to see who he was going to meet, she was now far away from the spot where she was supposed to be looking for the boat.

Brom! I need to leave!

He ignored her. Of course, he did, he was a memory with no respect for her needs whatsoever. This was the longest she had ever been stuck in a memory.

She remembered the sense of warmth in her chest. Was her gold flowing this entire time? How she wished she could gain control to try to blend a leaf. But Brom continued to wade through the forest, ignorant of her presence. His thoughts were a series of undecipherable images and foreign words. Bits and pieces she understood, like fire, and water, yet he thought about them in a way she could not comprehend. Why was he thinking about them so much? And what did it have to do with the urgency of finding someone with a golden heart?

Morning came and he picked up pace as the forest came to life with bird songs. He only slowed when the stars appeared above the trees. Herlot was exhausted, but from what she could tell, Brom was only tired. Every so often his mind would settle into a subtle hum above the sound of complete silence. It was actually quite fascinating. His thoughts were still present, but the hum numbed them. After about an hour his spirit felt replenished, and his senses sharpened again.

Another day. Another night. She was hopeless. What if she was trapped in this memory forever? She thanked the skies that she had not run into any trouble...yet.

Then there was the problem of finding her way back if the memory did stop. Was Movo following her, and she couldn't hear him? No. He would have shaken her out of it. She remembered how Ambro had pushed her, and the moment her bottom hit the ground she had been shaken out of the blend with Brom. Movo had definitely not reached her in time. What if the soldiers got him while he was searching for her? Oh, how she hoped that he had made it to the ship and was on his way to warn their friends.

She could sometimes hear waves. That meant that Brom had not steered her too far away from the coast. If she stirred out of the memory, she could follow the beach back. She had no idea what she would do once she did return. Was it even safe to try and go back? How would she find another ship?

"Nayeeta! Where are you?"

It was afternoon again and they had come upon a willow tree. Brom was circling it as if expecting to find something if he circled it long enough. At least they had reached the spot that he wanted. Herlot wondered where this Nayeeta was, and hoped that nothing had happened to her.

Brom wandered a ways from the willow and searched the ground for signs of footsteps. A few paces away, there was cloth resting upon a patch of wildflowers. "Oh, no," he said as he picked it up. The fabric was in a perfect shape to work as a blindfold. He flipped it over and Herlot gasped along with him when they saw the blood stain.

"Excuse me." Someone tapped her shoulder.

* * *

"There you are," Movo said as he spotted the boat hidden behind the bush. He pushed the branches aside to get a better look. He wrapped his hands around the fine wood of the rim and began to haul it out of its hiding spot.

Then Herlot's shout stabbed at his eardrums and he let the boat drop. Like a lightning flash he oriented to the direction from which her voice had come and raced toward it. He knew he was on the right track when he glimpsed a sight of her boots hanging off a branch. Why had she taken them off? He matched the volume he had heard and estimated how far away she must be. However, when he was sure he reached the spot, she was nowhere to be seen.

"Herlot!?" he shouted.

Where was she? He scanned the ground and searched for signs of footprints. From behind him he heard a rustling. Wrapping his fingers around his dagger, he spun and pointed the tip of the blade right at the chest of...

"Aleena? What are you doing here?" He kept the dagger pointed at her chest.

"I decided to come in case you needed help. I wanted to join you on the ship. Then I saw a swarm of fireflies protect two people from shooting arrows. Looked like pure magic. I speculated it before, but now I am certain. For years we have searched for something, someone to help us prepare for the war in the sky. Herlot is different, is she not?"

"I don't know what sick Iptan prophecies may be floating around in your head, but if you could see beyond your pursuits right now, you might notice that Herlot is missing."

Aleena's eyes widened. "She can't have gone far."

Movo didn't want to waste another moment speaking to Aleena.

The boots were a bad sign. From the stories she had told him about her past, it was more likely for the spontaneous blending to happen if she was barefoot. Out of all the times to have a need to frolic in the woods barefoot, she had to have picked now. He couldn't understand how the strong, intelligent woman who left him without words at every challenge she overcame was the same girl who would take her boots off when she was supposed to be looking for a boat.

He crouched down and looked closer at the ground until he finally made out a smaller imprint that had to have been made by someone who was barefoot. The next print was a long stride away. She had been sprinting. Why? Had she blended? His throat tightened at the thought. If she had blended, she wasn't in control of where she was going.

"Movo."

"Leave. Go get on your ship if you wish. I'm not coming."

"You might want to see this."

"Leave."

Something buzzed near his ear, and then three fireflies appeared in front of his nose. He ducked out of the way to continue looking for another footprint.

"Really, you must look. Bless the Emperor, this is absolutely astounding. What are you trying to tell me, little ones?"

The last thing Movo was in the mood to hear was a blessing to an Iptan Emperor. More fireflies clustered in front of his face.

"Movo, look."

Movo turned on his heel to make it clear to Aleena that his only interest right now was to find more of Herlot's footprints, but froze before he could speak his first word.

He frowned at the line of fireflies beginning near his chest and weaving off into the forest toward the seashore.

"I think they're forming a path. They're telling us where to go. They want us to go to the ship," Aleena said.

"You take directions from bugs?"

"These bugs saved your life just moments ago."

"You go on your ship. I'm going to find Herlot."

As he turned to look for more footprints, the entire fleet of flies appeared before him, blocking his view of the ground.

He couldn't believe he was about to speak to bugs. "Can you help me find Herlot?" he asked.

The fireflies glowed brighter. Once again, they began to form a line leading toward the shore.

"If that's not an answer, I don't know what is," Aleena said.

Movo took a long, deep look into the forest. Could he really trust that the fireflies would lead him to Herlot? For all he knew it could be an unexplainable coincidence. Surely the astrologers in Damalathum would have something to say about it—something along the lines of Venus meeting Mars at a certain time, and how that made fireflies act unnatural. Or it could all be Iptan magic, perfectly plotted to lure him to exactly where they wanted him.

"You go on your ship," he said. He swept a branch aside and walked deeper into the woods.

"You're making the wrong decision."

"Perhaps."

As he finished the words the entire swarm of fireflies buzzed by his face, forcing him to shut his eyes. Once he was certain the impact was over, he opened them again.

Aleena gasped at his side.

Amidst the darkness of the woods stood a unicorn figure, painted onto the forest scenery by the fireflies. The precision, the fireflies flew in a way that made the unicorn appear to walk, toward the shore, of course. He couldn't have received better evidence that, in fact, the fireflies knew where Herlot was. He was left with no other choice but to follow them to the shore.

"You win," he said to Aleena. Then he noticed her face. It was stern with an eager fire in her eyes.

* * *

She sighed in relief as she entered the darkness of the mound. With pride she teased the sun for not being powerful enough to follow her in here. She swung her long hair over her shoulder and shook her head.

Her Master stood erect, waiting for her when she entered the den. She began to hang her cloak up on the wall.

"She is on the next wagon headed for Elfolk. The plan has worked."

Her cloak fell to the ground and she spun to face her Master. "We found her? It's a woman?"

"Yes. I felt the gold disappear while you were in the village."

"Does she suspect you know?" she asked. She couldn't believe that soon they would meet the despicable human attempting to hide gold from her Master. She had always wondered if this person was aware of her Master.

"It does not matter. As soon as they arrive, you will end them."

She nodded. "All of them, or just the new ones arriving?"

"I leave that for you to decide."

She picked her cloak back up and went to the wall where a variety of her weapons hung.

She couldn't wait to rid the world of this pest once and for all.

CHAPTER 10

WARM SLIPPERS AND STEW

Herlot turned around to come face to face with an elderly woman with rosy cheeks and wearing a gray headscarf. "Are you lost?"

"Uhh..." Herlot had her own voice back. She looked down at her hands and realized the piece of fabric had disappeared. She was no longer Brom.

"Yes, as a matter of fact, I am. Could you let me know where I am?"

"You are near Elfolk."

That did not help. She had no idea where Elfolk was.

"Right. Uh—" she closed her eyes to see if she could hear the ocean, but there was no sound of waves. "Could you point me in the direction of the sea?" Herlot rubbed at her eyes. Tears of exhaustion were trickling down her cheeks.

The woman pointed behind Herlot. "That way. It's a bit of a trip. My dear, you look exhausted. Why don't you come and stay with me for the night? There's an awful lot of strangers in our village, Damalathum soldiers, too, a bit frightening, but at least you can get a warm bowl of stew in your belly and a good night's rest."

Strangers? Soldiers? "Why are there strangers and soldiers in Elfolk?" Herlot asked, although she already had an idea of where she had landed.

The woman's eyes narrowed. "Evil. Although our lives are meager compared to those of the city folk, never have we realized more than now how lucky we were to live so far from the King. We heard many stories, but this...ah, my dear, if only there was an explanation for such evil acts. These strangers from the other lands have suffered immensely, watched their families die of crowpox and their homes burned to the ground. And now they sit here and wait in our village, in our homes, given no explanation for what has happened and what they are here for."

Herlot cleared her throat. "I can't imagine." Brom had led her to the same place where Felix was holding the survivors. Could that be a coincidence? Could something related to Brom ages ago be related to this place now?

"What is your name, dear?"

She had to think fast. No way could she enter a village with soldiers and have her real name known. "Uh-Brom."

The woman raised her eyebrow.

"Elia? Yes, Bromelia. And yours?"

"Greta. But everyone calls me Getty, especially the children. I make a fine stew and am as swift as a squirrel with the needle and thread."

Herlot smiled. "It's nice to meet you, Getty. And if the offer still stands, I would love to have a taste of your stew."

"Well then, come on, dear. My home is a bit crowded since we house a few of the people from across the sea and three cats, but it is a kind place."

Herlot walked alongside Getty on the wooded path and listened to her speak about the village. There was a wedding to be held soon. As she listened to the list of preparations to be made, she thought about Manni and Ambro's wedding on the day of the soldiers' invasion. What was it specifically about her village that had made it a target for Felix? What did the people of Eraska have that the people of Elfolk didn't? Why couldn't Felix have succumbed people to crowpox who lived closer to him? There had to be something specific about the southern lands. But what? What?

They came upon a donkey tied to a tree. "Ah, my sweet boy, always so patient."

Herlot patted the donkey and scratched him behind the ears as Getty untied him.

"Too patient. He hates exercise," Getty said.

It was true. The donkey walked as if he were about to fall asleep. "I like him," Herlot said.

Herlot's steps faltered a bit as they reached a clearing. Several wagons made their way toward the village along a wide dirt path. They were filled with all sorts of crops. It was a busy village, far more people than in the villages in Eraska. And, of course, the soldiers. Everywhere. Near the entrance to the village, all around the border, she even thought she spotted one milking a cow.

"Come along, Bromelia," Getty said. Herlot felt Getty's hand grab at the side of her cloak as if she wanted to hold onto her arm. Then she heard Getty gasp.

"Getty..." Herlot started. A soldier with a potato sack slung over his shoulder was staring in their direction. "It's important that I don't bring attention to myself."

"Mhmm," Getty squealed. Her next words came in a whisper. "We have heard stories of a Herlot of Alonia who, along with the people of Eraska and Prince Movo, fought back...and won."

"I know the story very well, Getty."

"They say the girl lost her arm. She and the Prince were captured and taken to Damalathum, and by a miracle of the disappearing sun managed to escape execution. Do you know this story very well too?"

"Yes."

"My niece, Bromelia. If anyone asks, that is who you are. Understood?"

"Very understood."

Herlot coughed as dust kicked up from a wagon that drove past them.

"Here, hold the donkey's rope. You'll blend in more," Getty said.

Herlot held her breath as they entered the village. Most of the soldiers seemed incredibly bored. Several were sitting on barrels playing cards. They didn't even glance in their direction.

Herlot looked down the road that split the village into two sides. At the end of it were more soldiers. Both entrances were guarded.

"Getty! Who is this?" a middle-aged man, who was standing outside of a stable holding a pitchfork, asked.

"My niece, Bromelia," Getty answered and hurried ahead.

"I didn't know you had a niece! Slow down, I'd like to meet her."

Out of the corner of her eye, Herlot saw a man dressed in soldier's gear appear out of the stable with a woman at his arm. He chewed on a piece of straw, looking her way with curiosity. Herlot flexed her fingers, ready to reach for her dagger.

"Newcomers!" someone shouted, and a horn blew.

The soldier dropped the piece of straw and nudged the woman aside as he headed toward the entrance. Herlot snuck a peek behind her and saw several wagons approaching. These ones had soldiers on horses all around them. The wagons were packed with people wearing simple, gray clothing.

"Ah, when will this end? Our homes are full to the brim as it is," Getty said. "Poor souls."

"Are those people from the southern lands?" Herlot asked.

"Yes, dear."

How many villages had Felix invaded?

All of a sudden, the hairs on Herlot's arm and on the back of her neck stood up. A wave of fear swept over her from head to toe. She turned around again, and saw a woman wearing a black dress crossing one of the fields in the distance. She walked in a straight line headed toward the wagon, and ignored any of the people working the field.

"Who is that?" Herlot asked.

"None of us know. But she seems to be in charge of Felix's men. She comes every other evening when we are at dinner. She barely speaks. She's very beautiful, but the children don't like her, nor do the animals. It's a bad sign."

Movo had said that the reason Felix had undertaken his horrifying mission was because he would be granted assistance from a sorcerer in exchange. Was it a sorceress, maybe? Or was this woman related somehow to the sorcerer?

Herlot wanted to find out more. She wanted to see this woman up close and in the light. She even considered risking going near the wagon, but she realized her fingers weren't as eager to grab for her dagger, and her courage seemed to have gone missing. This woman carried no large weapon, yet the air about her spoke differently. "What's her name?"

"We don't know that either," Getty said.

"Any idea where she lives?"

"No. But she comes from the direction of Omen Mound. If her home is anywhere close to there, well, let me just say I can't imagine a good person able to live near such a haunted place."

"What is Omen Mound?"

"Omen Mound has been there for as far back as stories of our village go. It is a large field with a mound at the center. It would look nothing unusual of the sort, were it not for the skulls that make a circle around it as a warning. It is said that anyone who crosses over dies, as if the land itself were poisoned. We did our best to warn any traveler to not go near, but every few years an unlucky soul finds his way onto the poisoned soil." Getty shook her shoulders as she finished her words, as if she wanted to free herself of their burden. "This woman, though, she can walk the field."

Herlot felt incredibly cold all of a sudden, even underneath her cloak and wool dress. Had she heard this story as a young girl, she would not have been able to sleep for three moons, haunted by nightmares of the skulls. She had not expected to come across a person with mysterious abilities like the Iptans. Who was this woman, and why was she the only one who could walk this poisoned field?

"Here is my home," Getty said. "You can leave sweet donkey boy right out here. He is too lazy to wander off. His mother usually comes around to find him. Come on in, all friendly hearts are welcome, even ones with secrets." Getty winked at Herlot as she opened the door.

Getty's door did not even squeak as they entered. "Impressive," Herlot mumbled before she followed Getty in.

"Getty, is the new wagon filled with people like us?" one of two young girls coming down a wooden, creaky staircase said.

"We saw it out the window," the other one said.

"Yes, my dears, unfortunately, it is." Getty struck a match and lit a candle in the center of a wooden table. "This is Abby and this is Eleanora. They came from far away, but now will be Elfolkians for as long as they wish to stay with me, and I hope that is until the time I can prepare the meats and sweets for their wedding days," Getty said with pride. "Girls, this is my niece, Bromelia."

One of the girls wrinkled her nose when she heard the name Bromelia. Herlot could not blame her. The other girl, on the other hand, barely looked up from the cloth, needle, and string she carried in her hands. Her eyes were half closed and skin sagged. She didn't have the healthy, rosy cheeks of a young girl.

Herlot nodded with a gentle smile and left the conversation at that. The last thing she wanted to do was force politeness out of them. After all, she knew what they had gone through. Both were without parents, and she didn't have to ask as to how death came upon them. She had lost her own parents the same way.

Before she knew it, Herlot was sitting around the table with Getty and the girls, a wool pair of slippers on her feet, which Getty had gifted her, and chewing on stew meat, soft carrots, and potatoes with delicate hints of rosemary. She had tasted the most exotic of foods at the Iptan Headquarters, but this meal was the one that stirred a warmth in her belly that relaxed her entire body. When she finished, she sat back in the chair with her hand over her belly and a sleepy smile on her face.

Someone knocked three times on the door. "Is it a good time to finish?"

"Of course, come on in, a friendly heart is always welcome, even one with the driest hair in the northern lands," Getty said.

A man with red hair that stuck out in all directions entered. He carried a hammer and two short planks of wood.

"Getty, Abby, Eleanora." He nodded at the three women, and then his eyes rested on Herlot.

He dropped the hammer and planks.

Time stopped.

Hope fueled by the feeling of family pressed on the back of Herlot's eyes.

"Rudi," she sobbed.

She gripped the table and still tripped over its legs as she stumbled her way forward, reaching out her arm. "Rudi," she sobbed again as she buried her face in his chest and gripped the back of his tunic with her hand.

"Bless the skies for this miracle. Oh, my Herlot. There, there, I'm right here." By the sound of his voice, she knew he was crying as well.

"You're alive," she mumbled. "Don't die. Please, don't die."

He kissed the top of her head.

"Did he say... Herlot?" one of the girls said. "As in Herlot of Alonia? Rudi, you never said you were from Eraska?"

"Yes, Abby, but we must keep this a secret. They can't know she is here," Getty said.

Rudi put both of his hands on top of Herlot's shoulders and leaned back slightly. He tilted his head from side to side as if trying to recognize her. "Unbelievable. Well, actually, it is more than believable now that I think about it, but blimey, the little girl I once knew stands before me as a...my, have you fought. I see it in your eyes."

All of a sudden, Rudi frowned. "Herlot, why are you here? If they find out that you're here—"

"I'll be gone before they can. And you're coming with me. Are there any boats?"

"Elfolk has plenty," Getty said.

"Good. Rudi, we need to return home as soon as possible. Felix is planning to attack Eraska again, this time with an entire army."

"These boats aren't made for a trip across the sea."

Herlot gritted her teeth. "Then we'll have to find a ship."

"You know how to sail too?" Eleanora asked.

Herlot sighed. "No."

"Neither does anyone here. And you need a lot of people to sail a ship," Eleanora said.

Herlot prayed that Movo had found his way onto the Iptan ship and was headed to Eraska to warn them. Her only option seemed to be to return to Damalathum and find a way onto one of the war ships before they sailed for Eraska.

"Getty, may I take Herlot upstairs? There are important things I need to speak to her about," Rudi said.

"My, of course. I will be the last to stand in the way of long-lost friends reuniting. You both must have a wagon full to talk about. Just try not to be too long. I have a ginger cake for dessert."

"I wouldn't miss it."

"Even for Lorel's oat one?"

"Even for Lorel's oat one. Come, Herlot," Rudi said as he reached for a candle. The stairs creaked as if they had a story to tell as Herlot climbed them. "Oh, and Getty?" Rudi said as he reached the top. "Please don't tell Lorel I said that."

"Sure, sure. While she doesn't tell me that you like the oat one more than my ginger," Getty called back.

Rudi chuckled.

"Can you believe it? That we can still laugh?" Herlot said as they reached the top of the stairs.

Rudi's eyes drooped in the candlelight. "They would want us to," he said.

He opened a door and led her into a room with four beds on wooden bed frames.

Rudi walked over to the window and sighed. "Let's climb out here. Nothing like sitting on a rooftop. Of course, these are much higher up than at home, but you get used to it."

Herlot slung one leg over the windowsill and then the other. "I don't mind the height anymore. After being in

Damalathum I'm used to it. A night in Felix's dungeons was more than enough to convince me to avoid going below ground. Unless it's an Iptan library." Herlot took a seat next to Rudi and looked out over the rooftops. He wrapped an arm around her, and she rested an ear against his shoulder. An owl hooted and a nightingale sang in the distance.

"Ah, child. It will take me a lifetime to get used to hearing you speak of war, cities, and dungeons."

"As it will take me a lifetime to celebrate that you survived," Herlot said. The realization that Rudi was alive was beginning to sink in more, and a sob escaped her. And then another. She covered her face with her hand.

"No need to cry, I'm not going to disappear. I'm here," Rudi said.

"It's just that I'm so happy. After everything that has happened, finding you is a miracle. It's more than I could have hoped for." For a moment it almost felt like everything had never happened, as if just moments ago she, Ambro, and Elvin had snuck the strong ale from Rudi's home and were now sitting with him at the hearth, Rudi fully aware of what they had done. "How can someone have a future when everything they want is in the past?" Herlot managed through sobs.

"If it's not happy, it's not the end yet," Rudi said. "We have to believe this isn't the end."

Herlot couldn't believe that Rudi could say that, especially after having lost Lupert and Merle. She felt ashamed for breaking down. After all, in the most cruel way possible, she had Devotio back and had met Movo. Then there was her friendship with Enri and Mahtreeh. The Eraskan family that all the villages had created. And Ambro, she hadn't lost Ambro either. Rudi had only lost, and somehow he was still sane. To her, he was a hero.

The nightingale continued to sing, and Herlot watched as a woman wearing a ripped dress stepped out of a home and took a seat on a haystack. Her head drooped and her shoulders shook. She was crying.

"First time I have seen her step outside in the night."

"Who is she?" Herlot asked.

"I am not certain. She arrived recently. Barely speaks to anyone. The villagers that she came with do not recognize her either. Something awful happened to her, though. Her face is barely recognizable. Must have been a fire..."

They stayed silent, as if honoring the sobs of the woman.

"How did you do it? How did you keep going?" she asked.

"It's what I wanted to speak to you about. You. When I overheard the soldiers speaking about the rebellion, I knew it was you leading it. It had to be." He said the last sentence ever so slowly.

Herlot's eyes narrowed. "What do you mean, it had to be?"

Rudi let out a deep sigh. "I'm afraid you won't believe me if I tell you," he said.

She stifled a laugh. "Trust me, Rudi. Nothing could surprise me at this point."

"Hm. Could it be...you might be more aware than I think..." He seemed to be talking to himself.

"Tell me," she said. "Whatever it is, just start at the beginning."

"Yes. The beginning. The best place to start a story. Except... well, I'm not sure where the beginning of this one is. I guess I'll start with myself. You know that I was close with King Cloudian, everyone in Eraska did, Rudi the woodworker. What no one knew is that I was a bit more than that, as my father had been, and my grandfather, and great-grandfather, and many before. We all had a special task to perform for Cloudian, to be watchful for anything out of the ordinary."

Herlot wasn't liking the sound of this. "Go on," she said, although she wasn't sure she wanted to hear it. More secrets.

"For as far back as we can tell, every king of Eraska passed along an old letter speaking about an awful tragedy. Every king was urged to keep Eraska isolated and to not allow gold into the land. The writer spoke of an event that would take place, something to undo the tragedy that he had caused. And he said that if things unfolded according to his plan, nature would give a sign."

We were even fooled by our own king, was all Herlot could think.

"How could we have all been so foolish? How could our Kings have done this to us? We could have been armed, ready. And instead, we suffered because of a letter our Kings decided to believe?"

Rudi cleared his throat and spoke a pitch quieter than he had up until that point. "It seems that they may have had reason to believe..."

Herlot raised an eyebrow as the nightingale continued to sing.

"I witnessed that something-out-of-the-ordinary.'" I just never told him."

"And what was it?"

He glanced at her. "You."

"What?!" Herlot clasped her hand over her mouth and looked down at the street, making sure no one had heard. The only response was the nightingale.

"Let me explain—"

"Rudi, wait." The nightingale had sounded closer this time. Butterflies danced in her stomach as she remembered the walk from Lorfin to Temes, and how Mahtreeh had played with his bird calls. And then Movo, who had asked him to mimic a nightingale.

"Sing again, sing again," she whispered.

"What's going on, Herlot?" Rudi asked.

And there it was again. Now that she listened closer, it sounded more like an attempt at a nightingale song. She squinted her eyes to see better in the direction of where the sound was coming from. "Whistle with me, Rudi, like a bird."

It was as if the air that poured out from her lips was sent from her heart as she made the amateur sound Mahtreeh had tried to teach her. The nightingale sang back, and off in the distance a shadowed figure appeared on one of the roofs, heading toward them.

"Quick, we need to go back inside," Rudi said.

"No. It's a friend," she said, smiling wide.

The moment he stepped onto the roof that she and Rudi were on, she threw herself into his arms, not worried at all about knocking them over the edge. Movo kept his balance perfectly. "How did you find me?" she spoke into his chest.

"Fireflies and an Iptan ship."

She giggled. "I'll need more of an explanation."

"How did you find your way to Elfolk?" Movo asked.

"A golden heart and footprints."

Herlot delighted at the deep rumble that sounded in his chest as he laughed. "I had a feeling you'd say that," Movo said.

"There is someone very important I would like you to meet," Herlot said. Somehow she managed to part herself from Movo even though her body craved to be wrapped in his embrace for longer.

"Movo, this is Rudi, Rudi of Alonia. And Rudi, this is Movo."

Both of them spoke at the same time as they approached each other. "The famous woodworker of Alonia?" said Movo while Rudi spoke with excitement: "The Prince who fights for us?"

They both stopped in silence in front of one another and clasped hands. "It's an honor," they said in harmony.

Something felt whole in Herlot's heart at that moment. How much she would have wanted her parents to meet Movo. Having Rudi meet him was the next best thing. To see a man she could call a second father meet someone important from the time in her life where everything had completely changed, where she had completely changed, felt like a rope thrown across two strips of land previously impossible to connect. It felt more like hope.

"Herlot, the ship is waiting for us. Ready to take us home," Movo said.

Herlot sighed in relief. Their plan was still intact.

"It's not all good news, though, I'm afraid," Movo said. "The fireflies convinced her you're capable of helping them with their war in the sky. It seems they want you as much as my father now, except for other reasons."

"Do you think they'd sail straight for Ipta instead of stopping in Eraska?" Herlot's brows furrowed together. "If only we had another ship..."

"There's no other quicker way. Felix could set sail any day."

Herlot bit down on her lip and scrunched her dress with her fingers. "Before we make any decisions, I need to understand everyone's decisions for my life. Rudi, I need you to finish your story." She turned her glare at Movo. "And then you're going to tell me what it is exactly that Aleena thinks I can do for her. I need to make it clear to her that I won't compromise unless we stop in Eraska as planned."

She eyed Movo. "I was just learning about how the Kings of Alonia had been following the directions of an ages-old letter, a plea to keep the land isolated while awaiting a sign from nature, a sign to let them know that their plan of righting some man's wrongs had worked."

Rudi looked down ashamed and twiddled his thumbs.

"Oh yes, I forgot to mention that supposedly that act of nature had something to do with me."

Movo looked from Herlot and Rudi, clearly uncomfortable. Unfortunately, she was in no mood to lessen the awkwardness of the situation, although she did feel guilty for the harshness in her tone. She was grateful beyond the skies to have found Rudi, but she would not hide how displeased she was at knowing something like this had been kept from her.

"Herlot, please understand I never wanted to make things difficult for you, or to cause you any trouble. It's why I never told King Cloudian about you—I wanted you to be happy with your family in Alonia, a normal life."

Herlot tilted her head back and looked up at the stars. Her life stopped being normal the moment she learned to walk and caused the village to believe she could see and talk to ghosts. It stopped being even more normal when she blended through a tree and met a unicorn. Currently she had to save a unicorn family by blending their magical hiding place inside a leaf onto another tree. She almost felt sorry for Rudi in how much his intentions had not worked. She stopped at that thought as a tickle went up her neck. All of a sudden, she became terrified of the words she was about to hear coming from Rudi's mouth. Strange how words could create the same feelings as a swinging sword held in the hands of a soldier mounted atop a war horse. She placed her palm over her shoulder.

A warmth covered the top of her hand. She looked to her side to see it was Movo's hand covering her own as he pulled her closer to his side.

"It happened the day you were born, after your mother had escaped from Agatha's home to give birth to you in the forest. We were all out at the sea cliffs because the bells of Eraska were ringing."

Herlot remembered some of this story. "But the bells never rang in Eraska, right?"

"Yes. And I even confirmed it with King Cloudian after. He said it was a miracle. He had seen with his own eyes how they swung back and forth all of their own accord. As if the wind was pushing them back and forth."

"I don't understand how this has anything to do with me, though. Surely it could have signaled a variety of things besides a child's birth."

"I thought so too. But… when I handed you back to your mother, the wind…it wrapped 'round you. And—and you could hear the tone of the bells coming from it," Rudi said. His eyes gleamed apologetically.

"This letter you speak of—do you know who wrote it?" Movo asked.

"A man named Brom."

"Oh!" Herlot's knees went weak as she leaned heavily against Movo's side.

Brom. She could practically feel the words written on the parchment hidden in her pocket: *I have awakened a dark creature, dangerous beyond anyone's belief. If you are one who walks this world with a golden heart, I give you the responsibility that I was too weak to accomplish in my time.*

"I—I need to sit down, everything is spinning," she managed.

She slid down to her knees and rested her forehead onto the rooftop.

"Breathe slowly," Movo said as he rubbed her back.

"I think I'm going to be sick."

Rudi kept stuttering trying to say something that sounded like an apology.

"It's not your fault, Rudi. You couldn't have known." She lifted her head to explain more, but the spinning worsened.

"Oh…" she said as she brought her forehead back down again. "It's just that I've been seeing—or rather, being—this Brom man since I was a little girl."

"What?" Rudi asked.

"Have you ever seen this letter?" Movo interrupted.

"Yes, Brom wrote that he had done something terrible, and that our world suffers endless wars over gold because of it. He said that there was an enemy, one who had already won. For years he had studied this person, warned us to not seek this person out, and that a long time was required for crucial events to unfold in order to not allow our enemy to win forever. If our land was kept isolated and free of gold, these crucial events would possibly unfold," Rudi said.

Herlot rested her cheek against the roof and watched Movo pace as he rubbed his beard. His stare was focused intently downard, as if he were imagining things laid out on the rooftop to study. "Looking for someone immune to crowpox in the southern lands… that's who the sorcerer wants… A golden elixir from Ipta protects against the illness… could a golden heart do the same? An enemy from Brom's time who has already won. Crucial events must unfold to defeat him, so this person must still be alive? Omen Mound could have existed since Brom's time. Could it be connected?" Movo mumbled. He stopped in his tracks in front of Herlot and squatted down. He brushed a strand of Herlot's hair behind her ear. "What if the sorcerer my father met is looking for you? He's the one whom my father believes to possess the powers of Omen Mound. We need to get out of here."

Herlot threw up all of her stew over the edge of the roof. *I did not ask for this!* she screamed to the skies and the lands of the entire world with every heave that shook through her body.

"There's that damned woman who walks Omen Mound's field... she is back again," Rudi mumbled.

All of a sudden, Herlot was dragged back on her feet, all her weight supported onto Movo.

"We need to leave right now. That woman cannot get near Herlot," Movo said.

"Herlot is ill. We should take her inside," Rudi said.

"No. There's a story here. A long, ancient one, and somehow Herlot could be intertwined. And I will not allow us to stay in this place long enough to find out."

* * *

Just as Rudi was climbing out the window with Herlot's things, a trumpet sounded and soldiers began marching to each of the two entrances of the village. Villagers began piling out of the homes.

"What's happening, Rudi?" Movo asked.

"Everyone is ordered to line up in the street whenever the trumpet is sounded. It rarely happens, she usually observes us while we eat our dinner."

"What does she do when you're lined up?"

Herlot watched as the woman in the black cloak shouted orders at the soldiers.

"Counts. Asks questions. Looks at us closely. And then we are ordered back inside."

Herlot continued to watch as the woman made her way toward the first family standing outside.

"She's pulling out a weapon," Herlot said. "Is that normal?"

"No... she has never done that before," Rudi said.

"I have an awful feeling about this. We need to get down on the street right now," Herlot said.

"Wait—" Movo started.

But Herlot was already shuffling toward the edge of the roof. People screamed from below and out of the corner of her eye, Herlot saw the woman slice her dagger across a man's throat. Soldiers unwielded their swords and pointed them at the villagers' throats as the woman approached the next victim

Just before she leaped, she turned to Rudi. "Go along the roofs for as long as you can and meet us in the forest on the other side of the village."

Movo was right behind her.

She landed with a grunt and rolled. Swiftly she reached for one of the daggers wrapped around her leg and chucked it at a soldier's back.

"Run! To the eastern entrance, in the woods! Tell as many as you can!" she yelled to the families around her as she took the soldier's sword. Behind her emitted sounds of struggle and a grunt. She turned in time to see Movo snap a soldier's neck.

"You have a weapon?" she shouted to Movo.

"Two."

"Go east and clear the entrance. I'll go west!"

The moment she glanced up to see if she could see Rudi, it was as if she felt a wave of air coming toward her body, and she turned just in time to step sideways and avoid the strike of the sword. Lucky, but too close to the soldier's other arm. She winced as his fist made contact with her jaw, and her teeth rang with pain that spread inside her head. She leaned in closer and kneed him to knock him off balance before slashing at his abdomen.

Soldiers ran at her from all directions. Movo's situation couldn't be much different. They were outnumbered, and up ahead the unknown woman was creating a bloodfest of her own. How many more innocent villagers would she kill before Herlot would manage to fight her way through to her?

She let go of the hilt of her sword and then freed one of the powders rolled in fabric from her pouch.

She shouted to a family to move out of the way as she threw the ball at a torch outside of their home.

She picked up her sword and then kicked off her wool slippers as she raced toward a group of soldiers, paying specific attention to the bottoms of her feet. *Golden heart, if I ever needed your magic, it will be in the next moments.*

Just as Gold had explained, the whole area filled with smoke, making it impossible to see. The tip of someone's sword grazed against her shoulder blade.

Fear hammered in her temples as the blood trickled down. She had made an awful mistake. She was without the magical sword that could defend her in any situation. She was nowhere near close to controlling her golden heart skills, and couldn't rely on them to make her sensitive to the footsteps around her. Yes, she had blinded the soldiers, but in doing so she had blinded herself and all the villagers trying to escape as well. She crouched to the ground and squinted trying to get sight of anyone coming at her as she crawled toward what she hoped was the right direction.

Someone tripped over her, and her face planted with a crunch in the hard, dried dirt of the street. She shouted as the impact reverberated through her teeth that were still pounding from the punch. The taste of blood filled her mouth and a tooth swished in the pool. She spat it out. She tried to scramble to her feet, only to collide with someone else.

She crawled forward as best she could, rolling out of the way the moment her eyes caught a glimpse of a shadow coming toward her. She didn't even know how she would find the woman if she were in her vicinity. Maybe it was best to turn around and try to reach the exit where she had told Movo and Rudi to meet. But who was this woman, and why was she in charge of examining the villagers that were brought to Elfolk? No matter what the answers were, she was dangerous. Anyone capable of killing an innocent person with such swiftness was. She had to try and find her.

Out of the right corner of her eye she saw a black cloak skim by her side. Herlot kicked her leg out and smiled when she felt it collide with the cloaked figure's shin. As the person fell to the ground, a yelp escaped her. A feminine sound. Good. Herlot was more and more certain that she had caught her target.

She gripped the cloak, making sure the monster couldn't escape. Herlot pinned her knees on either side of the woman's waist and forced her to turn around. Then she brought her face down so it was just inches away, so she could look her in the eyes without the smoke fogging her view.

Piercing black pupils glared back at her. "It's you," the woman said as blood from Herlot's mouth dropped onto her eyes. She didn't blink it away. Just two words, and it felt like the woman had spat hatred in Herlot's face. That's when she remembered the woman had a dagger. A slight adjustment in the woman's side made Herlot certain of where the jab would be coming from, and she swung her arm out just in time to block it. She swung her leg around and stepped her foot onto the woman's arm. She heard the crunching of bones and the woman cry out. Having the woman's arm disabled, Herlot peeled the woman's fingers off the hilt of the dagger. She pointed the tip of the dagger at the woman's chest.

"Who are you?" Herlot yelled.

"Everything I ever wished to be," the woman hissed back. "More than you'll ever be."

Herlot shook her head in confusion. "Your name."

No answer.

"Your name!"

"Oof," Herlot sounded as someone collided into her back, pushing her body weight forward.

The woman cried out as the dagger buried into her chest.

"No," Herlot cried. She needed the woman alive still to get the information she needed.

She felt the woman tuck her arm between their bodies and pull at the knife. She screamed in agony as she pulled the dagger out of her own chest. Herlot rolled to the side to avoid an attack. She felt a cold liquid on her forearm where the woman's blood had already poured out.

She thought she heard the dagger fall to the ground, and with caution neared the woman again. The smoke was clearing a bit and Herlot was able to see. A black liquid flowed around the woman's neck.

"Wh-What is that?" she wondered out loud. "Is that your blood?"

Black blood?

"Lavinia. My name is Lavinia," the woman croaked. "Please, don't forget like I did."

And then Herlot felt it. The coldness. The emptiness. The hopelessness. The...nothingness. Cold sweat poured down her back as Herlot's body shivered in terror. She brought her arm up to her eyes and saw the black blood that also covered her arm. "Get it off me! Get it off me!" she cried. Without thinking, she stammered back, trying to get as far away from the woman and the awful feeling that was emanating from her.

"Miss, you're going the wrong way. Come, into the eastern woods," a man said as he wrapped his arm behind her back and guided her down the street. Her feet seemed to move without her consent.

"Is there water there? I need to wash," she said in a daze. That was all that mattered—to get the awful black coldness off of her.

"Now, now, I know you have been through a shock. I'm sure we will make it to the creek, but first we must leave this place. I don't want to imagine what kind of punishment those men will have in store for us. You will feel better once you're safe in the woods, Miss, that I assure you. Now come, let's keep moving along."

Herlot's eyes stung as she joined the crowd outside the village of people coughing from the smoke. Once they were in the woods, she let the tree-kissed air fill her lungs. She drank it in, thirsty, letting it wake her out of her daze. Her spine straightened the farther they walked along, and her hand tightened into a fist at her side. She soon heard Movo's voice calling her name and caught glimpses of his brown hair as he wove through the crowd. She frowned when she noticed a head of red braids following after him. Aleena. She didn't call out to them, even when they walked by her just several paces away.

Instead, she listened to the Elfolkians around her. How many more times would she walk among people displaced from their homes? How many more times would she need to hear a parent struggling for words to comfort their child about not being able to return home? And most predominant on her mind was the question: if they escaped to Ipta, who would Felix torture in their place?

No. More.

Something new awakened in her blood as she thought the words. No, it was certainly not gold. Whatever it was, it felt right. It felt powerful. It felt wild. Bloodlust, that's what it was.

Soon they reached a clearing where several Elflolkians were already working on building a fire. "If it wasn't for the light, I wouldn't mind several days without smelling smoke," the man who had walked alongside her said.

"Herlot! We've been looking for you!" Aleena said as she appeared at Herlot's side.

"You and everyone else. How can I be of service to your problems?"

Aleena frowned at Herlot's sarcastic response.

Aleena took a step forward "I don't know what you—"

Herlot extended her hand out in front of her and shook her head. She turned to Movo. "I'm going to find water. I need you to let all these people know that we will be joining Aleena on her Iptan ship.

"I—" Aleena started.

"I think there's something you desperately need from me, or else you wouldn't have followed some fireflies to find me here. If you want me, you're taking all of these people too. If you want me alive, you will take me to my home first so I can win a war on my land before meeting your emperor to talk about wars in the sky. Make a decision before I come back."

"War? I thought—" Aleena started.

"Enough." Herlot took a deep breath into her lungs, and then when she breathed out it was as if her decision engulfed the space around her. "Enough hiding. Enough running. Enough Kings, Emperors, and creatures."

She took another step closer to Aleena, to make sure she could feel every word on her face. "I don't care what your sky watchers see in the future. Your people have witnessed Felix kill thousands. Just now, his soldiers were going to allow a woman to slaughter innocent families." Herlot's voice turned into a hiss. "There is no excuse for your failure to make this stop." She spit at Aleena's feet. "Now, me and my untrained, armorless people are going to go to war because it's the one place worth standing up for in this world that you and your emperors and kings have created, even if it means I will die trying."

Movo started to protest but she walked away. No one was going to change her mind. She had made her decision. She was Eraska's leader and Eraska was going to war. She had seen enough of the suffering Felix had caused—in Eraska, in Damalathum, the other villages of the southern lands, and now putting people into the hands of a monster with black blood. It was time to show him, and all Kings, Emperors, warlocks, and whoever else might come along with an agenda, that they would rather die fighting for their life than run, hide or succumb, no matter how big the threat.

She wove her way through the crowd, learning the direction toward a nearby stream. She noticed Rudi with the group of girls from Getty's home. She was still grateful for having found him, but right now she needed to be alone.

There were enough others with candles heading toward the stream to make it easy to see. Nonetheless, she noticed a firefly dancing at her side the entire way.

The ground beneath her feet began to turn more moist. She couldn't wait to be back home. She wanted to feel the grass, stones, sticks, and pebbles of the land she would fight a war on, a land she would defend. *I'm sorry I ever thought of abandoning you, Eraska.*

Warmth sparked in her chest. A presence tickled up her legs and up her spine. Brom's voice spoke again, asking if he could share his memory. No, leave me alone, she thought, determined.

All of a sudden, the firefly's presence felt a lot bigger next to her. She turned to her right and saw a beautiful, tall unicorn. With wings. She wanted to express her shock, but found that she wasn't in control of her mouth. *I said no! Why aren't you listening?*

"Ah, aren't you glad we decided to go on an adventure? Imagine all the new places we will see, my Ola," Herlot said, but the voice she heard was not her own, it was Brom's.

Ola? This is Ola? Brom's unicorn whose heart shattered after he left her? Herlot couldn't even imagine forgetting such a beautiful being. Ola looked so right with her wings. How much she wanted to see what she would look like with them spread wide and flapping in the sky. They would have suited Devotio perfectly.

Her body temperature cooled a bit and Ola disappeared, only to be replaced by the firefly.

Thank the skies it didn't last longer. From what she could remember, Brom had always asked her if he could show her a memory. This time she had said no, but he had not listened. She began to wonder if she had ever had a choice.

She heard the water flowing over the rocks but didn't quicken her pace. She noticed a warmth in the bottoms of her feet beginning to form again. It is happening again, she thought. And just as her thought finished, she passively noticed how another presence seemed to be looking through her eyes.

Why, hello there, Brom. How nice it is to be you again for a little bit without knowing how, why, or when it will happen.

Brom skipped her body over to the stream.

Didn't even ask this time. Her rage was growing at the lack of control.

Just lovely. I'm skipping with joy among the Elfolkians who will probably never return to their homes again, she thought. *But of course, you could care less about that, Brom. After all, you had no hesitation running me into a battlefield once.*

Her voice hummed as she knelt and leaned over the stream. Brom scooped water into her hands and splashed her face.

The neck would be better, not that the black blood matters to you in your gleeful state.

Her thoughts stopped. Brom was in a joyful state, a state she had never witnessed in him before. Urgency, guilt, shame, and fear was all she had ever felt from him.

Brom looked down at his reflection in the stream. As enraged as she was to be forced into this memory, Herlot wondered at his beautiful features, large brown eyes and black curls that framed his face. And the glow. It was unmistakable. Even in the stream she saw the glow emitting from where his tunic exposed his chest. This was before he had lost his golden heart.

Brom leaned his face closer to the water. "How I wish I could see my own reflection better," he said. "If only the water would hold still, I could see myself clearly."

"I can show you your true reflection," a voice said from behind.

Brom spun around and saw a man dressed in a black cloak, his face hidden in the hood, standing next to Ola.

"You have an awful stain on your neck, my dear. Here, take this kerchief, it might help to scrub it off."

Herlot shook her head as her surroundings adjusted to the present moment.

"Thank you," she said. How strange it was that she could jump between what seemed like worlds, and no one around her was aware.

She dunked the cloth into the water and proceeded to rub it against her neck.

"Get off," she grumbled as she scrubbed harder and then dunked it back in. She swished it in the water until all the black blood was off of it before she brought it back up to her neck again, this time pressing even harder.

"Is it off?" she asked the woman next to her as she lifted her chin up to expose her neck.

"Just one more spot. Here, let me help you."

"Thank you," Herlot said as the woman scrubbed at the place just below her ear.

This woman didn't feel strange, although she was a stranger. She felt kind, alive, real. The way humans were meant to be.

Herlot looked around at the people drinking from the stream. She thought about the time Devotio had decided that they both needed to focus on protecting Eraska. He had said that if it wasn't for people like the Eraskans, the unicorns might never have a world to return to in the first place. What was the point of maintaining their secret world if there wasn't hope for a real world to return to with people who would love them?

It didn't matter what Rudi's story about the Kings of Eraska was. It didn't matter what the Iptans wanted from her. It did not matter how many obstacles and confusions this strange life would throw her way. She knew what she wanted to fight for. She knew what mattered to her. She knew what was real to her, and even if the obstacles kept coming, she would never succumb to them until she had the freedom to fight for what she loved. And that meant first killing Felix.

Good thing she was about to have an Iptan ship at her disposal, that is, if she played her pawns right.

"Time to go home," she said.

* * *

"We only have one boat to take us to the ship," Aleena said.

Herlot was right on the back of Aleena's heels and gave her a little nudge whenever she slowed her pace. She was followed by a whole group of Elfolkians who had decided that they wanted to come with them to Eraska after they all learned who she was.

"Then we will go back and forth as many times as we need to. And trust me, I'll be on the last trip," Herlot said. "I wouldn't put it past your people to sail off once you have what you want and leave all these people behind."

"Suit yourself. I don't understand why you have become so mistrusting all of a sudden," Aleena said.

"Ha!" was all Herlot replied.

As soon as they reached the beach, Movo silently helped Herlot set the boat into the water.

"First ten, please!" she called to the group. "That includes you, Aleena. Make sure to tell your Iptans the plan once you arrive at the ship." Off in the distance, below the sky split between sunrise and stars on a dark blue backdrop, she saw the Iptan ship. It was at least twice as large as the ship that had taken her and Movo to Damalathum. There was more than enough room for the Elfolkians, and there had to be plenty of weapons stored on it.

"Never thought I'd see the day where a villager bosses an Iptan around. The stories about you must be true, Miss Herlot," an Elfolkian elder said as he climbed into the boat.

"Sir, soon you will get the chance to do the same with King Felix of Isolda. I promise you, it will be an even better sight to see," Herlot said.

"You seem confident about winning," Rudi said as he adjusted the oars for the boat.

"I'm going to kill Felix," Herlot said, and then began to whistle a simple tune.

She noticed how both Rudi and Movo paused and exchanged glances.

Soon she was watching from shore as the first group rowed toward the Iptan ship with Aleena on board. Rudi and Movo were still at her side.

"Herlot..." Rudi began. "I—I know you have learned much since we last saw each other, and experienced much. And it was important, every fight you won, but...does the thought of killing someone, even if it's King Felix, really bring you a joy that causes you to whistle?"

"Yes."

She smiled at the thought.

"You don't mean that. That's not what Seum taught you. You were taught to fight with freedom, not for the joy of killing," Movo said.

"You're right, Seum did not teach me that. I taught it to myself."

Her heartbeat exhilarated as she spoke the words. No matter what anyone in the world expected her path to be, she could have power and control. She could whistle with joy about killing her enemy if she wanted to. It felt good. She soaked in the feeling of the sunrise light on her face as she reveled in this new sense of freedom.

The morning sunlight disappeared as Movo stepped in front of her, his chest and shoulders blocking her view. She leaned to the side, but he followed her instinctively.

He crouched down to come to eye level with her. She avoided his gaze. "Look at me," he said.

"Get out of my way."

"Not until you look at me."

"Do not tell me what to do!"

She whirled around and stomped toward the tree line.

"Stop following me," she yelled as she could sense Movo following her.

She found a stump underneath the shade of a tree and took her seat.

"Something is not right with you. In one night you have changed from a fierce warrior into someone full of vicious spite. I know the difference, and trust me when I say you are getting close to crossing a border that will be difficult to cross back again."

"Leave me alone," she practically hissed at Movo.

She noticed his cheeks sag as she spoke the words but still avoided his eyes.

"You really mean that? After everything we have survived together, you just want me to leave you alone?"

"Yes."

"Have it your way."

She covered herself in a blanket of numbness as he left. Several more boats made their way back, rowed by Iptans. She smirked. She couldn't believe Aleena had even tried that lie on her. Of course, a large ship like that would have more boats. Aleena didn't care about the others. The only thing she cared about was getting Herlot to Ipta. She honestly doubted them ever having made the stop in Eraska as promised. Good thing she had a plan.

Herlot focused her attention on the calm, morning breeze. Everything was fine. Everything was going to be fine. She repeated the mantra over and over again as the Elfolkians filled the boats for another trip to the ship. Only she, Movo, Rudi, and two families were left on the beach. She watched in satisfaction as the people from the boats made it onto the ship.

She rose to her feet when the last two boats were nearing shore. An Elfolkian mother told her children, who were singing a tune about rolling dough, to hurry up and finish building their sandcastle. Some of the older boys were cheering as they raced on the beach toward the boat. A bug crawled across the back of Herlot's neck. She brushed her fingers against her neck in an attempt to swat it away only to find nothing there.

Movo and Rudi were in the water helping the others get in when she felt the same prickle again. She slapped at the back of her neck, but the tickle didn't go away.

She turned around.

She squinted to see better.

She scanned the tree line.

A shadow.

No—a person.

A dark cloak.

Pain.

The pressure of an ocean on her chest.

She gripped her chest. She had to rip away whatever was causing her heart to burst.

Sand. The world turned sideways. She must have fallen.

Movo and Rudi in the water. She tried to yell for help, but the pain was too much—no strength to scream.

Their figures blurred.

Death was coming.

Rainbow-colored water shot into the air. A colorful fin. A beautiful last vision before death. The rainbow whales had been real too...

Her lungs exploded for breath as the pressure ceased and a sound resembling one of someone gasping for air after nearly drowning escaped her throat.

Every muscle in her body shook from the trauma of pain.

She tried to press herself up, but her heart felt like it was still waking up from the trauma of near death. Her chest was sore as if she had been wedged under a tree trunk for an entire day and night.

"Help," she whimpered. Too quiet for Movo and Rudi to hear. Surely someone had to have seen her fall.

Every muscle in her chest threatened to rip as she rolled her heavy body to her other side.

"She's alive!" she heard Rudi shout.

Herlot's breath caught.

A shadow lurked over her, and within moments Movo had two fingers pressed against the side of her throat. "Where are you hurt?" he asked with urgency.

"My chest," she said.

He hooked his finger under the neckline of her dress. "Let me know if I'm hurting you," he said.

She watched his expression turn into one of pain as he exposed her chest.

"Wh-what is it?"

She lifted her head up to see.

Her skin color had disappeared underneath a bruise that covered her entire chest and resembled the colors of tree rot.

Movo tucked a strand of hair behind Herlot's ear. "What happened?"

"I—I don't know. I was making my way to the boat when I thought I saw someone standing in the tree line, and then it felt like my heart was going to burst."

Rudi looked to the tree line, but Movo continued to look at her. That's when she noticed he had tears in his eyes.

"The bruising—I never saw it, but it's what they say happens to people at the mound," Rudi said.

"Are you sure you saw someone at the tree line?" Movo said.

Herlot nodded

How much she didn't want to say it or think it. "Could it have been the warlock?" she whimpered. The warlock. The same person controlling Felix, and even worse, possibly the same person Brom warned about.

"We can't waste another moment to find out. We need to leave straight away," Movo said. "Can you manage to put your arm around me?"

"Yes."

It was the first time Herlot had ever seen Movo acting like he was truly frightened.

She fought crying out as Movo carried her to the boat. The smallest movement of taking a breath hurt. She watched the tree line to see if the person would appear again

As soon as they were ready, Movo took hold of both oars and with swift, powerful strokes rushed them away from the beach.

"Did you notice anything else?" he asked.

"Whales. I saw the rainbow whales and it stopped."

"Rainbow whales?" Rudi asked.

Herlot couldn't believe that Movo knew more about her secrets and magic moments than Rudi, someone she had known her entire life and who was like a second father. "Rudi, I've had some secrets of my own. For a long time. I don't know if you'll believe them when I tell you…"

Rudi's eyes widened. "I will believe."

"I don't know the best way to say this…" How much she wished magical happenings could be easily woven into several words. Maybe it could be that simple? She closed her eyes so that no strange reaction from Rudi's expression would stop her from finishing.

She told Rudi about meeting Devotio, the fire, Emrys and the hidden world in the leaf, and about her golden heart magic and how she needed to use it to blend the leaf back onto a tree or else the unicorns' hidden world would disappear. She opened her eyes as soon as she finished. Rudi wore a gentle smile, like a child listening to a story.

"So, what do you say? Do you believe me? Do you need me to tell you again?" she asked as she bit her nail.

"Take a breath, child. Don't worry, yes, I believe you—but I would like to be quiet with what you have shared with me for a while, if that's alright." He chuckled. "I must say, this story makes up for your missed recitation."

Herlot laughed, and then winced as pain shot across her chest. "Time. Yes. More than fair." Had she really just shared her magical secrets with Rudi? Not only was Rudi alive, but this Rudi was now someone whom she didn't have to hide secrets from. From now on, when they saw each other and when they spoke, he could see and speak to the whole of her. How much she had wished for this feeling her entire childhood.

"I do have one question, though, right now... you didn't mention the whales. How do they tie into the story?"

Herlot almost laughed. How could she have forgotten the whales? "Rainbow whales. Ambro lost the new boat you had built. Devotio took us to the sea and they brought the boat to us. Devotio said that they know all the mysteries of the sea, and that they rarely show themselves to land creatures, especially humans."

"And you saw them just now?" Movo asked.

"Yes. At least, I think so. I saw their fins and their breaths."

"I didn't hear or see any whales... Then again, we were focused on bringing the boat in."

"The warlock, the whales, the mound. It all has to tie together too," Movo said.

That was possible, yet it seemed like an impossible task to untangle. There were so many pieces of information. To Herlot, it felt like an entire book had been ripped into pieces, and they didn't even have all the pieces to begin putting the story together, let alone know where or when it began, who was in danger and why they were in danger, or if there was any possibility of a happy end.

"The marks on your chest resemble those of people who have died when they walked onto the field surrounding the mound. I am certain that the figure you saw was the warlock. I hoped my father was insane, but everything points to the fact that there really is a man who possesses the power to murder from afar—the land isn't poisoned and at fault for the deaths after all," Movo said.

"This horrid power, the power to kill from a distance, would indeed be strong enough to conquer Ipta..." Rudi mumbled.

"And he is also the one looking for someone immune to crowpox in the southern lands. But why? Why?"

"You said it was Herlot he was looking for. Could this have something to do with this golden heart that she has? His power is the ability to make hearts burst from what it sounds like..." Rudi said.

Herlot wished this conversation would stop.

"Why wasn't he able to kill her?" Rudi wondered. "And he wasn't able to reach us, even though we were closer to him than we would have been if we were at the edge of the field..."

Herlot noticed Movo shudder after Rudi asked his question.

"And he couldn't travel to the southern lands to find and kill you himself," Movo said. "There has to be something about the sea."

Movo continued to row in silence, his gaze intently focused on the tree line of the beach. He kept stealing glances at Herlot's chest. She wished she could hide the awful bruise. She was battered enough as it was. The last thing she needed was another marking on her body of her inability to handle and understand the outrageous, horrifying circumstances that kept pulling her in with the force of a tide. She didn't know how to protect people from warlocks who could kill people at a distance. She definitely did not know how to help Iptans in a war in the skies. She didn't know how to blend and save Devotio's family.

But she did know she could use a sword.

And that meant she did know how to kill Felix.

She stared at the ship that was growing larger and larger as they rowed closer.

Yes. Soon she would get to experience the feeling of having Felix gone forever, and of her being the one to do it. As soon as the battle began, she would fight her way forward and look him in the eyes as she caused him to take his last breath. Goosebumps spread across her body at the thought of the victory.

"I've seen coldness in many people as of lately, but never have I imagined I'd see it in the daughter of Ernest of Alonia," Rudi said.

Herlot blinked a few times to return from her daydream. "What is that you say, Rudi?" She didn't like the way he was looking at her. She could not match the feeling. Rudi looked somewhat sad and concerned, but that wasn't it entirely. There was something else there. Fear. No. It couldn't be fear. Could it?

"You have changed much since last time I saw you. I-I just need to get accustomed to it, I think."

"As do I," Movo said under his breath.

Herlot nodded slowly. "How would you both like me to be, to better suit your expectations? I'm preparing to fight in a war and here you are, both looking like you wish I was sprinkling flowers around from a basket woven by someone who wakes to rooster songs. If that be the case, we can all dig our own graves when we arrive home."

"Even if you're the last one standing on the battlefield, you have lost the war if it makes you lose yourself," Movo said.

"That won't happen," Herlot said through gritted teeth.

"It's starting to," Movo said as he leaned back to push the oars through the water.

"No. I want to kill my enemy. I'm not like Manni who turns against her own. Rudi, did you know she helped the soldiers plan the invasion of Alonia?"

Rudi's eyes widened. "Impossible."

"It's true. Movo says she came to them and told them to wait, so they could invade when everyone was gathered in one place. And then she gave us away at the fortress after we rescued Ambro and our friends. Because of her, Movo and I were captured in the first place."

"I-I was kept in a room on the third floor of the fortress the entire time and rarely saw anyone. But if she was able to roam free in the fortress, why didn't she try to see me?" Rudi said more to himself than anyone in the boat. "And how did she know the soldiers were there? How did she know about what they wanted to do in Alonia? That does not make any sense. You have to be mistaken somehow, Herlot."

"She is not," Movo said. "I didn't remember her until we saw her at the fortress. It's as if our troop was hypnotized the day she approached and told us to wait."

Herlot blew at the bangs covering her eyes. She was so sick of questions without any answers. They couldn't get to that big, powerful Iptan ship fast enough.

She climbed over several boat seats toward Movo. "Let me," she said.

Movo slid to the side of his seat, opening up a space for her.

"No. I want to row alone."

He opened his mouth as if to speak.

"We don't have all day," she said expectantly.

He looked her straight in the eyes. "You need two arms for these oars."

"Oh." She had really wanted to row alone. She took her seat next to Movo and gripped the oar. Her chest burned at the first motion of rowing, but she forced herself to breathe through it.

"Maybe you shouldn't—"

"I'm fine." She rowed as hard and fast as she could, trying to stay a beat ahead of Movo.

"Slow down, we can't control the direction of the boat if you don't match your pace with mine," Movo said.

Herlot looked around and realized they were not heading toward the ship anymore. "Maybe you should match your pace with mine."

Movo sighed. "Fine."

Before Herlot could pull her oar back, Movo had already completed a full round.

"Keep up or we will miss the boat and row off into sea."

Herlot fought to keep up. Each breath helped her ignore the pain in her chest. Her arm began to shake from the strain, and she watched helplessly as her pace slowed more and more as she tried harder and harder to keep up with Movo.

Just as she thought her arm was going to give out, Movo's strokes slowed down. Their oars dipped into the sea water in harmony once again and they arrived gracefully at the Iptan ship.

Herlot released the oar, and her line of sight continued up the side of the boat until her head leaned far back in order to see the top. The thing was as tall as some of the buildings in Damalathum. Several heads peeked out over the banister, looking down at them. *Great,* Herlot thought. *They'll probably grab me as soon as I'm close enough to reach.*

The boat teetered as Movo stepped to one side and fastened a fat rope to the end. Herlot stood dumbfounded as he continued to fasten ropes to their boat. He waved and the boat jerked.

Herlot gripped the side of the bench and squealed.

"Flying horses, why not flying boats," Rudi said through clenched teeth. Herlot noticed that he was gripping the bench just as tight as she was.

"Unicorns, not horses. And Devotio doesn't have wings anymore. None of them do," she said with a smile. "You should have listened to Father's story better."

"I could use a story right about now. Something to keep my mind off of wanting to look down."

"Maybe try closing your eyes," Herlot said.

Rudi was silent a beat and then spoke quickly. "And that is even worse because all I can think about is what it would feel like to fall from this high."

"If we were to fall, there's nothing you could do to stop it, so why worry?" Movo said.

"Hm...in that case I'll keep my eyes on that cloud. Lovely hues it has. My, it almost resembles a mushroom, wouldn't you say?"

"Yes. Or a parasol," Movo said.

Herlot smiled. She hadn't expected Movo to care about comforting Rudi.

She looked up again and her smile immediately faded. She recognized Aleena, and next to her were several people dressed in comfortable fabrics, yet there were two with tunics cut at the shoulders exposing their muscular arms. Warriors.

She touched the dagger tied around her thigh, making sure it was still there.

"Welcome aboard," one of the men said as soon as they were in speaking distance.

"Aye, Captain, thank you," Rudi said.

"That's not the captain, Rudi," Movo said.

"Ah, wheat bugs, this is what happens when I try to make a polite impression."

If it were a different situation, Herlot would have laughed, but Aleena's concentrated expression, as well as the ones of the two warriors, stopped her. If only she knew what plan they had in store for her, but she wouldn't wait to find out.

"Let me give you a hand, sir," one of the men said as they helped a knees-wobbling Rudi out of the boat. Herlot's heart beat faster as formal introductions were made between Movo, Rudi, and the Iptans. With grace, Movo stepped over the gap between the boat and ship. Now it was Herlot's turn.

"Herlot of Alonia, I have heard much about you. It is truly an honor. Here, let me help you aboard." The man extended his hand in offering.

Now was the moment to make her move. She prayed her chest pain wouldn't affect her balance. She reached her hand out, but right before they touched, she grabbed hold of the banister, instead. She shouted out in pain as she used her strength to haul her feet on top of the banister. With a swift motion she freed her dagger and ran along the top of the narrow railing. She jumped just in time as one of the warriors reached to grab her leg.

The other one was right on her as her foot met the railing, but she was quick, having dislodged her dagger mid jump. She flung her weapon directly at his palm just as Aleena shouted. "Don't! We can't let her fall!"

Herlot smiled wide. *No, you can't, my friend. I'm of no use to your emperor dead.*

She practically skipped along the banister the rest of the way, until she was a fair distance away from anyone.

"Don't come any closer," Herlot said as Aleena began to approach her. Behind stood Rudi, mouth open, and Movo, eyes wide in horror. When Aleena didn't stop, Herlot knew it was time to test whether or not she could commit to her plan. She looked down at the waves bumping into the ship so far, far below. She wondered how quickly bones could shatter if someone fell from such a height. She couldn't do this. But then she thought of Felix, lifeless, a sword deep in his chest cavity. She could do this. She lifted one foot and hovered it above the sea. "I said stop." She glared Aleena deep in the eyes, hoping her warning would penetrate some sense into her mind.

"Herlot, what are you doing? You could kill yourself. Get off there right now," Aleena said.

"Take ten steps back and I'll think about it." She couldn't risk any one of them coming any closer. Who knew what Iptan tricks they had under their sleeves?

"This is ridiculous."

"So is a war in the sky. Seems like we both have ridiculous ideas that mean the world to us. Take ten steps back and we can talk about how we can both get what we want."

Aleena crossed her arms in front of her chest. "Fine."

As soon as Herlot was satisfied with Aleena's distance, she brought her leg back in. She lowered herself to sit on the railing. Feared by every kingdom in the world, Iptans controlled whatever land and people they decided on as easy as a snap of a finger. And here she was, attempting to do what most Kings would never dare to do, at least without the help of a warlock.

She straightened her spine. "Your star watchers foretell a war in the sky coming upon all of us. Your Emperor wants to win. I *am* the one he has been looking for."

At that, murmurs broke out among the crowd.

"And I *will* help him," she continued. "I have what he needs to win." *I have not learned to use my gold to blend yet, and he might already possess that power, and there is no way I will ever allow them anywhere near the unicorns, but since everyone has perfected the art of repressing truth, who am I not to stretch it?*

More murmurs.

"But first, you will take me and all of the Elfolkians to Eraska. You will give me your weapons, armor, shields, and manpower. We will defeat King Felix. And then, and only then, will you take me to your Emperor. And I'm not moving from this spot, and nobody is coming close to me, until I'm home. If you don't abide, I will jump."

The warrior with the dagger in his palm took a step forward, and as soon as he did, Herlot leaned her weight far back.

"Stop!" Aleena shouted. Aleena grasped and pulled at her braids. "Fine. Fine. But, Herlot, this is not a warship. I can get you home, but I can't give you the rest that you ask for."

"W-what do you mean, this is not a warship? I need shields and armor strong enough to protect everyone from the arrows."

"Not all ships are designed for war and carry an army. Yes, we have a few warriors, but nothing to assist in a battle. This ship is designed for the ultimate comfort of diplomats. In times of danger, it would be accompanied by the warships. Herlot, if you go to Eraska and face Felix's army, you will die. All of you."

This Herlot had not expected. She almost slapped herself for thinking the solution to all of her problems would have been that easy. Yet she didn't believe Aleena completely. She didn't believe an Iptan ship would roam the seas with no way to defend itself. It had to have something else, something like the magic of the powders Gold had shown her, to keep it safe."

"Then you might just have to find a better way to keep me alive by then," Herlot said. "Now we set sail for Eraska."

Aleena shook her head. "Do as she says," she said to the Iptans around her and marched off. Just before Aleena disappeared below deck, Herlot noticed her make eye contact and nod at the men sitting up high in the bird's nest.

She slid off the railing and leaned against it as Movo and Rudi approached her.

"You really plan on standing here the entire trip?" Movo asked.

"I'd appreciate it if you made markings on the floorboards that they're not allowed to cross."

"This is not a child's game. It's Iptans you're fooling with," Movo said.

Herlot shrugged. "What's done is done. I hope you both won't mind fetching me a bite to eat from time to time? Honey bread, if possible..."

At that Rudi smiled. "If you believe this plan of yours will work, so do I. We will cheer to fooling Ipta as we feast on honey bread."

Herlot managed a giggle but got serious soon after. "I will need both of you to keep a keen eye on anything out of the ordinary on this ship. Aleena is lying about the weapons, or perhaps there's something else we could use. She will definitely try to capture me somehow before we reach Eraska. Speaking of which, are we sailing in the right direction toward Eraska, Movo?"

"Yes."

"Good." She hated knowing how easily she could be fooled. She knew so little about the world and navigation, they could have been sailing toward Ipta right now and she wouldn't have known it. "Right. Well, it's best you both be off. Start looking."

"We'll be back with that bread," Rudi said.

"I wouldn't expect anything less from you," Herlot said.

They started to leave, but Movo stopped midstep, then he started following Rudi again. Once again, he stopped. He turned slowly and Herlot felt his gaze pierce her from head to toe. "Were you serious about jumping?"

"Yes."

"You'd rather be dead than have my father conquer your land? Did you even think about the fact that Ipta's predictions are true, and we have an enemy far worse than my father, and you might just be able to help?"

Herlot's breath caught. She hesitated, but then realized she couldn't lie to Movo. Everything he said was true. If she could learn to control the gold in her heart, she might just be who Brom sought, and who Ipta was seeking. But the truth was that she couldn't do it. She didn't know how to blend the leaf, she didn't know how to help Ipta, and she didn't know how to fix Brom's mistakes. When it came to her people and the unicorns, there was only one thing she had in her power to really influence the world they lived in. As much as she wanted to prove Movo wrong, she would tell him the truth. "I'd rather die than miss my chance of killing your father on my own soil."

At that, Movo nodded slowly, and without another word, walked away.

CHAPTER 17
THE CLOUD BREATHERS

For hours, Herlot looked at the clear blue sky, feeling the wind massage her body and the rocking of the ship ease her spirits. She couldn't remember the last time all she had to do was breathe fresh air and listen to the sea. She decided that she would have no struggle keeping up her rebellion for the entire length of the trip. Night hadn't even fallen yet, and she was certain she'd fall in love with her plan even more once she was able to see the stars. For several days, this was all she'd have to do besides the occasional warning glances she'd throw at anyone who came too close, or taking a break to eat the food that Movo and Rudi would bring her.

The sun set and the dinner bell rang. She watched peacefully and listened to the sailors gather and talk about the foods they hoped the chef had prepared before they made their way below deck.

She rested her head against the banister. "How lovely," she said as she delighted at seeing the first stars appear. A cloud of smoke from the sailors in the bird's nest blocked her view for a moment. They did not seem in a rush to get to dinner. She watched them finish smoking as they lowered the sails, and then climbed their way down to the surface. They waved at her before they, too, disappeared below deck.

Now she really had nothing to worry about with everyone busy at dinner. She doubted Aleena would strike now, and if she did, Herlot would hear right away as it was so quiet on the ship.

She yawned, and for the first time that day realized how exhausted she was. Maybe she could close her eyes just for a few moments. Her eyelashes felt immensely heavy, and she let them sink on top of her cheeks.

Someone slapped her, and she almost toppled to her side. Her eyes flew open, ready to defend against her attacker, but no one was there. It hadn't been a slap. Wind pounded against her side and she had to throw her weight against it in order to stay upright.

The ship creaked loudly. She glanced over the railing and saw how quickly the waves had increased in size. Then she looked up and gasped at how the stars were not to be seen anywhere. Only heavy, dark clouds. How long had she fallen asleep? There had been no clouds in sight just moments before.

The entire sea illuminated in light as lightning struck.

Before she could finish another breath, rain pounded down on top of her head and shoulders and her clothing became heavy with the weight of water. Thunder rumbled and rain pounded onto the deck. She didn't know which one was louder. Water dripped down her face, and she didn't have a free hand to wipe some out of her eyes. She feared that if she let go, the wind would take her.

She realized that she was scared. Terrified.

She cried out as the ship rocked to the side. She watched in horror as it tipped so far that she was almost at the level of the waves. Then the boat straightened again.

But it wasn't over.

This time it tipped toward the other side, and she cried out as she fought to hold on.

As the boat straightened again, she tried to get a view of where the entrance below deck was. Would she have enough time to reach it without losing her balance? She had just moments before she instinctively knew the boat was about to tip again. She didn't want to feel the awful feeling of tipping again. She didn't want to be so close to the angry waves.

Angry waves like the anger and hatred in Felix's eyes. She had to stay, she realized. If she made it below deck, Aleena would get to her, no doubt.

She took a breath and prepared for the next plunge. This time sea-wave water crashed onto the deck. Water gushed around her hand, making her grip slippery. How could she survive this?

Her chest muscles trembled as the boat straightened again.

"Herlot!!!" Movo's voice rang through the pelting rain. "Come here! Now!"

She could barely make him out, extending his hand to her from the entrance.

She shook her head. "No!" She would not give Aleena an opportunity to capture her, even in exchange for the dry and safe conditions of the ship below deck.

She took the time she had while the boat wasn't tipping to readjust her grip. Her palm was sore and fingers stiff. The ship started to teeter, and she still had not managed to secure her hold. She was going to fall.

A heavy weight slammed into her back. She cried out as her chest pressed against the banister, however, even though the ship had rocked to an extreme angle, she barely had to hold on. She was squished between the banister and the safety of Movo's body.

"Thank you," she cried. He didn't respond. For the next what felt like ages, all she could barely make out was Movo's forearms flexing through the pounding rain as he fought to keep them both glued to the ship while the storm and waves fought to flip the ship.

Herlot didn't know how much time had gone by, but each time the boat tipped she became less scared of the large, threatening waves. All because Movo was with her. She wondered about what the whales did during storms like this. On the surface it looked like the world was ending, yet who knew what magic was happening deep below the surface?

The first thing she noticed was that the wind began to calm, and the raindrops didn't splash as far off her skin. The wind slowed down to a point where it was possible to breathe out without pressure blowing against her face.

Movo's embrace was still strong around her, but his muscles were less tense. She could sense him looking around. "When did they have time to lower the sails?" he said.

"They did it right before they left for dinner," Herlot said.

Then, it hit her. "They knew the storm was coming." She wiggled just enough to turn around and be face to face with Movo. "They knew it was coming! But it was a clear night, no clouds. Movo, I could see the stars! I closed my eyes for a moment and then the storm was there." Then she realized something else. "And it came from a direction from which the wind hadn't been blowing!"

Her eyes filled with joyful tears. She knew that the Iptans had the power to control the weather, but never had she imagined they could evoke such a powerful storm. "I know how to defeat Felix. Those people in the bird's nest were smoking before they climbed down, and the smoke traveled to the sky. There is something special in that smoke, just like in the globes that Gold gave me. Of course, that's how they protect their land. Imagine the kind of sandstorms they can create if anyone unwelcome comes near their city, or the rain clouds they can manifest to follow their own... All we need to do is capture one of them, no, let's try to take all three to Eraska with us. We can destroy your father and his ships before they even approach land. And whoever is left, we'll be able to kill easily."

She smiled up at Movo. Rainwater dripped down his face and his clothing was soaked through, exposing the outlines of his chest. *He is so beautiful*, she thought. Emotions of joy pulsed through her veins. She stood up on her toes, wanting to kiss him.

But then Movo wrapped his fingers around her hand which was resting on his shoulder and lowered it back down to her side. "Rudi and I will bring you breakfast later," he said, and walked away.

What is wrong with him? she thought. Why wasn't he celebrating with joy that they had found their answer. "Movo, wait! We need to make a plan for capturing the men who sit in the bird's nest," she said.

As if he couldn't hear her, he left without stopping to look back at her.

Why was he acting like this? She pressed her palm against her forehead. *Silly me, he must be exhausted. He'll come back refreshed and then we'll make the plan.*

Something silky and smooth hit her from the side. She turned to her left and saw a beautifully woven blanket.

"Sorry to startle you. I usually don't throw blankets at people. Rain washed your markings away. Hope I'm not standing too close," Aleena said.

Herlot wrapped the blanket around her body.

"You need some dry clothes or else you'll get sick," Aleena said.

"I'll be fine, thank you," Herlot said.

Aleena raised an eyebrow. "You're shaking," she said.

Herlot looked down at her legs and indeed saw that her tremors were moving up from her ankles to her thighs.

Aleena crossed her arms in front of her body. "No matter what I do, even if I send a hundred more storms at you while you're out here, you're not going to give up, are you?

Herlot shook her head no.

"You'll fight me every step of the way, and even if I did manage to get you all the way to Ipta, you won't cooperate with the Emperor until you get your way…Herlot of Alonia, I ask you as a friend. If I take you to Eraska and let you fight this war, will you promise to stay alive and then serve my Emperor with as much passion as you showed this last night?"

Through shaking teeth Herlot spoke. "I want the men who use magic to control the weather."

"We call them cloud-breathers. You shall have them. Along with the few weapons and armor aboard. Can you trust me enough to cross these imaginary lines you drew and help you find dry clothing?"

Herlot marched over to Aleena and extended her hand. "We have a deal." Then, she smiled. "Only if I get my mother's dress back before we dock at Eraska."

Aleena shook Herlot's hand. Then her expression turned serious.

"You know, normally there would have been a very easy way to make you surrender, but I had to resign to try and force you inside out of fear of the storm."

Herlot frowned. "And what was that?"

"I could have threatened the lives of the Elfolkians, Rudi…Movo."

"But you didn't…"

Aleena shook her head. "No. I didn't." She tilted her head. "You wouldn't have surrendered, even for them. Something has changed about you since the first day we met in Da-malathum, Herlot of Alonia."

Herlot hugged herself, dumbfounded. "That's not true."

Aleena was silent.

"It's. Not. True," Herlot said, this time through gritted teeth taking a step forward into Aleena's space.

"Very well. It's not true. I guess I assumed wrong," she said. "Come, let's get you dry clothing."

It's not true. It's not true. I would have surrendered for them, she kept repeating to herself as she followed Aleena, yet she wondered why she needed that much convincing

Chapter 10

The Bell Tower

Herlot adjusted her wool leggings over the new pair of Iptan boots she had received as a gift and reached for a spear. "What about this?"

"Not enough time to teach anyone to use it. Leave it," Movo said.

"It's a sharp, strong metal object. Surely there's something we could use it for," Rudi said.

"If there were more, we could use them for a defensive barrier, but there's not enough," Herlot said.

Herlot, Movo, and Rudi were in the lower level of the ship where the weapons were stored.

"I like this..." Rudi said as he tried on an arm guard.

Herlot blew the dust off a sword blade. "Aleena said we'd dock by sunset. What will we need to do first to prepare?" Herlot asked Movo.

He was busy testing the sharp points of a mace. "Talk to Seum and Asm about structuring formations." He didn't look at her when he spoke. He hadn't looked at her in days.

"Look, I'm sorry I made you spend all night in the storm with me," Herlot said.

Movo stopped his inspection. He dropped the mace. "I need a breath of fresh air. Rudi, check the back corner for any more armor. Look for anything that might be able to be used as a shield."

Herlot sat back on her heels and sighed after Movo left the room. She understood that she had caused trouble, and that Movo had risked his life keeping her safe the night of the storm. She was grateful for it. She would have died had he not been there. She broke a piece of straw in half. Nonetheless, she was beginning to get angry with him for being this upset for so long. Surely they had survived just as bad together, if not worse.

"That boy cares for you an awful lot," Rudi said.

"Then he should care about winning this war as much as I do. I thought he did, turns out he would have rather had me surrender to Ipta." She threw the piece of straw at a haystack.

"That's not true. He would rather have you alive than drown."

"He didn't trust me. Yes, it was risky, but look where we are now. Felix will be lucky to make it to our shore with one ship. Had I not taken the risk, we wouldn't have Ipta's cloud breathers at our disposal. He should be happy."

A knock sounded on the wall.

"Aleena," Herlot said and smiled.

"I thought I'd come fetch you. If you look through the binoculars, you'll see the first glimpses of your land."

Herlot's eyes widened. She was home.

She waltzed through the ship as if she were a young girl out on the first day of snow. Once she was outside, she shielded her eyes from the sun. "I can't see anything," she said.

"Here, look through these. Like this." Alcena showed Herlot how to hold the binoculars.

"Ah-haha!" Herlot exclaimed as cliffs and a fortress appeared in front of her eyes. What an amazing feeling it was to see her home from this view. It was like the first sentence of an adventure story. And the closer the ship sailed, the more of the land's beauty would be revealed, its intricate details, and thousands and thousands of memories lived by its people, animals, and plants. And now, their stories still unfolding.

"Looks like it's not abandoned!" one of the men in the bird's nest shouted.

Herlot frowned.

"How many?" Aleena shouted back.

"Too far to tell—but there's someone in the fortress."

Herlot brought the binoculars back up to her face and adjusted the angle until she was focused on the fortress of Eraska. There, in the top window of the tower, was a hand waving back and forth. Who was this? There was no sign of another ship—the soldiers had abandoned the fortress and sailed back to Damalathum for the time being, and everyone else was hiding in the caves.

The closer they sailed the better she was able to see. Soon she was able to make out a long, white beard flailing in the wind. "Benyamin?" she wondered out loud. "What in the skies is he doing there?"

When she scanned the premises again, she saw that he wasn't alone. There were several people outside of the fortress's walls, dressed in typical Eraskan clothing. More and more showed up, and she could make them out pointing in their direction. Then two figures dressed in black showed up. "Seum and Asm," she whispered. "Why are they all here?" Based on the number of people she saw, it was at least half of everyone who had lived in the cave.

Around her, the Elfolkians were beginning to gather to help the sailors prepare boats to be lowered into the water. Herlot would be on the first trip this time around, that was for certain. The entire time she had imagined that nothing had changed in Eraska—that everyone was at the caves following the routine they had set in place before Herlot and Movo were captured. It seemed that this wasn't the case. What had happened while she and Movo were gone?

She noticed that Movo had joined in helping the others prepare the boats.

"Benyamin and the others are there," she said to him.

He nodded. "I saw."

She grabbed the oar he was about to lift and stepped into his space.

"Are you ever going to talk to me again?"

His eyes narrowed. "I just did."

She let out a strong gust of air. "That's not talking. I thanked you and I apologized to you, yet you still pretend as if I were invisible, unless it's necessary to speak."

Movo straightened. "Listen. The only thing that matters right now is winning this war by getting these Iptans to land so they can finish off my father's fleet when it arrives. Am I not right? That's what you wanted, is it not?"

Herlot looked sideways. "Well, yes. But—"

"In that case, you can help by getting these boats prepared." He turned on his heels and went to help with another boat, leaving Herlot standing by herself holding the oar.

I miss you, she wished she could say. She secured the oar to the attachment that was meant to hold it in place. Well, at least he had accepted the fact that they were going to stand up to Felix.

Soon she was climbing into a boat and being lowered down into the sea. As the first strokes toward land were taken, she couldn't believe that she had made it this far. From almost being hung in front of a crowd in Damalathum, she was about to be back home.

She noticed one of the Elfolkian women paying particular attention to her, yet it was difficult to make out her face through her hood. Herlot tried to get a closer look at her and gasped slightly when she saw the scars on her face. The woman raised her hand to lower her hood. Something struck Herlot about the woman's hands—even the way she had lowered the hood. Herlot had never seen a motion before with as much grace, it was as if the woman was petting a cloud. Her hands were dirty, but so smooth and flawless that the dirt settled on them like a glaze. They were the prettiest hands she'd ever seen.

One of the oars grazed against the rocky bottom. They had reached shallow water. Herlot stood in the boat and waved to the people standing at the shore. A few people gripped their heads and others pointed.

"Herlot!" she heard them shout.

She lunged out of the boat and ran through the water toward shore. Several people ran toward her, Seum in front.

She shouted in joy as she lunged into his arms.

He spun her in several circles as he squeezed her tight. "And my Iptans return our leader just in time for war!" he sang.

She knocked on his chest to signal for him to let her go. "War? How do you know about the war?" she asked as a crowd swarmed around her. She kept eye contact with Seum as someone wrapped her into a hug.

"Ah, yes, there are some things we will need to tell you about," Seum said with a wide smile. "Benyamin has a gift— he can see the stories unfolding in our world that the stars see. We were able to see and watch your entire journey, as well as the announcement for the war."

Herlot's mouth dropped open. This news explained so many of her curiosities about Benyamin. Yet it was another secret. The moment of first excitement had worn off, and now all she could think about was how Seum had tricked her.

"Oh yes, we will talk." The second she had space from getting another hug she lunged at Seum and connected her fist to the side of his cheek.

"We can start with why you lied to me from the first moment we met."

Everyone went silent.

"You tricked me," Herlot said. "I trusted you, but you were tricking me."

Seum shook his head and waved his hands in front of his body. "It's more complicated than that. If I had wanted to, you would have been on your way to Ipta right after I saw you fight at Lorfin. Even though I had my speculations about you, my father and I stayed. I wasn't honest about everything, yes, but we fought in good faith. You have to know that."

Herlot ground her teeth.

"Herlot. I fought with you. I trained you. I was tortured and still stayed with your people after you left. Answer me this: Did my father and I ever force you to go anywhere with us?"

Her eyes softened. He spoke the truth. Both Seum and Asm had stayed and dedicated their time to helping everyone learn to fight. She cringed remembering what Seum had looked like last time she saw him. That he was alive was a miracle after the torture Dartharus had inflicted on his body. And he still was here. However, all that aside, they definitely did have much to talk about.

Around her the Eraskans were beginning to welcome the Elfolkians.

"Rudi! Rudi!" she turned to see Ambro running through the water to the boat where Rudi sat. She smiled as she watched Ambro embrace Rudi the same way they had when they were children.

Before she knew it, she was wrapped in a hug that threatened to crush her bones. "I knew you'd come back. I would expect nothing less from a girl who can throw an ax with the precision of a hawk," Asm said. "It took those fools hours to find a way to lift that gate."

Holy basil, she had missed him. "Did you ever get it back?" she asked.

"No, unfortunately."

"Good. Because you'll get a new one. I made sure the battle axes were packed along with the other weapons."

"Is that—" Asm started as he watched the Iptan carry a gilded chest ashore. Supposedly, this was where their tools were stored that would help the cloud breathers create the storm.

"Yes. I'm aware of everything. The war in the skies, Ipta's secrets..." she glared at Seum. "People with unusual abilities that might help fight the war in the skies. The cloud breathers will help destroy Felix's fleet, but I made a deal, which I am sure you both will be happy about. After we win, I have to go to Ipta."

Herlot stood on her tiptoes and gazed out at the field. There were more friends her heart was beating to see, especially one. "Where is Devotio?"

"With Enri," Seum said. "Your horse has been a hero while you were gone. About a week after your capture, more than half of your people returned to their villages, including Benyamin, who was forced to go with his family. Devotio went on his own to Bundene to find him, just as he saw that Felix had decided to invade Eraska with a fleet. After they returned to our campsite, Asm and I took everyone who had remained to the fortress. Enri and Devotio are gathering those who went back to Temes and Lorfin as we speak."

Had it not been for Devotio, Herlot would have returned, not being able to gather everyone in time. How much she wished she could see him now and thank him. She couldn't wait to hear his words wrap around her ears, to see his beautiful white coat and the magic in his eyes, and most of all to feel the warmth of their friendship—and to finally see him believing wholeheartedly that he was real. She couldn't believe she would have to wait longer.

"And everyone believed Benyamin?" she asked.

"He scared their tree-climbing trousers off telling them the most intricate details of their lives, just to convince them his gift is real, and then told them that you were coming back, and that Felix had declared war."

"How could he not have shared about his gift sooner? Mahtreeh wouldn't have fallen in the trap."

Seum looked down ashamed. "He knew about our intentions. He didn't want to raise more of our suspicions about people with special abilities in Eraska. You will need to speak to him yourself, but Benyamin has a very obscure understanding of our dark star watchers. He will most definitely not want you to go to Ipta."

She couldn't wait to speak with Benyamin and learn more.

"And Mahtreeh?" she asked.

Seum lowered his chin. "We don't know. He and Lucinda made off into the mountains to see if they could find the allies, but we haven't heard anything since. There are places that Benyamin can't see, such as the mountains. Damalathum has been obscured, too, yet we were able to track you. We learned about the war by watching others in the city. Benyamin can only rarely see Felix."

Herlot pursed her lips and nodded slowly, digesting the information.

"Seven days until Felix arrives, based on Benyamin's observations of generals and ship captains."

Herlot sensed into the sand beneath her bare feet. *How many more forms of magic are hidden amidst the lands of our world?* she asked the sand. She had been handed another weapon against Felix, and it had been hiding among her own people all this time.

"We have an eye in the sky," Herlot said in a daze. "We'll be able to know exactly when Felix arrives." She looked up to see that Benyamin was still in the tower where she had seen him last. He waved at her. She waved back, hesitantly. Who would have thought that Benyamin, of all people, could play such an important role to prepare her for having Felix begging for his life at the tip of her sword?

"Speaking of Benyamin's skills, there's someone very special that you brought home with you. Ah, there... I think. Let me take that off your hands, your Majesty," Seum said to the woman with the hood who was carrying a chest.

The woman stopped dead in her tracks. "I-I've seen you before," she said. Her voice was just as beautiful as her hands.

"Movo!" Seum shouted. "Come here."

Movo grabbed a sack from a boat and slung it over his shoulder after which he came to stand awkwardly at Herlot's side.

"Don't be scared," Seum said to the woman. "Every person here will only respect you for what you did. Never before has there been a Queen with as much courage as you showed."

Herlot's stomach dropped. Had Seum said Queen?

Next to her, Movo's sack fell on the sand, the metal weaponry making a loud clank.

"Mother?" he said as he ran to the woman.

Head still bowed, the woman slowly lowered her hood. She raised her head to look up at Movo.

"Oh, Mother..." he said as he pressed his palm against her cheek. Herlot remembered the Queen's face from the execution. It was nothing like what she remembered. The silky-smooth skin was now covered in burn scars.

"Why didn't you come to me sooner?" Movo asked.

"My son—I'm sorry, I would have. I wanted to as soon as I saw you in the forest outside of Elfolk. I didn't know if it was safe, especially on the Iptan ship, to let them know that the Queen whom Felix has been looking for was with them. What if they turned the ship around and interfered with your plans?"

"W-what happened to your face?"

The Queen looked down. "Cora helped me. I needed a disguise, one that nobody in Isolda would ever recognize."

"She's a hero," Seum said. "She saved you both."

"What are you talking about?" Movo asked.

"There was a dream," the Queen said. "This man was in it, and a younger boy and an older man. They told me to change the time of your execution, and it just so happened to be right at the time the sun disappeared."

"Also Benyamin's working," Seum said under his breath.

Herlot couldn't comprehend how any of this was possible, and based on how wide Movo's eyes had grown, she knew he felt the same. Even though she didn't understand it, she did believe it.

"Queen Magdalene, it is an honor to thank you for what you did. I can't fathom the struggles you have been through since, and am grateful we can give you a safe home here," Herlot said.

Queen Magdalene bowed her head. "And it is an honor to meet you. As awful as the situations you and my son have found yourselves in..." she paused to look at Movo, "I have never been more proud. I can only hope your people and anyone in the southern lands will have their homes safe again as they deserve."

"Please, there is plenty of food in the fortress. Nourish yourselves to your heart's desires and let's celebrate this joyful reunion," Asm said.

"And after, we will meet in the tower," Seum said.

Herlot nodded.

She watched as Movo guided his mother up the beach. She yearned to walk next to them, but she had the feeling that she wasn't welcome. If anything, it looked like he wanted to get his mother away from her. Aleena's words rang in her mind. Had she changed? No. Aleena was wrong. She was making sacrifices and being strong. She had to be strong to accomplish killing Felix, and that would require sacrifices. How else could it be?

"Sister," Ambro said, appearing at her side with Rudi.

Never in her life did she think she would feel awkward about how to greet her own brother. She stepped in for an embrace, as did he, but they reached toward the same side and almost collided. She tried again for his other side, but the same thing happened. She sighed and leaned back.

"Ambro," she said with a nervous smile. Last time she had seen him, she'd threatened his life. He looked much better though, that she was happy about. His face was fuller and the bounce in his curls had returned. His eyes weren't sunken in, but they still weren't the adventurous eyes that made Ambro who he was. Or had been.

His lips moved as if he was trying to find the right words to say. Then he sighed and shrugged his shoulders. "I am ready to fight at your side."

Relief filled her chest. Maybe they were still brother and sister first, before their changed, adult versions. Once their reflections had mirrored back to them a girl and boy washing the dirt off their faces together after playing in the mud. She yearned for the same reflection, yet this time it would not be mud, but the bloodshed of victory that would flow into the stream, avenging the waters of Eraska that had been threatened by Felix. "Ours and Elvin's dreams were slaughtered, I would want nothing more than to have you at my side as we put this nightmare to an end. I am hoping that most of Felix's fleet will be destroyed with the storm the Iptans have promised to send to dismantle their ships. If they dare to approach still, we can finish them on this beach. We can do it, Ambro, I just know it."

The air filled with smoke as several Eraskans blew on a fire they were trying to start. One of the Iptans helping to bring supplies ashore squatted with both hands on his thighs and blew a strong gust of air at the fire. It immediately burst into flames and the Eraskans tumbled back. Several children clapped.

"Skies, who is this fellow? And what kind of training did he have to undergo to be able to do that with his lungs?" Ambro said.

Herlot peeled a greasy strand of hair that was matted against her forehead to the side as she laughed. Then she spoke in a mocking, low voice. "Our warriors learn to hold their breath for an hour on their first day of training."

Ambro rested his fists on his hips and puffed his chest. "By the second day, I could send the tide in the opposite way with a mere sneeze!"

Herlot pretended to be about to sneeze as she faced the sea. Ambro covered her mouth. "Now, now, let's not scare the fish away," he said. With that they both held their bellies as they fell into a fit of giggles.

Ambro's giggles hushed, and he cleared his throat. "Herlot," he said. "You were in Damalathum. Benyamin said that Manni had made it there, too, but he has troubles following her story. Do you have any information about where she might be?"

Herlot's lip curled. "No. And if I had known where she was, she wouldn't be alive now."

Ambro cringed as if Herlot had hit him.

"Ambro, you're my brother, but there is a limit to how much of your obsession with Manni I will accept. She betrayed us and hypnotized Felix's soldiers. Because of her, I was nearly executed. Unless she has returned to Eraska, you are not to even speak her name out loud on this land, do you understand?"

"You can't give orders like that," Ambro said.

"Oh?" She pointed to the Eraskans on the beach. "I've rescued these people from the crowpox and led them into battle, and am about to do so again. They trust me. And if I think it's for the best that you go to being locked away inside the fortress, because of a stupid mistake you might make based on the hypnotizing lure of a witch, I know there will be more than several hands to help me lock you in there."

Ambro took a step back and Rudi wrapped an arm around his shoulder. Rudi's eyes were wide as he stared at Herlot.

"Don't look at me as if I were a rabbit that made its way into the lettuce patch. All I ask of Ambro is to never mention her name or seek her whereabouts. Now, let's go eat."

* * *

Herlot examined the opening at the top of the stairs as everyone arranged chairs in the claustrophobic room of the tower. There was only one candle lit. Living in caves for so long made everyone accustomed to being in the dark. Movo and Seum seemed to be having a lively conversation about ridiculous

things people would steal during sieges, such as a goose believed to bless its owner with finding the love of his life. *He's
even being friendly to Seum, and they never got along well,*
Herlot thought.

"Rudi?" she tapped Rudi on the shoulder. "Is that where
the bells are?" She pointed at the opening.

"Yes."

"I want to see them."

She climbed the stairs, Rudi right on her heels, and then
pushed the door up when she reached the top. Up above her
hung two gigantic bells. A bat had made a home inside one of
them. As she took in their size, she was certain that she
wouldn't want to be standing under one of those bells if they
were ever to fall. She stood on her toes to get a closer look at
the bat hanging upside down. The bat stirred and flew away,
clearly disturbed by Herlot's presence.

"You see how impossible it was for them to ring without a
bell ringer? The wind had to not only push them one way, but
then the other for the ringing to be continuous," Rudi said
from behind her.

She couldn't imagine it. Yet it had happened the day she
was born.

"And King Cloudian thought that the wind causing these
bells to ring was the message Brom had written about in the
letter, the message that said Eraska's kings were on the right
path?"

"Yes."

"Absurd." She wished she could see how all these threads
tied together. Brom's people had lost their golden hearts, and
it just so happened that she had one, at least sometimes.
Brom's memories were looking for a golden-hearted human.
Yet how could keeping Eraska isolated from the world cause a
golden-hearted human to be born?

She sighed and let the door fall back down.

Below, Seum, Asm, Movo, Queen Magdalene, Ambro, and Benyamin sat in a circle, chewing on hard rolls and drinking wine. Herlot followed Rudi down the steps and took the empty seat next to Seum, making sure to avoid looking at Movo.

"Well, first of all, I'd like to understand how you did it," she started. "What I understand is that Benyamin is able to see events in other places in the world by watching the stars, and you all managed to contact Queen Magdalene in her dreams?"

"Yes," Seum started. "But you can't just enter the dream world and control what happens. We needed to maintain a balance between a state of consciousness and sleep."

Rudi could barely sit still in his seat. "How in the skies did you manage that?"

"Music. And someone to show us the way... well, Herlot, there is something else we need to tell you. Actually, I think it might be best if we just show you."

Herlot frowned as Seum unraveled a sack and took out Hans's psaltery. She nearly fell off her seat in shock when he positioned it on his lap to play. Seum could play the psaltery? The world had turned upside down while she had been in Damalathum, clearly.

As soon as the notes filled the air, Herlot was drawn to a spot in the room that started to look blurred and unfocused. Herlot rubbed her eyes—it was an awfully dusty tower. But the blurred spot was still there. Everything else seemed clearly in focus.

"Oh, Holy Basil," she whispered as the blurred spot began to take the form of a person. She covered her mouth. "Oh, Hans." She squeezed her eyes shut and opened them again, to make sure she was not imagining things.

"You're home! Finally," Hans said. He floated, *floated*, over to her.

"Is it really him?" she turned to ask Asm. "Are you seeing him too?"

Asm nodded. "It won't take too long to get used to, I promise. It's Hans, after all."

Hans. Someone she thought she would never see again was painted into empty space—speaking as if he were alive.

"I am so grateful to see you, dear friend..." she said. "But how is this possible?"

"It is unusual, indeed, but fairly simple, and complicated too. I was stuck after I died, between worlds. Seum played my psaltery, and because I loved it so much when I was alive, it created a path for me to this world."

Herlot took her time to repeat what Hans said in her mind. She thought of her parents. "I assume this is not possible for everyone who passes..."

Hans shook his head with sad eyes, as if he knew that she wanted to ask about her parents. "If they did decide to return to be ghosts, they'd be stuck like me. Herlot, I want to see this war over. I want to know Felix will never hurt another person again."

Herlot smiled at the thought. Hans's words stirred more motivation in her bones. "When I'm finished with Felix, he won't be alive to have any interaction with humans again," she said.

Hans smiled and nodded. "Good."

She turned to Seum and Asm. "I know neither one of you were completely honest with me during your time in Eraska. As much as I appreciate everything you have done, you should have told me the truth from the beginning. What exactly did you hope to find? How did you think I could be of any help to you?"

Asm twiddled his thumbs. "It's not a simple answer, Herlot. The dark star has shown our star watchers images of dark, winged creatures in the sky—ones that can fly above the clouds. Thousands of them. Many of us were sent to all corners of the world to seek help, not knowing what we would find... And you did clearly need help, we would have never taken you and left the other Eraskans to fend for themselves. You can imagine how we felt, though, when we met you, with a horse of the whitest color we had ever seen, and a sword that could defend its owner by magic."

"On the same land, with a cave that has winged horses painted on its walls," Seum added. "White horses."

Herlot's blood ran cold. Had they chained Devotio to the paintings of the winged unicorns on the walls They were too close to knowing the truth.

Movo cleared his throat. "You found a girl able to fight thanks to the fact that she believed the sword she had been given was magical. Based on your method of training Iptan warriors, it's humanly possible to develop skills in a short period of time if the person is able to reach a particular state. As for the horse, it's foolish to think the color of his coat could make him have anything to do with the paintings on the wall."

Herlot looked to Movo in gratitude for his attempt to instill doubt into Seum and Asm's ideas. She wasn't surprised that he did not look her way. He clearly had grown to despise her, yet why did he still care enough to protect her secrets?

"True," Seum said. "But it is potential we are looking for. We don't know when the dark star's prophecy will come true. Herlot's skills and her sword are a definite sign of potential that could unfold into something even stronger. We would like it if she were already with the Emperor, exploring her abilities if things were to develop."

Asm nodded. "However, we haven't seen any sign of these dark creatures—"

"It's because one should never watch the dark star, the star that sees the future," Benyamin interrupted.

"For centuries its stories have proven true. Not once has it lied," Asm said.

Benyamin laughed. He leaned forward and spoke in a half whisper, as if telling a secret he was too excited about. "You Iptans think you are so mighty, powerful, and intelligent. I already asked Seum, not one of you ever stopped to think that it may be imposing its will on the fools who watch it?"

Asm's face dropped. Benyamin had a point. Yet what kind of a will could a star possibly have?

"Can you explain this dark star more?" Rudi asked. "How can one see a star that does not shine?"

"It's something only our star gazers are trained to see," Asm said. "Our Emperor chooses the most promising astronomy students at a young age. I, myself, could not tell you where it is or how to see it."

"Benyamin," Herlot said. "How do you do it?"

"Hmm... It's not a how. It's an is. I always loved to watch the stars since I was a young boy. One day I just started seeing pictures. Each star showed something different, or the same but slightly different from the one next to it. It's not a method. I think if anything, it is a friendship."

Herlot smiled at that. She liked Benyamin's star communication much more than Ipta's. "Have you ever seen the dark star, Benyamin?"

"In order to see the dark star, one needs to develop a particular sensitivity to dark. Star gazers become accustomed to different colors of star light. The ones who watch the dark star do the same, but opposite. An awful state one must come into, to spend so much time in the absence of light."

Herlot agreed. She couldn't imagine being given the duty of watching the sky every night and not spend any of her attention on the twinkles and pulses of stars, and instead only the emptiness between them.

"Are we certain the Iptans' magic will work to create the storm that will destroy Felix's ships?" Queen Magdalene spoke for the first time.

"Yes, my Lady. I promise you that awful man will never come near you again. But I imagine a voice as beautiful as yours could bring the clouds to your command without the need of our magic," Asm said.

Herlot raised her eyebrows. Asm had a glimmer in his eye.

Queen Magdalene looked down and covered her cheeks with her palm, as if hiding a blush. As awfully scarred as her face was, everything about her shone royalty, at least the kind Herlot had imagined when she was growing up hearing stories about Kings and Queens. Usually, it was the princess who was the heroine. No one ever thought that a Queen could be miserable while married to her King. Not once did she have to save the Prince because the King wanted to kill him, and then disfigure her own beautiful features to escape his wrath.

"How does the weather magic work?" Rudi asked.

"Let me guess. Only specific people trained to do it know," Movo said.

"Correct, Prince!" Seum patted Movo on his back. "And much more complicated than watching the stars. You see, those needed for this task, need to know how to breathe."

"Breathe? Everyone knows how to breathe," Herlot said.

"Yes. But not everyone has mastered the art of bringing something into the lungs, stirring it with a vision, and then sending it out into the world."

He had her there.

"The cloud breathers brought that chest in earlier—the one in that corner," Rudi said.

Herlot and Movo were on their feet at the same time, rushing toward the chest.

"How eager everyone is to understand Iptan magic. It won't explain any more, I assure you," Seum said.

Herlot reached for the clasp on the chest and her hand collided with Movo's. She inhaled a breath at the sense of feeling his skin for a brief moment. She wished it would last longer. As the sensation lulled into a quieter and quieter echo on her skin, disappearing to a point where she yearned for more, Movo worked at unhinging the clasp.

Herlot leaned forward in curiosity as he opened it.

"Huh." She had expected more powders like the ones in the Iptan Headquarters' library, the two she still had in her pocket. But there were just three bottles filled halfway with a liquid. A golden liquid.

Rudi and Benyamin stood behind them, also peering in.

"Looks like the elixir against crowpox," Movo said.

"Looks like urine," Ambro said.

Herlot sat back on her heels. Once again, she was confused about whether or not the Iptan Emperor was able to blend. A golden liquid used to perform weather magic—what else could it be but golden heart magic? If the Emperor had a golden heart, had he found a way to extract the gold the same way Emrys did when she poured her gold into the lake? Yet if the dark star's prophecy was true, and Herlot really could play some role to help Ipta, wouldn't her golden heart and the ability to blend be it? What could the Emperor need her for if he could blend himself? Herlot's head pounded with confusion.

"Where do they get this golden substance?" Herlot asked.

"Now that only the Emperor knows," Asm said.

"Benyamin, can you see him?" Herlot asked.

Benyamin shook his head.

Damnit. Of course, the Emperor would be obscured. Herlot picked up a bottle and turned it around in her hand. Herlot wondered if she could somehow use it to blend the leaf. She wondered what would happen if she drank some. She bit the tip of the bottle and pulled to get the plug out.

"Not a good idea," Seum said as he plucked the bottle out of her hands. "You're not trained. Benyamin, have they set sail yet?"

Benyamin rose and limped toward the window. He stopped next to Seum and examined the bottle with a frown before moving on.

Herlot watched intently as Benyamin looked out the window. He just looked like a normal person looking at the stars. Magic, all of a sudden, seemed like a quiet endeavor. She wondered how many people in the world looked like they were doing something normal, but under the surface were experiencing something extraordinary. Could a simple wanderer in the forest be having a conversation with faeries? Anything seemed possible at this point.

"Looks like they will be ready to leave at dawn," Benyamin said.

"How many ships?" Asm asked.

"Twenty."

Seum clapped his hands. "Well, we have proven our ability to be perceived as a threat. Twenty warships for our merry group of armorless sword swingers. We should be proud of ourselves."

"We should be grateful that we have these bottles..." Herlot mumbled. She couldn't stop thinking about just taking the smallest sip to see if it would help her blend. If she could blend the leaf before Felix arrived, she wouldn't even have to go to Ipta to learn if the Emperor could do it. She could even go with Devotio and hide in his world, away from Brom's letter, warlocks, and a war in the sky. Away from Ambro's blind lust for Manni. And certainly away from Movo's cold heart.

Everyone was focused on Benyamin. She slipped a bottle into her dress pocket. She would sneak out in the night and see what would happen. *Just a sip,* she told herself. That way, if nothing happened, surely there would still be more than enough left to create the storm.

"What's taking so long, Benyamin?" Ambro asked.

Benyamin didn't respond. He raised a finger, and it looked as if he were painting something in front of him. He shook his head as if he didn't like it, and then tried again. "Is something wrong?" Seum asked.

"No. No. Enri should be returning in two days," Benyamin said. "Your Devotio is strong and healthy, Herlot."

How she loved hearing those words. How wonderful it would be if the sip worked, and she could tell him that she had finally completed the task. It would be the best apology for ever doubting his existence, for getting captured and leaving him, the best news to share after their time apart—that he could go and be safe with his family, far away from Asm and Seum's suspicions. They could go and find the perfect tree for the leaf together.

"All those people she has rounded up will sure be disappointed that they came all this way for no fight," Ambro said.

"Oh, there will still be a fight. One or two ships may survive, three, at the most. But that is nothing we won't be able to handle," Seum said.

"Mahtreeh, Lucinda, and Vincent made it out of the mountains. They're camped near the caves right now. They are without the allies. They didn't agree to help them, based on the conversation they exchanged since leaving the mountain."

"They reached the mountain," Benyamin said. "I haven't been able to see more. It is astounding how far starlight can reach—however, some places are limited. Our Eraskan mountains seem to be such a case. There are several places that have this strange occurrence—when a star looks at them, all they see is more stars."

"Like a reflection in a mirror?" Queen Magdalene asked.

"Exactly."

"Will they know where to find us if they make it out? What will they do if they reach the caves and see we are not there?" Rudi asked.

"We left a parchment with drawings showing that we would be at the fortress," Ambro said.

"What could Vincent have been doing in the mountains for so long?" Movo wondered out loud.

"I will learn more tomorrow, perhaps. They didn't trust him, from what I understand, but matters changed when Mahtreeh showed the ring and confirmed Vincent's story. Our friends have not been very talkative on their journey, though. They are disappointed that they are returning without news of the allies agreeing to assist us."

So that was that. "We still have your ability, Benyamin, and the storm breathers. We will do just fine," Herlot said.

Asm stretched back, yawning. He gulped the rest of his wine. "Well, I think we shall call it a night then, heh? Tomorrow we start learning to use the little armor we have."

Sleep. Herlot would finally get to sleep in her own homeland. Tonight, she wouldn't hope for dreams of being back home before she closed her eyes. But first she had to test the liquid in the bottle.

They said goodnight to one another and then Asm showed Herlot to her room. There was a wooden frame filled with a straw mattress, a window, and some pieces of wooden furniture. She wondered who had lived here during the times that King Cloudian had still been alive.

"Oh my," Asm said as he grazed the wilted leaf of a plant in a clay pot. "Would you mind if I took her with me? I might be able to revive her."

Herlot tilted her head. "Asm, I'm quite surprised. I would have never taken you for someone who enjoys plants and refers to them as women."

Asm poked his finger at the soil. "Hopefully one day we will have enough peace to know more about each other than our favorite guards and weapon preferences."

Herlot smiled. "Honey is my favorite food," she said and shrugged.

Asm chuckled. "Mine is a dish made of cooked red cabbage and apples." He tucked the pot under his elbow. "Goodnight, Herlot. It is a blessing to have you back," he said as he went out the door.

Herlot sighed in relief as she spread out on the mattress.

She turned on her side and looked at the candle on the small wooden table and told herself she would give herself time to rest, at least until it had burned down halfway. Then she would go outside and try a sip of the golden liquid.

It was so easy to breathe here. Her belly rose smoothly without the jagged quivers that so often happened in Damalathum—all the worries of not being able to make it back couldn't disturb her peace. Yet she noticed her chest was tighter than usual. Yes, it was still bruised and sore from her experience on the beach—she knew Enri could help with that as soon as she was back, but it was something deeper pressing on her heart. The room was so empty. She hadn't slept a single night without Movo in the same room since they had been captured at the fortress. The ship that took them to Damalathum, the dungeons, the Iptan Headquarters, and the room she, Movo, and Rudi had shared on the Iptan ship, Movo had always been there. If she were to follow her urges, she would have taken the candle and walked the halls of the fortress to his room, knocked, and asked him if it would be alright to sleep in his room. But she couldn't—he wouldn't want her there. He would shut the door in her face, and she would only know even more that everything they had shared didn't mean anything to him anymore.

Perhaps she could pretend. Maybe if she imagined hearing his peaceful breath in his sleep it would feel right. She closed her eyes so she didn't have to see how far from reality her imaginings were. That was better. She imagined breaking the silence and asking him if he was still awake. When he stirred and said yes, not complaining that she had woken him, she'd ask him to tell her something humorous. He would follow that by jokes he had heard in taverns of the vast lands he had traveled to. She could almost hear the sound of their chuckles intertwining and becoming quieter as they laughed themselves to sleep.

Chapter 19
Acorns

Herlot startled awake. The room was completely dark. The candle had burned out. How long had she been asleep? *This is what I get for reminiscing about Movo. I need to stop thinking about him. The more I'm distracted, the more mistakes I'll make. Pull yourself together, Herlot!*

Thankfully her eyes adjusted to the dark and she was able to find a match to relight the candle. Then she noticed that her pocket felt lighter. She reached her hand in. No bottle. "I know I put it in there...or did I?" she thought out loud. Maybe with all of the excitement she had imagined it. She wasn't looking forward to climbing the spiraling staircase all the way up the tower, but she had no choice.

She scolded herself for being scared as she climbed the spiraling stairs. She didn't like not knowing that the constant twist of their structure made it impossible to see far ahead. She kept imagining the dark-cloaked figure waiting just a few steps in front of her, and any next step would bring her face to face with him.

"Stop it," she said aloud. She was allowing her thoughts to get the better of her.

After what seemed like an eternity, she finally made it to the room at the top of the tower. She frowned when the candlelight illuminated an open chest. She rushed over.

"No!" All the bottles were gone.

She fell back on the side of her hip and stared at the empty chest. This had to be a nightmare.

"No!" she shouted again, as if ordering reality to change based on her protest.

"Who did this?" she shouted, looking around at the empty room.

She would ring the bells and wake everyone up and find out. As she made her way toward the stairs, she got a view out the window. Someone was out on the beach, illuminated under the moonlight. She sprinted to the window. She couldn't make out who it was, but she saw the faintest glimmer of gold.

She raced down the spiraling staircase, tripping and colliding into the wall. She managed to pound on several doors as she ran down the hall, shouting for everyone to wake up.

Once she made it outside the fortress, she gripped at her hair as she tried to decide which would be the quickest way to the beach. She would have to backtrack if she used the exit. Luckily, she had enough training from climbing buildings in Damalathum.

She kicked off from a barrel to reach the roof of the stable. The boards creaked as she ran across. She lunged across the gap between the stable and wall and hauled herself up. It was quite a ways down. She lowered herself until she was just hanging, holding on with her hand, and then she let go. She fell backward as her feet hit the ground and she let her body tumble backward in a roll.

She swung her arm with all her strength as she hurried toward the beach.

She could make out his long, gray hair now. Horror seemed to hit her in the face as she realized he was pouring the contents of the bottles into the sea.

"Benyamin, no!"

As she reached his side, she could feel death choking her and threatening every person on Eraskan soil—the empty bottles and the golden liquid mixing in a whirl with the seawater.

She threw herself into the water, trying to scoop up the golden liquid.

"The magic is bad. Don't touch it," Benyamin said.

"This magic was our weapon to winning!" She gulped the water she managed to gather.

"What are you doing?" Movo's voice practically roared through the night.

"Get off me!" she shouted as his arms wrapped around her waist.

"Do you know how stupid it is to drink sea water?"

Of course, she knew, but she needed the golden liquid. She twisted her torso side to side and kicked her feet to try to free herself from his grasp.

"No!" she shouted again and again as she felt the sand beneath her feet. "I need to go back in the water! Don't you understand?"

She extended her neck to bring her lips to his forearm and bit down hard. The taste of metal burst into her mouth.

Then she didn't know what hit her. All of a sudden, she was pinned to the sand, Movo's body wrapped around hers in a way that made it impossible for her to even wiggle.

"Did you seriously just bite me?" His voice was loud and threatening.

"The ships are coming! I need the gold!" she shouted.

"Herlot, it's gone. There's nothing you can do about it now."

The second she felt his grip lessen she fought to let herself free, and then that awful pressure was back, and she was stuck. She was trapped with the image of Felix's satisfied eyes as he drove a sword into her chest. No. No. No. It was she who was supposed to pierce his heart!

Her legs and arms began to go numb, and a tingling sensation spread all across her head. Her heart pounded fiercely. She didn't know if she was breathing. She couldn't feel her breath.

"Let go!" she screamed.

"You holding her isn't helping. Let go before she passes out," a voice said. It sounded like Seum's. Her vision was beginning to blur.

She thought she felt the pressure release, but she couldn't feel her body. Through her vision it seemed like she was upright. Seum's face came into her view, but her eyes couldn't hold still.

"Breathe very slow and listen. Your people are beginning to gather to see what has happened. It is better they do not see their leader like this. I need you to close your eyes and breathe slow. Pretend this is training and we need to act that we are asleep so the enemy thinks we are dead. I am going to count to three and then I will pick you up, are you ready to follow the plan?"

"Am I breathing?" Herlot asked. She needed to know that she wouldn't suffocate.

"Yes. You are breathing beautifully. Now, close your eyes. One... two...three..."

Herlot wasn't sure what was happening. There was a hint of floating, but she couldn't know for sure because it was so hard to feel anything. She wanted to open her eyes but Seum had said there was an enemy and they had to pretend to sleep. Maybe if she pretended to sleep long enough Felix wouldn't come either. Felix. He probably knew the gold was gone. He would make the ships go faster. But if she slept the ships wouldn't come.

"Seum, will you make sure everyone sleeps?" she said. She barely could hear her own words.

"Everyone is sleeping already," Seum said.

"Oh good. Ships don't sail when we sleep."

* * *

Herlot's vision focused as a bucket of warm water was poured on her back. As the water rose, she began to feel her toes and knees again. She realized that they were shaking. How long had they been doing that? She could make out the tub she was sitting in and the fire in the fireplace. The stack of wood. A bed.

She was breathing.

"You're lucky you decided to be delirious right when I decided the middle of the night was a fit time for a bath, or else this would be cold water," Seum said.

"Thank you." She couldn't imagine how her muscles would ever stop shaking if she were sitting in cold water now.

Seum swung an arm over the rim of the tub. "You have more fear running through your veins than the first day I started training you."

Herlot looked away to the side. That was definitely not true.

He splashed her in the face with water. "Look at me."

"Are you enjoying yourself, seeing me like this?" she said as her lips trembled. "I know I made a scene. Could you at least leave me in peace and quiet so I can pull myself together?"

Seum swirled his hand in the water. "If you can't pull yourself together in a bathtub filled with warm water, you won't be able to hold your ground with what's coming for you. You're about to face an invasion of twenty warships practically defenseless. Every single one of the people in this fortress, and the ones Enri is bringing back with her, will need to see you calm—that is, if you do not wish to surrender or run, which I would recommend at this point."

Herlot widened her eyes. "Surrender? Run? How dare you even suggest it?"

Seum nodded a few times. "I thought you'd say that. Hoped you wouldn't, but knew you would."

"How could he?" Herlot hissed. "He just poured them all into the sea. He said the magic was bad. What does it mean?"

"I don't know. It's saved thousands of lives from crowpox and protected our land for centuries. Benyamin is very special, but his mind is not always clear."

Herlot nodded. "He's a threat."

At that Seum frowned. "He wouldn't hurt a fly…"

"He has practically killed all of us!"

"Not intentionally."

"He needs to be locked away. Before he does any more damage," Herlot said through gritted teeth.

Seum looked appalled. "No. You can't do that."

"If you won't help me, Aleena ordered the three cloud breathers under my control. I'll have them do it. Now leave. I want my peace. I have a lot of thinking to do."

Herlot looked away again because she did not care to see Seum's disapproving expression. He could take his opinions about her and weave a basket with Movo. Two of the fiercest men she knew were acting like weak fools during a time she needed their support the most.

"Wait," she said as she heard Seum open the door to leave. "What are my chances, really?"

"We will suffer heavy losses. We have trained good fighters, but we will be too outnumbered."

"Can we win, though?"

"If someone manages to fight their way forward enough to kill the King, that would be the end of it."

That was all she needed to know.

She waited for Seum to close the door. "I can do it," she said, but her body began to shake again, as if it were laughing at her for trying to hide her fear.

She focused on the warmth of the water and imagined its comfort soaking into her muscles. She imagined a hug from her mother. After a while the shaking eventually stopped. She rested her head against the tub and closed her eyes.

Then she remembered the last time she had been engulfed in water and this relaxed. Ipta's bathing chamber. The never-ending darkness. The nothing.

She swung herself over the edge of the tub and toppled onto the floor, backing away from it until her back hit the wall. She hit the back of her head against the wall. "Come on, Herlot. Pull yourself together." She knew the only thing that could ease her fear of this darkness, this nothingness: killing Felix. There were twenty ships coming and she only had a few days to prepare. She had to start now.

* * *

When her body finally calmed down, Herlot dried herself off. She slipped on her dress. The water still dripping from her strands of wet hair cooled her neck. She swallowed her emotions about what she was about to do and headed out into the hall. She knocked on the door of the cloud breathers. "I might need your help. Follow me," she said when one of them opened the door.

"Come in!" Benyamin called after she knocked on his door.

She was surprised to find Ambro in the room with him. They were sitting on the floor with cups of tea in their hands.

Next to Ambro was a roll of parchment. Herlot raised an eyebrow.

"What are you doing?" she asked.

"Just reading a story."

"Sea monsters?" Herlot asked.

Ambro shrugged. "Old habits die hard."

She wondered how Ambro could find pleasure in reading their favorite childhood stories from when they lived in Alonia. Not that pleasure mattered at this point. She was here to get an important task done. She cleared her throat.

"Benyamin, I need you to follow these men. They are going to lock you in a room below for the time being."

"What?!" Ambro exclaimed. "Absolutely not. Have you lost your mind? Actually, forget your mind, have you no heart left? How dare you try to lock Benyamin away!"

Ambro knocked his cup of tea over as he stood.

"I'm sorry, but, Benyamin, you have threatened the life of everyone by pouring out those bottles. That was our main defense against Felix. I can't risk you hurting anyone else with your ideas. Not until the battle is over."

"Didn't you listen to him?" Ambro threw his hands in the air. "The Iptan magic in those bottles was bad."

"It has saved *countless* lives," she hissed.

Ambro curled his lip, but before he could speak, Benyamin interrupted him.

"The magic is bad."

"You have no proof."

"I know it doesn't feel right."

"Benyamin, I won't say this again. I need you to follow these men."

"No," Ambro said, taking a firm stance between Herlot and Benyamin.

Don't make me do this, Ambro.

"Step out of the way, son," Benyamin said as he rested his palm on Ambro's shoulder. "I will be alright. I could use a few days' rest. But, Herlot, I would like to give you a gift. He extended his palm and revealed a couple of acorns."

Herlot lowered her eyes. "I appreciate the offering, but I hope you understand that at the moment I don't want anything to do with you, especially receiving any gifts."

"Please. These are special—"

"Take him by force if he doesn't cooperate," Herlot said to the cloud breathers and turned on her heels to leave.

She walked faster and faster from Benyamin's room. She wanted to get far away from Ambro's exasperated cries.

She marched straight outside, out the gate, and then turned to head for the beach. She took a seat in the sand and watched the horizon as the sun rose. She tried to imagine what Felix's ships would look like as they appeared one after another where the sky met the sea.

At noon she left the beach and headed to the field between the fortress and the woods. She walked back and forth and imagined stepping on every possible spot it had to offer. And she thought endlessly about formations. She had managed to get men who could cause storms to form. Surely there had to be something else she could think of. But what? What? She still had the powders Gold had given her. They would work to her advantage, but would they be enough?

A girl her age brought her a plate of food in the evening. "Thank you," Herlot said. "Please let the others know that I will be addressing everyone tomorrow."

After that she returned to the beach and imagined the ships again, until she couldn't sit upright anymore. She fell asleep imagining that they would never appear, as much as she knew that they would. Soon now. Just a few more days.

* * *

"I missed you."

Herlot fluttered her eyes open. A gentle, warm wind played around her ears. She thought she had heard a voice.

Her eyes opened wider, and she shot up to her knees.

"Devotio!" she shouted.

She leaped forward and wrapped her fingers around his mane as she hugged herself against his neck. "I have missed you so much," she said.

She laughed as he nuzzled her back.

She felt more alive than the sun that was rising. She felt more free than the seagulls flying above. She felt like a giant of joy, as if she could stretch her hand out and it would touch the horizon.

She laughed again as she stepped back to take in Devotio.

Everything had been worth it to get her to this moment.

Devotio turned his side to her, and she didn't hesitate one moment to jump on. It felt so natural as if she had never left.

Devotio waded into the water. "Tell me your story," Devotio said.

"Don't you know most of it because of Benyamin?"

"Yes. And I sent the fireflies. But I'd like to hear it the way you tell stories, like you once did."

"You sent the fireflies? I don't know how—but I knew it. It was almost like you were there."

"It's easy to speak with them. They have the spirit of unicorns—of Ola. I asked them to help you. They sent their wishes to the sea, to the whales, and the whales told their wishes to the fireflies of the northern lands."

She leaned forward and rested her cheek against his mane. "Thank you. They saved our lives." She wished the fireflies could protect them against the arrows in the daylight.

"Will you tell me the story?"

Herlot shook herself out of her strategizing and began to tell Devotio everything. But most of all she told him about the moments right before she thought she was going to die, and how she knew she could never doubt his existence. In those last moments, she only had her most precious memories, ones of her loved ones, and ones of him.

She felt safe and free as she finished her story. And she loved how there was no saddle, like all the horses had that she had seen in the northern lands.

"Full speed!" she shouted.

Wind and seawater droplets swished around her as she lifted her hand up. The beach floor hummed as Devotio's hooves danced across. Herlot shouted out in joy as he began to run more in the water, and a particularly large wave crashed against their side. She shivered from the cold water, but it did not bother her one bit. She felt even more awake. She felt better than she had in a long time. How good it was to race without running away from someone or having a set place to reach. How good it was to race for the pure thrill of it.

The sound of flapping encapsulated her. It sounded like birds flying but slower and louder. She glanced down and gasped. Two enormous pairs of wings stretched out from Devotio's sides. She blinked and they were gone. Then she blinked again, and they were back.

"I think you have wings!" she shouted over the flapping sound.

"I can feel them, yet they're not there," Devotio's voice wrapped around her.

"How strangely beautiful. They're there one moment and gone the next," she said. "What should we do?"

"Keep running."

"Do you think you can fly?"

"No. But I like imagining I can right now."

"In that case, we keep running!"

Whatever was happening, she loved it enough to not try to decipher it. She wanted Devotio to enjoy every moment of it. It felt like hours as they raced down the beach, and even more as they raced back. Devotio did not tire.

Eventually when the fortress came back into view, Devotio slowed. The wings appeared less and less until eventually they didn't at all.

"That was absolutely astounding. Has that ever happened before?"

"No. I hope it does again, though."

"Me too."

She realized that all the Eraskans were crowded on the beach, many more than when she had arrived, since Enri and Devotio returned. They waved at her. They looked happy. And they also looked confident in her, that was most important now because of what she would ask them to do.

She noticed Enri break away from the crowd and run toward her and Devotio. Herlot slid down Devotio's side and ran toward Enri.

"Hello! Hello!" Enri cried, waving her arm up above her head.

They collided in a hug. "Oh, my friend, how I have missed you," Herlot said. "Thank you for everything you have done."

"It is so good to know that you're back. I didn't know if I could convince them to come back."

"But you did."

"Thank the skies. I've heard the news."

They released from the hug.

"Twenty ships on their way. And Benyamin is locked up?" Enri asked.

"Yes. I had to. As much as we care for him, I don't trust him right now. We could have all easily survived and won. It's going to be much harder now, and many of us are going to die."

Enri's expression turned serious, but Herlot could still see a glimmer of confidence in her eyes. Good.

"I—we all trust you to make the right decision. You've taken us this far."

"Thank you, Enri. Since everyone is here, now is a good time to set the plan. Devotio?"

Devotio appeared at her side and she climbed back on. They trotted toward the crowd of Eraskans.

"Eraskans! Next time we are on this beach, you will be outnumbered. Your enemy will have armor and weapons that you do not. And for many of us, it will be the last day in our bodies."

She nudged Devotio to stop so she could evaluate everyone's expressions. Some looked nervous, switching their weight from one foot to the other. Some looked down, as if sad about their future. And others looked her straight in the eye with their backs straight.

She leaned forward, resting her chest on Devotio's neck, as if she were leaning in to share the best part of a story. Her father used to do that.

"But you will be alive when you fight. And you will be alive after you die, every passion of yours buried in this land that you fought to defend. This land in a world where people fight wars for gold, will hold the souls of a people who fought to live free of tyranny. And I promise you, if you come to this beach with a song of freedom singing in your heart, Eraska will be forever ours."

Those who had been nervous and sad before now also had their backs straight.

"How can we win?" someone shouted.

Herlot straightened again. "You might think it's impossible, but this is the only place we can win. If we surrender, Felix will torture us and burn our land. If we run and find a new land to live in, he will only come again, and he will continue to do this to others. If we stay here and fight, we are creating a new law in this world— kings can no longer use the threat of death to get what they want."

She smiled at her army. "And we *can* win. I've been to Felix's world. It's a world where people fear their King, where children are put into dungeons at a young age and trained to live a life in despair because they shake at the knowledge of their leader's power. These soldiers come with better training, weapons, and armor than we have. But I promise you, every single one of them that you will face does not have the will and passion that swings a sword like you. Deep down inside they are more afraid of you than you will ever be of them, because the mere fact that you exist, willing to fight them, is living proof that their lives have been infiltrated by lies. They won't trust Felix's power as much as they have before. They won't trust what they believe to be the power they fight with. Eraskans...whistle if you trust your power."

Herlot closed her eyes and soaked into the song that erupted across the beach. She could hear the whistling of her people intertwining with the sound of the crashing waves.

"Remember this. Feel it in your being when the ships arrive, and Felix will be outnumbered."

At that her people erupted in cheers and battle cries. She made eye contact with Seum, who leaned on one leg, clearly amused, as he clapped.

Devotio and she trotted toward Seum as Asm ordered everyone onto the field for training. She searched the crowd for Movo but couldn't find him.

"Nice speech," Seum said.

"Thank you. Will it be enough?"

Seum shrugged. "We will see."

Herlot nodded. "Shouldn't we train on the beach? They'll be weak coming off the boats."

Seum shook his head. "Too many. And those paths leading down here are too narrow. You'll face hell trying to retreat, especially with the arrows."

"Those forsaken arrows..."

"Asm has a group cutting anything wooden in the fortress to a shape suitable to make more shields than the ones the Iptans gave us."

Herlot nodded. "Good. Good..."

"I'll be training a group within the fortress itself. That way Felix will feel pressure from behind, as well as from the front, once they come onto the field."

"Very good," she said. She would not have thought of that. Possibility of winning seemed a little more likely. She felt some relief, but it was mixed with doubt. She knew nothing of how to prepare for such a battle. All she could do was give a speech to ignite the spirits. For the rest of it she was dependent on Seum, Asm, and Movo.

"I have these," she said as she reached for the powders wrapped in fabric.

"Use them once you're in their lines, and there's little of our people surrounding you. They will help you clear your path to the King. You should be at the fortress, it will be the quickest path for you to reach him."

"What if he stays on a ship?"

Seum chuckled. "Then he's a coward. He won't want news to spread that he remained on the ship while his army battled villagers. No, Herlot, Felix will be here, I guarantee you that. He wants to see you dead as much as you want to kill him."

Her lip curled in anger. Felix would not get what he wanted.

"Herlot," Ambro said as he tapped her on the shoulder. "Benyamin keeps asking for you. He says he needs to give you a gift."

She rolled her eyes. "He can hold on to his acorns until after the war."

Ambro winced a little at her words. "Shouldn't we let him out, at least to watch the stars at night?"

"No. I don't trust the information he'll give us. Not after what he did. And that's the end of it. I don't want to hear any more about Benyamin. Just make sure he is comfortable and well fed. He can work on making shields if he wants."

Silence from her friends.

"Well," she started, "I'm going to grab my weapons and join everyone out on the field." At that she left Seum and Ambro and headed toward her room in the fortress. As she was dressing for training, a knock sounded on the door.

"Enri," she said, smiling as she saw her friend.

"I took good care of these when you were gone." Enri pulled off the necklace hanging around her neck, and hidden mostly beneath her dress, to reveal the leaf. From behind her, she unsheathed a sword and presented her the sword that Emrys had made for her.

"Thank you, Enri. You don't know how much this means."

"You think the Emperor will help you learn to blend when you go to Ipta?" Enri asked.

"Right now, I don't have any other options. I don't even know where to begin in trying to do it myself, I tried many times in Damalathum. Nothing happened. Maybe in Ipta I can at least find more information. Either way, traveling there is the smartest thing I can do while I keep trying. I have a feeling it will be much easier without Felix to worry about."

Enri put her hands on her hips. "Herlot, what if you die out there?"

Herlot sighed and turned to put on her boots. "I am not going to die."

"I think you should take Emrys' sword this time."

"I can't kill with it, Enri."

"You could fight your way all the way forward to Felix using it. It won't let anyone touch you. And once you reach Felix, just use your other sword."

"It doesn't work like that, Enri. I'd need someone at my side the entire time. If the soldiers aren't injured, they're going to keep attacking me, and I could be in a standstill for ages using that sword. The more people I'm fighting, the more likely it is that one of their slashes will kill me during the time when I am reaching for my other sword. And worst of all, the longer I fight them, the longer it will take me to get to Felix, which means the longer everyone else has to fight."

"I see. I'd still feel better if you had it."

Herlot's eyebrows furrowed as she noticed the concern on Enri's expression. "You're worried about something. Be honest with me."

"I just returned from looking at Movo's arm. Herlot. You really bit him. And I know you weren't completely...well last night. It reminded me of your fit when we were at Temes. And on top of that, what if you accidentally start blending during the fight? Movo said you ran all the way from Damalathum to Elfolk under Brom's influence."

"In that case, I'm dead no matter what. Brom won't think of using Emrys' sword to defend me, trust me."

"Yes, but had you at least been holding Emrys' sword at Ruelder, when you came out of Brom's trance, you could have defended yourself from the soldier while you were coming to."

She hated the feeling of being dependent on that sword for her life. Seum had taught her without it. A true warrior did not need a magical sword. If she was any good at anything, she had to fight with a real one.

"If you can't do it for yourself, do it for Devotio. That sword might be the deciding factor of whether you live to blend the leaf, or die to leave him defenseless."

Herlot nodded. "Fine. I'll take it. That's all, I hope?" She would do it for Devotio, but all of a sudden she wished for Enri to leave. She didn't like how Ambro, Rudi, and now Enri looked at her, as if they doubted her. She had had good reason to throw a fit, both times. Nobody else understood the pressure she was under.

"Y-yes."

"I'll see you out on the field, then."

Enri hovered for another moment and then let herself out. Herlot placed the leaf in a storage chest, and then rested the sword against the windowsill. The bed frame and table in her room had already been dismantled for shield pieces.

She adjusted all of her weapons and then took her leave. She turned to walk as she closed the door and nearly collided with Movo.

"Pardon me," she said.

Movo made some undecipherable mumble of approval. She nearly laughed. He wasn't even speaking words to her anymore. He walked ahead of her as if she didn't exist. She noticed the white bandage around his forearm. She might have apologized to him had he waited long enough to give her a chance.

Pride rumbled in her belly as she entered the field and saw the Eraskans. Asm was showing a group the angles of how to hold a shield above their heads. Seum's group was practicing dismounting riders. Seum tumbled off his horse, landing on his back with his chest exposed. A girl from Temes pointed the tip of her sword to his throat. He stood, patted her on the back, and jumped right back on the horse for another round. She was grateful for him. He'd be knocked off his horse for as long as it would take, until he felt confident in his students' abilities. He had changed immensely since the first time she met him.

She spotted Devotio. In another section of the field where Movo was gathering the best riders they had. He was the last person she wanted to train with, but it would be where she and Devotio would learn the most. "Are you sure you still want to fight? You don't have to if you don't want to," she said.

"I do."

Devotio was an asset, yet she hated the fact that he'd be fighting. "When the time comes, you'll get me as far as you can. As soon as I'm dismounted, you get out of here...wait for me in Alonia."

As soon as they joined the group, Movo lifted a saddle off the ground and began to lift it onto Devotio. "What are you doing? Stop," Herlot said.

"You need to get used to it."

"I can ride without it."

"Yes, but you won't be able to fight. You'll have to hold your sword, and you won't be able to hang onto his mane. The stirrups will help you stay on for longer."

She opened her mouth to protest, but Devotio stopped her. "Listen to him. I'm fine."

"Very well."

And then started an entire day's worth of hard work. Movo had wedged long sticks all over the field, and they had to practice swinging their swords as they rode by them. Herlot practiced until her legs shook from the strength it required to perform the skill while staying on Devotio.

Just as they were finishing, she thought she heard a whistling sound emitting from the forest.

"Who is that?" someone asked.

"Oh my skies, it's Mahtreeh and Lucinda!" someone else called.

"And Vincent," Herlot said.

"We didn't stop to sleep after we found the parchment in the cave," Mahtreeh said as he hugged Enri. Mahtreeh noticed Herlot as he looked over Enri's shoulder.

"You're back!" he shouted.

Within moments she was wrapped in Mahtreeh's hug. It wasn't as strong as Asm's, but just as warm. "You made it, you made it!" Mahtreeh sang.

"It's so good to see you," Herlot said.

"Tell us about the allies," Asm said, appearing at the scene.

"Well," Lucinda started. "Had it not been for us and the ring, they would've kept Vincent hidden away for who knows how long."

"Never approach mountain people without a ring," Vincent said, unamused.

"So why didn't they come?"

"That's where the only good news is," Mahtreeh said. "They offered us sanctuary for however long we need. Herlot, it is perfect. There's a lake, and gardens. It's protected. They're skilled fighters. And—and, oh, it is just beautiful. There are gemstones everywhere. And when the sun shines on them in the valley, oh it is another world, I tell you."

Herlot's head was already shaking as he spoke. "No. We're not hiding again."

At that, Enri began telling Mahtreeh and Lucinda about the warships sailing their way, and explaining about Benyamin's gift, and how he had managed to convince everyone.

Movo leaned forward and spoke near her ear. "My father wouldn't be able to reach them in those mountains. Ever. You could go off on your Iptan journey tomorrow if you wanted to."

"I don't think you were there to hear my speech this morning," she said through gritted teeth.

Mahtreeh and Lucinda's mouths dropped open as Enri began to share the details of how they were planning to fight Felix.

"But didn't you hear what I said? We can go to the allies and—"

"I did, Mahtreeh. And it is wonderful. But we're not hiding or running anymore. No matter what," Herlot said. "Vincent, I need to know that you are willing to fight for us. If not, I need you to leave this land."

"I will stay and fight." As he said it, he wrapped his hand around Lucinda's waist. Herlot thought she saw Mahtreeh's shoulders slump a little.

"Can I trust your word?" Herlot asked.

"I will vouch for him. He won't leave our side," Lucinda said.

Herlot nodded. "Then, it is settled. Please, there is plenty of food in the dining room, although the tables and chairs have been taken. There has been enough training for the day. Eat and rest, all of us. No ale. Enri, can you make sure anyone particularly sore gets some of your salves? And anything else you could conjure up that will help everyone be at their best for when Felix comes."

"Come on, Devotio. Let's find berries before supper," Herlot said as she began to lead Devotio into the forest.

"Salves won't help them stay alive in an overly outnumbered battle..." she heard Enri mumble.

She tried to keep walking into the forest but couldn't. She stomped back. "It's not a difficult task. I asked you to make salves, not strategize and let everyone know your opinions. If you can't complete your duty without spreading doubt, you can join Benyamin."

She froze after she spoke the words. Everyone's dead silence. Enri's lips trembling. She clearly was not welcome here anymore. Then, so be it, she could worry about friendships after the battle. She walked into the woods and noticed how the conversation between the group started up again the moment she was out of sight.

* * *

Herlot was deep into her dream. She knew she was dreaming because she was in Alonia, a fully blossoming Alonia. Everyone was still there—her mother, father, Agatha, Simon—all healthy, going about daily tasks with only another peaceful day to look forward to. She held a bucket in her hand, which she intended to use for milking the cows. Oh, how she would look forward to spending her dream time doing something as simple and relaxing as milking the cows.

"Good day, Herlot," Manni said, stepping out from the side of Herlot's home.

Herlot wanted to shake her fist at the skies. Did Manni *really* have to show up in her dream? She spotted a particularly jagged rock. She could have it be done and over with in a moment. But this was a dream, a nice one at that. Did she really want to turn it into a nightmare? She had enough nightmares to look forward to in her real life.

Herlot swallowed. "Good day, Manni."

Manni grabbed Herlot's basket and set it on the ground. "I thought we could go to the meadow and pick flowers."

Manni was actually being nice. She seemed genuine. Herlot decided to take her chance at the impossible that could only happen in dreams.

Manni took her hand and led them toward the tall grasses swaying in the wind.

"Oh, my, look at these!" Manni exclaimed. She swooshed up a cluster of purple flowers at the meadow's edge. "They would look beautiful in a headband in your hair."

They would look even better on your grave, Herlot wanted to say.

Herlot soon became enchanted, picking flowers of a delicate yellow. She brushed her fingers over them. The softness of their fluffy petals was mesmerizing. "Manni, look at these! I've never seen these yellow fluffy ones in our meadow before."

"We must show them to everyone," Manni said.

They strolled the village paths, Herlot carrying her bouquet of yellow flowers, Manni her purple ones.

"What a beautiful bouquet!" exclaimed Mayabelle, an elderly woman, as she came over to sniff Manni's flowers.

"Let's switch," Manni suggested when they arrived at the hearth. She shoved her bouquet into Herlot's hand and snatched the yellow flowers away from Herlot.

Herlot felt a hint of uneasiness stir in her belly.

"Darling! Come look at these delightful yellow flowers! Oh, I must go pick some of my own!" Bee exclaimed to her husband, who was working on their roof.

A crowd began to gather around Manni and the unusual yellow flowers. Herlot waited until they dispersed, after which Manni addressed her.

"I don't think you ever understood why it was better that I read your poem, so I decided it was time to show you, instead. You see, even if you had something beautiful to share, people wouldn't have noticed it, but they will if I do. Everyone enjoyed the poem because I read it. They probably would have barely listened to the end of it had it been you," she said. Then she dropped the yellow flowers into the firepit and walked off. "And you, you, of all people, really think you could ever perform magic?" She turned on her heels and walked away, laughing.

Herlot gathered the scattered yellow flowers. Many had lost their petals and were covered in ash. How could she have been so stupid, to believe Manni could actually be genuinely nice, even in a dream? She added the injured flowers to the bouquet of purple ones and held them to her chest.

"I think you're all beautiful," she whispered.

Thunder rumbled across Alonia. Herlot looked up at the sky. There were no clouds as far as she could see.

The ground shook and she stumbled left and right to hold her balance.

Her hand went up to shield her face as something incredibly loud crashed and rang next to her. She looked to see what it was. "What?" she exclaimed as she saw the fortress bells lying on the hearth.

The ground shook again, and this time she fell.

Chapter 20

The Mysteries of the Sea

Herlot startled awake as her body made impact with the ground. She scrambled to her feet as a rumbling shook the fortress. Her mind whizzed to understand what was happening around her. She screamed and covered her head as rocks fell around her. *What is happening?* She was too frozen with fear to move, but more rubble continued to fall.

Herlot, you have to go. Go!

She crawled toward the door and fumbled with the handle. She could hear screams and yelling outside of it.

Horror struck her in the face as the scene behind the door unfolded. The entire front of the fortress had been demolished. Felix's fleet floated outside. Soldiers swarmed the beach. To her right, the bells from the tower lay dead. She thought she saw someone's arm sticking out from beneath them.

A strange contraption sat on top of the ship closest to the beach. A group of soldiers were mounting a large, round object onto it.

"Everyone to the forest! Now!" Asm shouted. "My lady, please, come with me." He wrapped Queen Magdalene close to him and they disappeared out of Herlot's vision.

Herlot fell as she tried to take a step out. The fear was too overwhelming.

And then she cried. She looked around at the shattered fortress walls. Their plan to strike Felix from behind was just as shattered.

Movo slid down a hill of rubble toward her. "Your weapons! Go get your weapons!"

She understood his words, but all she could do was cry. The helplessness, the confusion, the impossibility to conquer what was happening was too overwhelming.

Movo pushed past her into the room. Soon she could feel him strapping something across her back. He tied a belt around her waist and slipped two daggers in.

"Come." He wrapped his arm around her waist and dragged her fear-struck body forward. After several steps, something whizzed by them.

She screamed again as she heard it make impact with what had been her room just moments ago.

All she wanted to do was wrap herself in a corner and cover her ears and eyes. She started fighting against Movo. Panic told her she needed to find a place to hide now. "Please, let me go, let me go," she cried.

Movo stopped and grabbed her shoulders. "Listen. We are not safe here. If we make it to the forest, we will be safe, I promise."

She wanted to hide. Needed to hide.

"Herlot, please, look at me." He held her face with both of his palms so she couldn't look away from him. "I love you. You can trust me. I'll get you to safety."

His words struck her panic into shock. Her heart steadied.

"Y-you love me?"

The horror around her seemed to freeze in another time as Movo leaned toward her. "I love you," he said as he brushed his lips against hers.

Warmth returned to her body. Her fear was soothed. Her senses steadied.

"Right. The forest," she said.

He smiled and grabbed her hand. "This way."

All her attention focused on each step forward to avoid tripping. Once they were on the gravel ground, she let go of Movo's hand and unsheathed her sword as a soldier lunged their way. She noticed she had two swords on her back. Movo had equipped her with Emrys' sword as well.

Once the soldier was down, she fell into step next to Movo. The gate looked strange standing by itself, not part of what little that remained of the fortress's walls.

"We need to get Benyamin!" she shouted.

"Right!"

They circled around right to the outside door that led below the fortress. The ceiling shook as they ran down the corridor. They reached a point where a pile of rubble blocked their way.

"Benyamin!" Herlot shouted. "Are you there?"

"Yes!"

Herlot and Movo wasted no time pulling the rocks off to create an opening.

"Benyamin, you need to climb. Hurry," she said the moment she saw Benyamin on the other side.

She urged time to slow as she watched him struggle to the top.

"I'm so, so sorry," she said as they pulled him through. "I never should have sent you here."

"Please, Herlot. Your gift," Benyamin said as he pressed an acorn into her palm. She shoved it in her dress pocket. He forgave too easily.

"They weren't supposed to arrive for another three days," Movo said as they rushed back up the stairs.

"It's the damned obscuration!" Benyamin exclaimed. "It's as if someone has manipulated the stars to tell lies!"

Herlot didn't even know how to begin to make sense of what that could mean. "What are these things Felix is using to destroy the fortress?"

"I don't know," Movo replied. "I haven't seen them before. They can't reach much farther than here, though. We need to get to the forest line as soon as possible."

Soldiers were swarming the premises of where the wall once stood. Especially around what had once been the wall supporting the gate—soldiers were blocking their way to the field, leaving them trapped. Trapped between soldiers and the objects being launched from the ship.

To her right, Seum pulled two people out from beneath a pile. He wiped sweat off his forehead, and then marched toward them.

"Ready to fight our way out of here?" he said.

"Archers!" Herlot shouted as she noticed several soldiers near the gate raise their bows.

"Seum, get Hans. Now!" Benyamin shouted. "Don't stand there and look stupid. Now!"

"This is not the time to play a psaltery," Asm said, appearing at their sides holding two shields. "Get behind me."

Herlot watched, terrified, as Seum did as Benyamin ordered, standing right in the line of fire. He struck a string, and Hans appeared instantly.

"This is what you wanted. Now is your chance, our Hans," Benyamin said.

Hans faced the soldiers at the gate. His body shook, becoming more vivid. Large red blotches grew on his shirt. Flaps of skin hung from his back.

Bile gathered in Herlot's throat as she watched his insides fall out his belly. And then with speed, he floated toward the soldiers. He screamed an awful pitch. Herlot could feel his pain in every nerve of her body. She watched as the soldiers at the gate toppled over one another, trying to get away from Hans.

"There you go, boy. Let them see what was done to you," Benyamin whispered. Then he raised his voice. "Now is our chance."

Asm roared as he swung his body forward and landed on one foot, launching his new ax from the Iptan ship at one of the archers.

Herlot and Movo followed in unison at two more with their daggers.

There was one more, but Hans lurched in front of him, giving Herlot enough time to reach for her other dagger. It pierced through Hans's ghost and caught the soldier right in the throat.

"Swords ready!" Seum shouted as he strapped the psaltery onto his back and unsheathed his two swords from his belt.

They ravaged their way through the rest of the soldiers. Herlot ran with relief as she noticed most of the people were already at the forest line as she sprinted across the field, Devotio included, Ambro standing right next to him.

* * *

All they could do was watch helplessly from the protection of the trees as Felix's army filed into a traditional formation in front of the ruins of the Eraskan fortress. Herlot could make out Felix from afar, right down the centerline and farthest in back, mounted on a horse. She had lost the advantage of attacking them from the rear. They had merely scraped their enemy in their attempt to escape. Her biggest fear about the battle had come true—they were going to fight it Felix's way, and only Felix's way, a way his army had had years of training in, and one that hers had just begun to practice.

Had she made a mistake? Was it better to wait and find a better way to kill Felix? If they did it now, perhaps they could still run to the safety of the allies.

She reached for a branch and hauled herself up. She balanced on top of it and reached for another branch. Once she was high enough to see everyone, she took a seat and allowed her legs to hang.

"Eraskans," she said, only as loud as she needed to for everyone to hear her. "We have been offered sanctuary by our allies in the mountains. Anyone who wants, it's likely that you will make it there if you leave now. Mahtreeh can take you there."

"I'm staying," Mahtreeh said.

"We're all staying," Lucinda said. She pointed at the fortress. "If we hide it's just a matter of time before that happens to another land."

"Agreed! They think they can scare us by destroying our fortress? Is fear of powerful armies worth who we are? I say no!" Cadby raised his fist in the air.

"I don't want to live in the mountains. I want to live in the forest, my home!" a Temesian shouted.

"Even if only a handful of us were to survive, like my sister said, if we show them that they lost their advantage of imposing the fear of death upon their victims, they will leave here weaker than they came," Ambro said after he climbed up on the first branch of the tree. He made eye contact with Herlot as everyone cheered. *I'm still with you*, his eyes seemed to say.

Herlot nodded. She could barely wrap her mind around the courage her people showed after experiencing Felix's wrath on the fortress. They were just as determined as before, if not more. Yet here she was doubting herself. Was their decision really based on what they wanted? As their leader, had she influenced them with too much confidence about something that was impossible? Was it right of her to still play the role of leader while she couldn't answer these questions herself?

She peered through the branches at the place where she knew Felix was sitting upon his horse. He was a disgusting excuse for a human being, waiting patiently as if he had no care in the world for the damage, the hurt, the terror he had inflicted on those defenseless. How could he dare to breathe the fresh air of her land? She wanted to protect the trees from his sight, the singing birds from his hearing. She didn't know if she could survive if she knew he'd taste the berries of a forest where once Rudi had led a group of children for tree sitting. No. There would never be peaceful people sitting around a fire telling stories, or children running freely through sunflower fields once he was here. There'd be children shaking in dungeons with markings on their arms. If she didn't kill him today, he would go back to his city and torture more people. Felix deserved to die.

Her people were still ready to fight. If they did this, they would have to do it without any advantage and only their spirits to rely upon. She had the two powders from Gold wrapped in fabric and sewn into her dress. Was that enough to offset the horsemen and archers?

Their spirit. They had their spirit.

"Right, Eraskans. Prepare your shields and get into formation," she said and jumped down off the branch.

Seum tapped Herlot on the shoulder. "I want Hans to lead the way."

Herlot nodded.

"A-and..."

Herlot raised an eyebrow. This was the first time she had heard Seum sound unsure of what he wanted to say.

He sighed. "I have an idea. I would never suggest it, but we need a miracle to gain any sort of advantage. If Hans could get more..."

Herlot shook her head. "I don't understand."

Seum strummed the psaltery, and murmurs broke out as Hans appeared among the Eraskans. Lucinda and her parents pushed forward.

"Hans?" Lucinda said.

"Oh, my son. Are you real?"

"My boy!" Hans's father exclaimed.

Hans held up his hand and avoided looking at them. "Yes. Please, my family, all will be explained after the battle. Right now, I need you to put everything into the fight, do that for me and, if you grieve me, win this battle. Now I need you to face away from the field until Seum says. I don't want you to see..."

"But—" his mother started.

"Mother, please. Look away."

Seum nodded to Hans's family in encouragement. "I'll explain everything after."

Herlot watched as Seum lowered his voice to a whisper as he spoke to Hans. "Am I breaking the most natural of laws of our world in even asking?" she overheard.

Hans never answered Seum, at least Herlot didn't hear.

"Benyamin, try playing the psaltery so Seum can fight," Hans said. "We will need the music to play the entire battle. I need to see if I can maintain connection with someone else playing."

Asm lifted Benyamin up to sit on a branch. Then, Seum handed the psaltery to Benyamin. Hans's image flickered for a moment of the instrument exchange, but then stabilized when Benyamin started to strum.

"Someone will need to stay back and shield him. I don't know if the music can reach as far as the archers, but the front lines should not be a problem."

Then, without another word, Hans stepped out into the field, and his figure changed again to the one he had right before his death—he wore Dartharus's torture for all to see.

"Let them all see what they did to us, and that even our ghosts won't stop fighting, Hans," Seum said, standing next to Herlot.

Herlot frowned and stared up at Seum. "Ghosts?"

Seum swallowed and he stared at the field.

Herlot turned to match his line of sight.

The entire field behind Hans turned into a blur. Herlot blinked several times until she saw hundreds, if not thousands, of ghosts, all dressed in villager clothing, most of it stained with blood, following behind Hans.

She gripped Seum's arm. "What is happening?"

"He asked them, the ones who crossed over, to come back. These are all the people who died of crowpox under Felix's plan."

Tears streamed down Herlot's face. She squeezed her eyes shut, promising herself not to try and look for her parents. "Th-they all become stuck like Hans now?"

"Yes," Seum said.

Hans's legs started to make the motion of running, but they never made contact with the grass. The other ghosts picked up their pace as they charged at Felix's soldiers. Herlot bowed her head in gratitude and then looked up to see the horrified faces of the soldiers.

The ghosts shouted in agony as they charged at them. Herlot imagined any spirit Felix's men had crushing as their formations split and tumbled apart. Across the field, the soldiers' shouts of horror were music to Herlot's ears.

"You're not the only ones who can inflict fear," Herlot hissed.

Of one thing she was certain: she would never understand the sacrifice these souls made, but now, more than ever, they had to win. She had to reach Felix.

"Now. As planned," Herlot said to Mahtreeh, who was going to be responsible for communicating the orders.

Mahtreeh whistled a specific tune, and they all stepped out onto the field—their heads and torsos now exposed to the archers.

Herlot heard an instrument sound from across the field, and within moments there was the sound of whooshing in the air. Hundreds and hundreds of arrows charged upward, as if they were headed to pierce through the clouds and then escape their world, but then, ever so gracefully, they changed their direction, the tips pointed at the lot of them.

Herlot crouched below Mahtreeh's shield with him.

Clampers of metal hitting wood and cries of pain erupted. Herlot thought she heard the trumpet sound again, and right away the same sound filled the sky. Already another attack was coming, and she hadn't even had the time to assess the damage the first round had done.

"We need to push forward, far enough to make their horsemen come out. Or else the archers will keep shooting the arrows," Asm called to Herlot.

"I know!" she shouted back.

She needed to see how bad it was first, though. More and more whooshing in the sky. They wouldn't pause. More and more cries of agony. Would they even make it halfway out onto the field without the arrows taking them all down?

"Herlot!" Asm shouted.

"He's right, Herlot," Mahtreeh said. "We can't stay like this forever. We either retreat or push forward."

Herlot dared to sneak a peek. She noticed the shadows first. Dashing lines slithered across the field like snakes. There were so many in the sky that they could have formed a cloud cover in themselves.

She had been wrong. It wasn't enough. Charging ahead right now was suicide. *Retreat, retreat! Say it!*

"Ah!" Mahtreeh shouted.

She looked in horror at the arrow sticking out of his shin.

"Retreat!" she called as she broke off the end part of the arrow in Mahtreeh's leg.

But before Mahtreeh could whistle, another whooshing sound flew ahead from behind them, and clanking sounded above them. Hundreds of arrows fell lifelessly onto the ground.

And then again, the trumpet followed by the field being covered in shadows from the arrows, and the whoosh from behind them. This time Herlot saw what had caused the noise. Strange objects in a curved shape that she had never seen before spun at the arrows. Once they had made impact with the arrows, their paths turned and headed back toward the forest.

"What kind of magic is this?"

"It's not magic, it's the allies! They changed their minds," Mahtreeh said. "I can't believe it!"

They erupted out of the forest in what had to be hundreds. They resembled the mountains—all tall with strong, defined muscles. Colorful light bounced off their gem-encrusted weapons and jewelry that adorned their bodies. Herlot watched in awe as they launched another round of the spinning objects.

Miracle.

"Herlot, orders!" Mahtreeh yelled.

No time to wonder about miracles. They weren't helpless anymore. Now was the time.

"Attack!"

Mahtreeh whistled the sound of attack.

Before Mahtreeh could finish the second note of the tune, Devotio was at Herlot's side. She jumped on and gave Mahtreeh a hand.

Mahtreeh held the shield up as arrows rained down on them, but not with enough force to penetrate the wood, thanks to the allies' method to ward off arrows. Luck was on their side. Herlot knew it.

"It's raining! Hahaaaa!" Ambro cheered. He was riding a horse with a girl from Bundene to Herlot and Mahtreeh's right.

"Ambro, focus! Up ahead!" Herlot shouted.

Herlot squeezed her legs against Devotio's sides and let her torso tilt out to the left as they approached two horsemen, one following close behind the other. Mahtreeh had one hand gripping her side as he leaned to the right. Since there were only stirrups for one person, Herlot had to be strong enough to support his weight and her own as they leaned out from opposite sides of Devotio.

The knights lowered their spears. Herlot and Mahtreeh extended their swords. Herlot pumped trust into Seum's idea, from her heart into every bone in her body. Only a few paces away now.

Just as they were getting ready to jump, she shouted with joy as several ghosts appeared right in front of the soldiers. Several even dropped their spears.

"Ready? Now!" she called. She heard the same order being echoed across all the others on horses. She tumbled off Devotio and launched at the knight's side, too close to his body for him to use the spear.

She scanned the field and saw that the Eraskan line of horse riders had been successful in their trick.

They had dismounted their opponents with ease. Too much ease? Herlot checked to her right. Ambro had not been hurt. Thank the skies. "That went much better than Ruelder. Let's do it again," Mahtreeh said.

"Devotio, forward!" Herlot called as she climbed back on. She was grateful their first strikes had been a success, but there were more mounted soldiers closing in who had seen their trick. Their element of surprise would still work because the soldiers had never practiced against such a method, but even if they broke through this line, they still had to fight forward for the unavoidable collision in the middle of the field. Fighting through there would be the real challenge.

As they got closer Devotio began to zigzag from side to side. The incoming soldier did not know from which side he would have to lower his spear, and whether or not he'd have to face Mahtreeh or Herlot.

Cheers erupted from her people as the ghosts once again appeared to obscure the soldiers' vision.

Herlot leaned to the side when they were just paces away, as did the knight with his spear. She glimpsed his head looking left and right, as if terrified of what would come out at him. Just in the last moment where the spear was a hand length from Devotio's chest, Devotio grazed to the other side, giving Mahtreeh a clear line of attack on the soldier's side. A female ghost materialized right between the soldier and Mahtreeh. She screamed in agony, and the soldier leaned back, making the angle of his spear useless. Herlot jumped off to get a clear line of sight as two horsemen charged at Ambro, then she swung a dagger at one of their backs.

"Herlot! Get back on!"

Herlot and Mahtreeh clasped forearms and he swung her back on Devotio.

Battle cries from behind and to their sides were confirmation that their side had succeeded again.

"We can do this. We can do this. We can do this," Mahtreeh chanted. "Damn Seum's tricks."

"Damn these tricks," Herlot said. This would be the most complicated, but if they did it right it would work. She leaned to the side to make room for Mahtreeh so they could both hold Devotio's mane. She kicked her legs underneath her. Mahtreeh leaned to the side. The next soldier lowered his spear.

"Now!" Herlot shouted

"Not yet," Devotio said.

Too close. Too close.

Just in the last moment that seemed possible, Devotio turned sideways so Herlot was facing the knight head on.

As Devotio leaped out of the way, she sprang and unsheathed her sword. The soldier fondled the spear trying to angle it up at her—in doing so he dropped it. She aimed her sword at the most vulnerable parts in his armor and then collided onto him, but not before her sword pierced through his body, and they clashed onto the ground..

She pulled her sword out, the blade dripping blood.

Another success. But the next line of horsemen was too close already. She'd have to do this on foot and hope for the best for Mahtreeh. Out of the corner of her eye she saw that the rest of her people were in the same situation.

Just as the soldiers neared, the sound of wind whipping sounded from above. The allies' spinning objects flew at the soldiers. Herlot didn't have to wait to see their distraction, she could feel it. She took her moment of opportunity.

This time she heard more cries of agony from her side. Allies on horses ran by as Herlot and her people attempted to regather. She was finally able to get a better look at them. Her heart pounded with hope as she saw what they had in their hands. Bows. Arrows. Aimed right at Felix's soldiers as they neared them. They would release and do their damage before the spears could touch them. Another line of allies ran past her, ready to take on more horsemen. She actually had time to wipe the sweat off her brow.

As she looked past the minuscule amount of horsemen left, she remembered this was only the beginning. There were far many more soldiers on foot that they would have to face.

The trumpet sounded. The ground shook from the impact of charging soldiers.

Skies, there were many. Diving into such a swarm of enemies went against her every natural instinct. Her mind was screaming at her—danger! Turn around! And how could they possibly fight through that many people, even with the allies? Even with having learned Seum and Asm's techniques, would that be enough—at least to give her time to reach Felix? She could see where Felix sat, but he seemed an ocean away.

"Help!" she heard Vincent shouting from behind. She whirled around to see Lucinda bleeding out her side.

"Argh."

She turned again, this time to notice Mahtreeh who hobbled ahead on one foot.

"Devotio, take Mahtreeh, Lucinda, and anyone you can and get them back to Enri!"

"No," Mahtreeh protested. "I can fight."

"Not like that." She hated to do it, they needed every last person, but Mahtreeh wouldn't last long in a ground fight with the arrow that was still stuck in his leg.

The pounding against the ground as the soldiers ran toward them grew louder and louder. The sound of Felix's men colliding with their allies, and the cries of pain that followed, nearly knocked her over—it was the sound of the beginning of massive bloodshed.

"Now! Go!" she yelled at Devotio and Mahtreeh.

She took off, ready to join the fight as much as her mind fought to make her understand that diving into a swarm of weapons was the stupidest thing anyone could do. Yet it was the only thing to do if she wanted to reach Felix.

To her right spread across the field, running just as fast as she, were Ambro, Vincent, Movo, Seum, and Asm. Behind them were the rest of the Eraskans. Ahead, Hans's troop of ghosts. She prayed that the seconds of distractions they could gain from the ghosts' tactics would serve them long enough for Herlot to reach Felix.

"Focus on your footwork no matter how scary," she shouted to Ambro. He had had the shortest amount of time training under Seum and Asm. *He shouldn't be here. Am I going to lose my brother today?*

And then she was in. It was a nightmare.

Footwork. Swing. Footwork. Slash. Screams. Footwork.

Blood blurring her vision.

Bite.

Footwork. Stab.

Merle, Rudi's wife's, ghost face.

Trip over a dead body.

Smell of blood and soil.

Slip on entrails.

Step over a leg not attached to a body. Then, a head.

The smell.

Ignore the vomit rising in her throat.

More footwork.

There was no way forward. There was no way back. Her soul screamed at the amount of death she had caused. So many dead. Too many dead.

Then there was the overwhelming heat of bodies and death. She wished she could jump and breathe in the air above the massacre she was engulfed in. If only she could get fresh air to enliven her footwork and jabs. But the heat only grew as the nightmare continued on without end.

The sun sat lower. Hours of heat and death must have passed. How many stories could Father have read during this time? She slashed at a throat. At least six. She stomped on a shoulder. Bones cracking. The nightmare had reached half-way into a night's sleep. Would it last that much longer? If so, and if anyone survived, how could they possibly live after?

Knocked off her feet. Face in the soil. A heavy weight collapsed on top of her.

She rolled onto her back and fought to push the soldier off her body. She was exhausted.

So many lifeless Eraskan bodies around her. This was the end. There were too many. She had made a mistake. How could she have pushed them into this nightmare? All of this to get to Felix, and she wasn't even near him. She had to get near him and end it. If she didn't, it was practically her murdering her own people.

The powders.

She reached for one, not knowing which one. She aimed at the fire of someone swinging a torch far up ahead.

Ringing in her ears. Vision straightening. Yes, more space. A quarter of the field on Felix's side was cleared, but it only took seconds for more soldiers to fill the space. She pushed forward.

She threw the second. Her body flew back from the rumble, and her ears rang as if her head was invaded with lightning strikes.

Clouds. Fog. She struggled to her feet. Remember which way is forward. Someone knocked the sword out of her hand. Less sounds of swords clanking. The soldiers couldn't see, but neither could she or her people. This weapon could give both sides a break, but both were equally at a disadvantage. Except for her. Emrys' sword—it would defend her and bring her forward as far as she needed.

Emrys' sword in hand, she closed her eyes and her body melted into the guidance of the sword that wove patterns through the fog of its own accord. It almost felt like taking a walk on a path in Alonia. Easy. Her mind was even free to drift.

She wondered how many were still alive. In the end, how much grief would there be? Did it even matter, it was already enough to torture any survivors for the rest of their lives. Was Movo still alive? I love you, he had said. Would she forever wonder if he had really meant it? Would he be alive to find out? And most of all, would she have a chance to tell him the same? How she wanted him to know.

She opened her eyes. The fog was less dense. She could make out the shadows that her sword struck at.

Her walk continued. The fog cleared even more. Sunlight. The green of the grass.

She had made it to their side. To *his* side. Felix stared right at her. She was close enough to see the details of his spiteful face.

A soldier charged at her and the sword's endless dance began. With the fog gone, and her clearly in the soldier's vision, he could attack her over and over again, and all she could do was defend against it. She was all alone here. No one to attack for her, and she didn't have another weapon. She could take control of the sword. She could break her promise to never use the sword to attack, and face whatever consequences awaited her if she did.

It will destroy you. You can't.

But what else could she do?

A shadow appeared on the soldier's figure, and before she knew it, two hooves came down on his shoulders. Devotio.

"Herlot, now, the King!" Devotio's voice embraced her.

Herlot moved to search for the weapon the soldier had used, but then she caught sight of Felix. He held a bow with the arrow pointing straight at—

"No!" She threw her body in front of Devotio right as Felix released the arrow.

The puncture barely hurt, at least not as much as she had expected. She could easily continue to fight. She twisted to reach for the weapon again.

But then her insides began to convulse. They shook, twitched, and churned to push out the foreign object inside her belly. It hurt. It hurt so much. Her stomach's contractions choked her as it tried to vomit the arrow out. Hopeless heaves. Every fiber of her being could feel the metal of the arrow stuck in her, its deathly texture. The more her insides contracted, the more it cut into her—endless cuts over and over in the same vulnerable place. Every fiber of her being also knew that this was her end. She was going to die.

She collapsed onto her knees and stared up at Felix. He was pulling another arrow back. No. She was going to die, and Devotio was going to live.

She was going to die, but so was Felix.

She knew Emrys' sword would kill him if that was where she manipulated it to go. She was already destroyed. She could do it.

With the very last amount of strength her body would ever feel, she raised the sword above and behind her, ready to throw it so it would spin and plunge into Felix's heart.

Her body wobbled with weakness. She fought to keep it steady for just this last moment. Just one more moment, even though the pain was so much. Oh, how much she wanted it to stop hurting. She wanted the end. She wanted to lie down and slip away forever. Anything to not feel the pain anymore.

Just one last bit of strength, just enough to release it and then I can go.

She held Felix's figure steady in her vision. She had to aim well.

She saw the snarl on his face. The saliva dripping from his mouth, as if her death were the most appetizing thing on a feast table. She saw the hatred in his eyes. That hatred would never see the light of day again. How strong his hatred was, impossibly strong. She kept staring. Why wasn't she swinging? She wanted to know how such hatred was even possible.

Why hadn't he released the arrow yet? She had waited too long, yet he seemed to be frozen in his glare as much as she was.

Why would this man try to kill a creature of such beauty as Devotio, in order to hurt a woman who was trying to protect her people? How could he hate so much?

A song of whales enveloped her. Was it real or was she imagining it? Was this the melody that would sink her into forever sleep?

How blue Felix's eyes were. Like the sea.

She blinked lazily, and when she opened her eyes again, she was in the sea. Sinking deeper into the water the color of Felix's blue eyes.

A whale swam by her and then wrapped around her. He swam in circles around her as she continued to sink.

Visions wrapped in bubbles rose by her as she continued her journey down. They held images of castles, fields, armies. Children in dungeons. Queen Magdalene. A man she did not recognize wearing a crown.

The whale swam below her and stopped her from descending as a bubble stopped in front of her. She saw two young boys dressed in royal clothing, one sitting across from a man wearing a crown, the same one she had seen in the bubble, and the other standing nearby. Between the king and the boy was a table with a chessboard on it.

The boy had lost several pieces already. It looked like it was his turn to make a move. He took his king piece and placed it in the most vulnerable place he could go, ready to be check-mated by the tower. The king's hand lashed out and grabbed the boy around the throat. "Why would you make such a move?"

"Thanks to the king's move, all his people will be saved," the little boy said through tears.

"The king," the man wearing the crown spat, "is always the last one standing. No matter what. If the other pieces don't die for the king, they are useless."

The man wearing the crown practically threw the boy toward the fireplace. A large candlestick fell on top of the boy as he tried to shuffle away from the man wearing the crown.

"Leave. The look of you disgusts me," the crowned man said. Then he turned to the other boy. "Robin, take your seat. Prove to me you're not a disappointment like your brother Felix."

The bubble popped.

After what felt like nights and days, her feet sank into a warm, sandy bottom. Among the seagrass stood a boy who held a small, wooden treasure chest in front of his heart. He looked exactly like the boy in the bubble who had sacrificed his king chess piece.

"I can't open it," he said. "Will you help me open it?"

"W-who are you?" Herlot asked.

"My name is Felix. Will you help me open my treasure chest?"

"You have done awful things as an adult, Felix. Are you aware of that?"

The boy nodded. "I see everything."

"I can't forgive you. Even though your father hurt you and you may have once had good intentions, no one can forgive you for what you have done."

"I know."

"Then why would you think I would help you open your treasure chest?"

"Because even though you can't forgive me, you can wait long enough to see the truth. You can know the truth that I have done evil, evil that can't be forgiven. But you can know that even though I have done evil things, I am not evil. You can also know that although I have done many wrongs, I can still do many rights."

"How? How could someone possibly create good after causing so much suffering?"

"If you open the chest, I can remember."

"Remember what?"

"My golden heart."

That she had not expected.

She trudged forward, her feet embraced by the sand. Could he be lying to her? Up above them the whale continued to swim in a circle. They held the mysteries and secrets of the sea. Felix having a golden heart was probably the biggest and worst mystery one could have imagined.

She was angry. Back wherever her body was, she was dying. Here, she was learning that Felix had a golden heart?

She had been brought to a strange realm of the sea right before her death. By all means, it was only logical to agree with what was presented to her. But even with the beautiful whale above, and the wonder of being able to walk around underwater without having to breathe, and the calming sway of the sea grass, she didn't want to help. It was not fair. He killed her. How come he got to have the golden heart? After a lifetime of struggle with this supposed gift that she had, Felix would get to be the one to have one? Felix, the one who murdered her family. The one whose fault it was that she needed to save Devotio's family in the first place

"No. I will *not* give this to you."

She looked up at the whale. "I want to leave. Let me go back to my body and let me die in peace."

"If you don't have the courage to see my good, how could you ever have thought you had the courage to kill my evil?"

"People like you don't deserve to have a golden heart. How dare you call me a coward after everything I have been through?"

"Because you would rather be dead, and me not have one, than be dead while I have the ability to perform a golden heart's magic."

Forsaken seas and whales and seagrasses. She wanted to protest but couldn't. He was right. If he were to perform golden heart magic, he would have the ability to blend the leaf. It wouldn't be her. Could she live with that? Could she rest in peace knowing that her biggest enemy would perform the deed most precious to her? She stopped herself. Was it her place to decide whether or not he was to be trusted with a golden heart? She had to bite through the pain of the truth and the outrageousness. Not only was her body in excruciating pain, now her feelings were doing the same. It was as if a dagger was slicing through every emotion she had. Could she push through this pain and do what was right based on the truths presented to her?

"Tell me, if you remember your gold, you will do good with it?"

"Yes," Felix said.

She forced herself forward. As she stood right in front of the chest and lifted her hand to open, she cried in agony. Her hand balled into a fist, and she bit into it as rage caused her body to shake. "Oh sea, give me the courage to do this. I don't think I can."

She pushed her hand toward the chest. "I can't. I can't. I can't," she chanted, yet her hand kept pushing forward. She cried out in despair as she unfastened the hook. The upper lid floated open.

Inside, cushioned on a bed of white flower petals, was a solid, golden heart. Its color was enchanting, strong and bold. Shiny, its surface so clear. She leaned forward, mesmerized. She saw a reflection of herself.

Her chest pulsed with warmth and a tune began to play, a beautiful melody. There were words and sounds she had never heard before. Where was it coming from? She couldn't figure out the direction where it was coming from... not right, not left, not forward, back, or above. Wait. Was it coming from her?

Some kind of light shined from below. She gazed down and gasped. A halo of golden glow encircled her chest. It rippled up and down. It was playing the tune! Oh, how she could feel it. Every part of it. She had a desire to stretch it. As soon as she thought it, the circle of golden light expanded.

Had she—? Was this—? She had done it.

She gazed up at Felix. "How is this possible?"

"You were going to kill me, but you chose to look further. You faced the parts of you that are afraid you might be like me. There is nothing stopping your golden heart from shining anymore," the child Felix said.

Herlot noticed a hint of sadness in his voice. Even though he held the chest with the golden heart, there was no golden glow around his heart. She could hear the beat of his heart, though—a tune, beautiful yet different from her own.

She allowed the sphere of gold around her to expand. It felt like singing a tune louder, only with her heart. Her song sang through the water until it intertwined with Felix's song. She closed her eyes and smiled and how much more beautiful the tune got with another melody intertwined with it.

She wasn't surprised when she opened her eyes again to see the same halo around Felix's chest now. He gazed down at it, his mouth open. He lifted his head. "Thank you."

The whale swam by her, and for some reason she knew she was supposed to hold onto it. She grabbed hold of his fin. Felix waved to her as the whale began to swim up toward the surface. "Goodbye," she called.

She felt more and more songs around as they traveled toward the surface. It was as if every bubble had a song. She stretched her golden heart toward each one, and as soon as her tune touched them, they began to glow as well. She saw images in each bubble—stories. She recognized many scenes from Eraska and Damalathum, at least of what she had seen of the city. She saw scenes with people she knew in one— Merle, Lupert, Ambro, and herself. It was as if the bubble was seeing from Rudi's eyes. Was this what these bubbles were? Were they the stories of all the people surrounding her?

They were almost near the surface. She looked down and was farewelled by a sea full of golden bubbles. It was beautiful.

The crisp air kissed her face, and she took a breath. She saw the sky above her and felt the ground below her.

She gulped for air, but even though it surrounded her, it was as if her body was surrendering the ability to breathe.

"Lower your weapons!" she heard Felix call. An instrument played a tune.

She turned her head to the right. The fog had dissipated. A tear rolled down her cheek as she saw the scene across the field. Most of them were on their knees, no more weapons in hand, staring down at the golden glow around their chests. Some were crying, some were laughing, some were simply smiling, hypnotized into an enchanted state.

She could still feel her tune. She knew her glow was still there, yet it was seeping out of her at immense speed. If only she had the leaf in hand, and if only she were by a tree, she knew exactly how she could blend the leaf onto the branch. All it would take was to flow some of her gold between the branch and the stem of the leaf.

She turned her head in the other direction to look at Felix. He gazed back at her. The cold blue of his eyes now with a hint of warmth. He bowed his head, as if in honor.

Devotio appeared above her against the background of the sky.

Her heart laughed because her body couldn't anymore. She hoped he could feel it. This is what he would look like flying in the sky with wings.

"I'm with you," Devotio's voice wrapped around her.

She thought she heard her name being called. Voices surrounded her, yet the words were jumbled together, and so was everything in her vision. She knew it was her friends.

She had to tell them one last thing. She had to.

Her lips were moving, and she hoped her words were decipherable. "Give the leaf to Felix."

Devotio's voice wrapped around her ears. It was so close, yet she could barely make out the words of his firefly poem.

What a beautiful way to go to rest forever. Thank you, my dear friend. May we meet again.

How much she wished she could stay. How much she didn't want it to be over. If only she could ride with Devotio through the forest. Just one last time. Just one more night by a fire telling stories. Just one more day with her family. Just one more embrace from Movo.

If only she could hide somewhere. She could feel her gold ready to free itself from her body as her organs went to sleep.

The acorn. She imagined reaching for the acorn in her pocket. She knew it could only be her imagination. Her body was not strong enough to perform such a task. She wrapped her fingers around it. It was as if Benyamin had known the future. He said he didn't watch the dark star. He said he didn't watch it, but that didn't mean he didn't sneak a peek from time to time.

The last lines of Devotio's poem hugged her.

She slipped into the peace of a golden light.

Light. Not darkness. She was so glad it was light.

And there were bells.

EPILOGUE

Enri pressed her hand over her heart. Light sparkled off the seawater below, as if celebrating. She rested her head against Mahtreeh's shoulder as he waved to Felix's ships sailing away. Had it all really ended in a silent peace? Had it all really ended with Herlot gone?

She wished she could still feel it, that warmth she had felt on the battlefield right below where her palm was right now. She wished she could still see it, the beautiful glow emanating from her chest. She wished she could hear it again, the blissful silence as every person on the field that day stopped amid the trap of the bloodbath they were forced to complete, and witnessed the magic happening within them. She wished Herlot could have seen how even after the golden hearts stopped glowing, and even though many were confused about what had happened to them, not one picked up their weapon again.

"Did she really say to give the leaf to Felix?" Mahtreeh asked.

"I really do think so," Ambro said. "But we all felt the gold. Any one of us should be able to do it."

Enri gazed up at Devotio. "We'll find it. It has to be here somewhere. With Asm's strength, we'll manage to look underneath even the biggest rubble."

"How many moons do we have left?" Ambro asked.

Enri looked behind her at the forest line where the leaves were beginning to turn orange. "Eight."

* * *

Manni let her head drop back in ecstasy as she gazed up at the night sky. All those stars, stars that since she had been a little girl only showed her beautiful princesses and queens who were far more powerful than she, all those stars that had made her life look pitiful, all those stars were now under her influence. Tonight she could laugh at the power of those princesses and queens, for hers was already more and would only continue to grow.

She practically floated with ecstasy as she made her way back inside the mound. She threw her cloak over her chest of the finest fabrics, and then spread herself on her layer of silken bedding. She hoped her Master would give her another taste of the gold before she went to sleep.

"I am so glad I followed your call," she said. He was off in the neighboring room, but she knew he could hear her. She knew he was pleased with her more than he had expected ever since he learned about her star-watching gifts. She liked that. His mastery of the dark star and now her mastery of all the others made them equals.

"If only you had been intelligent enough to watch your own village throughout all those years, you could have stopped the girl before it got this far."

A lump formed in her throat. She swallowed. "She's dead now, though."

"Her death is of no use to me when now hundreds have felt their own gold."

"They're too stupid to learn to feel it again."

"I need you to go back to the boy. Bring me the sword you saw her use."

She sat up. He expected her to travel without tasting gold for days on end? "I am not welcome there ever again. He does not love me anymore."

He was silent for a bit. "Tomorrow you will travel to King Robin's kingdom. You will enchant him and marry him. The boy will come once he hears the news of you being soon-to-be wed. You will get him to trust you and bring you back to Eraska. And then, you will take and bring me my sword."

"I said he does not love me anymore," she said through gritted teeth.

"He will come. Rest now and leave before the sun rises."

She opened her mouth to protest, but then a strong pressure began to form in her chest. She fell on her back, writhing in pain. The pressure released, and she didn't dare to open her mouth again.

Coming Soon: Book 3 of the *Herlot of Alonia* Series

For release date announcements,
please sign up for the newsletter
at www.mariarosestone.com

THANK YOU

Thank you to Kira Henschel for welcoming Herlot's story and me into the HenschelHAUS family. Stories travel to distant places and it mean so much for the *Herlot of Alonia* series to have found the perfect home. Thank you to Victoria for your creativity, detail, and talent in bringing the covers to life.

I am forever grateful to the wonderful persons who have continued to support Herlot's story coming to life. To my husband, your belief in me astounds me as we journey through life's ups and downs. Thank you for being my rock. Numerous thanks to my family, friends, Jacque, and Mary for your sweet excitement and curiosity in every step forward. Alexa, Elaine, Elizabeth, and Mike, every character in the story celebrates your valuable input and editing! And of course, Robyn and our art journaling book club, you have taken the experience of sharing a story to places I couldn't imagine myself. Thank you!

ABOUT THE AUTHOR

Maria Rosestone is a historian, instructional designer, and science student who can always be found with a book. She particularly enjoys ancient and medieval history. If she is not researching or writing, she loves to go for nature walks with her family and dogs.

Website: www.MariaRosestone.com
Contact: mariarosestone4@gmail.com